Dead Pretty

£2·49

C2/5

Dead Pretty

A Novel

by

Candy Denman

DEAD PRETTY © Candy Denman
ISBN 978-0-9933815-7-7
eISBN 978-0-9933815-8-4

Published in 2017 by Crime Scene Books

Book design by Clockwork Graphic Design
Cover design George Foster Covers
Printed and bound in Great Britain by Marston Book Services Ltd, Oxfordshire

Dedication

For Bob, who is happy to talk about how to kill people,
on walks, in restaurants and even in bed.

Acknowledgements

A huge thank you to all the doctors, nurses, policemen and crime scene investigators who have given their time to chat to me and answer my many questions. Any mistakes in this book are mine alone and I apologise for not listening properly. People who know Hastings will recognise that I have changed the name, descriptions and locations of the hospital, wards and surgeries in order to underline the fact that this book is fiction and in no way reflects the dedicated health care professionals of Hastings.

A big thank you to the Crime Scene Books team and, in particular, Sarah Williams, who nursed me through this process and trusted me to come up with a finished article at some point, and Katharine May my editor who removed all those excess commas.

And finally, a great big thank you to my family who have put up with me hiding in my garden shed for long hours and to Bob who has been dragged round the country to various crime festivals without complaining too much, yet.

Prologue

She lies there, on the dishevelled bed, mocking him. Her scrawny, naked body covered in old scars and bruises, courtesy of her job, her profession. And there she is, this hag, this whore, laughing at him and his limp dick. Soft as ice-cream, unresponsive to her sucking and wanking. No use to man nor beast, let alone a woman, she laughs. Cackles. Her mouth gaping wide. Stained, uneven teeth. Furred tongue. Lipstick all gone. Left on the glasses of vodka and coke he's been buying her all night. He's paid out for this pathetic body, this diseased bit of stubble covered cunt, but it's her that's laughing at him.

He has to shut her up, shut up the stream of humiliation from her mouth. Going on and on. Ringing, echoing, in his ears. He reaches for her discarded tights, her grubby, laddered tights, wraps them between his hands and winds them around her neck, tightening, straining, until the abuse stops, replaced by a hoarse, terrified, rasping noise. A croak. A silent scream. She scrabbles at his hands, scarlet nails ripping in vain at the cord around her neck, breaking off, useless fakes in her fight for life. The tights are buried too deep in the flesh of her throat. Eyes bulging, she lashes out with her bare feet, landing bruising blows to his legs, but only making him pull tighter. Slowly, inexorably, her frantic but pathetic attempts to stop him become weaker and then cease.

Her body twitches and lies limp. Limp as his dick. Still he keeps the pressure on, until he can be sure. Sure she is dead. Sure she is silenced forever.

He loosens his hold, slowly unwinding his hands from the tights. A skein of drool hangs from her mouth. He looks at the body. The stillness of the flesh. The cool slackness. At last he feels a stirring, and looking down, sees his cock getting hard.

1

The sun was not fully up and the last vestiges of sea mist were still lingering around the sea front kiosks as Jo made her way along the promenade, shivering slightly in the cool morning air. It was normally deserted at this time of day, apart from the seagulls wheeling overhead, but today she could see a small knot of people ahead, waiting for her by the public conveniences. There were two undertakers, lounging against their grey unmarked van, smoking and laughing over some undoubtedly tasteless joke. After all, this was a council pick-up job, an unknown corpse for delivery to the hospital mortuary, as opposed to a private call-out by a grieving family. No need to put on a veneer of professional empathy.

Closer to the modern, squat, concrete building were two PCs, the first to be called out and grateful to be able to move away as she approached. The younger policeman, new to death, looked concerned and faintly green about the gills, but the older one, although still only in his late twenties, had seen it all before and was simply fed up that they were unlikely to get off duty on time.

Jo paused a moment to take in the scene before she knelt beside the body of the young woman lying slumped against the outer wall of the toilets, next to the drinking fountain. She was careful to keep her distance and not to get too close to the body fluids that had pooled beneath the corpse. She put down her medical bag just within reach, but as far away from the immediate vicinity of the body as possible.

"Who found her?" she asked.

"Cleaner. Unlocks the toilets every morning at five thirty. She's in the caff over the road, getting tea and sympathy and telling everyone the gory details, no doubt." It was the older policeman who had answered.

Jo took her time, she liked to fully assess the situation before touching the body, making sure this was not a crime scene before potentially destroying or altering the evidence. The girl looked scarcely out of her teens, but her ravaged face told Jo a story of drug abuse and

11

addiction. Her short Lycra skirt didn't cover the essentials, revealing the greying thong she was wearing, suggesting prostitution as a career choice, and lower-end-of-the-market prostitution at that. There were nicotine stains on the first two digits of her right hand and a length of rubber tubing still drawn tight around her left forearm. A small globule of blood had oozed from the needle-hole on the dorsal aspect of her left hand. This addict had already knackered the veins in her antecubital fossa, the veins of choice for a junkie, even if they didn't know the name for their precise anatomical location. Jo leaned over and looked at the far side of the girl's torso. The one ml hypodermic syringe, with orange cap needle attached, had fallen to the ground, a small amount of brown liquid still in the barrel. The liquid, or draw-back as it was called, would almost certainly be a mix of heroin and blood. At least they would be able to analyse the contents and check the strength. If this overdose was due to an unusually strong batch of smack, they would be able to warn other users, maybe prevent any similar deaths. A stained teaspoon, a small piece of aluminium foil, a cheap Bic lighter and a filter torn from a cigarette lay next to the syringe, completing the drug user's kit.

Tucking a loose strand of her straight, shoulder-length blonde hair behind her ear, Jo turned back to her medical bag and took out a pair of latex gloves, pulling them on and then, holding up her tailored jacket with one hand to make sure the hem didn't dip into the mix of faecal fluid and urine around the body, she reached forward to feel for a carotid pulse. It was a formality; this girl was dead and had been for hours, killed by the habit that made the job that paid for her drugs bearable. With a slight sigh of regret for a life lost so pointlessly, Jo took out an evidence bag and gingerly picked up the syringe.

"Don't touch that!"

Startled by this sudden order, she almost dropped the syringe and turned to glare angrily at the person who had just shouted at her. He was a man in his early forties, she guessed, striding purposefully towards her from the car park. Dressed in a dark blue suit, pristine white shirt and subdued silk tie, he looked more like a businessman than a policeman, but the older man, scurrying along behind him, trying to keep up, was definitely, unmistakeably, CID. His crumpled suit and the loosely knotted tie that failed to cover the tea stains on yesterday's shirt, no doubt hastily grabbed as he was roused from his bed, were a dead giveaway.

"Are you the duty Doc?" Mr Clean said brusquely, as the two PCs looked on with barely disguised interest.

"Dr Hughes. Jo Hughes, Forensic Physician," she corrected him, as she stood up to discover that he was surprisingly tall, at least six inches taller than her, unlike his sidekick who must have struggled to make the minimum height restriction, still used in the days when he would have joined.

"Oh. You're Dr Hughes?"

Jo nodded and smiled inwardly. She had caught another closet chauvinist out. It never ceased to amaze her that so many men, especially policemen, assumed that anyone with her job had to be a man, and she knew that having a gender ambiguous name like Jo didn't help them at all.

"And you are?" she asked.

To give him credit he recovered himself quickly and held out his hand.

"Detective Inspector Steve Miller." Jo waved her gloved hands to explain why she wasn't about to shake his ungloved one, and he quickly dropped it. "And this is DS Jeffries."

Jo nodded, and noted that, rather than the scent of beer and stale smoke she had come to expect from policemen, DI Miller exuded a fresh and pleasantly soapy smell, as if he had just this minute stepped out of the shower.

"As a forensic physician, you should know better than to touch evidence at a crime scene then, Dr Hughes."

The shower image disappeared like a cloud of steam and the look Jo gave him was blatantly hostile.

"I am delighted to hear that the police are finally taking the town's drug problem seriously." Her voice was flat and clipped with barely restrained anger, and if Miller had known her longer than a minute he would have apologised and backed off- if he knew what was good for him, that is. Instead, he looked down at the body and was unable to disguise his disappointment.

"A bloody junkie."

"Yes, Detective Inspector, just another bloody junkie. Nothing interesting, like a nice murder, I'm afraid."

Her sarcasm was evidently lost on Miller, so she ignored him and turned back to her work, extracting an evidence bag from her case, placing the syringe inside and sealing it, before storing the bag in a rigid plastic container so that no one could be accidentally injured by the needle. Miller continued to stare at the body.

"We were told that it was a dead prostitute. You're sure this is just an OD?"

A further slight hardening of Jo's features, and a cold glint to her eye, should have warned Miller that she did not take kindly to having her professional judgement questioned. A slight twitch of Jeffries' lips showed he had seen her irritation and that he was enjoying it.

"Yes, Inspector, I am quite sure."

Miller said nothing, staring her out, until she returned to the corpse and crouched down beside it, her back rigid with hostility.

"If you are thinking that this might be connected with the prostitute killing last month. There's no sign of restraint, bruising or ligature marks on the neck." She lifted the girl's head so that he could see. "The residue of froth around the lips that you can see here and which, if I am not mistaken, is slightly bloodstained- but we can check that in the mortuary- is indicative of pulmonary oedema, almost certainly due to heart failure brought on by an overly large intravenous shot of heroin."

She was gratified to see that Miller was taken aback. The slightly green PC was looking worse, but fortunately had the presence of mind to turn away before he threw up.

"I understand your victim was strangled with her own tights," Jo continued as both she and Miller looked down at the body's bare legs and scuffed white stilettos. "I think you'll find this girl isn't wearing any." She pulled the body slightly over and lifted the skirt even higher, then raised one of the legs up and peered underneath. "Lividity is present under the legs and buttocks, suggesting she died in this position." She straightened and looked him in the eye. "Face it, she came here to jack up but the cut was too strong for her. Same old story. Nothing to interest you. Now, could you stand back and let us get on with our job?"

Miller moved back obediently as Jo picked up the remaining drug paraphernalia and a small fake leather clutch bag she found half tucked under the body, placing it all in evidence bags before waving the mortuary attendants forward.

"You can take the body to the hospital now. Make sure you don't lose the tourniquet. I'll deliver the syringe to Dr Dunbar myself." She glared at Miller. "Can't have the chain of evidence compromised, can we? Even if it is just an overdose." She started to strip off her gloves, as the two undertakers lifted the body and deposited it onto their trolley with a bit of a thud. She glanced round anxiously; you never knew when an early morning jogger might be passing and the last thing she wanted was to have to deal with a complaint about insensitive or rough handling of a corpse. Seeing that the young girl's skirt had ridden up even further, Jo couldn't stop herself from leaning across and quickly pulling it down to retain at least a modicum of decency, before the mortuary attendant zipped up the body bag and wheeled the trolley towards the van.

She turned back to spot the two young policeman who had attended first already getting in their car and Miller and Jeffries walking towards theirs.

"Don't you think someone ought to be sent to hose down the area?" she called after them. Miller looked at her blankly, but Jeffries cast an eye over the dark stain around the toilet door.

"Council job, love. Give them a call." And they left, but not before Jeffries had seen Jo's reaction to being called love.

Angry and exasperated, even though she knew he was right about who had the responsibility for cleaning up, Jo checked her watch and saw that it was still early. She was not due at morning surgery for more than an hour. The cleaning lady had left her mop and bucket where she dropped them on discovering the body and there was a cold water tap on the side wall. If Jo was very careful not to splash herself, she could at least sluice the worst of the malodorous puddle away before anyone else came along. It was a health hazard after all, and she did hate to leave a mess.

The mortuary had been built slightly apart from the hospital, and an attempt, of sorts, had been made to hide it from view by planting a row of Leylandii between the main hospital block and the entrance, presumably to screen the sick and dying from the physical reminder of where they themselves would end up. The trees had not prospered;

perhaps their proximity to the incinerator chimney had choked the life out of them. Whatever the cause, the result was that these specimens, whose family are renowned for their hardiness and hyper-virile growth, were so thin and spindly that the closed metal trolleys which they were supposed to be shielding from public view could clearly be seen as they came and went with their lifeless cargoes.

Jo ignored the main door marked "Chapel of Rest" and instead entered by a small, anonymous side door. Behind it stretched a windowless corridor with naked, expressionless walls interrupted only by an unmarked door on the left- the back entrance to the chapel of rest- and terminating in a set of plain steel, double lift doors. Once inside the lift, there was only one direction to go: down.

Having descended, Jo stepped out into the subterranean mortuary where she could hear the clank and chink of metal instruments being laid out on metal trolleys as she headed for the autopsy suite. Looking through the porthole window in the door to the first room she could see the Chief Technician, whose name she struggled to remember but whose pale and pasty bulk led her to always think of him as Doughboy, after a television advert for bread mix she remembered from her childhood. Doughboy's enormous stomach stretched the operating theatre greens he was wearing to the limit, and Jo tried not to think about the consequences of them splitting as she watched him prepping for a post mortem, the shroud-covered body already lying on the table. He looked up as Jo pushed open the doors, having to press hard against the positive air pressure, the cooler atmosphere and smell of disinfectant hitting her simultaneously.

"Is Dr Dunbar about?"

"In the office with the Coroner's Officer, Dr Hughes." He waved latex-covered hands at her, gesturing in the general direction of the corridor, and smiled. "I heard you attended an OD this morning. You're not expecting us to be posting her yet, are you? Only she hasn't even arrived and we are chock-a-block."

"No, no, don't worry. Just delivering the ancillary evidence." She held up the sharps box.

Doughboy hurried across to take it from her and she wished she could remember the man's name. She must ask Ian Dunbar before it became blatantly obvious.

"Thanks," was all she could say under the circumstances. "I've just labelled it with the evidence number, location, date and time I pronounced her death, as we don't have a confirmed name."

Having handed over the syringe, she ducked back out of the autopsy suite, leaving the technician who had gone back to opening sterile packets of instruments out onto the already loaded surface. As the post mortem he was preparing for was a not a criminal case, using the sterile instruments was more to protect him and the pathologist from possible infection rather than to prevent contamination of their already-dead subject.

Back out in the corridor, Jo opened the office door to see Dr Ian Dunbar, seated at the well-ordered desk, checking the details on the body he was about to post. In his early sixties and fighting any suggestions of retirement, Dr Dunbar was also dressed in theatre greens, but he was a thin and spare man in direct contrast to his obese assistant. Mike Parton, the Coroner's Officer, a man of great physical dignity with the bearing of a funeral director, was waiting patiently as Dr Dunbar read the reasons a referring doctor had put forward for requiring a post mortem on his patient.

"Hello, Jocasta, how nice of you to drop in on us." Dr Dunbar always liked to use Jo's proper name, and was always telling her it was lovely and that she shouldn't let it be shortened. Jo wondered if he had helped choose it, having been a family friend from before she was born, and being her Godfather to boot. Someone had to take the blame for saddling her with such a ridiculous name. One thing was for sure; if she ever had children, especially a son, she'd never let him or his friends know what it was or where it came from. She had no intention of setting up any child of hers to be teased mercilessly by his more educated mates.

Dunbar turned to Mike and waved the paper at him.

"The old dear found dead in her chair up at Rosemount. If her ruddy GP had been doing his job and seeing her regularly, he wouldn't be needing a P.M. on her now. Blatantly obvious she'd had heart failure for years. Still, keeps me in a job, I suppose."

"Don't think there's much risk of you being made redundant, Dr Dunbar."

Jo was surprised. That was almost a joke, and she had always believed Mike Parton to be completely devoid of humour.

"Are you here about the OD from this morning, Mike?" The pathologist asked.

"No, no. Christine Trent again. The ligature strangulation," he added unnecessarily as he brought a few pieces of neatly folded paper out of his inside breast pocket. "We need to organise a second post mortem for the defence in case we ever charge someone and then release her body to the family. I've spoken to Professor Wadsworth about an independent forensic pathologist and he's been in touch with a colleague in London."

"And who has Wally Wadsworth foisted on us this time?" Dr Dunbar had never liked the local forensic pathologist who covered the south east coastal region, feeling, probably quite rightly, that Wadsworth believed himself to be superior because he handled the criminal cases instead of just the 'unimportant' sudden deaths due to natural causes. Both Mike and Jo had already had the Dunbar lecture on every life being valuable and every death a personal tragedy for someone. Several times. Mike checked his notes for the pathologist's details.

"Ah, here it is. A Dr Andrew Lister will be down here tomorrow for a ten o'clock start."

Dr Dunbar frowned.

"That's pretty short notice."

"It was the only time he could spare."

Dr Dunbar leant slightly towards the door and called out: "Did you hear that, Dave? The Very Important Home Office Pathologist is coming to do the second P.M. on the ligature strangulation tomorrow, so we'll have to do the old dear found in her chair at the residential home today, as well as the two-day post-op and the OD."

Dave Ball, of course! That was Doughboy's name. Jo mentally stored the information: she really mustn't forget it again. Dave appeared at the door, looking disgruntled.

"Haven't you got a pathology dinner to get to, Dr Dunbar?"

Dr Dunbar stood.

"Hmm. I'd forgotten that." He turned back to Jo. "Looks like your OD will have to wait until tomorrow afternoon, Jocasta. Is that okay? Maybe you could come and watch? See what real medicine is all about? Hmm?"

"Actually, yes, that would be interesting." She looked at Dave, "But maybe we can send off a sample from the fluid in the syringe today? Only, I'm anxious to know the strength in case we need to issue a warning to prevent further deaths."

Dave beamed back at her, happy to help.

"No problem, Dr Hughes, I'll send it off straight away."

"Right then, young Dave. Chop, chop. Let's clear the deck and get ready for tomorrow. Can't upset the man from the Home Office and anyway, we don't want that poor young woman's corpse hanging around indefinitely. It will be the flu season soon and we'll need all the room we can get."

2

Somewhere in the building a baby was crying. Not a mere whimper, or even a wail, but a full-throttle, all-out, bellow of rage. The sort of noise only made by a six week old infant who has suddenly discovered that life isn't all about being kept warm and dry and being fed on demand. Life also comes equipped with ladies in blue who jab needles into your leg and nobody even tries to stop them. Welcome to the real world.

Jo tried to shut out the noise and consider her options. She was getting nowhere. The woman in front of her had a stubborn set to her jaw, telling Jo that nothing she said was going to make the slightest bit of difference, so perhaps it was time to bring in the big guns. Do something drastic. Against all her training, she honestly believed she had little choice but to break the rules of patient confidentiality.

Jo stood up and went to the door. Striding quickly into the waiting room before she could change her mind, she surveyed the room full of expectant faces suddenly looking up at her.

"Mr Jennings?"

Never having met him, she had no idea what her patient's husband looked like, but she knew he always drove her to her appointments. Jo hoped he waited inside rather than out in the car.

She searched through the expressions of disappointment until she identified a middle-aged man with a surprised look on his face and a back copy of the Angling Times hanging from his hands.

"Mr Jennings?" she repeated, directly to him.

"Er, yes." He seemed embarrassed at being singled out like this.

"Would you come through, please?"

She turned and went back into her consulting room, leaving him to make his way through the massed envy of waiting patients. Some, the few who had really been ill at some point in the past, realised that this was a serious development and flashed him looks of sympathy, but for most it was simply irritation they felt for this man being called through before them, before his turn.

"You've no right," Mrs Jennings hissed but said no more as her husband came in, anxiety seeping from every pore.

"Everything all right, is it, doctor?" he asked.

"Just have a seat, Mr Jennings and I'll explain things to you." She hardly dared look at Mrs Jennings who, already pale and anaemic, had pursed her lips so tightly that she was now almost white with anger.

"Your wife is a very sick woman. Very sick." Jo emphasised. "I can't make you any promises that she will get better, but her best chance is to go into hospital. Today. I've spoken to the Consultant taking all the admissions this week, a Mr Kane, and he's found her an emergency bed on Winchelsea Ward. She'll need a blood transfusion first of all, to make her feel a bit stronger, but then they need to find the cause of this bleeding."

"Oh." He struggled as her words sunk in before turning to his wife, attempting to keep his tone bright, knowing this was serious. "We'd best get you over there then."

She didn't move, didn't look him in the eye, just played with a tissue, already shredded and disintegrating, in her hands.

"I don't want them messing me about. I don't want an operation."

He stared at his wife as if seeing her for the first time, and Jo crossed her fingers. This was the crux of the matter, and the cause of the gamble she had taken. Would he be able to persuade his wife to have treatment, when she had failed?

"Don't be so daft."

"I don't want them touching me."

"But you're sick. You need their help."

"No. I don't want it." But the voice was less insistent. Jo almost held her breath. Would it work?

"But, why? I mean, why not let them touch you? Never heard anything so bloody stupid in my life."

He met the same brick wall Jo had been hitting for the last few months.

"I just don't want all this."

A vague wave of her hand towards Jo indicated what she meant. Doctors. Hospitals. Interference.

Jo tried again in a firm but soothing voice,

"I know it's hard for you, but it really is for the best, Mrs Jennings."

The thin, middle-aged woman in front of her was terrified. More terrified of doctors and hospitals than she was of dying. Looking at her lined, troubled face, her pepper-and-salt hair, Jo found it hard to believe she was only forty five. Old before her time. Ground down by worry, fear and disease. A startling contrast to the man by her side. Her husband. Brimming with rude health. Brusquely taking the matter in hand.

"Of course you'll go into hospital. They'll get you sorted. You'll be right as rain. You tell her, doctor."

He looked at Jo, challenging her to give his wife the reassurance she needed. Jo hesitated.

"Mr Kane will be able to tell you more, once he's seen her." Passing the buck. Knowing her patient's chances were slim, at best.

"But I don't want to see him."

Jo could feel the fear pouring off Mrs Jennings in waves, hot, sweaty, sickly waves, but this was a half-hearted protest, almost petulant. The point had been conceded. Jo willed Mr Jennings to touch his wife. Reassure her with some sign of affection, but none came.

"We all have to do things we don't want." He simply overruled her. Didn't try to persuade her, reason with her or beg her to go to hospital. Just told her, then stood and turned to Jo. "I'll take her straight there."

Mrs Jennings pushed on the desk, helping herself to stand, shaking with the effort even such a small movement took. Jo breathed out with relief. Game over. For months she had been telling Mrs Jennings she needed referral, but the woman had refused. Refused to go to hospital and refused to let Jo speak to her husband about it. Now Jo had taken the matter into her own hands and gone against her patient's direct wishes, broken the trust, but it had worked and Mrs Jennings was heading for hospital. Whatever her fears, founded or not, she couldn't argue with her husband's decision, it wasn't that sort of relationship. A victory for Jo, of sorts. She just wished she felt better about it.

"So," she tried to sound bright, reassuring, firm, "take your wife up to Winchelsea Ward, then she can settle in before they have to get the transfusion started. Mr Kane will be round to see her as soon as he's finished his afternoon list, to examine her, organise tests and such like." She faced her patient. "All right?" Jo looked down before Mrs Jennings could disagree, even if only with a look.

Mr Jennings walked through the waiting room, looking neither left nor right, his wife walking slowly behind him, staring at the floor. No one in the room took any notice of them; their eyes were all focused on the information box, hoping desperately that the light would come on against their doctor's name, that they would be the next one in. Too busy to worry about the couple leaving, or to wonder about the problems or ailments of anyone but themselves.

A buzzer sounded and the light came on against Jo's name. A small smile of triumph flashed on the lips of a fussy looking man as he hung his number on the hook and hurried down the corridor, leaving a collective sigh of disappointment behind him. He walked fast and knocked on the door, going in immediately. He knew from past experience that it was better not to give a receptionist or a nurse the chance to stop him and ask him to wait whilst they had a word with the doctor. It was always more than a word. Often needing the doctor to see something or someone urgently and he would be sent back to the waiting room to stew again.

"You're running late, doctor. My appointment was scheduled to begin seventeen minutes ago precisely."

Jo looked up and tried not to let her irritation show. Why did it have to be this particular patient when she was already having such an awful morning?

"Hello, Mr Herring. Haemorrhoids playing you up again? You should bring a cushion." She closed the door, but not before seeing the smirk on the practice nurse's face as she hurried past, heading along the corridor to the waiting room. They all knew Mr Herring and what he was like. Everyone's least favourite patient. As she observed the irritation on Mr Herring's face, Jo permitted herself a tiny smile. It was only a small victory, perhaps, but a sweet one.

Later, after her final patient- a singularly inadequate personality, struggling to cope with his remarkably simple and uncluttered life- had left, Jo sank back in her chair and closed her eyes. Dr Jocasta Harriet Hughes MBChB MRCGP DipFMS to give her her full title. Jo to her friends, never Jock. Absolutely, categorically never Jock. Tall, slim, elegant, in an understated, natural way, she was a New-England-crab-cakes-on-a-bed-of-rocket-with-sweet-chilli-sauce-on-the-side sort of woman. A glass of Pinot Grigio with one cube of ice. Cool, precise, well-ordered, in looks and in life. With just a hint of fire, a slight glint in her eye, a slight twitch at the corner of her mouth, that let you know there was a lot more going on than she was prepared to let show from under that steely exterior. It seemed a lot more than just twelve hours since she had examined the body of the young prostitute on the sea front. At least the poor girl had a name now, a debit card having been found in the small clutch bag that was discovered with her. Ellie Smith. A name and, presumably, a grieving family. Jo slowly let out a deep sigh, letting the tension go, blowing it away, but the throbbing in her temple remained and she rubbed at it.

It hadn't been a good day all round. An early start with Ellie. Two packed surgeries. Patients whose problems were either all in their head or so bad they were beyond help, and a visit list that had included a gangrenous leg ulcer, the unavoidable necessity of sitting on a sticky, flea-ridden sofa whilst talking to an alcoholic, and an impacted bowel, with overflow. She looked down and nodded with satisfaction; the oatmeal coloured, linen mix trouser suit had survived quite well. She was more in need of resuscitation than her clothes, which was exactly how it should be. Jo hated to look creased, crumpled, or, heaven forbid, grubby, even if she felt it, like now. She sighed. What she needed more than anything was a shower. And a large glass of wine. And Albinoni. Or Pachelbel. Something light and airy, well-ordered and uncomplicated by emotion or drama.

What she got was a knock on the door, bringing her back to the real world with a bump.

Linda Crompton, Practice Manager and mother hen, opened the door and poked her head around it.

"No sleeping on the job allowed."

"I'm finished. Off duty." Jo protested.

"Ah well, that's where you're wrong, Doctor Hughes," Linda corrected her. "I've one more home visit for you." She paused as Jo groaned, "Oh, and you're needed at the police station."

3

As she entered the large modern building that was the East Sussex Police Headquarters, Jo was not exactly sure what she was about to face. On the telephone all the duty sergeant would say was that a prisoner had been slightly injured during arrest and that he wanted her to check and document said injuries. Whilst most of her work for the police was mundane, there was always the possibility of something more interesting, something other than the seemingly endless parade of drunks and the aftermath of petty violence. She could count on one hand the number of people whose life she could honestly say she had changed, or investigations that she had moved forward, but it was that hope of these happening again that kept her coming back.

She knew most of the uniformed sergeants and many of the constables by sight if not by name, but was much less familiar with the detectives, as had become all too evident at this morning's scene. Her world and theirs rarely coincided and, as a relative outsider, she was not privy to their gossip; all she heard were the moans and groans about them from the uniformed officers, who she suspected, were biased. She nodded at the civilian at the desk as she entered and was buzzed through the door into the body of the police station, where she walked briskly along the corridor and down the stairs to stop at another locked door, buzzing for attention and smiling up at the CCTV camera. The lock clicked open and she passed through into the reception area of the custody suite, stepping up to the desk and only just managing to stop her face from showing her dismay as she saw which custody sergeant was on duty this evening. He greeted her with a nod grunted,

"'Evening, Dr Hughes."

Sergeant Barlow was a well-known jobsworth with only three years to go until early retirement. He would be polite, do things rigidly by the book and not let her forget to dot an i or cross a t. Absolutely nothing was going to come between him and his pension.

"The prisoner is this way," he gestured, leading her down a narrow, brightly-lit corridor to the cell area, where he unlocked the gate and ushered her through before turning and locking it again behind them. Even though she knew they were being constantly watched on the camera screens at the desk, Jo always felt a slight frisson of excitement and fear that she was locked in with the mixture of thugs, sad cases and hardened criminals held in the cells.

"I'll bring him down to you." Sergeant Barlow told her as he began to unlock a cell, and Jo headed towards the treatment room at the end of the corridor.

The custody suite treatment room was slightly smaller than her consulting room, but felt much more spacious as it had less clutter and a somewhat different array of equipment. No box of toys by the door or cartoon posters on the wall. Nothing to soothe the troubled soul. Here the emphasis was on the job in hand: syringes and tubes for taking blood samples from drunk drivers in one cupboard, first aid equipment such as dressing packs, plasters and steristrips, to patch up both prisoners and policemen, in another. A sink to wash your hands, complete with the obligatory notice reminding her to do so frequently. As if she needed reminding. Most of the patients she saw here hadn't bathed in recent memory and were sweating off an excess of alcohol anyway. It always took a good soak in scented bathwater before she could get rid of the custody smell.

As well as two chairs and a desk, the room also had an examination couch so that patients could lie down, if it was absolutely necessary, but this was currently covered with several boxes of swabs for taking DNA samples. It was more like a nurse's room than a doctor's and that was what the job was most of the time. In some areas the police employed nurses to do the routine blood tests and dressings, cutting down on how often the forensic physician, as police surgeons had been renamed, had to be called out. Nurses come cheap and it was a case of anything to save money.

Jo had been thinking about giving up her three days a week at the surgery for some time, but, although those days and her occasional stints doing out of hours cover meant she often worked long hours, she was loth to stop when the police authority might decide to reduce her main job to the sort of walk-on part that had happened just up the road in Maidstone. What with paramedics and nurses even being allowed to pronounce death as well, it was getting to the point where being a forensic physician could end up a very part-time job indeed.

Jo looked up as her patient, Jimmy Allen according to the custody record sheet Sergeant Barlow handed her, came in, and tried not to wonder what he might have done. She preferred to think of him as just another patient at this stage. Knowing whether a prisoner was a suspected rapist, or a wife beater, would colour her attitude towards them, no matter how hard she tried not to let it. She might even be tempted to feel they deserved to suffer a little unnecessary pain, which would be human but distinctly unprofessional. So, staying ignorant of his possible crimes, she tried to examine Jimmy just as she would have done if he'd presented to her in her consulting room at the surgery rather than in the custody suite of the local nick.

She gestured to him to sit down and, pulling on surgical gloves, looked closely at his battered face. It clearly wasn't the first time his features had been re-arranged. There was a scar across one eyebrow, and the suggestion of another on his chin, though it was hard to make that one out clearly because of the two-day stubble that covered the lower half of his weaselly face. An unpleasant-looking person if ever she saw one, Jo thought to herself as she pulled down his swollen and split lower lip with her vinyl-covered finger. The frenum was intact. His lip would be sore for a few days but nothing more. She moved her hand up to his bloody and swollen nose and tweaked it.

"Fuck!"

Jimmy flinched away, but there had been no give or crunch when she tried to move the nasal bone.

"Not broken, Mr Allen. No need for you to go to hospital."

She dipped a cotton wool ball from the dressing pack in sterile saline and firmly wiped all the blood away.

"You a fucking sadist or what?"

"Or what, Mr Allen. Definitely an or what." She bundled up the used pack and threw it in the contaminated waste bin, stripped off her gloves and chucked them in after it.

The door to the examination room was open and she leant out, catching the custody sergeant's eye.

"No major damage. Fit to be detained." She came back in and sat

29

at the desk, writing up her examination on Jimmy's custody sheet as Sergeant Barlow approached.

"I want to make a complaint." Jimmy said.

"Oh yes?" She barely looked up, still busy documenting her findings.

"It was that bastard D.I. He did this. Hit me when me hands were cuffed. He can't do that, can he? I mean, I know my fucking rights."

"No need to swear, Mr Allen."

But he had Jo's attention now. She looked at the doorway, where Sergeant Barlow stood, looking as if he wanted to use a few choice words himself. His shift had just got complicated. So close to knocking-off time, and yet so far.

Like Sergeant Barlow, Jo was not happy about this turn of events and her dismay showed. She ushered Jimmy out of the treatment room and thought longingly of her bed. And a bath. But both seemed a very long way off now. Whilst she waited for Sergeant Barlow to return with the officer involved, she tried not to think about how difficult this could turn out to be. A bit of a disaster all round. Whatever else, she had to work with the police and was employed by them: she didn't want to suddenly find herself ostracised, considered an enemy rather than a friend. That was exactly what would happen if she found Jimmy's accusation to be true. She was under no illusions about her job. Many officers considered that she was only there to support their side of the story, not the scumbags they arrested. That said, she never had been and never would be on the same side as the sort of policeman that went around thumping people already subdued or restrained, unable to hit back. There was nothing she hated more than a bully.

As she rubbed at a place on the bridge of her nose that seemed to be the focus of her fast-developing tension headache, rolling her shoulders in an effort to loosen them, there was a sharp rap on the door.

"Come in," she called, hastily sitting straight and putting on her serious professional face.

Miller opened the door and came quickly into the room, almost doing a double-take when he saw Jo sitting at the desk.

"Oh, great, Doctor Hughes, I didn't realise it would be you."

"Only one police surgeon on duty at any given time in Hastings, Detective Inspector Miller. Have a seat."

He sat, and appeared to rapidly try to regroup his thoughts.

"If I had a pound for every prisoner who said I'd used unnecessary force…"

"And if I had a pound for every policeman who said he never touched the bloke…"

They looked at each other, both knowing exactly where the other stood. Jo took the opportunity to size up the man in front of her.

He still looked good. Clean, neat, nothing flashy and as if he was, in general, a solid and reliable sort of bloke. A man's man. Closer inspection showed him to be on the downward slope towards forty, but his once taut, rugger-player physique was only sagging a little. He obviously kept up some sort of physical exercise other than propping up the rugby club bar. Squash, Jo thought, he probably plays squash. His hair, a rich brown, still thick and with a tendency to curl where he had let it grow a little longer than he should, had developed a sprinkling of grey above his ears- not that it was likely he would have noticed, she thought. He didn't seem the type to be overly troubled by either vanity or introspection. Like many men, he might worry a little that his hair may start receding one day, but Jo was willing to bet that that was as close as he got to navel gazing. As he sat in front of Jo, giving her an unashamedly appraising look, he appeared unworried by what she might think of him, but she suddenly found herself feeling less secure about the impression he was getting of her. She looked away, tucked her hair behind her ear, and mentally kicked herself for letting him get to her.

"Hold out your hands, please, Inspector."

Miller held out his hands, well aware that the grazed and swollen knuckle at the base of his right little finger looked exactly like a punch injury.

"Caught it on the car door," he explained, "as we were putting the prisoner in the back. He tried it on; my finger got whacked against the edge."

Jo pulled on gloves and took his hand. Gently feeling along the fifth metacarpal towards the knuckle. Miller winced.

"You ought to have it x-rayed."

"It's fine, honest."

She looked him in the eye.

"I would expect there to be a line, or ridge across the injury, if you

hit it against the edge of the car door. This," she indicated his hand, "…
is more indicative of hitting a flattish surface." Like a face, she left the
words unspoken, but still hanging in the air.

"The edge of the door, the side, whatever, makes no difference; it
was the car I hit, not Jimmy Allen."

"And how did he get the bloody nose?"

"Struggling. Resisting arrest. My hand went into the car door; his
nose met the car roof." Miller looked her straight in the eye. Challenging her to rebut his version of events. "He should have been a
good boy and got in the car when he was told. Have you finished?"

She had, but she certainly wasn't going to admit it now.

"I should clean the graze."

"It's fine. I washed it as soon as I got back."

"As you wish."

"Is that it?"

"Yes. You can go now, Detective Inspector."

He stood.

"And what are you going to put in your report, Dr Hughes?"

She gave him her most impenetrable smile. Small, cold and getting
nowhere near her eyes.

"You'll have to wait and see, won't you?"

He looked at her, weighing up his next move.

"Jimmy Allen is a rapist. A torturing, perverted, violent rapist who
finally went too far and killed his victim. If I don't prove it before we
have to release him, he'll do it again. Think about that and the amount
of time we've already wasted with this when you make your report,
doctor, not to mention the added pressure for an early release if you
support his ridiculous claim." And he left.

Jo felt her colour rise. This was exactly what she didn't need to hear.
If he was so worried about giving Jimmy a get out of jail card, why
had he hit him in the first place? Because she was pretty sure that that
was what he had done. And why blame her? The moment a complaint
was made there was a set procedure that had to be followed and he
knew that. The doctor had to check the alleged assailant, Miller, for
wounds that might be consistent with the injuries inflicted on the alleged victim, Jimmy Allen. End of story. It wasn't her fault all this had
happened, it was his. She slammed the pen down on the desk and took

a deep breath, considering what to put in her report, when there was another knock at the door.

"Yes?" she almost shouted before getting herself under control. "Come in."

The door opened and Detective Sergeant Bob Jeffries came in. He'd managed to put on a clean, roughly ironed shirt but that was as far as he had been prepared to go to smarten up for work.

"Doctor Hughes? I just thought I'd let you know that I was a witness. To the alleged assault on Jimmy Allen."

"How convenient. Don't tell me, you support DI Miller's story?"

"Exactly."

Jo looked at the sergeant, and weighed up the options. Should she try and get the real story out of him? He was one of the few CID men she had heard about even if she hadn't met him before. Older than his boss, more experienced perhaps, his once-ginger hair now faded and laced with white. If his boss was Man at Marks and Spencer: middle-of-the road, good quality, always smart, Jeffries was Man at Matalan: you got what was available whether it suited or not. Everyone, except possibly Jeffries himself, knew he would never make it beyond detective sergeant because of an inability to play the political game or to keep his mouth shut when a smart remark came to mind. Tact and diplomacy were foreign territory to Detective Sergeant Bob Jeffries. But he was loyal to the force, and to his boss, in his own way.

Jo sighed. If it was the case of two officers' word against Jimmy Allen's her report would make very little difference. Besides, it could have happened the way they were telling it, even if her gut reaction was that it hadn't.

When Jo came out to custody reception with her report, she saw Miller and Jeffries at the desk along with a man she recognised as Harry Worthing, a legal executive rather than a qualified solicitor and almost certainly there to represent Jimmy Allen. Harry had been a policeman once and had even got to the heady heights of duty sergeant until a slight misunderstanding about the social club accounts ended his career prematurely. Harry never hid the fact that he felt he had been treated unfairly, or that he bore a grudge. It was this grudge that had led him to make a radical change in his choice of career. He had crossed to the other side. The dark side. The Defence. No longer being on the job, he had run to fat, and the buttons on his cheap nylon suit and polyester shirt looked as if they were in imminent danger of giving up the struggle to stay fastened. His face was an unhealthy choleric shade with hints of purple on his bulbous nose and his greasy hair could have done with a cut. Harry hadn't hit the big time with his new job; his pay was less than when he was in the police force, and that didn't make him happy either. What made him happy was revenge. He counted every petty vandal and thief released without charge as a personal victory against the bastards who made him resign over a few poxy quid.

Harry was smiling now, as he turned to Jo.

"Ah, the good doctor. I trust your report makes it clear that my man was punched whilst already under restraint?"

Jo was irritated, her dislike of Harry almost as strong as her negative feelings towards Miller and Jeffries.

"My report makes no such judgements, Mr Worthing. I am a doctor, not a clairvoyant. The only people who can tell you how exactly your client got his injuries are Jimmy himself and the two arresting officers."

Miller looked relieved and Jeffries grinned.

"Bad luck, Harry."

Worthing scowled. "You won't be smiling half an hour into a no-comment interview. You've nothing on Jimmy and you won't get it whilst I'm around, of that you can be sure. He'll be out of here first thing in the morning, you'll see." He turned to Barlow. "I'll speak to my client now, sergeant."

He nodded at Sergeant Barlow to let him through into the custody area so that he could make sure that Jimmy was well-schooled in repeating the words "No comment". Probably a lesson Jimmy had no need to learn as he was hardly a virgin to police interviews.

Jo slammed the report down on the desk in front of Sergeant Barlow and turned towards the exit.

"If you could let me out first, sergeant." And she walked towards the door with Sergeant Barlow scurrying after her. She didn't see Miller's appraising stare as she went out but she could feel it, hot on the back of her neck, and she was uncomfortably aware of a flush coming to her cheeks. Thank goodness she had her back to him.

4

Hastings Police Headquarters had been built on the outskirts of the town in the eighties, on the Town Centre side of the West Hill, along with the hospital and the council buildings, all part of the administrative stranglehold that the residents of the Old Town, the medieval fishing village that nestled in the Bourne Valley between the East and West Hills, resented so much. The police building stood back from the road, and the visitors' car park was screened from public view by several large trees, showing either an uncommon degree of discretion and sensitivity from the planners and architects or, more likely, that they had failed to get permission to fell such old and well established specimens. Whatever the reason for their presence, many were grateful for the cover as they parked their cars, anxious not to be seen in this place under embarrassing circumstances.

It was late September and summer was coming to an indecisive end. One day warm and sunny, the next cold and damp. Impossible to second guess. Darkness was falling fast as Jo hurried through the light drizzle towards her midnight blue convertible Audi TT. A frivolous car, her father had told her disapprovingly. Not a suitable car for a serious person, a career woman, a doctor. Jo loved it. Her little piece of rebellion. God knows what he would have said if she had bought the scarlet version, and she had been sorely tempted.

She slipped into the driver's seat, glad she had put the roof up before leaving the car earlier. There were few things worse than driving home with a wet seat, and it happened to her regularly. She slammed the door shut, still seething about her second encounter with DI Miller.

"What an arrogant -" She struggled to find a word that was acceptable, but finally chose: "prick!" The nearest to a swear word that she could bring herself to use but, she told herself, entirely justified in the circumstances.

She switched on the wipers and punched buttons on the radio, in no mood now for anything soothingly light and airy. She wanted something angry and discordant but that didn't seem to be available. So she hit the off button and drove away with nothing to distract her thoughts from Jimmy Allen's bloody nose and DI Miller's classic punch injury. A bully in uniform- even though he wore plain clothes now. She realised that he must suspect Jimmy Allen of killing the prostitute who had been found strangled in her own home three or four weeks back. The ligature strangulation. She remembered reading all the grisly details in the local paper. Jo shuddered. Krissy, the poor girl had been called. Although some of Jo's patients certainly sold their bodies on the street or in cheap hotels, Krissy hadn't actually been one of hers. That didn't make it any easier, though. She had tried to get across to some of the working girls, particularly the younger, less hardened ones, just how dangerous prostitution could be. If the sexually transmitted diseases didn't get you, one of your punters might, but the older ones accepted the risks and the younger ones refused to believe it could happen to them. Delusions of immortality. It was intensely frustrating.

She drove fast down the hill and along the seafront, past the strip of amusement arcades and fish and chip shops that linked the Old Town to the Town Centre. Past the mini-golf, the toilets where Ellie had died and then the kiddies' fun fair, and further on to the fishermen's beach, where the largest beach-launched fishing fleet in Britain stood, the boats looking strange and awkward on the stones, like fish out of water, with the net shops towering, black and menacing, close by. There was no doubt in Jo's mind that the heart, and particularly the soul, of Hastings were housed in the Old Town, where she lived. She slowed to make the left turn up the valley, feeling the tension slowly slip away from her shoulders on the familiar road up the East Hill.

Jo left the car parked at the back of the square, brick-built, Georgian manor house that she called home. With its tall windows and graceful lines it stood out as different from the Victorian villas more common in this part of town. The house was situated in a commanding position high up on the East Hill and at some time in the past twenty years it had been converted into flats, or apartments, as the Estate Agent had insisted on calling them when Jo bought the one that was up for sale on the top floor. It was just three rooms: a bedroom, a bathroom and a living room with a kitchen area along one wall, divided from the living area by a breakfast bar. The rooms were large and well-proportioned, the conversion having been sympathetic, not like the amateurish efforts she had seen elsewhere: plasterboard walls sectioning off bathrooms in the corner of the bedroom, chopping through ornate ceilings, making a mockery of the original features. But it wasn't the ceilings, the sympathetic conversion or the size of the rooms that had sold the flat to Jo the moment she walked into it: it was the views. From the main living room you could see the coast, the funfair and promenade she had just driven along, almost as far as St Leonards. Down and to the right was the Old Town nestling in the valley, crowded and compact, and further, across to the West Hill, the castle ruins, and the swathe of green parkland crested by a terrace of white houses. It was a view that never ceased to impress her, whether it was early morning with the rooftops floating in a sea mist, the castle backlit by a setting sun or, like now, with the street lights in the valley twinkling invitingly below.

Jo switched on the lights as she came into the living room, throwing her bag onto the cream sofa, and purposely ignored the flashing light of the answer phone as she headed straight for the modern beech wood and stainless steel kitchen area. She took an open bottle of white wine from the fridge and poured herself a glass. Sipping as she stood at the breakfast bar and looked out at the lights shimmering in the rain on the window, she wondered if she should risk the wet and walk down to the town for something to eat. Or perhaps she should get back in the car and head for the supermarket? A brief glance at what was on offer in the fridge hadn't inspired. A carton of milk that was several days past its best, half a lemon, slightly shrivelled, some un-salted butter and an open packet of mixed salad leaves that, on closer inspection, had begun to get slimy. Maybe someday soon they would genetically modify salad leaves to last long enough to be eaten. And perhaps the rain would stop, too.

Jo enjoyed cooking; it was the shopping she hated. Wandering around soulless supermarkets, which always seemed to be filled with screaming children, and God knows she had enough of screaming children at work; then there was the muzak and tinny announce-ments, all combining to give her a headache within minutes of her ar-rival. Not to mention the risk of running into a patient. On more than one occasion she had been quizzed about test results in the middle of the frozen food section, desperately trying to remember the person's name, let alone their results.

She checked out the cupboard. Passata, garlic paste, extra virgin olive oil, freeze-dried basil, not as good as fresh, but a reasonable compromise. All the ingredients for chicken Parmigiana. Except the chicken. And the buffalo mozzarella. And the shaved parmesan. Not to mention fresh salad and crusty bread. She opened the freezer door and looked at the stack of frozen ready meals that were her only choice. As usual, they didn't appeal. They seemed so appetising, not to mention quick and easy, when she was doing the shopping, but when it came down to it, she never fancied them. Some of them must have been in the freezer for months. She was too tired to play salmonella and listeriosis roulette. She closed the freezer without taking anything out and refilled her glass, wandering reluctantly over to the answering machine. Jo had a mobile phone, but only work and Kate Ward, her best friend, were allowed to have the number, and Kate knew better than to use it for anything except emergencies. Her father also had the number for emergency use, on the proviso that he never let on to Jo's mother that he had it. He quite understood her reasoning. The thought of being at everybody's beck and call every second filled Jo with horror. She hated the thought of people constantly accusing her of not answering her phone and liked to be able to pick and choose which calls she would answer. She pressed play and a synthesised voice announced that she had three new messages. The first, as usual, was her mother, fishing for news on the boyfriend front; whatever happened to that nice young man from the city? Could she mean the rich, brash commodity trader, who admitted to rotating his "women" on a weekly basis to stop himself from getting bored? Jo had thoughts on exactly how she'd like to rotate him, and from which part of his anatomy. The second message was from her friend Kate, suggesting they meet for an exercise class or, failing that, a calorie-laden meal out later in the week, tomorrow maybe? And the third was silent apart from some audible breathing. Jo replayed the last message. Was the breathing threatening? Or sexual? It seemed too quiet for that. Just gentle, silent, somehow reproachful breathing. Jo erased the messages and looked around the room. The stillness, the emptiness, seeming less peaceful and more accusatory to her now. No cat or dog, not even a goldfish to welcome her home. Maybe her mother was right, maybe it was time she got a husband, or changed her life in some way, or at least changed her phone number.

She went into the kitchen and poured herself another glass of wine whilst she gave it some thought.

5

Jo was making a much-needed cup of coffee in the tiny staff kitchenette on the top floor of the modern surgery building where she worked as a part time general practitioner. While she waited for the kettle to boil, she was checking out the cupboards in the hope of finding a biscuit.

"Skipped breakfast again, Jocasta?"

Dr Hugh Grantham, the practice Senior Partner, was watching her with an amused smile. In his fifties, with his hair still thick and stylish, if almost completely grey, Dr Grantham endured a reputation as a bit of a ladies' man. This renown was enhanced by the minor scandal, albeit from twenty years ago, of marrying a young and beautiful woman who, inconveniently, had been a patient- until they started seeing each other, of course. Dr Grantham was very strict about protocol; he knew that many a doctor had found themselves in unnecessary trouble by not observing protocol. So his beautiful young patient moved to another doctor at another surgery and, after a decent interval, became his wife. Not that his precautions stopped the gossip mongers for one second; the General Medical Council might not have been able to touch him, but many a female patient who thought marrying a doctor might be glamorous, or that at least seducing one might prove lucrative, tried it on. Dr Grantham had developed an efficient line in firm but gentle rebuffs and had only once had to resort to refusing to see a patient ever again, insisting that she be removed from his list. Even then, he had only felt the need for such drastic action because she was always coming to see him with chest pain of unknown cause, and would strip off for an examination despite Dr Grantham's insistence that it really wasn't necessary on a daily basis. And just the top half would do, anyway.

"Didn't have time to do any shopping yesterday. So no bread or milk in the flat."

She poked around in the only biscuit tin that had rattled when she shook it, but she was disappointed.

"They've all gone soggy. I'll have to persuade Linda to let me have one of hers."

"It has always seemed profoundly unfair that the practice manager keeps an emergency supply of chocolate biscuits in her room, for the use of ladies only. How does she know that men don't get PMT too?"

Jo thought for a moment.

"No, I'm sorry Hugh, Neil's story about being a chocolate addict in withdrawal got close to working, mainly because of his very realistic jitteriness, but male PMT? I don't think so."

"Neil is always jittery. I think he's thyrotoxic."

Jo poured milk into her coffee. "You could be right." She peered at the insipid liquid in her mug. "We should get a proper coffee machine."

"Then you would all take too many coffee breaks and the patients would never get seen."

Jo could see his point as she took another quick look in the biscuit tin, but it still only contained a few very old and broken custard creams. "Maybe I should have brought the cereal packet with me and had breakfast here."

Dr Grantham took the milk bottle from her.

"We don't have enough milk and anyway, why didn't you have time to shop, hmm? Get called out to the police station again, did you?"

Jo looked uncomfortable.

"How did you guess?"

"Because I had a complaint from the out of hours service that a call for a visit had come through to the surgery at a quarter to six, but the patient was told to wait quarter of an hour and then to call again, because the duty doctor was otherwise engaged."

Jo had the grace to look guilty.

"It wasn't an urgent visit. Could have waited until today."

"But it didn't. She called out the emergency doctor and I'm sure I don't have to remind you that the service is not there to do routine visits that you don't have time to do yourself."

"I'm not the only one to -"

"No, but maybe you should have told Mrs Cartwell not to mention it to the doctor who finally visited. Or maybe you should stop messing around playing at being a police doctor. Rushing here and there and not doing a good job for them or for us." He stirred his coffee vigorously. "Time to decide where your future lies, Jocasta. We could offer you a full time position here, partner even." He made to leave but turned at the doorway. "Oh, and if you do manage to get some biscuits out of Linda, bring one down to me, would you?"

He left Jo to her thoughts. He was right in many ways, of course, and being a partner was tempting, if only for the feeling that she would have arrived, have made something of her life, something tangible, her mother might even approve- but the thought of spending all day, every day in the same place, seeing the same patients, wasn't so appealing. She could see herself twenty years down the line, still reassuring Mr Herring that there was nothing seriously wrong with him. She needed the two jobs, not for the money so much as for her sanity.

Jo wiped the last crumb from the corner of her mouth with only a tinge of guilt that she hadn't taken one to Dr Grantham and thought that she must try and persuade Linda to stock plain chocolate digestives rather than the milk chocolate variety, they were so much nicer. One last sip of coffee and a quick check to see that there were no more crumbs on her lap or desk and she was ready for the second onslaught of patients. She looked at her computerised appointment list. Next in line was the ten-forty patient. She was only running five minutes late- that was a turn up for the books. The name, Timothy Lockwood, meant nothing to her, so at least he wasn't one of her regular, heart-sink, patients. That elite group that every doctor has, and wishes he didn't. The hypochondriacs and the genuinely sick but those for whom, whatever the doctor does to help, it is never enough. Like Mr Herring. She pressed the buzzer and double clicked on Timothy's name to reveal his records, flicking through what little information there was in them.

There was a light tap on the door as she read that Timothy Lockwood was aged nine and had only recently registered with the practice so there was no past history to go on, yet.

"Come in," Jo called and Timothy and his mother appeared in the doorway. She smiled reassuringly, as both mother and child seemed apprehensive.

"Have a seat, Mrs Lockwood. Hello, Timothy. What can I do for

45

you?"

She listened as Mrs Lockwood, in her thirties and good-looking, in a high maintenance style, explained that Timothy had been feeling increasingly unwell over the last few days. Lethargic, nauseous, listless, she said and the woman was clearly irritated by the fact that, even when she persuaded him to go to school, they were sending him back home.

"It's not like it's anything specific, doctor. He just isn't feeling well. Of course," She glanced at Timothy but he sat quietly, apparently not listening to what she was saying, "he's not helped by all the stress. My situation. My husband and I, well, we're in the process of getting divorced. We are legally separated for now, and I have an interim settlement. I'm in the middle of changing lawyers because my last one was useless. That's why I'm here. Hastings was all I could afford thanks to him."

Jo swallowed the remark that sprang to her lips and kept it professional.

"What about Timothy? You have sole custody?"

"Joint, supposedly. Not that Philip's ever around to do his fair share."

Jo turned to Timothy, deciding that he was probably going to be more use.

"So, Timothy, let's take a look at you, shall we?"

Whilst he was taking off his shirt, Jo warmed her stethoscope in her hand. She listened to his chest, front and back, felt for glands in his neck, peered in his throat and ears, took his temperature, and all the while he was quietly cooperative and polite but listless. Listless was definitely the word, Jo thought.

"Have you been drinking more than usual? Been thirsty?"

Timothy shook his head.

"Can't seem to get him to eat or drink anything much."

"Up on the couch, young man, so that I can feel your tummy."

He did as he was asked and lay back, letting Jo palpate his abdomen.

"Does it hurt anywhere?" She asked, but he shook his head.

"Right, off you pop and get your shirt back on."

"It's nothing, isn't it? Just the stress?"

"It might be that, Mrs Lockwood, but I always think it's best to be sure" Jo was already pulling out blood test request forms, filling them in.

"There's nothing in his past history I should know about? Anything that could be relevant? His old notes haven't arrived yet," She explained.

"No, he's been quite healthy. But sensitive. That's all." Mrs Lockwood seemed more surprised Jo was taking it seriously than she was worried that her son might really be ill. "What could it be? If he has got something wrong, that is."

"It could be any number of things, Mrs Lockwood, but he isn't showing signs of anything acute. We'll wait and see if the picture gets clearer, or if Timothy gets better, and, in the meantime, these blood tests will narrow it down if he doesn't."

She held out the form to explain it.

"I've asked for liver function tests, full blood count in case of anaemia, although I saw no signs of that when I checked his eyes, and ESR, to see if he shows signs of fighting an infection, blood sugar for diabetes, Us and Es, they tell me how his kidneys are doing. And I'd like a specimen of urine, too, in case he has a kidney or bladder infection brewing." She opened a cupboard and took out a specimen bottle.

Mrs Lockwood turned and checked Timothy had finished getting dressed.

"Just wait outside for a minute, all right?"

Timothy went outside obediently and Mrs Lockwood turned back to Jo.

"You don't think it's all in his mind then? Just a bit of attention seeking?"

It was clearly what she wanted to hear. What she wanted to be able to tell the school so they didn't keep sending Timothy home. Jo took a deep breath.

"It might be, Mrs Lockwood, but that doesn't mean we should ignore it. Whatever is causing Timothy to feel so unwell will need to be treated, one way or another."

It was gone one o'clock by the time she had finished her paperwork and went into the cluttered main office to leave the audio tape of letters for the secretary, and a sheaf of test request forms and repeat prescriptions to be left for collection by her patients. Linda was checking something on the computer as Dr Sinha, a lovely, unflappable, middle-aged Asian woman who had been a partner at the practice for many years, looked on.

"Can we chase up this lad's old notes?" Jo asked, placing Timothy Lockwood's details on the desk. Linda glanced at them.

"Sure, oh, and by the way, I've told Hugh. We're going to need another meeting."

Linda had on her stern voice which warned Jo that this was not good news.

"We aren't anywhere near reaching the eighty percent mark for smoking status recorded in the last fifteen months."

"Oh." Jo found it hard to work up much enthusiasm over this catastrophe.

Dr Sinha sighed.

"It's not the end of the world, you know, Linda."

"I know, Dr Sinha, but just don't blame me when we don't get as much money from QOF as we anticipated. It really doesn't take long to ask whether a person smokes or not." she turned to Jo," And you aren't very good at it either, in fact you have the lowest percentage."

Jo held her hands up in mock surrender.

"Mea culpa. Mea culpa. I promise I'll ask everyone tomorrow."

"You're doing a baby clinic tomorrow."

"So I'll ask them if their parents smoke, okay?"

Linda smiled and left the office.

"Questions, questions." Dr Sinha sighed. "We spend all our time asking questions of our patients. About diet, about smoking, exercise, alcohol intake. Maybe if we ignored all that we would have time to find out what is actually wrong with them." She took a fresh sheaf of letters from her basket and started sorting through them. "Do you have a lot of visits, Jo?"

"Not too many. Just as well, really," Dr Sinha gave her a questioning look, There's a post mortem I want to watch."

Jo hurried out, and Dr Sinha shook her head.

"Rather you than me," she said to the empty room.

6

Jo watched carefully as Dr Dunbar did an external examination of the body whilst it was still fully clothed, carefully removing the rubber tourniquet and depositing it in a plastic evidence bag, before instructing Dave to strip the corpse. He stood back, double-gloved hands held close to his plastic-apron-covered stomach, whilst his assistant carefully cut away the flimsy top, skirt and thong, and put them in the property bag along with her shoes. The pale, pathetically thin body spoke volumes about a life of misuse and abuse. How could she have done this to herself? It was a question Jo had asked many times, but never managed to answer.

"The malnourished body of a young woman, aged approximately eighteen." The medico-legal formality and precision of the language used by Dr Dunbar as he spoke into the small microphone hanging above his head soothed Jo, and took the sting out of what was about to happen. Dr Dunbar continued, starting at the head and working his way down.

"No visible injuries to the head and neck." He lifted each eyelid in turn. "No petecheaie. Some froth on the lips, can you swab that please, Dave?" He paused to allow his assistant to do so. "No visible scars on the thorax, small scar in the right iliac fossa, consistent with an appendectomy, scarring and track marks of varying age over the veins of both arms. Two recent puncture marks to the dorsal aspect of the left hand." Jo looked up. Two? Dr Dunbar set the girls' hand down and continued, oblivious to her interest. "Old scar on the left knee, a blister on the left heel, and bilateral incipient Tailor's bunions. Why do these girls wear such inappropriate footwear?" Jo and Dave both decided this was a rhetorical question and didn't answer as Dr Dunbar continued: "Let's turn her, Dave, roll her towards you."

Dave slid his hands under the thin body and turned her onto her side facing himself so that Dr Dunbar could inspect the girl's back.

"No visible scars or bruising. Lividity present on the back of the legs and buttocks, consistent with death occurring in a sitting position.

Roll her back, Dave, and let's start cutting."

As Dr Dunbar sliced a broad Y incision from the tip of each shoulder, arms meeting at the base of the sternum and following on down the length of the abdomen, Jo couldn't suppress a shudder. No matter how many autopsies she had seen, the first cut, the first defilement of the dead body never failed to fill her with disgust. She wondered if anyone ever got used to it and looked up to see Dave Ball watching her. She smiled at him reassuringly. He was probably wondering if she was about to throw up or faint. Well, she wasn't. She hoped.

Later, Jo sat in Dr Dunbar's office, drinking Earl Grey tea from the delicate china cup and saucer provided by the pathologist. A quick glance under the saucer whilst he was out of the room had told her the tea set was genuine Limoges. Nice as it was, she would have preferred something less valuable, less of a breakage worry, and put it down, very gently.

Dr Dunbar bustled back into the room waving a piece of paper at her.

"She has yet to be formally identified, but it seems certain that her name is Eleanor Smith, known as Ellie. You can never be sure just from cards found on them, in my experience, she could have borrowed a friend's, or stolen it, but Mike seems to think it is her. She worked the street, lived in a hostel and didn't have a pimp as far as anyone knows. The heroin solution found in the syringe was certainly somewhat stronger than usually hits the streets, but I also sent the foil wraps- there were two pieces of foil rolled up together, suggesting two doses- for analysis so that we could check the strength. One of the doses was slightly stronger than normal quality, but not worryingly so, and the other much weaker. What did for young Miss Ellie, therefore, was probably the fact that she must have taken the two hits in one go with only a short space of time between them."

"A double dose? You're thinking suicide?"

"Possibly, although we can't totally rule out an accidental overdose. If she took the weaker dose first and it wore off too quickly, or didn't do enough, then she might have taken the second stronger one thinking it would be the same, perhaps. We will never know for certain." He stopped for a moment, trying to piece it together logically. "I suspect her blood alcohol will prove to be raised as her stomach contents seemed to be blue and alcoholic in nature. Perhaps she was too drunk to realise what she was doing."

"What a waste. She was only eighteen. Why on earth did she have to go and kill herself? Accidentally or otherwise. You haven't had reports back on any of the other tests have you? Was she HIV positive?"

"Won't know for a while yet."

Dave Ball popped his head into the office.

"I've got a Mrs Brierly in reception, Dr Dunbar. The mother of Ellie Smith."

Dr Dunbar grimaced.

"I'll speak to her if you like," Jo volunteered.

"That would be very kind." Dr Dunbar was obviously relieved. "She can have the body once she's done the formal identification. The family just need to let Dave here know which funeral directors they want it released to. No point keeping her any longer than necessary." He sounded tired for the first time since Jo had first met him. "You know that other poor lass, been here for weeks waiting for the second autopsy, and when we finally told her family, a brother, he could have the body he didn't want it, so she's off to Gilberts' this afternoon or tomorrow and the council will have to pay. A pauper's grave, just in case anyone wants her body for a third post mortem."

"Maybe he hasn't got the money to pay for it. Burials can be expensive."

"That's no excuse, Jocasta. There are grants, charities. She was still his family. It's one thing for some spinster of ninety to have no one to bury them but she was still young, compared to me at least." He really seemed to have taken Krissy's fate to heart. "Speaking of getting old, haven't seen your father at any LMC dinners of late. Just because he's retired doesn't mean he doesn't have to attend, you know. I need at least one other old bugger I can talk to, the others all seem impossibly young."

"I'll tell him." Jo smiled and Dr Dunbar stood up.

"I hope you two youngsters are both going out to enjoy yourselves tonight. If ever you needed reminding that life can be all too short, working down here should do it."

He went out and Dave and Jo exchanged looks. Dave shrugged.

"Guess it's been a bad day. You going out at all tonight, Dr Hughes?"

Jo picked up her bag.

"Having dinner with a friend, but I've one more call to make first, and that's after I've spoken to Mrs Brierly. How about you?"

"Oh, I have plans, I certainly do. I will be tripping the light fantastic, don't you worry. So if the earth moves, it's not an earthquake, just me boogying on down." And he gave Jo a private display of his skills as he went down the corridor, a wobbly, disco-dancing green giant, light on his feet despite his great weight. Jo laughed, and he turned at the end of the corridor to give her a grin and a wave before disappearing into the post mortem room, his natural habitat, leaving Jo to make her way upstairs to the Chapel of Rest reception, where Ellie's mum was waiting to hear why her daughter was dead.

"She seems to have died from an overdose of heroin. The final test results won't be back for a day or two, but I don't think there will be any surprises. Did you know she was using?"

Mrs Brierly nodded but couldn't seem to stop crying and her words came out in brief bursts between sobs.

"She started, you know, injecting, a few months back."

"Did she try and get help? Get off drugs?"

"Don't think so. She said she would do. When she was ready. I told her that might be too late. I told her drugs were a risk. But she just laughed, said she was careful. Knew what she was doing. I don't understand it."

"Understand what, Mrs Brierly?"

"How she could do it."

"Inject drugs? Well a lot of -"

"No." She interrupted, "I mean, how she could overdose?"

"Well, the batch might have been stronger than she was used to."

"So someone might be responsible? Might have caused her to die?" Like many a bereaved relative before her, Mrs Brierly desperately wanted someone to blame for her daughter's death.

"Well, it's possible. We'll look into it, of course."

"And let me know?"

"Of course." Jo hesitated, not wanting to give the woman false hope. "But, even if it is a strong batch, the chances of being able to prove it, to charge someone, well, they are very remote indeed."

"I don't care. I just need to know what happened, Doctor. Promise me you'll find out how my baby died. Please?"

Jo patted her on her hand.

"I'll do my best, I promise."

Mrs Brierly sniffed.

"You must think it's odd, me crying like this. After all, it was me that threw her out, put her on the streets. I mustn't care about her, that's what you think, isn't it?" She sobbed again and looking at the already drenched hankie the woman was clutching, Jo fished in her bag for the small pack of tissues she always carried.

"Not at all."

"But I did. You know. I did care. It's just that she didn't get on with Terry, my husband."

"Her stepdad?" Jo ventured, wondering how many dozens of times she had heard a similar story. Mrs Brierly nodded. God, it was depressing.

"Made his life hell, she did. I know it's not right, but I don't blame him for hitting her." She looked up anxiously. "Just the once it was, I think, and she drove him to it. She'd been such a sweet little girl and then, well, you know what it's like with teenagers."

Especially when mum moves a new man in.

"She seemed to change overnight. I had no choice but to kick her out. It was her or Terry."

'So you picked your new lover over your own daughter,' Jo thought but didn't say. She just smiled blandly as she patted Mrs Brierly on the hand.

"You mustn't blame yourself," she said and wished she meant it.

7

Jo pushed open the doors into Winchelsea Ward and, making her way through the assorted hoists, drip stands and wheelchairs that litter every hospital corridor, headed towards the ward sister's office. The office was supposed to be guarded by the nurses at their station, but the desk was currently unmanned, so there was no one to stop Jo going straight into see Sister Ojo.

"Dr Hughes. What can we do for you?"

Jo smiled. Sister Ojo-Burunde was a larger-than-life Nigerian woman who had lived in this country for many years and worked at the hospital almost as long. She ruled the gynae wards like a benign dictator and took no nonsense from anyone: patients, relatives, Chief Executives from the Hospital Trust, or consultants. Especially not from consultants.

"I came to ask how one of my patients was doing, Sister Ojo. A Mrs Jennings."

Sister Ojo's face grew immediately grave. If Jo hadn't already realised that it was not looking good for her patient, she certainly did now.

"That poor woman. Why she didn't come for treatment earlier, we will never know. Mr Kane and his team were just here and they've decided not to put her first on the list for tomorrow, she's just not strong enough, but they can't wait long, it's almost certainly spread already."

She gave a heavy shrug that spoke volumes.

Sister Ojo looked up at the door and Jo turned to see a good-looking man standing in the doorway.

"Do we have the result on Mrs Ahmed's FSH level, Sister Ojo?" He asked and Jo automatically gave him the once over as she waited for Sister Ojo to finish letting him know about his patient's result. He must have been in his early forties, but was well-preserved and dressed in what Jo suspected was a bespoke shirt and suit trousers. An expensive silk tie, held in place with a gold tiepin, completed the ensemble. No lowly white doctor's coat for this consultant. He was busily doing up his gold cufflinks, having obviously rolled his sleeves up to examine a patient, and once the cuffs were secured he turned to the office door and retrieved a suit jacket that he must have hung there before doing his rounds, and not just slung on the hook. Jo was impressed: there were not many men she knew who cared enough about their appearance to bring a clothes hanger to work. He left the door open having recovered his jacket, and Jo could see out into the ward. By the time he had put his jacket on, Sister Ojo had finished her report.

"This is Mrs Jennings' GP. Dr Hughes." Sister Ojo introduced Jo. "Mr Kane is the consultant in charge of her case."

"Pleased to meet you, Mr Kane." Jo stood and held out her hand and he took it in both of his.

"Jonathan, please, Dr, er, Hughes, was it?"

"Jocasta. Jocasta Hughes." Jo was unusually hesitant and felt the need of something more formal than Jo. Mr Kane definitely fancied himself as a bit of a charmer and the look he was giving Jo was an open evaluation.

"Jocasta? What a delightful name. Almost as delightful as its owner."

Jo tried to extract her hand and he seemed to suddenly realise that he was still holding it between his own.

"I'm so sorry. Do have your hand back. I was getting a bit carried away there, and who could blame me?"

Jo smiled; that little trace of humour, of self-awareness that almost amounted to self-mockery, even though she suspected that it was a well-practised line, redeemed him in her eyes. He wasn't just another hopeless smoothie.

"That's all right, Mr, um, Jonathan." Jo corrected herself. "I understand Mrs Jennings is not on your list for tomorrow?"

"Ah, yes, Mrs Jennings. No. I have spoken to her, and her husband, too, and explained the seriousness of the situation. How she really ought to have come to us sooner. I'm afraid that the cancer has almost certainly spread; the scan seems to suggest considerable pelvic involvement, and she's really very weak. We're going to do a second transfusion, and ask the oncologists for their opinion before we open her up, make sure she's up to it. It's possible they may suggest some chemo to shrink the tumour before we operate, if we can wait that long."

"I've been trying to persuade her to let me refer her for some time."

"I'm sure, I'm sure. But sometimes patients don't take our advice, do they?"

"Sister?" A staff nurse was standing in the doorway clutching a chart. "Lisa Blaney? In bay C, bed four? Her temperature is up, should I slow down the transfusion?"

Sister Ojo briefly excused herself before hurrying out and Jo moved towards the door, brushing past Jonathan Kane as she did so.

"Would it be frightfully presumptuous of me to ask if you'd like to go for a drink with me? Tonight?" Jonathan asked and Jo hesitated, surprised by the request. "I'm sorry. Of course it would, ignore me, I'm being a bore."

"Not at all. I have other plans tonight but maybe some other time…" Jo startled even herself.

"Terrific. What about tomorrow? About eight? Or do you have something more interesting to do?"

Jo was caught on the spot. It had been a while since anyone had asked her out quite so directly and she hadn't prepared her excuses. She thought for a moment and realised that it might actually be nice to go out for a drink with a charming, intelligent, good-looking man who was unlikely to be short of money. He saw her waver.

"A country pub? Or a wine bar? You choose."

If she was seriously going to meet him for a drink, she had best make it home territory, she thought, and walking distance from home.

"Porters." She told him. "The wine bar in the Old Town High Street." At least then she might persuade him to stay there for dinner as well, if the evening was proving a success.

Jonathan Kane smiled and Jocasta, feeling uncomfortably self-conscious, slipped past him into the corridor, only then realising that Mr Jennings was standing at the entrance to the four-bedded bay opposite the office, watching them.

She hurried away feeling vaguely disquieted although she wasn't sure why.

Jo had arranged to meet Kate for a quick drink in The Stag that night, so that they could discuss where to have dinner over a drink. It would be a calorie-laden, wine-drenched meal if Kate had anything to do with it, even if she constantly professed to be on a diet. The Stag was a convenient place to meet, close to both their homes in the Old Town and to the restaurants that they were likely to visit; besides which, it had everything you could want from a pub: a warm welcome and an open fire, beer that met Kate's rigorous standards and a display case containing an ancient mummified cat for some obscure reason.

The evening had turned out warm but damp and they sat in the window seat, far enough away from the fire not to roast but sheltered from the door and the people coming in and out, shaking wet umbrellas.

"So, what do you feel like?" Jo asked Kate. "They've got a jazz pianist at the wine bar, a Spanish guitarist at the tapas bar and muzak at the bistro."

"Can't say that I'm fussed what the music is like, so long as it soothes the fevered brow; much more important is the food. I'm thinking braised lamb shank at Porters or an Italian. I could quite fancy an Italian."

"Nothing new there, then." Jo looked affectionately at her friend as Kate took a swig of her pint of Spitfire. If Jo was a tall, thin glass of Pinot Grigio, Kate was a large, round bowl of a glass, filled to overflowing with Merlot, warm, dark and full bodied. Kate swirled the inch of beer that was left and looked at Jo's almost untouched white wine spritzer. "You want another drink to play with while we decide or do you want to talk about what's bothering you? Is it because you're supposed to be going to stay with your parents, whenever it is, is it this weekend?"

"There's nothing really bothering me. And I am going to see them next weekend, not this."

Kate did not look convinced.

"Plenty of time for you to change your mind, then."

"I am going to see them. Honestly. I may not stay the whole weekend but…"

"So what's the matter?"

"I'm just feeling dissatisfied with life at the moment. You know, being a GP can be.." she struggled to find the right word.

"Trying?" Kate suggested.

"Yes, that and, well, boring sometimes too."

"You could always go full time as a police doctor."

58

"Not enough work and anyway, that can be trying and boring at times too. Maybe I need a complete change. Or at least a new challenge."

Kate finished her pint and put it down decisively.

"I vote for the Italian." She stood and picked up her coat. "What you really need, my girl, is a man."

And depressing as that was, Jo thought, she was probably right.

"Just as well. I've got a date in Porters tomorrow night, as it happens, and I don't want to go there two nights in a row. They might think that I can't cook for myself," Jo confided as she shrugged on her coat.

"Fantastic. Tell me all about him. Come on, come on. Is he rich? Good looking? And has he got a brother?"

Jo was laughing as they headed for the door. It was an undeniable fact: an evening spent with Kate always made her feel better.

"Bye, Jo. Good luck tomorrow, and you'd better call me and give me all the gory details about this consultant bloke after your date. And don't forget to ask if he has a brother, right?"

"I promise." Jo waved and hurried up the narrow flight of steps that led up from All Saints' Street to the lanes on the hill above. In the nineteenth century, as Hastings town grew, house owners had sold their gardens for building plots and sometimes several homes would be built on the land between two houses whose gardens had previously backed onto each other. The only way of reaching these in-fill houses was by a complicated network of steps and alleys called "twittens" and "cat creeps". Jo knew her way round these sometimes dark and unlit paths like the back of her hand; she often had to visit patients who lived down them and had never found them scary but, as she walked up the steps towards her home she thought, for a moment, that she heard footsteps further down the hill. She stopped, thinking that if someone was hurrying up the steps behind her they might want to get by and, after the enormous meal she had just eaten, she didn't want to race up ahead. She'd probably throw up if she tried. As she waited to see if the person wanted to get by the footsteps stopped. Maybe they had turned off, gone down one of the side passages or into a house, Jo thought as she started up the steps again, listening carefully as she climbed. She could be imagining it, but she was sure she could hear the footsteps start up again after a pause. For the first time, Jo felt frightened by the darkness of the alley and had to remind herself that the houses on either side were very close. If she screamed someone would hear, she was sure, but she wasn't about to hang around and put it to the test. She leapt up the last steps two at a time, despite her full stomach. It was amazing what an adrenalin surge could do for your energy levels. She reached the well-lit street above with relief and hurried on towards her flat, and safety.

8

Jo took a long hard look at the woman sitting next to her desk at the surgery. In her late thirties, Marcy had not had an easy life, and it showed.

"I know I'd done well, cut right down, but these last few weeks, it's been bad, Doc."

"It's bound to happen, some weeks you feel the withdrawal worse than others."

"Don't I know it. But it's not just the withdrawal, I really have had a bad few weeks."

Jo had heard this one before. Many times.

"There are always reasons, excuses, to fall off the wagon, Marcy. A bad day, an argument, a court appearance."

"Don't worry about them any more." She was dismissive.

"Addicts often deliberately provoke confrontations to give them a reason to slide."

"I know all that, but I mean it. Look, two of the girls have died in the past few weeks. I knew them both. One was murdered and the other topped herself. I haven't made that up, and it's bound to unnerve me."

Jo was interested.

"You knew Krissy Trent and Ellie Smith?"

Marcy fiddled with her cigarette packet, looked as if she was thinking of lighting up before remembering where she was and putting the packet away again.

"Ellie not so well. I admit that. She was newish on the street. I tried to give her some advice, but she didn't like taking that from anyone. Thought she knew it all, that one. But me and Krissy went way back." Marcy's lower lip trembled despite her well-cultivated, hard-as-nails image. "We were going to get out of the game. Buy a house and run it as a B and B. With extras, if you know what I mean. We'd put some money aside where no one could touch it. Okay so it's not enough yet, but we would have got there. Honest truth, but I can't do it now, not on my own, can I?"

"Why not?"

"It was Krissy who had the business sense, worked out the money side. I'm hopeless at that sort of stuff. What am I going to do, Doc?" Jo tried to look reassuring, but there was little she could say that would help and she knew it.

"She can't even be buried 'cos they have to keep the body, so I can't even get what's it called? Closure. That's it. Closure."

Marcy looked as though she was about to cry.

"The police are ready to release the body, Marcy, but no one has claimed it yet."

"What do you mean?"

"Her brother was informed but he didn't want to organise the funeral."

"That worthless bit of shit. So what happens to her? Do they keep her forever, like?"

Marcy was getting increasingly hysterical and, if the noise reached a level where they could hear her in the waiting room, someone was bound to come knocking sooner rather than later.

"No. They'll send her to Gilberts', the funeral directors on Catherine Street, and the council will pay for a simple burial. If you go round there they'll be able to tell you what the funeral plans are." Jo hoped that was enough to placate Marcy and it seemed to be, for now at least. She turned to her computer keyboard and keyed in M for medication. "I can't give you any more temazepam, but I will let you have some diazepam to tide you over the next few days." She typed in the drug name, dosage and frequency and pressed P for print, ripping the prescription off the printer as soon as it was done, and signing her name along the bottom.

Marcy sniffed and took the prescription.

"It'll have to do, I suppose. Better than nothing."

"Try not to mix it with anything, Marcy, okay?" They both knew that was a forlorn hope, so Marcy didn't bother to reply, she just sniffed again and then wiped her nose on the back of her hand.

"I'll use our savings to give her a proper send off. I don't want her being given a council ceremony, without any, you know, class. I want her to have the works. We can afford it." She folded the prescription and put it in her bag.

"Maybe you'd be better off using the money to get yourself off the street, like you planned. It's a dangerous game."

"That's what gets me. I mean, I know it is, but that night? Krissy wasn't even working."

"Maybe she changed her mind, decided to earn a bit extra?"

"No. She couldn't have been working."

"How do you mean?"

"She was strangled at home, wasn't she? Her flat up on the Priory. Krissy wasn't stupid. She never took punters there. Always took them to the place we used on Wigmore Street. Other people around, see. Other toms. We look out for each other there. If she was in danger she woulda screamed and someone would have come to help."

Jo had been to the dilapidated four-storey Victorian terrace on Wigmore Street where the working girls rented rooms by the hour. It had been when a man had died "on the job" and, remembering the place, she realised that what Marcy was saying was true. The rooms, just big enough to accommodate a bed and a basin, had been divided off using sheets of plasterboard nailed into place, and everything that was happening in one room could be heard in several others. A turn-on for the clients and a built-in safety feature for the girls.

"No, if she was at home, she was killed by a bloke she picked up on the side, like. A leisure fuck." Marcy stood up and pulled at her micro-mini in an attempt to make herself half-decent, missing Jo's wince at her choice of language.

"Have you told the police that, Marcy?"

Marcy seemed indignant at the suggestion.

"No."

"Don't you think you ought to? I mean, anything that would help catch the man who did this has got to make you and the rest of the girls safer, hasn't it?"

Marcy hesitated.

"They're not going to listen to me. I'm a junkie whore with a record."

"You have relevant information. They'll listen."

Marcy didn't seem convinced.

"Probably bang me up on some soliciting charge."

Jo realised where the problem lay.

"Is there an outstanding warrant on you, Marcy?"

Marcy was defensive.

"There might be, I'm not sure I made it to a court appearance. Hard to keep up with things, you know?"

Jo did know, only too well. The working girls seemed to be in and out of the police station with monotonous regularity, and Jo was often called in to certify them as fit to be detained if they were high or in withdrawal, or to patch them up if they were injured.

"What if I went to see them for you, to explain the situation to the detective in charge, and arrange for him to meet you somewhere neutral." She held up her palm to stop Marcy's anticipated interjection. "He's really not going to be interested in you missing a court appearance for soliciting, Marcy. Believe me, I've met the man."

Marcy still didn't seem too sure.

"Look, if you get done I'll pay the fine, okay?"

Marcy smiled.

"You're on, then, Doc. If you got a monkey to throw away don't let me stop you."

Jo's smile was a little taut as she wondered just what she had got herself into: meeting Miller again, voluntarily, and risking losing five hundred pounds into the bargain. She wasn't sure which was worse. Why on earth did she get herself into these situations?

9

As Jo was shown into the Incident Room, Miller was in his shirt sleeves, watching the cheap office desks and chairs being stacked up ready to be moved out. He looked towards the door and managed a tight smile.

"Dr Hughes, to what do we owe this unexpected pleasure?" But his expression made it clear that it was no pleasure. "Don't tell me, you suspect me of beating up another prisoner."

"And how is Mr Allen?" she replied coldly.

"Free. And quite possibly out looking for his next victim. I wouldn't know as he seems to have disappeared."

Jo frowned. It was typical of the man that he seemed to blame her for Jimmy Allen's disappearance, rather than his own lack of restraint. Like every other bully she had ever met, he blamed everyone but himself.

"Maybe you should have concentrated on collecting evidence against him rather than attempting to 'persuade' him to confess."

"Look, is there a reason for you being here, or have you just come to gloat?"

"I don't think losing a murder suspect is any reason for me to gloat."

"Neither is the fact that my squad is being disbanded and a team from another force is coming to examine everything I've done from the moment the body was discovered, just to see if I've made any mistakes or omitted anything- other than charging the murderer."

Jo had the tact to look sorry. It had to be a difficult time for everyone involved when the investigation was scaled down and the murder book was reviewed by an outside team, looking for errors. Even if they didn't find anything wrong, it was depressing for those involved. There was relief that they hadn't cocked up, of course, but there was also no joy in the situation because it meant that there was nothing new to work on.

"I have some information for you, actually."

"On that ruddy junkie?" Sergeant Jeffries cut in, startling Jo because she hadn't seen him under the table where he had been unplugging a computer.

"No." She replied, rather shortly. God, the man irritated her.

He stood and coiled the wire as he pulled it up.

"No, I have some information on Krissy Trent." She had their undivided attention now. "It comes from a patient. So it's a slightly sensitive area."

"This is a murder case and murder isn't sensitive." Miller gave her concerns characteristically short shrift. "What's the information and who is it from?" Whilst Miller had no time for niceties, Jo wasn't about to let herself be pushed into giving them Marcy's name, not without her say so.

"I will need certain assurances before I give you a name."

"I don't have time to argue the semantics of patient-doctor confidentiality. I don't have the time, and certainly not the energy. Just tell me what she has got to say, doctor. I'm assuming she's a she? That you got the information from a tom?"

Jo felt herself redden, but kept her voice steady and calm.

"Krissy had a room in the house on Wigmore Street that she used for work."

"Most of them do."

"She never took her work home to her flat. It was an absolute rule with her. That was her sanctuary away from it all that. Ergo, the man who killed her was not a client."

"Bet she didn't use the word ergo." Jeffries muttered under his breath, but both Miller and Jo ignored him.

"This patient of yours? Did she know Krissy well?"

"Yes. They were good friends." Jo hoped Marcy hadn't been exaggerating their friendship, or her reputation would be worth even less if Miller found out.

"Is there any chance we could meet her?"

There was a cough behind them, and they turned to see Mike Parton, The coroner's officer, standing in the doorway. Like most coroner's officers, Mike was an ex-copper who hadn't managed to get fully away from The Job when he retired. It was his responsibility to take possession of the body in all sudden deaths, ordering post mortems where necessary, compiling the reports from which the coroner had to decide whether an inquest should be held or not, calling in the police if the death was suspicious or unnatural. And dealing with the relatives. The part that every policeman hated. Keeping them informed about what was happening if their relative's death didn't warrant a family support officer on the police team. Only major investigations had big enough teams to allocate a person to help support the family. In this case, a WPC had been named family liaison officer on top of her other duties, but one meeting with Krissy's brother had brought her to the decision that this was one family that didn't need liaising with or supporting, so it had fallen once more to Mike to talk to him.

Sombre, concerned and reassuring as Mike doubtless was with the bereaved, he was like a spectre at the feast when he had to deal with his colleagues. He irritated the hell out of them. Silently disapproving of how they spoke and acted towards the dead, his presence had the effect of restricting conversations. Of course the dead should be treated with respect and dignity, they all had to concede, but a certain level of sick humour was to be expected from police officers, particularly Bob Jeffries, and Mike should have understood that. His possession of absolutely zero sense of humour did not help him and his pride in the fact that he was teetotal was unlikely to improve his standing amongst his colleagues.

"The second post mortem on Christine Trent, the strangulation victim, has been completed and I have informed the family that the body is ready to be released for burial, although I understand they are not interested."

"Typical." Jeffries muttered.

Mike hadn't moved, he seemed to be deciding whether to say more.

"And?" Miller prompted.

"Miss Trent's brother was asking about the crime scene. When will you be finished there?"

Jeffries wasn't taken in for a moment.

"You mean he was asking when he can get his hands on her possessions. I've met the man. Took his initial statement about finding the body. You remember, Guv? He wanted to have her purse to make sure none of us nicked the cash out of it. First thing he said to me wasn't: how terrible, my sister's been strangled, but: can I have her purse, because I know what you lot are like."

"He's still her next of kin, and in the absence of a will…."

"He's sole heir to her condom stash, I know, I know."

Mike's upper lip curled in distaste at Jeffries remark and even Miller looked embarrassed and sneaked a look at Jo to see how she was reacting. Her face was impossible to read. He rubbed the back of his neck and looked like he was wondering why he'd bothered to come into work today. Maybe it would have been a good day to develop flu, or food poisoning, let his colleagues handle things and come back when it was all over. He sighed and looked at Parton.

"We'll meet him over there this afternoon, after we've taken a last look round, okay? Say threeish?"

Parton nodded to Miller, but couldn't bring himself to even look at Jeffries, as he went out. Miller turned to Jo. "Would your client, or patient or whatever, be willing to meet us at the flat too? Earlier than the brother? She might notice if there's anything missing or out of place."

"I can try." Jo wasn't overly optimistic. "She said she might speak to you, so long as I was present, and so long as I got an assurance from you that you wouldn't arrest her for any warrants that might possibly be outstanding. Or not."

"Typical!" Jeffries snorted, but was silenced by a look from Miller.

"No problem. Tell her I won't have time to check outstanding warrants. I don't even know her name, right?" His voice was softer now, less antagonistic. "It would be really helpful if you could persuade her."

"I'll do my best. We'll see you there if I succeed."

Miller smiled and Jo turned to leave.

"Tasty bint, I'll grant you." Jeffries said, not quite quietly enough, as he watched her leave the room. "But got too much of a mind of her own for my taste."

Miller just rolled his eyes heavenward and said nothing.

10

The Priory Estate was in the process of being renovated. Two of the four blocks had been finished, and now boasted little balconies in blue plastic and brushed steel stuck incongruously onto the front of the buildings, partly to make the flat concrete slabs of the original design look less dismal but also to give the residents somewhere to hang their washing or stick their rubbish. What was more important was that the blocks that had been refurbished all had new windows to keep out the cold, wet, seaside air and security doors to keep out the muggers and burglars that operated on the estate. At least, the security doors would stop them provided they weren't also residents, which they were more often than not. The Priory Estate wasn't popular, having been run-down and crime-ridden for years, with the result that any self-respecting person on the housing list would suddenly find they no longer needed council accommodation when offered a flat there. This meant that the only people housed on the estate were the sort of people who didn't mind its condition because they tended to lower the tone of any area they inhabited anyway. They chucked rubbish out of the window instead of down the chutes and burgled each other on a regular basis, and if the council thought that adding balconies and security doors would change anything, they were sadly mistaken.

"Just Krissy's luck," Marcy said, as she and Jo looked up at White-friars House. "She lived on this poxy estate for years but managed to get herself killed just days before the council were due to move her to a new flat and start doing up her block. She would've liked a balcony. She coulda sat out there with a glass of wine and pretended she were somewhere flash like Ibiza. When it wasn't raining, that is."

Marcy and Jo climbed the open stairs, littered with fag ends, empty beer cans and polystyrene takeaway cartons and turned the corner at the top. As soon as they started to walk along the dimly lit corridor that led to Krissy's front door, they could see her brother Darren waiting for them, jiggling about from one foot to the other. Dressed in a grubby sweatshirt and jeans that seemed too big, Darren sniffed loudly and wiped his nose on his sleeve, unaware that he was being watched.

"Selfish little runt," Marcy muttered.

"He's not supposed to be here yet." Jo explained. "Do you want to wait until he's gone?"

"And he's nicked all Krissy's stuff? No way."

"He is the next of kin."

"Yeah, I know. We get to choose our friends, but family, we're stuck with what we're given." Marcy shook her head. "I was always telling Krissy to stop giving him money. But he was her little brother, the baby of the family….."

Darren turned and spotted them and started towards them aggressively.

"What are you doing here? You can't have anything, it's mine."

"And you're welcome to it, you ungrateful little tosser." Marcy was not intimidated.

"So piss off then and take your social worker with you."

He was closing in on them and Jo was just wondering whether or not to grab Marcy, who seemed to be spoiling for a fight with the man, and run for it, when Miller and Jeffries appeared behind her.

"Oi, Darren, learn some manners, will you? We asked the ladies to meet us here. Hello, Marcy, nice to see you again." Jeffries said in passing as he grabbed Darren, none too gently, by the arm. "You are not supposed to be here for another hour."

"Yeah, well, I thought you might be trying to pull a flanker. And I was right, wasn't I? You were going to let the whore have first pick of Krissy's stuff. Weren't you?"

Jeffries shook his head as he started pulling the police tape off the front door of the flat.

"You know what? You are a sad and suspicious individual."

Miller got out the key and unlocked the door.

"If we could just have one last look round before you take anything, Mr Trent, okay?"

Darren followed them into the flat, with Marcy and Jo bringing up the rear.

"Just don't take too long about it, all right? I ain't got all day."

"Yeah, right." Marcy was unsympathetic. "Meaning you ain't got no money as usual and you've got to flog some of this stuff to get your next hit."

"Takes one to know one."

"At least I work for mine."

"Yeah, right. On your back."

"Kneeling, more often."

"That's enough."

Jo was thankful that Miller had had enough of their bickering, because she had too. In fact, she could feel another headache coming on and rubbed at the spot between her eyebrows where it always seemed to be centred.

"Darren, sit down and shut up, or I'll make you wait outside. Marcy? It is Marcy, isn't it?" Miller asked, and she nodded, sullenly. "Can you take a look round, tell us anything that might have been moved, out of place, whatever."

Marcy nodded again, and Jo followed her as she went slowly through the flat, taking her time, looking at everything. Many people must have been through the flat before them, checking and logging the contents. Every inch had been dusted and photographed by the crime scene investigators; their grey fingerprint powder covered almost every surface. Although she had never met Krissy Trent, Jo tried to picture the person who had lived here as she went from room to room. Somehow it made her feel less of an intruder.

The living room was quite comfortably furnished. Nothing flash, but homely. Not a bordello, or a brothel, just an ordinary living room, the sort that she had seen many times when visiting patients. Large telly, not new but a good quality make, a green patterned sofa with a cream throw over it, and assorted cushions artfully arranged. Prints of African elephants, lions and giraffes on the wall. Maybe she had dreamed of going to Africa one day, on a safari holiday, to see the animals in the flesh.

The kitchen was clean and tidy, the bathroom spotless. Nice fluffy pink towels on the rail. Jo hadn't expected Krissy to be quite so house-proud, showing that she was as prejudiced by Krissy's profession as anyone else would be. Jo could feel Marcy steel herself before stepping into the bedroom, almost as if she expected the body to be still there. Miller stood by and watched them and Jo was relieved to see that the

71

bed was stripped of its sheets and that even the mattress, which would most probably have been stained with the body fluids involuntarily released at death, had been removed. It had gone to the forensic laboratory to be sampled and scraped, she supposed, just in case any particle or cell from the killer remained.

"Krissy's clothes, what she had been wearing that night we think, were on the floor by the bed, where they must have fallen as she undressed." Miller explained.

Looking at the bed now, Miller could still see Krissy's body as he had that first visit, her naked body, legs akimbo, head lolling, and he suppressed a shudder, looked up and realised that Jo was watching him, surprised to see him moved. He turned away quickly, taking a last look at the rest of the room. The cheap furniture, all MDF and laminated chipboard, the pink swirling patterns on the nylon carpet, the teddy bears lined up on the window sill. The only things in the flat that pointed towards Krissy's profession was the large collection of half used make-up scattered in front of the mirror, and the sort of clothes only a tart would wear neatly hung in the wardrobe.

He had been hoping intensely that Marcy would spot some vital clue, but she shook her head.

"No. It looks like it always did. Apart from the mattress being gone, of course."

Miller couldn't hide his disappointment as they left the bedroom and Jeffries jerked his head to Darren.

"You can start on the bedroom." Darren didn't wait for a second invitation and they could hear him opening and closing drawers as they stood in the lounge.

"Did she suffer?" Marcy asked and Miller wished that he could say no.

"She put up a bit of a fight, but not for long."

Jo's interest was piqued.

"What about under her nails? Strangulation victims often claw at their assailants." Jo looked up at Miller and read his expression that spoke volumes about teaching grandmothers and egg sucking, but Marcy hadn't noticed.

"She used those stick on ones, kept pinging off. It was so she could still take them off and bite her nails when she wanted. Disgusting habit, but not as bad as some, I suppose." She looked at Jo, acknowledging that drug dependence was probably worse. "Me? I prefer the acrylic nails, much harder to shift, although they are expensive." Marcy looked down at her talons.

"There were some traces of glue on her nails, which were bitten down, but there was no sign of the false nails we assumed she was wearing."

Jo was perplexed.

"Her killer took them with him? He must have realised that he'd been scratched and known the significance."

"Doesn't mean much these days, every bugger watches CSI." Jeffries was unimpressed.

"But it does mean that the killer was cool headed." Jo persisted. "Cool enough to collect any damning evidence even though he'd just killed her."

"Cold-hearted bastard." Marcy said under her breath.

"Organised and calculating, yes." Miller agreed with Jo. "Which is what makes me believe that this isn't an isolated incident. This killer will strike again, and I don't think he'll wait all that long."

Jo shuddered. She hoped he was wrong, but something about this crime told her that he wasn't. It wasn't a rage killing. It wasn't a one-off. This was just the start.

"There's nothing worth having in the bedroom." Darren's return to the lounge had, thankfully, interrupted her train of thought. "Can I start in here now?"

"You can take it all, Mr Trent. If that's what you want."

Darren looked round the room and shook his head.

"What would I want with most of this stuff? Worthless crap. Nah, I'll leave it for the council to clear, that's their job, innit? Unless you want any of it, Marce, a memento of your best friend." Marcy looked like all she wanted was to punch him on the nose. "I just want the telly, video, stuff like that."

"Stuff that's easy to sell, you mean. You never did give a monkey's about her."

Darren ignored Marcy and picked up the telly.

"Don't lock up or nothing, will ya? I'll be back up for the rest in a mo."

They watched him stagger out of the flat under the weight of the television.

"Hope he drops it." Marcy voiced what they were all secretly wishing.

Miller took the opportunity of Darren's absence to ask her a few more questions.

"Where would she have gone on a night off, so to speak?"

"There are a few places she used to go. The vodka bar on George Street. The sports bar, and that new place near it, in the town centre, Bateman's, or Yates's. Those are the most likely."

Jo had gone to the window and watched as Darren carefully placed his haul onto the back seat of a decrepit H reg Ford Orion. She saw that Jeffries was watching too.

"Could run a vehicle check on it," he said, but Miller shook his head.

"No point. So what if we bring him in for possession of a stolen vehicle, or we slap a producer on him," he turned to Jo to explain, "get him to bring his car documents into the station within two weeks. We know he's unlikely to have anything as expensive as insurance or an in-date MOT, but even if he can't produce his documents, all he'll get is a fine."

"And a ban if he's got enough points." Jeffries still seemed keen to give it a go.

"He won't pay the fine, or stop driving if he's banned. His sort just laugh at bans. And he'll get away with it. That's the way it is. Always has been." Marcy sighed.

"Only the law-abiding middle classes ever pay their fines, not the likes of you or Darren, eh, Marcy?" Jeffries was disappointed not to be allowed to do anything.

"So why do you bother running us working girls in all the time?"

"Fun." Jo could believe that someone like Jeffries would do it for fun, too.

Darren came back into the flat and started collecting together the video, mini hi fi, and the few CDs on the rack.

"What about the body? I understand the coroner's officer told you, you can have Krissy's body now." Miller asked.

"What would I want with her body?"

"To bury it, Mr Trent. It is the normal procedure after death, I've

74

found." Miller was unable to keep the sarcasm from his voice.

"Can't afford a funeral, right? So, if I just leave it, like, the council have to do it an' all, don't they?"

Neither Miller nor Jeffries felt the need to answer. The man was right, of course he was, someone always pays up in the end.

He backed out of the flat laden with the last bits he wanted.

"That's it, you're welcome to the rest," he told Marcy as he paused in the doorway. "You're wrong, I will miss her you know, she was always good for a bunce." He said as he left.

Marcy waited until he had gone before turning to Miller.

"It's okay, isn't it? If I see to the funeral? I went to the funeral directors and they thought it was okay."

"Fine. No problem at all," he replied.

"Won't tell him when it is, though." She jerked her head towards the door. "Don't want him to spoil it."

Marcy turned to leave, with Jo following her.

"And if there's anything else? Anything at all that you remember, you will tell us, won't you?" Miller asked her.

"Depends. If I think it will help catch the killer of course I will, but I might not feel too helpful if I'm under arrest or anything."

Marcy looked at Jeffries pointedly and left.

11

It was nearly ten past eight when Jo pushed her way into Porters wine bar and it was packed, as it always was on a Friday night.

'No chance of a table' she thought to herself, but then spotted Jonathan, reading The Daily Telegraph and ensconced at a small table for four in the corner, with his coat, a newspaper and his briefcase spread proprietarily over the other chairs to fend off anyone else who might get ideas about sitting there. Jo smiled. He definitely got brownie points for getting a table, and extra points for having a bottle of red and two glasses ready and waiting.

She wound her way through the heaving masses, towards the table.

"Sorry I'm a bit late. Visit that went on a bit," she explained as he stood and cleared a chair for her to sit.

"Don't mention it. I know how difficult a GP's life can be." Jo tried to suppress a smile; he was going to have to stop being quite so smooth. Jonathan noticed.

"Too much? Sorry," he said. "Let's start again, shall we? Sit down, have a glass of wine and relax. I got red, but I could get white as well, if you'd prefer?"

"Red is perfect."

Jo sat as Jonathan poured her a glass and passed it to her. He then raised his own.

"The weekend starts here." They both took a sip of wine and Jo could immediately feel it easing the tension of her stressful day.

"Or are you on call?" he asked.

"Only for the police, and even then, not until tomorrow."

He looked surprised and Jo explained about her work as a forensic physician.

"I had no idea. Now that must be really interesting. Come on, don't stop there, I want to hear some gory stories or, at the very least, some salacious gossip."

Jo was surprised by his interest and she entertained him for quite some time with stories of unusual injuries and their unconvincing explanations, tiddly old ladies who insisted they'd had nothing but sherry trifle, and the weird and wonderful things that drunks get up to.

"You clearly like your job very much." He commented when she ran out of stories, and Jo realised that yes, she did. She also realised that the wine bottle was almost empty and she didn't think that Jonathan had drunk much of it.

"I'm sorry," she apologised, "I've monopolised the conversation and drunk all the wine. Let me order another bottle." She stood up, but Jonathan placed a hand on hers and stood up himself.

"I'm really sorry, but I have to go."

Jo couldn't hide her disappointment. She had been enjoying herself.

"Can I give you a lift home? My car's just up the road."

"No, that's fine. I could do with a walk. Clear my head."

Jo was embarrassed, wondering if perhaps all her talk about working with the police had put him off, and not sure what she should do as he hastily put on his coat.

"I've bored you. I'm sorry. You should have stopped me going on and on like that."

"No, not at all. I've found it absolutely fascinating, I think your enthusiasm is wonderful, it's just that I have something that I need to do, and I'm going away for the weekend so I have to do it tonight."

"I'm not sure I believe you." She admitted.

"It's true, I'm afraid. Sad and boring, but I have some work I need to finish. An article I'm writing. But look, I've really enjoyed this evening, Jocasta." Jonathan took her hand. "I mean it. And I'd love to do it again, only maybe next time we can make it dinner as well? Next week, perhaps? Damn, my firm's on call all week, let's make it the following week. I don't want to be called out to an ectopic halfway through the first course." He smiled and Jo found herself believing him. "How about Wednesday? Here? I had a look at the menu and it made me feel quite hungry. How does that sound?"

Jo smiled back. If he had been bored rigid, he wouldn't have suggested a specific date, would he? Jo was useless at reading the signals given by men; contrary to common belief, she thought women were much easier to understand.

"That sounds terrific, Jonathan. I can certainly vouch for the food here. A week on Wednesday. I'll look forward to it."

And, as he gave her a smile and a quick peck on the cheek, she realised that she was looking forward to it already. And also that she hoped that it would go a bit further than a peck on the cheek next time.

Outside Porters, Jo was relieved to see that at least it wasn't raining. She hesitated. She could turn right, to the sea front and the more direct route up the steep steps and twittens, or she could turn left and use the well-lit main road. Silently telling herself she was being a wimp, Jo took the longer, safer route. She still felt as if she was being watched all the way home, but she saw and heard no one. As she locked her front door behind her she felt a wave of relief, then gave herself a mental slap. It was stupid to live your life in fear, particularly as she had no proof or even genuine reason to believe that she had ever been followed or at risk at all. It wouldn't do, she told herself, it really wouldn't do. She'd end up with agoraphobia like one of her patients, a little old lady she visited every week, a spinster who never left her home for fear of what might be out there. Too frightened of death ever to live.

He saw her at the karaoke night at the Jolly Sailor, a large, soulless pub out on the London Road. She was on her own, although she obviously knew a few people in the bar to nod to, to say hello to, to pretend to herself she was friends with. Plain and fat and scarred by acne. The fat was all too obvious under her tight synthetic top, bulging either side of the crease of her bra strap, and over the waistband of her low-cut jeans. Her dull, straggly, mousy hair was at least clean, but when she laughed, imitating happiness, being one of the gang, he could see that her teeth were yellowed and stained from the cigarettes she smoked endlessly, thinking they made her look cool perhaps. Probably never had a boyfriend in her life, he thought. Not a proper one. Not a bloke who wasn't blind or drunk, anyway. The look on her face when he caught up with her on her way home, suggested they go back to hers for a coffee. She'd been pathetically grateful. Tried to hide it, tried to make out she wasn't normally that easy, but there was no doubting it, she was astonished and flattered to have a bloke come home and fuck her. Someone to tell her mates about without having to lie. If only she'd known, Fat Denise, shelf stacker and check-out girl at the supermarket, if only she had known just what she was going to get once they got back to her pathetic rented basement flat.

She wouldn't have been grateful then, she would have been terrified. She'd thought it was a joke at first, a dressing up game and happily went along with it, giggled at the outfit he put on, and sniggered dirtily at the latex gloves. Doctors and nurses, now this really would be something to tell the girls. It was a shame she hadn't got any tights on, she chuckled coyly when he'd asked about that, said she always wore trousers and socks, so he'd had to use his key chain. Next time he'd be more prepared, bring some tights with him, or something better perhaps. It wasn't until he'd got the chain wrapped round her neck that she began to realise it wasn't a game, and by then it was too late. Her eyes bulged and her tongue stuck out as she gasped, almost got cut off when she bit down on it. Didn't bleed much though, because she was dead soon after. Cooling fast, almost as fast as his prick rose. Strong and hard. He unwrapped the chain from her neck and tried to put the tongue back in, but it kept flopping out. That put him off her a bit. It stopped her looking so nice. Not that she was ever going to be pretty, and there was no denying it, she was fat. He looked closer at her fat thighs, dimpled with cellulite, her pubic hair- wild and untrimmed, leading up to the stretch marks crossing her sagging belly. He'd felt disappointment then, as he looked down at her, and quickly lost his erection. She just wasn't good enough. Even in death, Denise was disappointing. If only she knew.

12

Jo wriggled in her chair. It was hard and uncomfortable, guaranteed to discourage her from spending long at her paperwork. Perhaps she should have taken her box of letters and reports down to her consulting room; at least she had a proper adjustable seat in there. Up in the main office the secretaries got the good chairs and, even though Jo knew that was only right and proper and she had no wish for the surgery to be sued for industrial injury if one of them developed a back problem, she couldn't help feeling that the partners could have run to a few extra ones for the doctors. She signed the sick-note in front of her and reached for the next item, groaning when she saw the thick wad of previous notes that had been forwarded to her for the young boy with the mystery malaise, Timothy Lockwood. She waved the reams of computer paper at Linda.

"When are we going to get direct electronic transfer of patient records?"

"We're on the list, Jo. Just got to wait our turn."

"So we'll get it about this time next century, the way that Connecting for Health, or whatever it's called this week, is going," Dr Sinha cut in, to Jo's surprise.

"Unlike you to be so cynical, Gauri."

"It's not cynicism, it's experience, young lady. You wait until you've worked for the NHS as long as I have. You'll see I'm right."

Jo smiled as she started to read Timothy's notes, highlighting diagnoses she wanted their summariser to transfer onto his new computer record as she went through. Once she had checked all his immunisations, and weeded out the routine visits, health checks and run-of-the-mill childhood illnesses, she could see that he had little of importance in his history apart from atopic eczema, which went through a really quite acute stage before settling down for no apparent reason, as it so often did. There had certainly been little sign of it when Jo had examined him. There were a couple of mentions of his parents' split in the notes, and the fact that he seemed to be taking it badly. Perhaps it was just the stress of the divorce that was making him ill, Jo thought, as she put the notes into the summarisers' basket.

"Police station, Jo," Linda called, waving the telephone at her, and Jo hurried over.

"Hello, Dr Hughes speaking." Jo spoke into the receiver as Dr Sinha pulled a face at Linda.

"She's off to play at cops and robbers," Dr Sinha said in a stage whisper that had Linda giggling.

"And what sort of state is she in?" Jo tried to ignore them. "Okay. I'll be right there."

Jo handed the phone back to Linda.

"Actually, it's a young girl who is claiming that they can't detain her because she's an asthmatic and hasn't got an inhaler with her. So I'd better take a nebuliser and puffer pack in case." She looked at her watch. "Gauri?"

Dr Sinha looked up with a sigh.

"How many visits have you got this time, Jo?"

"Just the two. And I wouldn't ask only it's Krissy Trent's funeral later this afternoon and I promised Marcy I'd go. She's worried sick she'll be the only one there."

"Go on then. Can't have Marcy Draper singing hymns all on her own." Dr Sinha held out her hand for the visit book and quickly added, "so long as neither of them is Mr Herring. I'm not visiting that horrid little man ever again."

"Don't worry, Dr Sinha," Linda said before Jo could reassure her, "We don't let him through the net. I have a Mr Herring alarm. If he rings up for a visit the alarm goes off and the phone self destructs in five seconds."

They laughed, both wishing that Linda was telling the truth.

"No, just a couple of call-ins on the frail elderly. We could always reschedule them...."

She looked at Linda.

"By we, I presume you mean me." Linda was resigned: she'd had to do it many times before when Jo was called to the police station and she was certain to have to do it again, if not today then one day soon. They both looked at Dr Sinha.

"No, no. That's okay. You go and see the girl and go to the funeral. I've nothing better to do this afternoon than see your patients." They both looked at the mountain of paperwork still on the desk in acknowledgement of the lie.

Jo thanked her again and slipped out of the office, blushing slightly as she saw that Dr Grantham was in the corridor outside and must have heard everything. He said nothing, just raised an eyebrow, and watched as Jo scurried guiltily away.

In the custody treatment room, Jo watched Charlotte, or Charlie as she had firmly told Jo she preferred to be called, a plain and slightly tubby girl with a number of piercings and a whole lot of attitude, blow into the peak flow meter for the fourth time.

"That's right, hard as you can. Ok. That's better." At last the girl had managed more than a half-hearted puff and Jo looked at the meter. "Three hundred and eighty. Not bad for a someone as badly asthmatic as you say you are." Jo was wholly unconvinced that Charlie was now, or had ever been, asthmatic. The only wheeze she had was the wheeze she was putting on, pretending to have asthma so that she couldn't be detained. Her first three attempts at the peak flow meter had been pathetic, but her lungs had been completely clear when Jo listened to them.

"Now take a couple of puffs of this," Jo handed her a salbutamol inhaler, "and we'll wait a couple of minutes and try again."

Charlie took a couple of sullen, and inexperienced, puffs of the inhaler.

"Didn't know they called a doctor, I thought they'd just let me go. That's what my friend said, said she'd pulled that trick when she was arrested once."

"Hmm. Well, she wasn't telling the truth, then. Is she arrested often, this friend?" Jo didn't want to miss the opportunity for a lecture on sexual and personal health if, as she suspected, this girl was drifting down the path to prostitution or serious drug abuse. Charlie might only be seventeen years old, but she clearly considered that age to mean she was fully adult, and that she knew it all.

"Not any more."

Jo was about to suggest that maybe Charlie's friend had learnt the error of her ways when the girl continued: "Topped herself last week. Down by the toilets on the sea front."

Jo was temporarily lost for words and just handed her the peak flow meter.

She waited for Charlie to blow again and looked at the meter.

"Three hundred and seventy five. So it's irreversible."

"What does that mean?" Charlie was worried. "Does it mean I've got something you can't treat?"

"What it means, young lady, is that you don't have asthma but that your lungs are slightly affected by something not helped by asthma medication, probably the fact that you smoke." She handed Charlie a card. "If you ever decide to give up smoking, ring that number and they'll help."

Charlie took the card reluctantly and Jo hesitated before broaching the subject of her friend who was dead.

"This friend of yours, Charlie. Was her name Ellie, by any chance?"

"Yeah. How do you know?"

"Because I was the doctor who had to certify her dead."

Charlie pulled a face.

"Wouldn't want your job. Not for all the tea in China. That's gross."

"Yes, yes it was. It's not something I like doing. She was young. She had everything to live for. Just like you."

"Yeah, right. My life's just a bundle of laughs." Despite her bravado Charlie couldn't meet Jo's eye and was staring down at the floor, looking suddenly very young. Very alone. Jo softened her tone and placed her hand gently on Charlie's arm.

"It's too late for Ellie but it's not too late for you, Charlie. Don't go down the same road. Don't get involved with hard drugs like her. The risks just aren't worth it. It's too easy to make a mistake. She proved that."

"What makes you think it was a mistake?"

"Why would she kill herself deliberately?"

"'Cos her life was shit, that's why."

"Maybe it was," Jo hesitated, trying to find the right word, "unsatisfactory, but need it have been? She chose to earn her living selling her body and risking all the sexually transmitted diseases from chlamydia to HIV. And she clearly wasn't happy with that choice or she wouldn't

84

have needed smack to get her through the day, would she?"

"She didn't have much of a choice. Not like jobs are two a penny round here."

"But there are some, and there are shelters, hostels for kids your age. Don't go out on the street, Charlie. Don't let some pimp take your money, or put you on drugs. You're worth more than that."

"I'm not stupid." Charlie said sullenly. "I'm careful who I get involved with and I wouldn't let anyone force me to do something sick, not like Tomas did. I'm not stupid like Ellie."

Charlie shut up quickly, immediately aware that she had said too much.

"What do you mean? Who is Tomas? Why was he forcing Ellie to do something sick?"

But Charlie wasn't going to say any more. She seemed almost frightened about what she had already said.

"Nothing. I didn't mean nothing. You gonna tell that bastard of a sergeant that I'm fit to be detained or what?"

"Are you that keen to go back to your cell?"

"You think this place is better? I'd rather be on my own, catching up on my zeds."

"Ok, I'll call the sergeant but listen, Charlie, if you ever want to talk to me, call me." She gave the girl her card. "About anything. Sex, drugs, rock and roll, whatever you want. Okay? Just call me." But Jo had little hope that the girl would, she had the adolescent "I know it all" look back on her face as she waited to be escorted to her cell.

The rain had started in earnest by the time Jo got to the small chapel in the corner of the cemetery. Marcy had arranged for Krissy's funeral to take place here rather than at the municipal crematorium in the hope that it would be more intimate, given that the numbers expected to attend were few. Jo was running late as usual, but she was relieved to see that they hadn't yet taken the coffin inside, and also that Marcy had resisted the temptation to go for a horse-drawn hearse, a lone bagpiper or anything over the top like that.

She hurried inside the chapel, shaking the worst of the rain off her umbrella as she sidled into a pew at the back and was surprised to see several people in the chapel. Marcy was at the front in a dramatic black hat and full length leather coat, regularly dabbing at her eyes with a lacy handkerchief. Behind her were two men in suits who turned as they heard Jo come in. Miller and Jeffries.

'Probably here in case the killer turns up,' Jo thought scornfully, 'as if life is ever that simple.'

There were three or four other working girls, a couple that Jo recognised, but all of them easily identifiable by their clothes. Battered stilettos, mini-skirts and an awful lot of cleavage for a funeral. They can't have been planning on taking the whole afternoon off then. And Edna. Jo wasn't surprised to see Edna there. Edna went to pretty much every funeral service going, said she liked to be sure nobody went without at least one mourner, but Jo suspected that her real reason was the after-funeral drinks. Most people felt it only polite to ask her along, even if she had never met their Aunt or Dad or whoever the deceased actually was, and they quickly discovered that Edna was very partial to a glass of sherry.

There was also a slim, elderly man, sleek, silver hair cut stylishly, and wearing a slinky black polo neck jersey, tucked into neat black trousers. An aging trendsetter, stuck in the sixties. At first Jo thought he must be a relative of Krissy's but, as the coffin was carried in to the chapel by the pall bearers provided by the funeral director, she realised that he was actually taking the service. Jo was relieved that this wasn't going to be religious; somehow she couldn't believe that Krissy would have wanted hymns and prayers. The humanist service arranged by Marcy turned out to be short, simple and very moving. A couple of inspirational readings, the Auden poem made famous by Four Weddings and a Funeral, and the silver-headed man then read out a sanitised version of Krissy's life, that somehow left out pretty much everything that Jo knew about her.

As they all followed the coffin out, to the inevitable Robbie Williams song *Angels*, Jo thought she would try and slip away, but Marcy took her hand and gripped it firmly before she could escape.

"Thank you so much for being here, Doc. You've no idea how much your support means to me. Just got the actual burial bit to get through now, then we can all go back to The Hastings Arms and raise a toast to Krissy. Eddie's laid on some food. You will stay, won't you?" And she didn't have the heart to refuse, even though the rain showed no sign of easing off. She put up her umbrella and followed the dismal procession to the graveside, where the freshly dug soil was already turning to mud.

The Hastings Arms was a traditional English seaside resort pub. It had fishing nets dotted with shells and plastic crabs hanging from the ceiling, a cheery feel and during the summer it was always packed. On a wet autumn afternoon in midweek, Eddie, the landlord was probably delighted to have the funeral group in there, otherwise he would have been on his own apart from Old Jim on his favourite stool in the corner. By the time Jo re-emerged from the Ladies, having removed the worst of the mud from her shoes, most of the working girls had gone back to work, or to get ready for the evening rush at least, but Marcy, Jo, Miller, Jeffries, a neighbour of Krissy's whose name Jo had forgotten if she had ever known it, and Edna had stayed. Edna, of course, was already clutching a nearly empty glass of sweet sherry. Half a dozen people at that time of day were a good crowd as far as Eddie was concerned, even if some of them were only drinking mineral water.

As she sipped her fizzy water and exchanged pleasantries with Edna, Jo saw Miller looking over in her direction more than once.

"I always think rain is good for a funeral. There's something wrong about laying someone to rest when the sun's out, don't you think?"

"Mmm, yes, I suppose you're right." She looked at her watch. "Going to have to go in a minute, Edna. Evening surgery."

Edna didn't seem to have heard.

"Shame about the turn out though. I do like to see a packed chapel. Makes for a livelier do afterwards." Edna tossed back the last of her drink and looked meaningfully at her empty glass.

"Can I get you another, Edna? Sweet sherry, is it?"

"That's very good of you, doctor. I don't mind if I do."

At the bar, Jo was joined by Miller as Jeffries headed off to check out the facilities.

"Always attend the funerals of your patients do you, Dr Hughes?"

"She wasn't my patient." Jo glanced round at Marcy, who seemed more relaxed now that she was on her second large glass of Chardonnay. "I came to support Marcy, that's all, and I have to go in a minute. Evening surgery awaits. How about you? Do you always attend the funerals of your victims? I mean, do you honestly think her killer is here? Or is it just standard procedure?"

"Standard procedure. And more in the hope that a friend or relative we don't know about attends rather than the killer. Speaking of which," he indicated Edna, "Is she…?"

Jo shook her head.

"Never met Krissy. Just here for the free drinks."

"Oh." Miller was disappointed.

Jo paid for Edna's sherry and was about to head back with it when she paused.

"I know you're not interested in the girl who killed herself," Miller looked set to protest but Jo didn't give him a chance, "but I saw another girl today who knew her, and she mentioned a Tomas? Apparently he was -"

"Tomas Czernak?" There was no doubting Miller's interest now, and even Jeffries, ambling back from the Gents, spotted it and quickened his pace to make sure he caught the rest of the conversation.

"I don't know the surname, she just called him Tomas. Apparently he was forcing Ellie to do something she didn't want to, something sick, according to this girl."

"Sounds like him. Tomas Czernak is a sick, sadistic, son of a bitch. He runs a dozen or so girls."

"He's a pimp?"

"Amongst other things."

"He wasn't Krissy's pimp, though, was he, Guv?" Jeffries interrupted.

"No. We're talking about the OD." Miller told him before turning back to Jo. "Are you suggesting he deliberately gave her an overdose?"

"I'm not suggesting anything, merely reporting what I was told. In fact, if anything, this girl suggested that Ellie might have deliberately taken the overdose rather than do what this man wanted."

Miller was disappointed.

"And she didn't know what it was he was making her do?"

Jo shook her head, and she could feel his interest waning.

"But you'll look into it? I mean, you don't want him turning his attentions to another girl, do you?"

"Of course we'll look into it." Jo wasn't convinced by this reassurance. "Meanwhile, the best thing you can do is warn all the prostitutes you treat to keep away from Czernak." Miller put his half-empty glass on the bar and headed towards the door.

"Not that most of them need warning against the little bastard, not the smart ones anyway." Jeffries followed his boss out, leaving Jo wondering whether the pair of them practised irritating the hell out of her or if it just came naturally.

Since her drink with Jonathan Kane, Jo hadn't been able to stop thinking about Mrs Jennings. How had the operation gone? Was her situation as bad as Jo expected? She had intended to ask him when they met for a drink but he had left before she had a chance and anyway, some doctors didn't like bringing their work out on the town with them, and she didn't, as yet, know Jonathan well enough to be sure that he was not one of them.

She often popped into the hospital to see how her patients were doing, if she had the time. Try as they might, hospitals could never guarantee that a patient would see the same doctor twice, let alone the same nurse, so it was reassuring for them to see a familiar face. They could ask questions of their GP that they might not feel able to ask a busy surgeon. Jo had intended to go and see Mrs Jennings but work had conspired against her, especially today, and it was preying on her mind. That and, she had to admit, accidentally bumping into Jonathan would be nice. She knew that it was eight o'clock in the evening, and it was unlikely that he would still be around, but she could live in hope. He had said that his firm was on call, and that was why he couldn't see her, so he might just be there, called out to see a sick patient in A and E, or to review one who had taken a turn for the worse on the ward. If she saw him, then maybe she would know if he was just fobbing her off and had every intention of cancelling their next date, or not. She couldn't quite bring herself to phone him; that could be too humiliating if he had changed his mind, did not want to see her again, and it could make their continuing professional relationship awkward. Her instincts, normally so reliable, were confused after the night at Porters. Perhaps she had imagined that he was attracted to her, that he had enjoyed himself as much as she had. Wine could throw your instincts right off base, she knew, but she was sure she was right. They had clicked and seeing Jonathan again, even briefly, would tell her how things were between them. She hoped.

She parked her car in a side street near the hospital, just outside the zone where permits were required. During the day, when hospital workers battled for free parking because there were never enough staff spaces provided on site, she knew she would not have stood a chance of finding a place to park but at this time of the evening she found a space easily. Visitors trying to avoid the heavy parking charges in the hospital car park had not found their way to this street just yet, but they would if the charges went up again. One day soon, she was sure, the council would have to respond to pressure from the residents and extend the restricted parking zone but, for the time being, it was only a short walk through an alley to the back entrance of the hospital.

The ward was busy, with visitors at almost every bedside and as Jo made her way down the central corridor she looked left and right into each of the bays for Mrs Jennings. She didn't see her, or Mr Jennings, and, as usual, there was no one at the desk. She turned back to the sisters' office.

Sister Ojo looked up as Jo came in, and raised her eyebrows.

"What brings you here so late, Dr Hughes? Don't you have a home to go to?"

"I came to find out how Mrs Jennings was doing and couldn't get here earlier. I've been a bit busy. I looked in all the bays but I couldn't see her."

Sister Ojo sighed.

"That poor woman. I put her in a side ward to let her, and us, have a little peace and quiet."

"That bad, huh?" Jo had known deep down that it would be, but it was still hard to have to admit it to herself.

"Oh, no, not that, it's just that her husband is getting in the way. Keeps stopping the doctors and nurses, no matter if they know about his wife or not, and asking them what they think. Going on and on and on. No one's going to come to my ward if we don't stop him badgering people, and we can't send the poor woman home; she needs her strength building up. So we put her in a side ward for now. The oncologists say there's nothing they can do until Mr Kane has removed the tumour, that if they start trying to shrink it Mrs J will never be fit for surgery. So, it's a high cal diet, plenty of rest and more transfusions. Then Mr Kane can operate, maybe next week or the week after. Can't put it off longer than that."

"If only I had -"

"You can't go living your life thinking if only this or if only that," Sister Ojo interrupted, "What has happened, has happened, and there's nothing you nor I can do to change it."

A sound philosophy, Jo knew, if only she could get herself to believe it.

"But if I had managed to convince her to have a smear, to accept treatment earlier…"

"She's an intelligent woman. She knew the risk she was taking and it was her choice. Don't blame yourself, Dr Hughes."

Jo looked at Sister Ojo's kind, sensible face and knew she was right, but it didn't stop her feeling guilty.

"I'll just pop in and say hello. If that's ok?"

"Of course it is. Her husband's with her, of course. Definitely a strange man, that."

Jo paused to think about that. She had thought so, too, but wasn't sure why.

"Can't say that I know him that well. I only met him when I told him that I was referring his wife and, though he wasn't as sympathetic as I would have liked, at least he grasped the urgency of the situation and persuaded her to come in. He obviously cares."

"He certainly does care. No doubt about it. I've hardly been able to get him to go home, but there's something wrong there, just can't put my finger on what."

Sister Ojo smiled and shrugged. She wasn't going to waste her precious time on figuring it out, whatever it was.

"She's in side ward B. Second on the left."

Side ward B was set back from the main corridor and the door was half-open, so Jo gave a slight knock and went in without waiting for a reply. She was surprised to see Jonathan Kane standing by Mrs Jennings' bed as a staff nurse helped make her more comfortable.

"There you are, Jean, love," The nurse said, "You'll be more comfortable now."

It took a moment for Jo to realise that Jean was Mrs Jennings' first name. She had always been Mrs Jennings to Jo and, somehow, Jo felt that Jean didn't fit this woman, particularly now that she looked so old, and sick, and frail. She noted with dismay the grey skin, the sunken, dull eyes, and the dry, cracked lips on her patient. This was a very sick woman indeed.

"I'll pop in again later, Jean, and settle you down for the night." As the nurse turned to leave Jo could tell by the way Mr Jennings reacted, as he sat in the visitor's chair next to the bed, that he didn't approve of this familiarity either.

"I'm so sorry. I don't want to interrupt anything. I just thought I'd look in and have a word."

The nurse was on her way out and Jo would have followed her but Jonathan gave her a smile that stopped her in her tracks.

"Nonsense. I was just explaining what was going to happen next. We're all hoping Mrs Jennings," he looked pointedly at the door closing behind the nurse, "will be well enough to have the operation next week. But it's down to her: plenty of rest, plenty of fluids, more blood. Then, when she feels fit and ready, we can try and sort her out."

"Are you sure it wouldn't be better to operate now? Before it spreads?" Mr Jennings clearly desperately wanted them to do something, anything, to make his wife better.

Jo knew that it was too late, it had already spread, and wondered how Jonathan would cope with that question, but he handled it well. He smiled at Mr Jennings sympathetically.

"I'm afraid she's just not strong enough. The stress of surgery could kill her," he patted Mrs Jennings hand and looked at her, "and we wouldn't want that, would we?"

'No,' Jo thought, cynically, that would mean it going down as a peri-surgical death.

And she knew what that meant: it would count on Mr Kane's death rate statistics, and he, like all surgeons, would be anxious to avoid patients dying on the table or shortly after. It didn't inspire confidence in their other patients, particularly the private ones.

Jo smiled and looked at this desperately ill woman. Her eyes were unfocused, probably as a result of the painkillers she was on, but she wasn't out of it. Indeed, it seemed to Jo that she understood exactly how bad her prognosis actually was, more so than her husband. Jo knew from her talk with Sister Ojo that no one seriously thought that Mrs Jennings would ever feel ready for an operation, but there was no point in saying that, of snuffing out all hope for Mr Jennings, even if his wife no longer had any expectations left.

"No, it's best to wait until you feel better." Jo played along. "A couple more units of blood and you'll feel like a new woman."

Once outside the room they moved into the main corridor, and Jo and Jonathan were at last able to drop the fake cheeriness that they had both adopted in front of the dying woman.

"I'll have a chat with the husband, make sure he understands just how bleak her chances are," Jonathan assured her.

"Thank you. It will make things easier if he knows. If he can accept it, though I don't hold out much hope that he will. He looks like he's in denial to me."

Jonathan nodded.

"It's always worse when they are. It would make life much easier for him if I could get him to understand that she is terminal before she actually dies. I'll just have to do my best."

Jo desperately wanted to broach the subject of their date but couldn't quite bring herself to ask him. Thankfully, he brought it up first.

"About next week?"

Jo's heart sank: he was going to pull out.

"Is Wednesday night still all right? I could book a table at The Dining Room. It's in the Old Town, so your neck of the woods, so to speak and more intimate than Porters."

Jo was relieved but tried not to look or sound it.

"That would be lovely."

He smiled, and she smiled back.

"Keep it cool, girl" she told herself, even though she would have liked to have given him a hug, she was so pleased.

Sister Ojo leant out of her office.

"Mr Kane?" She called and Jonathan held up a hand in acknowledgement before turning back to Jo.

"Eight o'clock?" She nodded. "I'll see you there then." And he hurried over to the office.

Jo turned to leave as well, noticing as she did that the door to side ward B was open and Mr Jennings was standing there, in the doorway, silently watching, or listening, to them. He looked distinctly angry. Jo wondered if he had heard what they said.

'Not exactly a professional exchange,' she thought guiltily and she would have said something, asked him about it, but he firmly shut the door and, as she hesitated about whether she should still go in and speak to him, he snapped the blind covering the porthole window in the door into the closed position. He clearly did not want to talk to her and she had to respect that, so she left.

13

As Jo brought her Audi to a gentle stop on the sweeping gravel driveway of her childhood home she could feel the tight ball of anxiety growing, deep down in her stomach. The dread she felt about going home was disproportionate, she knew, but it had been there, steadily building, since she had got up this morning. She loved her parents dearly, but she knew she was a disappointment, to her mother at least. A mother who, Jo reminded herself when she was feeling particularly unfairly victimised, had never had a career, had only managed to produce one child and had few, if any, real friends. A mother who still managed to make her feel a failure because she was unmarried, had no children, couldn't cook, and was a mere GP. Jo often wondered, if she suddenly became all the things Diana Hughes professed to have always wanted her to be, exactly what her mother would find to be disappointed about next. Probably that the grandchildren were not well-behaved enough, or clever enough, or that Jo did not bring them up in quite the right way. Deep down Jo knew that she would never please her mother and that she should stop trying but it was easier said than done.

She took a deep breath and stepped out onto the drive. The Old Vicarage was a beautiful house, symmetrical and graceful. Its dove grey stucco would be festooned with pale, lilac-blue Wisteria blossoms in spring, but now was decorated only by the twisted, woody stems, with a few dying leaf sprays and velvety seed pods hanging from them, clinging to the walls around the front door and the ground floor windows.

Jo took the time to look around her as she went to the boot and pulled out her weekend bag. As usual, the gardens were immaculate even though it was autumn. No dead bedding plants or fallen leaves were allowed to mar the perfection here. The small window box of dead herbs that Jo had planted in a fit of domesticity always made her mother wince on the rare occasions she found time to visit her flat in Hastings.

Jo closed the boot, checked her brown cord skirt wasn't creased and her boots were not scuffed, took a deep breath and fixed a smile on her lips as the front door opened.

"Jocasta! At last. Was the traffic awful? Silly question. Come on in, darling. We'd all but given up on you."

As Jo proffered her mother a cheek to kiss, she bit back a retort. She was only ten minutes later than she had arranged, but she knew from past experience that rising to the bait this early in the weekend, blaming road works or unusually heavy traffic when they all knew she had delayed leaving, half in the hope something urgent would come up and prevent her from making the trip, would just make matters worse. She followed her mother into the house, and, after leaving her bag neatly out of the way in the hall cupboard to be taken upstairs later, she hurried through into the morning room to greet her father.

Charles Hughes was sitting in a large armchair just to the side of the open fireplace, where a log fire blazed. His half-moon spectacles perched on the end of his nose as he read The Times.

"Hello, Daddy." Jo bent forward to kiss him on the forehead.

"Jocasta! How lovely to see you. I was wondering why your mother was fussing round, tidying things up." He struggled to his feet, dropping the paper and, as she bent to pick it up, Jo thought he looked older than the last time she had seen him. It was only two or three months ago, surely? And she had arranged this visit weeks ago, had spoken to both of them on the phone, she was certain. She shrugged it off mentally. Maybe the days were all running into each other now that he had no work to fix them in his mind.

"How are things then, Daddy? Ma been keeping you busy?"

Charles Hughes had retired from his job as a consultant orthopaedic surgeon almost a year ago now and had struggled with the loss of purpose to his life. He had always said that he looked forward to retirement, to pottering in the garden, playing more golf, visiting places he had never had time to see before, and had even said he would take up watercolours again now that he would have the time. But since actually stopping work he didn't seem to have done anything at all. When pressed, he said that golf more than once a week got boring, that Diana was better at the gardening and had a nice young man to help with the heavy bits, that he didn't want to waste time in the car, let alone an aeroplane, and that he had lost his eye for painting. Excuses all, and Jo didn't know why he was making them. Why were the hobbies that he always complained he had no time to indulge suddenly so unattractive now that he had all the time in the world? Perhaps he was depressed. Or maybe no pastime was as interesting when you had all the time you could want to indulge in it.

"Oh, you know. Takes me most of the morning to do the crossword these days. Can't seem to fit much else in." He smiled but Jo wasn't convinced. "Now, what about a drink? Your mother will want her pre-prandial G and T."

"Just a sparkling water for me, Daddy."

"Why don't you pop through to the kitchen and help your mother? I'll bring the drinks through."

So, with sinking heart, Jo trudged obediently to the kitchen to face the first of many skirmishes, part interrogation and part criticism, that made up her relationship with her mother.

"I thought he was such a nice young man." Diana was saying as Jo covered her glass with her hand to stop her father from topping up her wine. "I simply don't understand why you didn't agree to see him again."

"He just wasn't my type." Jo was still firmly refusing to rise and concentrated on her monkfish in Pernod sauce instead.

"But do you know just what exactly is your type, Jocasta, darling?" Diana waved her perfectly manicured hand. She had hardly touched her food, she rarely did, but God help Jo or her father if they didn't clean their plates.

"I know what isn't my type, Ma, which is halfway there."

"Hardly."

"Now, now, Di. Stop pestering the poor girl about her love life. She's young yet, plenty of time to settle down."

As usual, her father was playing peacemaker, as he had done throughout her life. Jo hoped her mother would back off, it was too early in the weekend for a full-on row, but she knew equally that any truce would only be temporary. Her mother would just wait until they were alone to bring up the husband topic again.

"I just want her to be happy, that's all."

Jo was relieved; her mother's reply did at least signal a reprieve, for now.

"Have another potato, Jo. Can't let them go to waste." Food had always been Diana Hughes' way of making amends, or of bribing people, and sometimes she even used it as a weapon.

"Thank you." Jo accepted the peace offering.

"I wish I was like you, not bothered about my weight." Diana sighed and patted her very flat stomach, and looked at Jo's waistline pointedly. Jo grimaced at this, but once again bit back a reply. She might not be quite as slim as her mother, but there was no way she was overweight. She sometimes wondered if Diana tried to feed her up in an attempt to make her fat, and therefore less attractive. A psychologist friend had once suggested that she might see Jo as competition, and the theory did seem to fit, but Jo was not so naïve as to think it was that simple. After all, if she was overweight wouldn't she find it even harder to catch her mother's idea of the perfect man?

Later, having cleared away lunch, and once Diana had retired to her bedroom for her afternoon rest, Jo suggested a walk to her father. Diana could be relied upon to remain in her room until at least four, often later, in time for a reviving cup of tea before starting to prepare dinner.

Walks with her father had always been their special time. Even in the days before Diana needed her afternoon rest she had never been keen on walking, or exercise of any kind other than issuing orders to the gardener, and Jo and her father used the time to talk, asking each other questions about work or discussing interesting articles in the BMJ or the state of the NHS, all topics that Diana would call "boring" as she banned them from further discussion.

Jo had suggested a circuit through the fields to one side of the house, skirting the church and, as it had been raining recently, both were wearing Wellington boots, which they would be able to leave outside the back door when they got back. God help anyone who tracked dirt back into the house. As they cheerfully splashed through the puddles and the mud, trying to be careful about not getting any on their clothes, they chatted amiably about the latest NHS re-organisation, introduced before the last one had had time to make any difference.

"I tell you, I'm glad to have retired. I couldn't take one more Department of Health white paper. Or another Health Care Commission audit. One more set of targets or standards or whatever they are calling them this week. Complete chaos."

"You can say that again. I think they've lost the plot. Well, if they haven't the rest of us poor souls have," Jo agreed. "So, how is retirement? You aren't bored?"

"Oh, you know what they say. You wonder how you ever found time to work. There's so much to do."

But Jo wasn't going to be brushed off so easily this time.

"Like what?"

"Oh, this and that. Nothing much, just pottering really." He seemed to be evading the issue.

"I was chatting to Ian Dunbar the other day. He was asking after you, saying he hadn't seen you at any LMC dinners for a while."

Charles looked surprised.

"I went to the last one, although I may have missed the one before that." He thought for a moment. "I spoke to him, about an article on death rates following hip replacements. I remember it distinctly." He shook his head. "His memory must be going. Poor old sod. Fancy forgetting. He's older than me, you know. He should retire before they make him." And he picked up the pace, as if to prove that he was as young and fit as ever.

It wasn't until the next morning that Jo finally snapped. Diana had probed and questioned her about men friends over dinner but Charles had always managed to change the subject before she got too persistent. After dinner, when they always retired to the morning room for coffee and a whisky nightcap, Jo had excused herself, claiming tiredness, and went to her room. It had been way too early to sleep but Jo needed to be alone, or at least away from her mother. So she sat up in bed, reading a novel and gazing round the room, unchanged since her schooldays. Jo was glad she had never been one for the pink, frilly and flowery styles that her mother favoured. At least the apricot that they compromised on, with very plain brown and cream accessories, no patterns or chintz, was easier to bear. Beginning to feel sleepy at last, she had closed her book and clicked off the bedside light: an early night would at least restore her strength for the morning, or so she thought.

But it was the next morning that Jo cracked. She was supposedly helping Diana with an arrangement of flowers from the garden but Jo had never been any good at flower arranging so Diana was getting more and more critical of her efforts.

"No, no. That's completely in the wrong place. I mean look at it. You need to put it over here, to balance." And Diana moved the offending spray of greenery to a place that looked, to Jo, no different from where it had been before.

She took another spray and tentatively held it up where she thought it should go and stepped back a little to see how it looked. Her mother snatched the spray.

"If you are not going to take it seriously, Jo, just let me do it. Honestly, how you think you are ever going to get yourself a husband when you can't even do a simple flower arrangement, I don't know."

"I have yet to meet a man who gave a toss whether or not a woman could arrange flowers."

Jo leant back against the worktop and gave up any pretence of helping her mother with the arrangement.

"That says more about the sort of man you meet than anything else."

"And what's that supposed to mean?"

"All those criminals and policemen." The way she said it made it sound as if she considered the policemen to be worse than the criminals. "I don't understand why you would want to be a police doctor. It really isn't a suitable job for a woman."

"Why not? Are you saying women are too weak, or too easily shocked to do the job? Shouldn't be exposed to that sort of person?"

"Of course not, darling. But you're hardly likely to meet a future husband in a police station, are you?"

"There are more important things in life than getting married, Ma."

"You might think so now but you wait until you are middle-aged and your looks have gone. All alone and no hope of having children. You'll regret it then, my girl."

"Well, I've a quite a way to go before I get to middle-age."

"Time has a way of creeping up on you before you know it. You

100

should get a job in a hospital, you might meet some nice surgeon, a consultant even. I mean, where does an NHS GP get to meet anyone worth marrying? You'll marry someone unsuitable or die an old maid, you mark my words."

"Actually, I'm going out with an Obs and Gynae consultant at the moment and I met him in my humble role as an NHS GP."

As soon as the words came out of Jo's mouth she regretted them.

"Darling, but that's wonderful news! Why didn't you say before? How long have you been seeing him?"

"It's early days, so don't get too excited."

"Nonsense." Diana went to the kitchen door; she really did seem genuinely delighted.

"Charles, darling? Jocasta's got something to tell you."

"Ma!" Jo was cross and embarrassed. All this fuss would make it ten times worse if things didn't work out, and how could she tell them now that they had only been on one date and that was ridiculously short. They hadn't even kissed. She really shouldn't have said anything. She kicked herself, mentally. Idiot!

Charles Hughes came into the kitchen, still holding the Sunday paper and peered at her over his spectacles.

"What's that?" He gave Jo a mischievous grin, "Am I going to be a grandfather, or something?"

"Daddy!"

"Don't be so ridiculous, Charles. She isn't even married yet, but she soon might be. To a consultant gynaecologist."

"Ma. For goodness' sake! Give the poor man a chance. If he heard you say something like that he'd run a mile."

But her mother refused to believe it.

"Nonsense, Jocasta. You wouldn't have mentioned him if it wasn't on the cards."

Jo sincerely wished she hadn't mentioned him.

Charles gave Jo a searching look, but Jo couldn't quite bring herself to look him in the eye.

"Hmm." He seemed to realise the situation immediately, which just made Jo feel worse.

"You will have to bring him here to dinner, meet your father. Let me get the calendar-" But Charles stopped her, gently putting a hand on her arm as she hurried towards the hall.

"I dare say Jocasta will bring him to meet us in her own good time, Diana."

He spoke firmly, but Jo was still surprised that her mother allowed herself to be persuaded.

"But that will be ages, knowing -" She looked at her husband and saw the look on his face. "Of course. Mustn't rush things." She was still too excited to let it go completely, though. "What's his name? Where did he train? You must tell us so that your father can look him up in the Medical Directory."

And so, with reluctance, Jo told them.

Later that night, Jo was in The Stag, comfortably settled on a bench seat near the fire conducting a post mortem on her weekend with her parents.

"Honestly, Kate, I could have bitten off my tongue. How could I have been so stupid as to mention Jonathan to her?"

"I don't know. You are supposed to be a bright woman, for God's sake, but you let your mother push all your buttons and run your life. Always have. You wouldn't let anybody else in the world get away with what she does on a regular basis."

Jo groaned.

"What am I going to do, Kate?"

"Well, doctor, I think that what you need is to work this through with a therapist."

"I meant about Jonathan. And anyway, you ought to be my therapist so it's you who have failed."

"Therapist, priest, confessor, counsellor, I am all of these things, but I have to admit that this mess is probably beyond even me. You might well be able to string her along for a month or two but she is going to demand to meet him sooner or later and if it's all gone tits up in the meantime your mother is going to go mental."

"That's why I think, when the time comes, you should be the one to tell her."

"Oh, no." Kate shook her head, vehemently. "Not on your Nellie. In fact, I want to be warned well in advance so that I can be out of the country when you tell her this one."

"And you call yourself a friend?"

"A friend who knows and cares about survival."

"Please?"

"No."

"Not even for a year's supply of Shepherd Neame beer?"

"Not even for a year's supply of beer and a lifetime's supply of chocolate cake."

Jo sighed. She knew when she was beaten. If things didn't get serious with Jonathan soon she would have to face her mother, alone.

14

The relentless drizzle that seemed to have settled on the town in the days since Krissy's funeral was showing no signs of lifting as Jo hurried up the steps towards the address, high up on the West Hill, that she had been given. As she reached the top and looked along the road she assessed the run-down Victorian terrace, each four storey house divided into as many flats as could be crammed in to the available space. The upper floors would have a nice view over the town centre to the sea and would bring in good money, but the lower floors, even the so-called "garden flat", with its bit of concrete patio out back, where the residents stored their wheelie bins and chained their bikes to the railings, looked dark, damp and dingy. A flight of cracked concrete steps led down to the basement flats in each house. There was no mistaking the address that she was supposed to be visiting. Apart from having a police car parked outside, a cluster of interested neighbours and onlookers had gathered on the pavement, and a middle-aged man was sitting on the steps, head in hands, with a young police constable, looking unsure and awkward, next to him. Jo was surprised that the witness-comforting was being left to a rookie, until she spotted the more experienced policewoman in the panda and could tell from the look of her that she had been the one who went in and discovered the body. She didn't look like she would be eating again any time soon.

The constable stood up to let Jo pass and she patted the other man on the shoulder as she went by. She was not sure that he noticed, he was so engrossed in his misery and shock. As she went down the steps to the tiny concrete area that allowed a modicum of light in to the basement rooms as well as giving access to the front door she could understand why. The smell of decomposed human tissue was unmistakeable. There was a small splattering of vomit over the steps and Jo trod carefully round it, glad that she was in jeans and easy-to-clean, dark leather shoes; she wouldn't want the mess from this death scene on her cream suede Ballys or her dry-clean-only silk-mix suit. She would want everything she was wearing today to be thrown straight into a hot wash to get rid of the smell as soon as she got home. She paused on the bottom step by the open front door, the broken glass on the doorstep and missing window pane revealing how the policewoman had gained access, and fished a pot of vapour rub out of her medical bag. Taking a large dab, Jo smeared it under her nose knowing that, even if she stuck a whole pot full of menthol and eucalyptus up there, there was no way it was going to disguise the smell from this body. With one last, deep, breath of not-so-fresh air, she entered the flat.

The hallway had no natural light except for what was coming through the open front door and a second door at the end. It took Jo a few moments to adjust to the dim light, before she could make out the hallway. The floor, covered by a well-worn, stained carpet, led to the back of the house and she could make out three doors off the hall-way, all closed, except the one at the end which was slightly ajar, and through which a muted light and a terrible smell emanated.

"Hello?" she called out and was relieved to see Mike Parton appear from the doorway.

"She's in here, doctor."

She hurried along the hallway and followed Mike through the open door at the end, pulling on a pair of gloves as she went.

Standing in the doorway, Jo looked round the cheaply furnished bed-room. Mike Parton, aware that she liked to do this, stood silently to one side, waiting for her to take it all in. The curtains were drawn across, but a weak light was seeping through the gap where they did not quite meet in the middle. Behind them she could glimpse dingy, grey nets that looked as if they had hung there, unwashed, since the flat was first built. The central ceiling light was on but the bulb was dim, probably only twenty five watts and insufficient to light the room properly. The furniture was a mix of second-hand junk and cheap flat-pack pieces, inexpertly put together. It was an unloved and utilitarian room, typical of cheap, rented accommodation of this type, a type that Jo had often seen when visiting the sick and poor of the town. The council put homeless people on the housing waiting list in this sort of place, when they could find it. Students, the unemployed, the old, the vulnerable; this was where they often ended their days, overdosing on drugs or alcohol, or just giving up the struggle.

The room was warm, despite the cool temperature outside. There was a night storage heater under the window. It would be on a timer and would have continued to come on regardless, speeding up the body's decomposition. There were several flies buzzing at the window. Jo was thankful it wasn't summer or there would have been several hundred.

She finally turned her attention to the bed. This was clearly the source of the smell. The naked, bloated and partially decomposed body of a woman was lying on top of the covers. It was hard to tell if she had always been overweight or if it was just the effects of the putrefaction gases building up inside her bowels and abdominal cavity that gave her such an obese appearance. Probably both Jo decided, as she moved closer to the body, checking the surrounding area for anything that might give her a clue as to why this lady was deceased.

"Do we know anything about her?" Jo asked Mike.

Mike looked down at his notebook.

"Her name is Denise Gardner. Twenty two years old. Lived alone. Worked in Morrisons, on the checkout. Hadn't turned up for work for the last two weeks. That's her manager outside, came round as he hadn't been able to reach her on the phone and it was out of character for her to no show for more than a couple of days. I think he was just covering his bases before forwarding a P45."

"Next of kin?"

"Her manager didn't know of any but I went through her bag and found her driving licence, still with an address in Croydon, and there's a telephone number for Mum in her address book."

Jo nodded. Mike had been as thorough as always.

Close up, Jo could make out more of the girl's features but light was still a problem. She flicked the switch on the bedside light but the bulb had gone so Mike opened the curtains and pulled back the nets. It was a grey day and the already weak sunlight was no match for the many years' build-up of dirt on the windows. It wasn't going to be easy to see what she was doing.

Jo stooped over the body and checked for any obvious signs of trauma. There were no apparent wounds or limbs at odd angles. Her mouth was open and her tongue was lolling out slightly. The girl looked as if she had died in her sleep but healthy twenty two year olds don't usually die in their sleep, not even obese ones, not without some kind of help. So Jo looked round for any signs of drugs or alcohol. There was nothing on the bedside table. The top drawer was sticky and difficult to open and contained nothing more than a pack of contraceptive pills, some condoms, a vibrator and several used tissues.

Jo pulled down the girl's lower jaw. There was a pool of blood in her mouth from where she had bitten her tongue but no sign of vomit, and if there had been froth on the lips it was hard to tell now that decomposition was so advanced. Jo tried to keep the revulsion from her face as a single maggot crawled out from under the tongue.

"Any history of epilepsy? Fits?"

Mike shrugged.

"There's no anti-epileptic drugs in the drawer, were there any in her bag? Or the bathroom cupboard?

"None in her bag. I'll check the bathroom." He went out.

Jo gently moved the head to one side and stopped.

"Just some paracetamol," Mike reported as he came back in. Jo held up her hand to stop him and indicated the girl's neck.

"Have you got a torch, Mike?"

He moved back towards the door.

"There will be one in the panda."

He went off to fetch it, leaving Jo with the body. There was no point trying to examine it any further without light and she didn't want to disturb anything or touch anything if what she suspected was right, so she stood still and patiently waited for Mike to return. It was less than two minutes but seemed like an hour before he hurried back in and handed her a black police issue Maglite. She shone it on the girl's neck and tilted the head slightly to one side, aware of Mike leaning close, trying to see what had obviously caught her attention.

"There." She pointed at a slightly darkened line around the neck. It was hard to see as the skin tone was already unnaturally dark due to the putrefaction process. "Looks like it could be a ligature mark to me."

Mike leant back.

"Right. Best call for back-up then."

And he went out, Jo following, making sure that she took all her things with her and left everything just as she had found it. If her suspicion that young Denise Gardner had been murdered was correct then she wanted to disturb as little as possible and leave as little evidence of her presence as she could, in order to give the crime scene investigators a clean a field on which to work.

As she waited for the back-up to arrive she spoke to Denise's manager, who was still feeling very sorry for himself.

"I didn't notice the smell at first. It wasn't until there wasn't any answer at the door and I opened the letter box to shout that I smelled it. Now I can't get rid of it. I don't think I ever will."

Jo handed the manager her pot of vapour rub.

"Here, a touch of this helps, just pop it under your nose."

He took the pot gratefully and stuck a large glob of the stuff right up his left nostril before digging his finger in again and getting more to stick in the right. He went to hand the pot back, but Jo shook her head. Did he really think that she would want it back after he had contaminated it like that?

"It's okay. You keep it."

They were sitting on the kerb a little along from the flat, where she and Mike had moved the manager and, realising how distressed he was, she felt obliged to attempt to comfort him. A thin, almost scrawny, man in his early forties with thinning hair and a care-worn expression, Jo rather doubted that he would ever go looking for any missing employees again.

"So, how come you were visiting Denise?" Jo asked, just searching for something to break the silence, get the man's mind off the lingering smell.

"I was coming to see what the problem was. Why she hadn't come into work for the last two weeks." He looked down at the pavement, absentmindedly scraping at a lump of discarded chewing gum with his cheap plastic shoes. "Thought it might have been something I'd said."

He was shifting his position nervously, guiltily.

"Did she kill herself?" He looked directly at Jo.

"What makes you think that?"

"The last time I saw her, at the end of her shift on the Saturday before last, she asked me to go to a karaoke night with her, up at the

Jolly Sailor."

"And you turned her down?"

"No. I said I'd go, meet her there, like, but…"

Jo let the silence linger on, knowing that he'd fill it sooner or later. He only left it a few seconds.

"I know she had a bit of a crush on me, but well, I mean, fraternising with the staff is looked down on. You know. From head office."

"So why did you say you'd be there?"

"Because it was getting embarrassing. She kept asking me to things and I'd run out of excuses. It just sort of came out and she looked so happy. It just seemed kinder."

"To let her go to the karaoke and then let her down publicly?"

He went back to digging at the gum with his foot.

"I'll never forgive myself if she killed herself because I stood her up."

A silver Toyota Avensis pulled up, and Jo stood as she saw Miller and Jeffries get out.

"We'll have to wait for the post mortem but I don't think she did."

He looked at her with a mixture of relief and disappointment. God save her from the egos of men, Jo thought.

"I've got to go," she told the manager, "Just remember to tell the police everything you told me." He nodded and she hurried towards the steps down to the basement, already several paces behind the two detectives.

Miller and Jeffries were standing just inside the bedroom door as Jo came in. Both men exuded pent-up excitement and anticipation, convinced that this second death would be the break they were looking for, had been waiting for.

"You say you think you saw a ligature mark on the neck, Doctor Hughes?" Miller asked.

"That's right. It's hard to tell with the decomposition, but I thought it better to be safe."

"Have you touched anything?"

Jo glanced at Mike Parton, who was looking slightly uncomfortable.

"We opened the curtains to let in more light, that's all." Mike answered for her.

110

Miller nodded.

"And I opened the bedside drawer, looking for signs of drug use." Jo added.

"Did you find anything?"

"No. Just contraceptives."

"Okay. Show me the mark." He almost ordered Jo.

She moved forward, pulling on a fresh pair of gloves, tilting the girl's head slightly to one side and pointed.

"Here. It's faint, but I'm sure." Jo tried to sound more convinced than she was. The line seemed even less obvious now than it had when she first saw it.

But it was enough to convince Miller. He turned to Jeffries.

"I want the full team out here, everything, and get on to Professor Wadsworth, not the local pathologist, see if you can persuade him to come out to the scene. Now let's get everybody out of here until the crime scene boys have done their bit."

They all traipsed back to the front door and Jo wondered if they all felt like naughty schoolchildren, or if Miller only had that effect on her.

Jo was not sure if she should hang around, see if she could do anything else to help, or if she had been dismissed. Jeffries and Miller were questioning the manager and she didn't want to interrupt and ask but, on the other hand, she had things to do, places to go. It was her day off from the surgery so she couldn't claim an urgent need to leave but she really needed to do some food shopping, take several weeks' worth of clothes to the cleaners, go to the bank. All the little jobs that, one way or another, she never quite found time to do. She knew the investigation took priority, the dead girl deserved that, but this sitting round waiting was beginning to irritate.

She saw Mike Parton returning from having made a telephone call from the privacy of his car, presumably to brief the Coroner about this case, and went over to him.

"Hi Mike, do you think they are likely to need me any more?" She nodded towards the two detectives.

Mike frowned.

"Hard to say. Professor Wadsworth will be here soon but -." He shrugged.

Jo sighed. Best to wait until class was dismissed. She glowered over towards Miller and was embarrassed when he turned and looked straight at her, as if he had felt the force of her ill will across the twenty or so yards that separated them. Jo dropped her gaze hurriedly but looked up again when she heard footsteps approaching. It was Miller. He paused and turned back to Jeffries, who was a few yards behind him, as if he had suddenly remembered something.

"Get uniform to pick up Jimmy Allen if they can find him, would you, Bob?" Then he turned back to speak to Mike Parton.

"Is the Home Office pathologist on his way?" he asked.

"Yes, should be here within the hour."

Miller turned to Jo.

"No need for you to wait then, Dr Hughes. There's nothing more for you to do now. Professor Wadsworth will take over from here on in." He turned to leave and Jo could feel a flush of anger reach her cheeks.

"That's so kind of you." She muttered sarcastically to his retreating back, "Arrogant, patronising..." Jo was embarrassed to see that a female police constable standing by one of the police cars that had arrived with Miller and Jeffries had overheard her and was smirking in recognition of her description.

Jo stalked off towards the steps down towards the town, still angry at being so summarily dismissed without so much as a thank you. She knew it was silly, that she had merely done her job but done it well, and Miller was right, Professor Wadsworth did have to take over from here. Anything that she did or touched at the crime scene could cause contamination or a break in the chain of evidence, muddy the waters for any future prosecution, but he could have suggested that she wait for Professor Wadsworth and report her findings direct to him and then wait to see if he agreed, if her suspicions had been correct. After all, it was she who had flagged the death up as suspicious in the first place. It would have been common courtesy to allow her to stay and hear the experienced pathologist's expert opinion, surely? She knew that she was being contrary, having wanted to leave a few minutes earlier, but that didn't change the way she felt. She had been disposed of as unwanted and unnecessary, and it grated.

At the top of the stairs she took one last back towards the house and was interested to see Miller still watching her, obviously aware that he had irritated her. As she brazenly regarded him he shook his head, as if giving up trying to work out why she was angry with him, and turned back to where Jeffries was busy on his mobile, probably urging his colleagues to rough up Jimmy Allen once they found him.

Jo practically stomped down the steps to where she had left her car, fuelled with righteous indignation. If he didn't know why she was upset he couldn't be much of a detective, she thought. She decided to go home and clean the flat then take a shower; she didn't want to go food shopping until she had got the smell of death, mixed with menthol and eucalyptus, out of her nostrils.

15

Jo was surprised to see Charlie, the not-really-asthmatic from custody, sitting on the wall outside the surgery the next day. She looked as surly as ever, swinging her legs and smoking as she waited. A small pile of cigarette butts below her on the pavement indicated that she had been waiting some time. It was a cold, quiet Tuesday afternoon and there was a slight, intermittent drizzle, although Charlie seemed oblivious to it. It was not a day for hanging around outside a doctors' surgery unless you had a good reason.

Jo crossed over to stand in front of Charlie and waited for the girl to speak.

"Did you mean it, then?" Charlie finally asked.

"Mean what?"

"That I could come and talk to you anytime."

"Yes, I did. Do want to come inside? You might not mind getting wet but I do." Jo ambled towards the surgery door, giving only the slightest of glances back to make sure that Charlie was following her. Charlie waited a moment, either not wanting to seem too eager or not sure that she wanted to do this, but then stubbed out her cigarette, dropped the end on the pavement to join the others, and slipped off the wall. She didn't seem to make any effort to hurry after Jo but still managed to catch the swing door before it closed.

It wasn't until they were settled in Jo's consulting room, clutching cups of tea to warm them up, that Jo asked what Charlie wanted to talk to her about.

"I was, you know, thinking. About what happened to Ellie?"

It was half-question, half-statement and Jo decided to keep quiet, let her get round to saying what she wanted in her own good time. Charlie was cradling the mug of sweet, milky tea in both hands, looking at the floor, the posters, the window, anywhere but at Jo.

"I saw her. Before she went off and, you know, topped herself. And I keep thinking, like, could I have done something, said something, to help?"

"You think it was deliberate, then? Suicide?"

"Yes. No. I don't know." Charlie sighed, and Jo felt sure she wasn't telling the truth. Not the whole truth anyway. "She was really worried."

"About what?"

Charlie hesitated.

"About what Tomas was telling her to do."

"And what was that?"

"I don't know, honest. I just know that she said it was fucking sick."

Jo didn't even want to begin to think what a drug addict and prostitute would call sick.

"Why didn't she just say no? Refuse to do it?"

Charlie looked at her, amazed that anyone could ask such a stupid question.

"You don't say no to Tomas. He can be a real bastard. He could cut your face, or slice your tits off, if he wanted. You just don't fuck with Tomas. He's a madman."

Jo shuddered. What were the police thinking of? Letting men like Tomas Czernak prey on young girls and fill them with such fear. She was sure they must be able to get something on him, preferably legitimately but, she acknowledged, however they did it, they needed to get something that would mean they could lock him up and get him off these girls' backs for a long time. It was all very well maintaining that the law needed to be applied correctly and impartially no matter what but, when kids were being frightened to death, even Jo had an urge to do something drastic, although she could also see that she couldn't have it both ways: allow Jeffries and Miller to fit up Tomas and then complain that they had nothing on Jimmy. At least she was consistent in her dislike of brutes and bullies, she thought.

"So she told you she was going to do it? Whatever it was that Tomas wanted her to do?"

"Yes." Charlie was staring into her mug, swirling what was left of the tea around. Irritated, Jo took the mug from her.

"Come on, Charlie, spit it out. What's worrying you?"

"She said that she needed something to help her get through it."

Jo sighed.

"You gave her some gear?"

"Only a bit. A mate gave it me to try but I'd never had the nerve."

"Mate?" Jo asked. "We both know that "mates" don't give you gear to try, Charlie. Dealers do, to get you started and get you hooked so that they have more customers."

"All right then, a dealer. But that's what I gave her and she must've used it and it was too strong. Don't you see? It could have been me. But it wasn't. Instead, I killed her."

Jo sat back in the chair with a sigh. Charlie was looking her in the eye for the first time and a tear slowly spilled out and trickled down her cheek to join a dewdrop from her nose. Charlie honestly believed that she had been at least part to blame for Ellie's death.

"We sent the little bit of liquid from the bottom of the syringe to be analysed. It wasn't too strong."

Charlie was looking bewildered.

"So why did she die then?"

"We think she injected herself twice in a short space of time. Maybe one dose wasn't enough. Anyway, it added up to a larger dose than she usually did."

"Or maybe she decided she couldn't go through with it. With whatever that bastard Tomas wanted her to do. Killed herself rather than face him." Charlie was angry now.

"Perhaps."

"Or maybe he forced her to take a second dose because she wouldn't do as he said."

Jo didn't like the way this conversation was going.

"There's nothing to suggest that, Charlie," she hastily told her. "No signs of force, and why would he have killed her in the public toilets?"

"He could've dumped her there. Later."

Jo shook her head.

"No. You can tell when a body has been moved after death. You get what is called liver mortis, lividity. Pooling of the blood in the lowest parts of the body. It settles there so you can tell the position of the body at death. Ellie died where she was found."

Charlie thought about it for a while, before nodding her acceptance.

"He's still the reason she died, though, isn't he? Even if he didn't actually give her the injection? She only did it 'cos she was frightened of him and what he was asking her to do." She seemed young again. The child that she still undoubtedly was.

Jo leant forward and took her hand.

"Neither of us can know what was going on in her mind when she did this, Charlie, but I can tell you one thing: she wouldn't have wanted you to get mixed up in it too. Wouldn't have wanted you to put your life in danger. Wouldn't have wanted you to make the same mistakes she did. Do you understand?"

Jo was hoping that Charlie would look on Ellie's death as a warning and change her ways before it was too late but, even more than that, she prayed that Charlie wouldn't go off and do something stupid, like try confronting Tomas Czernak. Tell him that he was to blame for Ellie's death. She didn't think Charlie would, she seemed healthily frightened of the man, but she wanted to be sure.

"You won't go near him, will you, Charlie? You'll give Tomas a wide berth?"

"Too bloody right." Jo was relieved that Charlie seemed to be being straight with her. "That doesn't mean he's letting it go, though. I heard he was asking round, trying to find someone else to do his little favour, as he calls it. So everybody's trying to keep out of his way but he'll find somebody. You wait and see, he'll make somebody else do it."

"Just don't let it be you, Charlie."

Knowing Charlie as she did, Jo didn't want her putting herself in danger but that didn't mean that she wanted anyone else to either. She was going to have to go and see Miller again, she realised, get him to take it seriously but if he wouldn't then maybe she would have to try and find out more about Tomas herself or at least make sure she warned all the working girls she knew to stay clear of him. That was a compromise, she thought. Much as it would be wonderful to go and present Miller with irrefutable evidence of whatever Tomas was up to, and wipe the smile off his face for once and for all, she knew there was no way she would ever be doing that. She would still have to be very careful though; if Tomas got to hear about her telling girls to keep away from him he wasn't likely to appreciate it and, whatever else, she wasn't going to put herself in danger. She certainly didn't want to get too close to a man as unpleasant as Czernak sounded, even to prove herself, but there was nothing to stop her digging around a little, asking Marcy and some of the other girls about him, seeing if she could find out anything useful. Anything that would help Miller or his colleagues to get Tomas Czernak off the streets and away from the Ellies and Charlies of this world. Legally, if at all possible.

Charlie's visit had inevitably delayed Jo so she was late for her first patient of evening surgery and she hadn't even glanced at her paperwork- the pathology results, the repeat prescription requests, the hospital letters- let alone dealt with any of them. Up in the office, she rifled through the pile in her basket, trying to pick out anything urgent.

"Have we had Timothy Lockwood's results back yet?" she asked, knowing he was due in later.

Linda checked on his electronic record as Jo continued to sort through the paper copies.

"Yup. They're there." Linda told her and Jo came over to the computer screen to look at them. She frowned as she read them.

"Good thing he's coming in."

The phone buzzed, indicating an internal call, and Linda picked it up, glancing almost immediately at Jo, who was still engrossed in young Timothy Lockwood's blood results.

"Helen on reception says Mr Herring wants you to know that you are now four minutes late starting surgery and he is your first patient."

Jo groaned. Why did it always have to be him?

Timothy was not looking well. Jo wasn't sure if she was seeing his complexion as sallow and jaundiced with the benefit of the insight that his blood results had given her or if she would have noticed it anyway. She pulled down his lower eyelids. The whites definitely seemed a bit yellow today and she knew they had not been before.

"Up on the couch, young man," she ordered and turned to his mother as he obeyed. Mrs Lockwood was looking as expensive and immaculate as ever, with her perfectly polished and manicured nails, her thick, shiny, blonde hair showing not one iota of the darker roots that Jo was sure would be more her natural colour, and with plenty of solid gold jewellery visible, for all her protestations of poverty.

"His test results are back and there are one or two abnormalities."

"And what does that mean? Do you know what's wrong with him?"

"His liver function tests are raised, which suggests that he might have a problem there."

"His liver? What do you mean, a problem?" She seemed more irritated than concerned, but maybe that was just the way she came across, Jo thought.

"The most common reason in boys his age is hepatitis A. A viral hepatitis that you can get from eating infected food, usually seafood, or from contaminated water. Has Timothy been abroad recently?"

Mrs Lockwood thought for a moment.

"We haven't been away since Koh Samui last year, thanks to the divorce. I can't possibly afford to take him on holiday. Could it be from that long ago?"

Jo didn't say that if she could afford as much on clothes and beauty products as she clearly spent, she could afford a holiday with her son, but the thought sounded very loud in her own head .

"No. I don't think that's possible. Has anyone at his school been ill?"

"Not that I know of." Mrs Lockwood continued to think as Jo went over to Timothy and felt for his liver, sure now that it was enlarged.

"When we went out to Thailand last year we all had loads of injections. Isn't hepatitis A one of those?"

Jo turned back to Mrs Lockwood.

"Yes, but there's nothing on his notes about having had travel vaccinations."

"We had them done at a travel centre. It was more convenient."

"And he had the full course?"

"Just a booster that time, I think. We'd been abroad a few times, my ex-husband works in Hong Kong and we've lived there, off and on, until the divorce, that is, so he'd already had some of them. I can check his card."

"Please do. You can get up now, Timothy." She told the boy, before coming back and sitting at her desk.

"But what else could it be, if it's not hepatitis A?"

"That's a good question. I'll take some more blood." She saw Timothy pull a face. "Sorry, but it has to be done, I'm afraid," then turned back to the mother, "I'll send it off for viral studies and antibodies, see if we can identify if it is hep A, or maybe another sort of hepatitis, and I think we should get him seen up at the hospital. As soon as possible."

"You'll write a letter?"

"I'll call, tonight or first thing tomorrow, get some advice from the paediatrician."

This, more than anything seemed to bring it home to Mrs Lockwood that there might be something seriously wrong.

"These other forms of hepatitis- some of them can be dangerous, can't they?" Mrs Lockwood seemed suddenly vulnerable, almost soft, despite all the expensive veneer and lacquer. Whatever else she was or was not, this woman was still a mother.

Jo stole a glance at Timothy, who was listening intently, a serious expression on his face. Jo didn't want to alarm him but, equally, she didn't want to lie. To either of them.

"They can be, as can hep A, but there could any number of reasons why his liver is playing up, let's just try and find out why, quickly." She turned and spoke directly to Timothy, "Then we can getting you feeling well again."

"Don't worry, darling," Jo was pleased that for the first time his mother was addressing Timothy directly, "I'll call your father as soon as we get home." She turned to Jo. "I'll tell him we need to go privately. I've absolutely no intention of hanging around an NHS hospital, all that waiting in uncomfortable chairs, not to mention the infections you can pick up these days. There must be a decent hospital around here somewhere and he'll have to pay up or I'll get the lawyers onto him again. Let me know what you've arranged as soon as possible. Hurry up, Timothy, it's already late in Hong Kong so I'll just have to wake your father up, won't I?" The prospect seemed to please her. "Goodnight, Dr Hughes."   And she ushered her son out of the room, leaving Jo gobsmacked: was there no end to this woman's selfishness?

Jo had picked up the local weekly paper when she did the shopping in the Sainsbury's up on the Ridgeway on her way home. Sainsbury's was not actually on her way home, she had to admit; in fact, it was significantly out of her way but she had not wanted to go to Morrisons in case she bumped into the manager. Silly really. Much as she was curious to find out more about the body from the basement flat in Keyfield Terrace she didn't want to be forced to talk about it with someone who probably knew less about it than she did, and, selfishly, she didn't want to have to spend yet more time being sympathetic; she did far too much of that in her official hours to want to do it in her off-duty time. She was sure that the local paper would have a report on the death and she was not wrong. Unsurprisingly, it was front page, lead story. "Supermarket checkout girl found dead" in large capitals filled half the page above what looked to be an old school photo of a plump, verging on the obese, young girl with limp mousey hair framing a very plain face with a forced smile and a bad case of acne. Poor girl, no wonder she developed a crush on her singularly uncharismatic manager, Jo thought, as she kicked off her shoes and settled on the sofa with a glass of wine to read the report. What she really wanted to know was if the police had anyone "helping with their enquiries" as they liked to call it. In other words, had they picked up Jimmy Allen again?

The full results of the post mortem would not be through for a while yet but she hoped that the police, Miller, that was, might have let something slip if they had had any kind of preliminary report. Was this a second strangling victim as Jo thought or had she got it wrong?

She skimmed through the newspaper report once and then read it again more carefully. Nothing was said specifically about cause of death but the police were treating it as suspicious and they didn't have anyone in custody. Jimmy Allen was either guilty as hell and in hiding or innocent and had decided that the best thing was to keep his head down but she suspected that Miller would favour the first interpretation. A sudden thought hit her. Maybe they had found Jimmy Allen and he had a cast iron alibi. That would seriously piss Miller off, she thought with a slightly mischievous smile, and resolved to ask him when she went to speak to him about Tomas Czernak in the morning, more for her benefit than his. Much more.

The paper had dug up a bit more background on the victim, Denise. She was the eldest of four children, one boy, three girls, from Croydon. Her mother was a school dinner lady, her father worked for the local authority parks department. A solid, unexceptional family, "devastated by the loss of their much-loved daughter and older sister", according to the report. She had apparently always loved Hastings after years of family holidays in the seaside town and had decided to move there soon after leaving school. Various old school friends were quoted as saying that Denise would be sadly missed, that she was a great girl, good fun. Maybe she should have stayed in Croydon, Jo thought, because she didn't seem to have had much of a life in Hastings. There was no cause of death noted or any similarities drawn to Krissy Trent's death but the final line of the report mentioned the prostitute's unsolved murder so it was clear that the press were beginning to link the two. It was just a matter of time before the public would, too. It was no coincidence either, Jo thought, that the opening and adjourning of the inquest into the death of Eleanor Smith was mentioned in a short report adjacent to the story on Denise and Jo thought about that for while. Could Ellie's death be connected? The method of killing was different, and it would be difficult to prove anything, but it was possible, wasn't it? Perhaps she should tell Miller that tomorrow. The syringe and wraps had all been kept and treated as exhibits the same as they would have been in a criminal case, thank goodness. Any sudden death was routinely treated in the same manner as a suspicious one, until proven to be due to natural causes and, although they had not yet been sent for forensic testing or fingerprinting, perhaps it would be as well to do that, they might lead the police to a known dealer if nothing else. Jo decided to ask Miller if that could be done. Just in case. It had to come out of somebody's budget, after all, so it might as well be his. God knows, he was going to love her admitting that maybe, just maybe, there was something more to Ellie's death than had at first seemed the case.

She put the paper down and went to pour herself a second glass of wine whilst she sorted out some dinner. Chicken fajitas. Quick, easy to cook, and not too bad on the healthy eating front. She'd stocked up on a few ready meals for the freezer again as well. They might be loaded with salt and fat but at least they were better than nothing sometimes. Although experience told her that they would just sit in her freezer for months, never quite matching what she felt like eating, until she threw them out in exasperation and started all over again.

As she thinly sliced the chicken and vegetables, Jo thought ahead to tomorrow night. Dinner with Jonathan. She was looking forward to it. He was, after all, good-looking and good company and very charming, unlike a certain detective chief inspector. Her few meetings with Miller suggested that he would be anything but good company. Going out with Jonathan would be good for her, she thought. He was a great catch, as her mother had pointed out. It had been a while since she had gone out with anybody other than Kate, and best friends didn't count anyway. She chucked everything into the wok to stir fry and surveyed the room. The flat was perfectly tidy and clean but maybe she ought to change the sheets tomorrow, just in case.

Suddenly there was a racket from outside, the sound of something ceramic being hit, or kicked, but not breaking. Flower pots maybe, or some bricks? A dog was barking and there were shouts of "Down!" and "Heel, boy". Jo looked out of the window and saw a man grabbing his snarling dog and putting it on a lead, literally dragging the animal away from the deeply shadowed recess where she put out her dustbin on collection days. Maybe the dog had found a cat and it was cowering in there terrified, or had jumped down into the garden beyond. Or maybe it was a rat. She would have to take a look, make sure there was no food or anything lying around that might tempt them to make it a regular haunt. But as she looked she saw something move, something too big to be a rat or even a fat, pampered cat.

A fox maybe? she thought, as she peered harder into the shadows and switched off the light to help her eyes adjust to the dark. There was some movement again, then nothing. Jo shivered and told her self not to be so silly. It was almost certainly just a fox. If she must live this close to open land it was hardly surprising that a bit of wild life came round. She had read that foxes, increasing as they were in numbers, were getting more and more bold, moving further into towns and cities in their search for food. It wouldn't be anything to write home about if she had seen one in central London, let alone on the outskirts of Hastings.

That said, Jo closed the curtains before switching on the lights again. She had been unsettled by what she had seen because the shape had been big and bulky and she couldn't get the idea out of her mind that it was too big even for a fox and that the way it moved had been more human than fox-like. She kept seeing something that, the more she ran the pictures through her head, had looked like an arm moving to pull, what? A hat or a hood, over its head. But maybe that was her imagination playing tricks. Maybe she was inventing it now, inventing the pictures to match her fears? Try as she might to get her thoughts back to Jonathan and her forthcoming date, she couldn't get rid of the feeling that there was a man out there, watching her. She would never be able to sleep.

Finally, telling herself that she was being very, very stupid, she grabbed a torch and coat and went out to see if there was anyone out there.

It was dark and damp as she crossed the road, clutching her coat round her and suppressing a shiver of fear.

"Come out, come out, whoever you are," she said, acutely aware of just how ridiculous she sounded as she shone the torch into the recess.

There was no one there but the top brick of the wall around the area had fallen. It had always been loose, she told herself, could have been knocked off by a cat, or a fox, or a man, trying to get out of the way of a dog.

She hurried back to her flat, double locking the door behind her. She wished that it made her feel safer but it didn't.

He hurried along the road, anxiously checking behind him to see that he wasn't being followed. His heart was beating so fast he thought it must surely burst. How could he have been so stupid? He tried breaking into a run but his breathing was so laboured that he was almost sobbing in his attempts to drag air in and force it out. If anyone saw him like this they would know something was wrong and probably think he was having an asthma attack or something. The last thing he needed was to end up in the back of an ambulance. Not here. Not so close to her home. He stopped and gripped his side, bent double. A stitch, that's all it was, he knew, but that didn't make it any less painful. He forced himself to breathe slower, taking deep breaths, regular breaths, and slowly it worked, the sharp pain of the stitch beginning to fade. He started to walk again, slowly. He'd so nearly been caught, concealed in the shadows by the dustbins and gazing up at her as she stood by the window, preparing vegetables. Slicing and dicing them like a surgeon. So cool, so calm. Oblivious of the fact that he was there, watching every move. Taking it all in, absorbing every detail. Didn't she know that anyone could see her? Or maybe that was what she wanted. Maybe she liked to be watched. He smiled and felt a small shiver of excitement run down his spine.   They were made for each other, he felt sure. She was so still, her movements so small and yet so precise, and she liked to be watched. His perfect love.

125

His soul mate.

A smile suffused his face as he remembered how she looked. A magic moment indeed, but he had been so caught up in watching her that he hadn't paid attention. It had been close, that fucking stupid mutt sniffing him out like that. If he did come back he would have to be more careful. A lot more careful. Be better hidden and bring some pepper spray or something, something that would make the most inquisitive dog back off, howling. If he came back. When he came back.

Because he knew he would. Maybe next time he'd find a place to the side of the house, where her bedroom window looked out over the open ground towards the cliff top. Maybe he'd see her undressing. See her pale skin. He imagined the blue-veined whiteness of her breasts and the pink of her nipples and he touched himself. Just imagining Jo undressing in front of an open window was getting him hard. He should get home now, didn't want to be seen like this, rubbing himself in the street, but he would return. He had to return. After all, it was what she wanted, deep down, he was sure. She was so much better than the others, the cackling hag, or the lump of lard. Much better. They were just rehearsals, practice runs. He needed to get everything ready, to prepare himself, and then one day, one day soon, he would be ready for the main attraction, the best: Dr Jocasta Hughes.

16

Jo had expected a bit of a wait when she turned up at police headquarters without an appointment but was still irritated that Miller kept her kicking her heels for more than half an hour before she was called through to speak to him. At least the waiting area in reception was almost empty, as most of the usual customers were probably not out of bed yet. The detective constable who called her through was not anyone Jo had met before and was an inconspicuously motherly-looking woman, with a homely face and a twinkle in her eye as she assessed her boss's visitor.

"This way, Dr Hughes. The DCI can see you now." She led the way and opened a nearby door, ushering Jo into Miller's office, a light and airy room at the back of the building, with views over the town centre to the West Hill.

"Dr Hughes. Come in. Um, have a seat." Miller stood, awkwardly, as if he was not sure whether he should do so, as she entered the room.

He was dressed in a light grey suit, the jacket casually hung over the back of his chair, and his usual plain white shirt and a grey and blue flecked tie. Jeffries, lounging against the wall by the window, was wearing a pair of slightly-too-long black trousers, scuffed brown shoes and a blue checked short-sleeved shirt, no tie. No style makeover there then, Jo thought.

She sat down, careful to ease the fabric of her trouser suit over her knees so that it didn't get stretched, and crossed her legs, revealing the low heeled shoes she always wore to work. Several years of experience as a forensic physician for the police force had taught her that skirts and high heels were not always practical when she did not know what she was going to have to do next. It had taken only one occasion, a body on a building site which she couldn't move because health and safety were on their way, to learn that lesson. She could clearly remember, as she leant over the half-built wall that had collapsed and trapped the victim, checking for the non-existent pulse, the chorus of wolf whistles that came from the scaffolders opposite. It might have been dubiously gratifying but it was hardly seemly, in the circumstances.

"What can we do for you?"

Jo hesitated for a moment, steeling herself.

"Ellie Smith. I've been talking to some of her friends and work mates." Miller raised an eyebrow and Jeffries smirked.

"Other tarts, you mean."

"Yes," she conceded, reluctantly. "From the scene and the post we know that she injected two separate doses in a short space of time. That's an unusual thing to do and the question has been raised as to whether she injected both times herself, or if.."

She hesitated and Miller leant forward.

"There's a possibility someone gave her the second injection. Killed her. Is that what you're saying?"

"Well, yes. Although there was no sign of force having been used. I was thinking that maybe the syringe and wraps should be sent for fingerprinting."

Jeffries pushed forward from the wall, hands in his pocket.

"Already done, Doc. No one's prints other than her own."

"We had a word with Dr Dunbar as well." Miller told her. "Just to be absolutely sure. He said she was using quite difficult veins. If someone else injected her they would have picked an easier site, her other arm, for instance. The veins were in much better nick there."

Jo was relieved. She'd hated the thought that she might have missed something and that Ellie was another murder victim. She was pleased, too, that the police or, rather, Miller, had taken the death seriously and gone to the trouble to look into it, despite her original confidence that it was just an overdose. She was cross that he hadn't thought fit to speak to her, of course, but relieved.

"I don't suppose you've managed to find out what this Tomas character was trying to persuade her do, have you? What she was so frightened of that she took the overdose?"

"I have a killer out there targeting prostitutes, Dr Hughes. I'll get round to Tomas Czernak when I have the time and the manpower. Now, much as I appreciate your input, is there anything else I can help you with?"

It infuriated Jo that, every time she met Miller, he dismissed her and

128

she wasn't going to let him do it again.

"Prostitutes? Plural? I thought it was just Krissy who was a prostitute, the other girl, Denise? She was a checkout girl, wasn't she?"

Jeffries smirked unattractively.

"Didn't have the looks to make a full time job of it."

Miller silenced him with a look.

"There are," he hesitated delicately, "certain indications that she may have been supplementing her income."

"What indications?" Jo wasn't going to be fobbed off that easily.

"The Jolly Sailor is a well-known haunt for girls on the game," Miller explained.

"Is that all you're basing your theory on?"

"It's a knocking shop," Jeffries put in.

"It's also a popular pub and meeting place. It was karaoke night. Lots of single people were there looking for company and maybe more, but that doesn't mean they were intending to pay for it."

Jo stood, angrily.

"She was an ordinary girl, not a prostitute, and she was out that night looking for Mr Right. What she got was killed and she didn't deserve that," She started to leave but then turned back, "And that doesn't mean that Krissy did either." She corrected herself quickly. "I mean, she wasn't even working that night."

Jo left the room, head held high, but not before noticing that Jeffries had spotted her error, the subconscious suggestion that Krissy might have got what she, in some way, deserved or, at least, would have deserved if she had been working. It took every ounce of her control to resist the temptation to slam the door behind her, as she made her exit.

The motherly DC was sitting at a desk outside and raised one eyebrow at Jo with a wry smile of amusement.

"Goodbye, Dr Hughes."

Jo merely nodded in acknowledgement, hoping she wasn't too red in the face, and left.

Jo was walking fast and steam was practically coming out of her ears as she headed to the car park. Why did policemen have to be so sexist? It was such a cliché. And, more to the point, why did she have to accidentally suggest that Krissy had brought her murder on herself? Got what she deserved? She didn't for one moment believe that one person's life was worth more than another. She didn't think that women were "asking for it" when they got attacked wearing short skirts or skimpy tops. She didn't think anyone deserved to be murdered, be they street walker or nun. And whilst inviting a stranger into your home could be considered to be taking a risk, it was also a risk to get behind the wheel of a car, or cross the road, even on a pedestrian crossing. Or to walk home alone, down dark alleys, late at night. Something that Jo often did. That certainly gave her pause for thought. It wasn't far from the Old Town back to her flat but the shortest route, through the maze of unlit cat creeps and twittens, could hardly be called safe and even the longer route involved walking the last few yards along a dark lane. Her converted house was the last in the road and open parkland was all that stood between her and the cliff top, and then the sea. What had seemed secluded and scenic until now could also be seen as isolated and unsafe. Jo shook her head. This was no good. She refused to live her life in fear. She would not change her ways except, perhaps, to consider the option that she might be wise to invest in a good, strong torch, heavy enough to give someone a good clump if they decided to mess with her. Reassured by this eminently practical solution she got into her car.

Back at the flat, Jo held a dress up in front of her and looked in the mirror. She had a second outfit in her other hand and was alternating between the two. The red jersey wrap number or the little black dress? Both were subtle and expensive. Was red too daring? Or black too boring? It surprised her how much she wanted to make a good impression on Jonathan. She certainly didn't want him rushing off and leaving her in the lurch again. She held up the red dress again. On the plus side, it was a good fit, clung in all the right places and the crossover gave her a satisfyingly deep cleavage, but it was cut below the knee and her long, shapely legs were possibly her best feature. The black dress, whilst higher at the neck, was shorter and, with her ultra high black heels, made her legs look like they went on forever. She held up the red again. Her legs would be under the table for most of the evening and her cleavage clearly visible, so she plumped for the red.

When she was finally satisfied with how she looked, every hair in place, her make up smooth, subtle and flawless, she picked up the matching red bag she intended to take for the evening and began to pack it with everything that she would need. She finally got to the torch. It was a small, powerful, handbag sized torch but it still was not going to fit in this bag. The red evening bag struggled to accommodate a purse, brush, makeup, keys and mobile, a torch was asking way too much of it. Jo dithered. She could take her black leather bag, which was bigger but less elegant, or she could leave the torch behind, which rather defeated the object of buying it. Eventually, she made a decision and left the torch. After all, she was having dinner with Jonathan and she was sure that he would see her safely home, whether or not he stayed. At least, she sincerely hoped he would.

Jo paused outside, hand on the restaurant door, taking a moment to compose herself. Her last-minute indecision had left her running slightly later than she'd intended and, although the taxi she had ordered so that she wouldn't have to teeter down the steep hill in stilettos had made up some of that time, she still felt a little rushed and breathless. Perhaps that was the prospect of meeting Jonathan again she thought, as she peered into the restaurant. The Dining Room was busy but, unlike Porters, there was none of the noise, bustle or raucous laughter of people enjoying themselves audible from within. It was the sort of restaurant where the clientele spoke in hushed tones, either because they didn't want to disturb the other diners with loud conversation or because they didn't want to be overheard. The Dining Room was a serious restaurant, or at least it certainly wanted to be taken seriously. It was the sort of place that Kate always said made her want to shout out "Knickers" just to shake things up a bit.

Jonathan was sitting at the bar, and Jo quickly checked her watch as she pushed open the door. Five minutes late: perfect timing.

Jonathan looked up and smiled as he saw her enter. Sliding off his bar stool to greet her with a kiss on the cheek, he stood back and swept his gaze over her.

"You look wonderful," he said with genuine appreciation. She smiled back and thought that he did too. He had swapped his work day suit for cream chinos and a light blue Oxford shirt, open at the collar. The epitome of stylish smart-casual wear. She arranged herself on a stool next to his and, as he settled himself and signalled to the barman that he would like to order drinks, she was acutely aware that his knee brushed against hers. She hoped that he had been too.

They had one drink at the bar, ordering their food there before moving to a table. Jo wondered why they waited when another table was free, but it seemed that Jonathan wanted one particular table, to the right of the door, on its own. The secluded table was tucked in by the curtained window, and set with linen napkins and silverware, sparkling in the candlelight. Very romantic.

Their dinner was excellent, lightly seared scallops wrapped in bacon and set on a bed of rocket, rare fillet steak, sautéed potatoes and perfectly crisp vegetables, followed by an absolutely flawless crème brulee served with fresh raspberries dusted with icing sugar, all accompanied by a smooth Sauvignon blanc and a mellow Chilean Merlot. Everything just as Jo liked it. Perfect, in fact. And Jonathan had kept her amused and interested with a raft of salacious and scandalous stories about colleagues and friends. Jo had had a wonderful evening and, as they lingered over coffee and Elizabeth Shaw bitter mints, she knew that she didn't want the night to end here.

Jonathan insisted on paying the bill and, for once, Jo didn't put up too much of a fight. She firmly believed that women had to pay their way if there was any hope of having an equal relationship but she also knew that Jonathan earned considerably more than she did and was old fashioned enough to need to be led gently to the issue of equality. So she let him pay. This time.

He helped her into the black pashmina which she had brought instead of a coat and opened the door for her to leave the restaurant. His manners were impeccable and as she stood in the pedestrianised road outside, looking up at the stars, she felt almost giddy with anticipation. Mentally she checked her flat, ticking off her usual failures. Yes, she had made sure that all the towels in the bathroom were straight and neat, yes, she had put away all the washing up and wiped the draining board and no, there was no underwear drying anywhere. She smiled and relaxed into him as he put his arm round her and started to lead her towards the main road where he had left his car.

"Are you all right to drive?" she asked, surprised that he was even contemplating getting behind the wheel of a car, knowing that he had drunk four or five glasses of wine during the evening. "We could walk back to my flat for coffee," she suggested.

He shook his head.

"Can't leave my car where it is overnight." He smiled meaningfully and she smiled back. At least he intended to stay the night, then.

As they walked along the street Jo let the slightly fuzzy feeling from the wine she had drunk envelop her and she leant further against him. He stopped and bent down to kiss her. A long, slow, delicate kiss. A tease. A taster. A promise of what was to come, interrupted by a gaggle of drunken youths falling out of a pub.

Jo pulled away from Jonathan, startled back to reality by the sudden noise.

"Come on," he said. "The car's just here. Let's continue this somewhere more secluded."

So he led her over to the car park, and opened the door of his top-of-the-range, racing green, S-Type Jaguar and, as she slid into the car and settled back into the champagne coloured leather seats, she felt a frisson of excitement and anticipation.

17

It was early the next morning, grey dawn seeping through the curtains, when Jo was woken by Jonathan slipping out of bed. She glanced over at the digital clock on her bedside table to see that it was only half-past five. She turned over and sat up. Jonathan leant over and kissed her.

"Sorry, tried not to wake you. "

"Do you have to go?" She reached up and kissed him back, letting her hands stray down to the waistband of his boxers. He hesitated before removing her hand.

"Much as I would love to stay, I've got to do an early ward round before theatre."

She let herself drop back on her pillows with a sigh.

He pulled on the rest of his clothes and came round to her side of the bed for a farewell kiss.

"What about Saturday? Any chance of a repeat performance?" he asked between the light kisses he was planting softly on her lips.

"Mmm. I'll have to check my diary," she teased, "but I'm sure I could squeeze you in somewhere between the leg-waxing and the manicure."

He stood again and, despite the gloom, she could see he was smiling.

"How about a trip on my yacht? It's only small, a thirty-two footer, nothing too flash I'm afraid, but easy to handle with just the two of us. Sailing is the best ever way of winding down after a long week, I find."

Jo was caught, still half asleep and unable to think straight. Before she knew it, she found herself agreeing.

"Yes, sailing, that sounds fun." She hoped she didn't sound too insincere but, whilst she loved to watch the sea from the safety of dry land, going out on it was another matter entirely. It was very hard to keep up a look of cool sophistication as you leant over the side, throwing up everything you had ever eaten. But if Jonathan had detected her less than enthusiastic response, he ignored it.

"Great. I'll check the weather forecast and tides and let you know what time I'll pick you up."

And with a final kiss he was gone. Jo closed her eyes with a groan and prayed for a hurricane on Saturday. Anything to get out of setting foot on board a boat. The trouble was, if sailing was so important to him, it was too early to refuse and risk scuppering things before they had fully got off the ground but equally, letting him believe she enjoyed something she loathed was hardly building an open and honest relationship. Oh well, she thought as she snuggled back under the duvet, last night had been good enough to risk a little subterfuge. She'd buy some Dramamine at the chemist and try not to disgrace herself too dramatically.

The custody suite was quiet for once. Early Thursday morning wasn't known as a peak time for either brawling in the street or drink driving. It was just Jo's bad luck that one of the regular homeless people who committed petty crimes simply to get a bed for the night and what they, unlike the rest of humanity, considered a decent breakfast, had been taken ill in his cell.

The day shift custody sergeant turned out to be one of Jo's favourites, Jayne Hales. Jayne was in her late thirties, on the bulky side and on the plain side. Not that that was the way some of the lads described her when she wasn't around. They weren't nearly so polite. Rumour had it that her nickname was Shrek, which was a little unkind, although even Jo had to admit she could see the resemblance, but it wasn't her looks that made Jo like her so much, it was her down-to-earth attitude coupled with a level of empathy uncommon in those who had been in the job more than a year or two. Whilst most of her colleagues would have to admit to a grudging appreciation of her skills, it didn't stop them wondering how she'd managed to get herself a husband, let alone three kids, or idly speculating as to whether or not said husband would be able get it up with the light on, but it did mean that they were usually polite to her face.

"I'll take you down to him, if that's all right, only he's an awkward sod and he's really not looking too well."

"That's fine, Jayne. Lead on."

As Jayne led the way through to the cells, the duty inspector, a sour-faced man that Jo secretly believed must suffer from chronic dyspepsia, as there was no other real excuse for his bad temper, stopped them.

"You got rid of that dosser in cell nine yet, Sergeant?"

"Just getting him checked out first, sir. Fulfilling our duty of care and all that. Can't be too careful in these litigious times. Even dossers get legal aid."

"Quite so, quite so." He looked Jo up and down and nodded. "Carry on, Dr Hughes."

And he left them to it.

"Got to hand it to you, Jayne. You know how to handle the tossers of this world."

"Tossers or dossers, they're all the same to me," Jayne said with a smile and unlocked the cell door. "Doc's here to see you, George. Okay?"

George looked up from where he was curled up on a thin, plastic covered foam mattress laid on the low concrete platform that served as a bed. He had wrapped himself in the well-worn blanket provided by the police and obviously still had on the several layers of grimy clothes that he habitually wore on the street. Even from the door Jo could see the sheen of sweat on his brow and the bouts of shivers that wracked his body at regular intervals.

"Can't you turn the fucking heat up? I'm frigging freezing in here," he said and covered his head with the blanket again.

Jo sighed. Why did everyone in a police station have to use such foul language? She came into the cell, placed her doctor's bag on the floor near the door and opened it up to remove the electric thermometer. Taking out a fresh ear piece and going over to George, she bent down and pulled the blanket away from his face.

"Okay, George, I just want to take your temperature. I'm going to put this in your ear very gently, it won't hurt."

She could feel how hot he was even before the thermometer beeped and told her that it was thirty nine point two degrees centigrade. His breath was audibly rattling in his chest and she suspected that this was the cause of his fever.

"Can you tell me how you feel, George?" she asked, as he huddled under the blanket again.

"Bloody awful," was all he replied.

"Do you hurt anywhere?"

The blanketed mound seemed to shake its head.

"A bit, in me chest, maybe."

"Have you got a cough?" It seemed to give more of a nod this time.

"Can I listen to your chest, George?"

There was no reply for a moment, but the blanket came down and George looked out at her.

"Go on, then. Listen to it if you want."

"I'll need you to sit up, and maybe take some of those layers off. Can you do that for me?" Jo took her stethoscope out of her bag as Jayne helped George out of the outer layers. Once they got down to the lower ones, it became clear that they hadn't been taken off in a long time. Jo spotted something very small and black moving hurriedly out of the light and pulled out some gloves for herself and Jayne. Positioning herself as far from her patient as the procedure would allow, Jo slid the stethoscope up under the front of his T-shirt and listened to the man's breathing before getting him to turn around so that she could listen to the back. Jayne was gingerly sorting through the man's clothing whilst she did this.

"I'll see what clothing we've got in the store in a minute, George." Jayne told him as she indicated some of his rags. "I think some of these have had it."

George turned back to face them, pulling down his brown-stained vest as he did so, and gave a sudden staccato burst of coughing. Both Jayne and Jo quickly stepped back out of range.

Jo turned to Jayne.

"He's got a nasty chest infection. I can prescribe him some antibiotics, but I'd really rather he was taken to the hospital for a chest X-ray. Any chance of him getting a lift? I don't think he'll make it on his own."

"He'd almost certainly forget where he was going," Jayne agreed and hesitated. "I'll have to call an ambulance to take him, is that okay? Only they won't allow us to take him in a squad car, not when he should really be being kicked loose."

"Besides which, it will mean de-lousing the car." Jo smiled and Jayne nodded, ruefully.

"I'd not be very popular, it has to be said."

"Okay, then." Jo agreed and turned to George who was back under the blanket. "We're going to organise some transport to the hospital,

George. You'll be nice and warm there."

She got nothing but a grunt by way of thanks.

As Jo walked back towards the custody desk with Jayne she asked if they had any working girls in.

"Only, I could give them a check-up and a health promotion chat whilst I'm here," she explained.

If Jayne was surprised by Jo's dedication she didn't comment.

"Two. One calling herself Angel Stubbins and an old hand, Maria Tyler. You must have come across her before now. They're both up before the bench this morning so they'll be leaving in about an hour. Why don't you go to the treatment room and I'll bring you a coffee and see if either of them want to come and see you?"

"That would be great, Jayne, but hold the coffee, okay? I've had what passes for coffee round here before." Jayne laughed and left Jo to make her way to the treatment room.

First up was the exotically-named Angel Stubbins, although Jo suspected it was more likely that she had been christened Angela. Angel was one of the names that had suddenly become popular amongst young working girls, like Scarlett, Candy and Crystal a decade or so before and Jo was regularly called to the police station to see Angel this or Angel something else. Jo wasn't sure if the name was fashionable because of Robbie Williams' song or because of some American television programme, but perhaps it made the girls feel in some way better about the job they were doing. Helped them to disassociate from the sordid reality of their lives: it was Angel who was giving a fat, sweaty, bald bloke, old enough to be her father a blow job in the back seat of a Ford Fiesta, not Angela, and it was Scarlett being humped up a wall in a damp back alley, not Mary. Or maybe it was the other way round. Angela was plain, unloved and unwanted, but Angel was attractive, glamorous and had loads of lovers, even if they paid. Jo didn't know the answer and she probably never would but, whatever the reason, there were a lot of Angels about at the moment. This particular one turned out to be in her late teens and not in the least angelic to look at whatsoever. She had frizzy, brassy-blonde hair with several inches of dark roots showing and she breathed through her open mouth the whole time, probably due to either an adenoid or sinus problem. Whatever the cause, it gave her an air of stupidity that was only reinforced when she spoke.

"What's that clam thingy you just said?" she asked again.

"Chlamydia. It's a sexually transmitted disease that you can catch," Jo explained.

"I don't have a discharge so I'm all right, aren't I?" Angel gnawed at her already completely bitten down nails.

"As I said, you can have chlamydia and not know that you have it. That's why I recommend a screening test. To see if you do, so we can treat it."

"But if it don't give you a discharge, why bother?"

"Because if you have it and you don't get it treated it can cause problems later. It can make you infertile, stop you from getting pregnant, that is." Jo was doing her best to be very tolerant.

"I don't want to get pregnant."

"No, but you might do, one day."

This seemed to require far too much imagination for Angel to comprehend, so Jo finally gave up, exasperated.

"Okay, you can go back to your cell, Angel. I'll get Sergeant Hales to take you."

"Is that it?" Angel asked. Jo was already reaching towards the bell to ring and let Jayne know she had finished.

"Yes, that's it," she agreed but then, on impulse, changed her mind.

"I don't suppose you've heard of a Tomas Czernak, have you, Angel?"

"Tomas who?"

"Never mind."

Jo sighed and pushed the button.

Angel played with her hair and Jo wrote up her notes while they waited for Jayne to arrive and knock on the door. Jayne waited patiently with folded arms as Angel stood up and they'd almost got out of the door when the prisoner suddenly remembered that she had heard the name Tomas before.

"Do you mean Tomas the bloke from Albania or Romania or somewhere really weird like that?"

Jo looked up attentively.

"That sounds like him. Tomas Czernak, his name is. Do you know

140

him?"

"Think so. Sort of. He's always been okay with me, whatever they say. I think they're just trying to warn me off, like, 'cos they want to keep him to themselves."

"I'd heard he was looking for a girl to do something really strange. Bad, maybe. Did you hear anything about it?"

Jayne raised her eyebrows and gave Jo a funny look but let her carry on.

"It's not that bad."

"What's he planning on doing, Angel? It's important."

"He's making a video, that's all. A real professional job he said. Might get us work in proper films or on the TV. And, like, he's offering a lot of money for doing it, too. He was looking at me when he told us, I know he was. That's why they're all so, like, jealous."

"Angel, you know, it might not be a good thing to get into. I mean, if he's offering a lot of money why aren't they all rushing to do it?"

"Maybe he's turned them down. I think it's me he wants."

"This is not as good as it sounds, Angel, believe me. What he wanted to film, well, one girl has died over it already."

Jayne looked startled, but Angel just looked sceptical and shook her head.

"No. I know about her. She just took an overdose, that's all."

"Because she had changed her mind about what she was asked to do, Angel, but couldn't get out of it." Jo was desperate to get Angel to understand the enormity of what she was considering, even if she didn't know exactly what it was.

"He could want you to do anything. You could end up getting hurt."

"He said it wasn't anything too kinky, no pain and no animals, he promised. I mean, I'm an animal lover, but that's really sick, isn't it?"

"Are you sure it's not S&M? Tomas has a certain reputation. Not to mention a record."

Jayne's question seemed to suddenly make Angel aware of the policewoman and she became acutely uncomfortable.

"Nah, look, I shouldn't have said anything. Tomas would be cross. He just wants a sexy film to watch, that's all. And I don't know if I'm going to do it, like, so let's just drop it, okay?"

Suddenly Angel couldn't get out of the room fast enough, and Jo knew she'd missed her chance. She'd have to try and find Angel again once she was out of the station and back on the street. Try and convince her that Tomas and his film were not as good as they sounded. God only knew what he was asking, but Jo suspected that Jayne was right and he wanted to film himself hurting someone, S&M for real, with himself cast as the sadist and Angel as the masochist, whether she liked it or not. As she waited for the next patient Jo had a sudden awful thought: maybe Tomas was making a snuff movie. She wasn't sure if they actually existed, other than films of executions in the Middle East, although she suspected that they did and she also expected that big money would be paid for one of them. From what she had heard, Tomas sounded just the sort of man who might consider it a good way of earning a living.

The second working girl was older, wiser and if she knew anything about Tomas Czernak and his directorial aspirations she certainly wasn't saying and, once Jayne had shown her back to her cell, she and Jo walked back to the custody suite's main desk.

"What's your interest in Tomas the Albanian, then?" Jayne asked her.

"Ah, he's Albanian, is he?" Jo asked, stalling for time.

"So they say, and he's a very nasty piece of work from what I've heard. Unofficially, that is. No one will talk about him officially, probably because they value their health."

Jo thought for a moment before replying. There was no doubt she could trust Jayne, but she wasn't entirely sure whether or not her fears were based on a real risk or completely unfounded. What was the chance of a man deciding to make a snuff movie in Hastings? It was ridiculous. Then she remembered what Charlie had said about Tomas not thinking twice about slicing your breasts off and she shuddered. She knew she couldn't forget about it, she had to find out what he was up to and stop him from harming any more vulnerable girls like Ellie. And maybe save Angel.

"I'm pretty sure he had something to do with that girl who took the OD. Ellie Smith. She talked about having to do something awful for him and then…"

"She wound up dead." Jayne finished the sentence for her. "It certainly looks like he's up to something unsavoury but then, I think

142

we already knew that." Jo was relieved that someone was taking her fears seriously, even if that in some way validated them, making them more real. "You should take this to the DI, Dr Hughes, not go poking around yourself." Jayne told her firmly.

"I have but he wasn't interested."

"Why am I not surprised?" Jayne grimaced. "Look, I'll have a word, tell him what Angel said, just leave it alone yourself, will you? Believe me, you don't want to have anything to do with Tomas Czernak. Okay?"

Jo nodded, relieved because she really didn't want to face Sergeant Jeffries and his humour again. She could just imagine what he'd have to say if she told him she thought Tomas Czernak was planning to make a snuff movie; after all, she had absolutely no evidence to back it up. She was also relieved to be able to hand this over to Jayne because she found Miller irritating and, in some way, unsettling and she wasn't sure why.

They had reached the desk, when two uniform constables came in, laughing.

"Watcha, Sarge, you hear about Jimmy Allen then?"

Jayne looked at them.

"Please tell me it was nothing trivial."

"Not at all trivial, no." They could hardly contain themselves, they were so pleased with their news.

"He was picked up in Cardiff." The young, baby-faced boy telling the story put on a Welsh accent to add atmosphere to his tale. "Seemed like he'd done his usual, gone to see this Welsh prossie…"

"Was her name Dai?" His mate interjected.

"That's a man's name, you twat," the story teller objected, "and anyway, he tried to do a runner without paying, like."

"Only he made the mistake of not getting his clothes on first." The other constable cut in, again.

"So this tart grabbed his todger, she did, and wouldn't let go, even when he punched her."

"They say he's going to need reconstructive surgery." Both men winced and checked out their groins, imagining what that would be like.

"Do you think they could make it bigger at the same time?"

"They'd need something bigger than yours to work on."

"At least I've enough for a Welsh tart to grab, unlike -"

"Boys, boys, can you leave your organs alone for one minute, please?" Jayne had reached the end of her patience and both constables stopped obediently but seemed completely unembarrassed.

"Sergeant Jeffries has gone off down to Cardiff to pick him up soon as he's bailed, Sarge." The story teller finished.

Jayne was clearly delighted with the story.

"First bit of good news I've had all week. Fantastic. Seeing as George is on his way to hospital, we'll put Jimmy in his cell when he gets here."

"Shall we clean it out then, Sarge?" the baby-faced one asked, innocently. Jayne looked across at Jo and held her gaze with a mischievous smile.

"No, don't bother. I'm sure George didn't have anything contagious, like lice." And she grinned.

Jo felt really quite happy as she left the station, not just at the thought of Jimmy Allen catching lice from George, but also because he was off the streets of Hastings and that had to be a good thing for the safety of the female inhabitants. She just hoped that this time Miller and Jeffries would play it by the book and get this particular killer off the streets for good.

She switched her mobile phone back on as she walked across the car park, and saw that she had a voicemail message. It was from Jonathan. Thanking her for a fantastic night and making a few suggestions for things they could try next time they spent the night together. Things that made her blush and look round anxiously, as if anyone else could hear what he was suggesting.

The sun was making a determined effort to break through the gloom and it looked as though it might be a nice day for a change. The only cloud on her horizon was that Jonathan mentioned in his message that his car had been scratched by some passing oik whilst parked outside her flat. She was surprised to hear this; not only had she never suffered anything like that in the two years she had lived in the house, but there was no reason for anyone to be passing. She was at the end of the street, on the way to nowhere. She shrugged and thought that it had probably happened whilst the car was parked in the car park by the restaurant and that they had been too preoccupied to notice. She smiled mischievously as she thought about it. They had both been in quite a hurry to get back to the seclusion of her home, and particularly her bedroom, as she recalled.

She was in such a good mood that she had temporarily forgotten about Tomas Czernak and didn't see Miller until she was almost at her car, when she heard him call her name.

"Dr Hughes?"

She looked round, startled, and saw him standing by his car.

"Detective Inspector." She acknowledged him, coldly, as he made his way over to her. Unsurprisingly, he was looking pleased with himself.

"I just thought I'd let you know, we've caught Jimmy Allen."

"So I heard. Although, technically, I think you'll find it was the Cardiff Police who picked him up." She couldn't help a little smile, not quite a triumphant one, but definitely a slightly self-satisfied one, as she turned back to her car and opened the driver's door, sliding into the driver's seat.

"Okay," he conceded, putting his hand on the door of her car so that she couldn't close it. She looked up at him, expecting him to be put out by her remark, but he was smiling, genuinely pleased. And it was a nice smile, she thought. "The Cardiff Police caught him, but the end result's the same. He's off the streets. Which should please everyone, Dr Hughes, including you."

He really had very nice eyes, with crinkles at the corners, Jo thought before she suddenly realised that she had been staring at him in silence and that he was probably expecting her to say something.

"Yes, indeed," she said sharply. How could she do something so embarrassing as look at him all gooey eyed like that? She was so cross with herself. "And they even managed to arrest him without beating him up."

His eyes hardened and Jo looked away.

"I think he'd had all his fight squeezed out of him by the time they got there, or so I heard." He took his hands off the door and stepped back to allow her to close it.

I've got to go," she said hurriedly but he had already turned and was walking away. She slammed the car door.

"Why does he always make me so cross?" Jo asked herself as she drove away with a little more aggression than was strictly necessary. And it was only when she was well on her way home that she thought that maybe it would have been a good opportunity to talk to him about her concerns with Angel and the film, even though Jayne had said she would do it.

"Damn." But it was herself, not Miller, whom she could have cheerfully kicked for letting such a good opportunity pass. She was unlikely to bump into him so opportunely again.

18

The mortuary was quiet as Jo walked along the corridor but she could hear whistling from the storeroom as she passed on her way to Dr Dunbar's office. Someone was happy in their work.

Ian Dunbar was sitting at his desk, writing up a report on the computer.

"Jocasta! What perfect timing." He said looking up from his intense scrutiny of the keyboard. "Put me out of my misery and let me take a break from this wretched machine. I swear someone comes in at night and moves the keys around to confuse me."

Jo glanced at the keyboard.

"They all look in the right place to me."

"Hmmph." Dr Dunbar was unconvinced. "Have we got a case you're interested in?" He was looking puzzled. "I'm pretty sure they've all been referrals from the hospital the past few days."

"The girl found in her flat? I thought it might be strangulation? I know you won't have done the PM, but I thought you might have heard some gossip."

"Gossip? We don't indulge in gossip, here." Dr Dunbar pretended to be scandalised, before calling out to his assistant. "Dave? Have you got a mo? Only Jocasta wants to hear all about that PM you assisted the Prof. with. The ligature strangulation."

"Dave assisted, did he?"

Dave came waddling in, surprisingly quick on his feet for such a big man.

"They needed an extra hand. It was great, Dr Hughes," Dave told her eagerly, "a bit pongy, but really interesting."

"And was it strangulation?"

"Yeah. The Prof thought it was done with some kind of thin chain. Narrow. Killer must've taken it with him. He said you were pretty smart to have spotted it." He glowed with pride at the complement bestowed on Jo by the Home Office pathologist.

"We don't need Wally Wadsworth to tell us that, Dave."

"No, Dr Dunbar," Dave agreed before turning back to Jo and carrying on with his unofficial report. "And there didn't seem to be much trace evidence either, just like the last one. Vaginal swabs were negative. There was a bit of skin under her nails but Professor Wadsworth thought that might have been her own because she had scratched her neck, trying to loosen the belt, I suppose. He sent it off, anyway."

"So, do the police think it's the same killer?"

"Hardly likely to have two stranglers operating in a small town like this at the same time, are we? At least I certainly hope not." Dr Dunbar was dismissive and Jo had to agree that it seemed unlikely. "I heard they had someone in custody so I sincerely hope that will be the end of it."

Jo silently agreed.

Marcy was sitting slightly apart from the other patients, and her skin-tight, lycra leopard print outfit, set off by incredibly high, fetish-style stilettos, was getting a fair number of disapproving looks, particularly from Mrs Lockwood, although Timothy was clearly fascinated by her. Marcy would never pass as a member of the general public, even to those with a high degree of myopia, and Jo couldn't suppress the smile that came to her lips. It always made her day, even though she knew that Hugh Grantham would prefer it if she moved her professional sex worker patients to another surgery. He didn't want them frightening the parents of young children and, given Marcy's outfit of the day, he had a point.

Jo hurried into her room and turned on the computer. She always liked to have a quick look through her list of patients before she called the first one in so as to prepare herself for any possible problems, even though that did mean the inevitable feeling of dread if she saw the name of any of her more obnoxious patients, like Mr Herring.

Timothy was her first and Marcy was fourth on the list, so she must have arrived early. Jo prayed it wasn't one of the days when Marcy was hyper and found it difficult to sit still. The last thing she needed was her creating a scene in the waiting room, especially dressed as she was.

Jo pressed the buzzer for Timothy and his mother to come in and took a moment or two to look at the latest blood results and the letter faxed through from the private paediatric consultant who had seen

Timothy a few days earlier. It wasn't looking good. There was little doubt that the boy was in early liver failure and the cause remained unknown. The blood results had not revealed any infectious element and Timothy was being urgently referred to the specialist liver unit at Kings College Hospital in London for their advice and treatment.

"Hello, Mrs Lockwood" Jo smiled encouragingly as the mother came in. She was surprised that Mrs Lockwood had come in alone, leaving Timothy outside, and waited whilst the woman settled herself and fidgeted about before getting to the point.

"What can I do for you?"

"I wanted to know what was wrong with Tim. The paediatrician told me but, you know, it all sort of goes over your head when they talk and it's only after you've gone home that you think of all the questions you should have asked. Philip, Tim's dad, he's flying over to be here and I'll need to tell him what's going on."

Jo read through the consultant's letter again, which had been scanned into Timothy's computer records, and she pointed to it on the screen.

"Did you get a copy of this letter?"

"Yes, but I'm afraid it doesn't mean much to me."

"That's okay, I'll do my best to explain but basically all Dr Mitchell could say was that Timothy's liver isn't working properly and none of the usual suspects seem to be involved. He shows no sign of any infection and she did some tests to see if she could find any other cause but, so far, there's nothing showing up."

"But what other things could it be?"

"Well, there are quite a few substances that are toxic to the liver. Paracetamol, for example, and alcohol, of course, not that anyone's suggesting that Timothy's been drinking," she added hastily before Mrs Lockwood could protest. "But again, nothing specific showed up on the tests. Of course, it would take quite a while for the liver failure to show up, so the toxic substance causing the problem could have all gone, or they might not be looking for the right one."

"Paracetamol?" Mrs Lockwood had latched onto that, probably because it was something that she was familiar with.

"Is it something that you give Timothy? Or could he have got hold of some from somewhere?"

"I have it in the house, of course. Children's strength. But I don't think that any has been used. He hasn't had a temperature or been in pain. I'll check that Myra, the help, hasn't given him any, but I'm sure she would have said, asked me first, I mean."

"What about at school? Could they have given him some?"

"God no, they ring and ask for permission before they so much as put a plaster on a graze. They are absolutely paranoid about being sued, I think."

"It's understandable."

"I have to take Tim to King's College Hospital tomorrow with his father but can you tell me what's likely to happen, what they are going to do?"

Jo thought for a moment, not because she didn't want to tell the woman, but because it was hard to know exactly what would happen.

"As the failure isn't acute yet, I suspect that they will just monitor him for a while and do more tests to see if they can find a cause."

"And if they can't find one? If it gets worse?"

"Let's not worry about that just yet."

"I need to know, doctor. I need to know what could happen."

Jo hated having to speculate like this, especially as what could happen was quite frightening, but she couldn't refuse to answer, not when she had been asked a direct question like that.

"Well, worst case scenario, if Timothy goes into acute liver failure, they will have to admit him and use supportive measures to do the work of the liver for him."

"And if that doesn't work? I mean, if his liver fails completely? They can't keep him on a machine, or whatever, for ever, can they?"

"If that happens, he'll need a transplant but let me stress, Mrs Lockwood, that he is a long way from needing that, okay?" Mrs Lockwood nodded, frightened by the seriousness, but grateful for the small drop of reassurance that Jo had been able to give her. Jo hoped the woman believed her although, in actual fact, she wasn't really sure that Timothy was that far off needing a transplant. According to the letter, his liver failure seemed to be progressing pretty rapidly.

After a brief discussion with Helen, the girl at reception, Jo agreed to see Marcy next, because she was apparently pacing up and down in the waiting room talking to herself.

"Using the sort of language that upsets the other patients, not to mention Dr Grantham," she warned Jo, who groaned inwardly. Marcy had presumably fallen off the wagon. Big time.

Marcy came in and sat awkwardly on the edge of the chair, chewing gum and fidgeting. She moved her bag from one hand to another, adjusted her clothing, inspected her finger nails, picked up a paperweight from Jo's desk and put it down again; she could not sit still for a second. From checking her records, Jo could see that she wasn't due another prescription or check-up, so she took the bull by the horns and asked:

"What are you here for, Marcy?"

And prepared herself for a tirade.

"That DI friend of yours is a pillock, that's why. He's got it into his head that Jimmy Allen did it. That Krissy picked him up in the vodka bar, 'cos they know that's where she was that night now but they don't know who with. What they're saying, guessing more like, is that it was Jimmy Allen and that she took him home like she was simple or something. No fucking way. She knew Jimmy Allen. She wouldn't have gone near him with a bargepole unless it was to hit him round the fucking head with it. She weren't stupid, unlike your mate Mr High and Fucking Mighty policeman."

Jo had spent years trying not to let bad language upset her but had eventually given up and now just concentrated on not allowing her face show any outward signs of distress or distaste. After all the practice in recent months, she was getting very good at it. Marcy had barely paused for breath and, although Jo would have liked to cut in to tell her that Miller was no friend of hers, she knew it was useless, Marcy was on a roll and was quite obviously on something else too. She was high, no doubt about it. Jo looked her in the eye. Judging by her pupils it was coke or some sort of amphetamine-based drug. Whatever Marcy's choice of drug of the day, clean and sober she was not.

"Krissy had had dealings with Jimmy before, see, he'd done a runner on her, not paid. Gave her a split lip and all, a year or so back. She knew his rep. He's a vicious little fucker and she certainly wouldn't take him to her place. The pigs have got it so totally wrong, as usual, and you've got to fucking tell them. There's a killer out there, don't they understand that? And while I wouldn't put anything past Jimmy

Allen, I got to say they're wrong here, he didn't kill Krissy, no way, and what with all the time they're wasting trying to pin it on him, someone else is going to get killed. Tell them, go on, tell them they're wrong." She stood up abruptly. "Gotta go to work."

And she left. Jo hadn't even had time to argue. She sighed and rested her head in her hands for a moment or two, feeling one of her headaches coming on. There was a gentle knock on the door and Linda poked her head in.

"It's okay. She's gone. And I don't think Hugh heard anything, so you're in the clear as long as none of his patients mention her visit to him."

Jo continued to massage her temple and closed her eyes.

"Want a coffee?" Linda asked.

"I think I need something stronger."

"A chocolate biscuit, then. Back in a tick."

Jo smiled in gratitude as Linda went off to fetch the required sugar shot.

"Please God, let the rest of the surgery be more straightforward." Jo prayed to the higher being she didn't really believe existed and was, surprisingly under the circumstances, apparently heard. The rest of the evening was filled with blood pressure checks and medication reviews, a viral upper respiratory tract infection, and a smear test. The sort of evening surgery that normally had Jo climbing the walls with boredom but tonight she accepted the routine consultations with relief and gratitude.

"So, come on then." Kate coaxed her, as she put the two glasses and a packet of plain crisps down on the table. "Tell me all about the amazing gynaecologist. Does he know his female anatomy or what?"

They were in their usual window seat in The Stag, although they had actually planned to go to an aerobics class. Kate's excuse this time was a bad knee, although Jo had seen no sign of it as her friend carried the drinks over from the bar.

"You are so crude, Katherine Ward. And anyway, how would I know?"

"You held out? But why?" Kate was surprised but she saw the little smile on Jo's lips and realised immediately that her friend was not telling the truth. "Liar. I knew you were too desperate to resist the advances of Doctor Lurve." Kate opened the packet of crisps and split the bag the whole way along one side, opening it out on the table so that they could share the contents. She always did this, even though Jo rarely got to eat more than one or two because Kate moved so fast.

"I was not too desperate. I just didn't want to resist. There is a difference." She took her sip of her wine and picked up a crisp. The pile was already visibly smaller.

"Come on, come on, do I have to resort to torture? What was it like?" Kate was impatient to hear.

The smile on Jo's face said it all.

"I knew it. He's a sex god. You lucky, lucky girl." Kate emptied the last crisps and the residual crumbs into her hand and sat back, content.

"You are as bad as my mother." Jo protested.

"No, I am not. She wants you to get married, I just want you to get laid."

"Well, I did and very nice it was, too. Thank you very much."

"I want more detail."

"Well, you're not going to get it."

"I'm your best friend, Jo, you can talk dirty with me." Kate was teasing and Jo knew it.

"Absolutely not. You know I can't do it. It's just not me."

"God, you are hopeless woman. How on earth do you talk to the prostitutes who are patients?"

"That's different, it's medical, and it's not like they discuss the sex bit." Jo could feel herself getting embarrassed just thinking about it, "just the side effects."

"You are such a prude." But Kate was smiling as she shook her head in mock dismay. "When are you seeing him again?"

Jo grimaced.

"Saturday. We're going sailing."

Kate almost choked on the crisp crumbs she had just poured into her mouth, she was laughing so hard.

"Sailing? You? Are you mad? The relationship will be over before it's begun. You've got to get out of it somehow. Remember that gorgeous hunk who took you to Cowes week? Couldn't believe anyone could throw up that much?"

Jo looked miserable.

"Why are people, and by people I mean men, by and large, so obsessed with boats? If God had wanted us to go to sea he would have given us webbed feet and stronger stomachs."

"It's not just men. Look at Dame Ellen Mac Thingy and the other one, went round backwards, you just think it's men because there's no way you would agree to get on a boat if a mere woman asked you."

Jo was about to protest but stopped. Kate was right.

"God, that makes me really pathetic, doesn't it? That I am willing to put myself through torture for a man?"

"It certainly does," Kate agreed.

They sipped their drinks in contented and companionable silence for a few moments, watching the flames of the open fire and contemplating life, the universe and men.

"So, how are things with you and your love life then? Anyone on the horizon?" Jo asked.

"Nothing interesting in absolutely ages. I shall either shrivel up or start stalking young boys if something doesn't come along soon, or maybe I should finally accept that I can only have a sex life vicariously through you, so you owe it to both of us to have a good one." Kate seemed happy enough, but there was a little sigh after her words and Jo wasn't taken in.

"Go on with you, what about that teacher? That was only a couple of weeks ago."

"And over so soon, I know. Let's just say he didn't live up to his initial promise. Personal hygiene issues."

"Oh dear." Jo wrinkled her nose in distaste.

"Indeed. Kept washing it, over and over again, I think he was phobic about catching a disease. Either that or he just like washing his bits."

"Ah. Obsessive compulsive disorder."

"You can give it a fancy name, but it's still irritating as hell. Not to mention a little insulting. I mean, I'm not riddled with disease and anyway, we used protection."

"Too much information." Jo laughed. "I can't believe that here we are, two successful-ish career women, not too bad looking although admittedly in our mid thirties, and we have such difficulty finding men."

"But that's the problem, isn't it? We've put our careers first and not snapped up the eligible men in our twenties. All that's left are commitment-phobes, the frankly unloveable and recently divorced rejects."

"That is a very depressing view."

"It's the truth. Every bloke worth marrying is married before he's forty and stays married, unless he has honestly made a horrendous mistake, and those are few and far between. Divorcees of the masculine persuasion are, generally speaking, on their own for a very good reason. Believe me, I know, I've been a divorce lawyer, remember? You get a better standard of clientele in criminal law."

"At least we're not forty yet." It was a small consolation.

"But every year, month, week, day even, the number of unmarried men our age or older and under forty, gets smaller. Think about that, but not for too long. It's a shrinking market."

"I've had lots of patients who have met new partners in their fifties or so and been very happy."

"Ah yes, but that's when they've accepted that all they want is companionship. Are you ready for that? No, let's face it, Jo, your gynaecologist might be your last chance. And me? Well, I might just have missed the boat."

"Rubbish. You are depressed, that's all. It must be lack of food."
Kate looked at her watch.
"You are sooo right, doctor. And my stomach is saying another snack won't do, it's definitely dinner time. What do you want to eat?"

"How about we have a quick something or other and go to a karaoke night?"

Kate was more than a little taken aback. She couldn't remember Jo ever having suggested something like that.

"Karaoke?"

"You know, where they play the backing track of a song and you sing along?"

"I know what karaoke is, I just wondered if you had gone completely mad or if there was a reason behind your sudden interest in community sing-songs? Does this gynaecologist like it or something? Is he a closet Elvis impersonator?"

Jo spluttered at the thought.

"I have no idea but I can't see it somehow. He's got far too much dignity."

"And we don't?"

"Of course we do."

"So why are we going?"

Jo stood up.

"I have my reasons, as they say. Come on, we can stop off some-where on the way up to the Jolly Sailor." Kate began gathering her things: she could tell that Jo wasn't going to be talked out of whatever she was up to because she had grabbed her coat and umbrella and was already walking towards the door.

"We could pick up fish and chips. Eat them out of the paper as we walk there, if you like." Kate suggested, knowing that Jo would hate it but, after all, it was her own fault for dragging Kate off to a karaoke night in some dire hole of a pub which probably wouldn't serve decent beer. Jo pulled a face. As Kate well knew, she despised the aggravation of eating out of the wrapper as you walked along the road. Bits of fish, or kebab, or whatever you were attempting to eat always ended up escaping, dribbling grease as it slid down your clothes so that you arrived at your destination smelling of your food rather than your expensive designer scent but, on this occasion, she was prepared to admit it was the most sensible option and, if it meant that Kate was willing to come with her, then it was a sacrifice that had to be made.

"All right, the Blue Dolphin chippy it is, then. Last one there pays." And they hurried out of the door, laughing and jostling for position.

Karaoke night at the Jolly Sailor had not proved to be as popular as the manager had hoped, but at least there were more people in the bar than other weekday nights. Except for nights when the football was showing. That always drew in a good crowd. The place suffered from being one of those purpose-built pubs that supposedly catered to the middle classes. Large and spacious, clean, recently refurbished according to the chain owner's interior décor vision, the pub could have been anywhere. In a town full of local, character pubs, serving good beers and only a short walking distance from their homes, who was going to travel further to a soulless barn of a place that sold freez-ing cold, fizzy beer and overpriced cocktails? Unless it was to drink said lager and watch the football. Or to find some easy company and maybe show off a bit, or embarrass yourself, depending on how you rated as a singer.

Jo and Kate pushed through the doors and looked round for a place to sit, preferably a quiet and unobtrusive place. Neither wanted to attract the attention of the single men hanging round the bar, drinking their pints of Stella and looking for someone, anyone, to take home for a shag. Kate indicated a free table in a dim corner and Jo nodded, it being hard to talk over the racket. The karaoke night was already in full swing and a man old enough to know better was busy massacring My Way. Jo pointed to the bar, meaning that she would get the drinks if Kate sat at the table to prevent one else taking it. Kate nodded and headed over there, unsurprised that she then saw Jo head straight for the ladies rather than the bar. She must have been desperate to wash her hands and get rid of the smell of fish and chips.

Once they were both settled with their drinks, Jo looked round and took stock. Four cheaply-dressed, middle-aged men were leaning against the bar, trying to ignore a couple of women well past their sell by date who were making eyes at them and giggling from a side table. A woman wearing far too much make-up and far too little clothing was perched on a barstool in the corner, nursing a coke and looking awkward and out of place. A group of teenagers were at a large table, talking loudly and excitedly about nothing worth hearing, and a single man in his thirties, dressed in jeans and a T-shirt, sat at another, smaller table. None of them looked like killers to Jo, but what did she know? The only killers she'd ever met were drunk drivers and arrogant surgeons and she was pretty sure she wasn't looking for either of those here.

A young girl hopped up from the teenage table and went up to Big Les, the Karaoke King, according to the poster on the amplifier. She was dressed in jeans cut low enough to show her ample love handles, and she pulled at her shirt, trying unsuccessfully to tug it down over them, as she told Big Les her name and what she wanted to sing.

"Please, God, no one decides to do Bohemian Rhapsody," Kate said as she took a suspicious sip of her beer. It could not have been too bad because she took another, longer drink. Jo had opted for a spritzer, so that it would not matter about the quality of the wine.

"Or that one from Grease, you know, Summer Loving I think it's called. Where John Travolta sings really high and everyone squeaks," Jo agreed.

"Oh, God, yes. Awful. I warn you now, one screech of a falsetto "Mamma Mia" or a wella wella warm up will have me out that door pretty sharpish, so," she gave Jo a long, hard look, "you had better tell me why we are here, Jocasta Hughes. Right now, this minute. Tell me all and no bullshitting."

So Jo did. She told her about the three deaths and how Miller insisted on discounting Ellie's death as connected, just because of the minor matter of little or no evidence, and how he insisted that the killer was targeting prostitutes but that there was absolutely no evidence to suggest that Denise was one. About how Jimmy Allen was in custody, being questioned by Miller about killing the two women, but that Marcy was adamant that Krissy would never have taken him home. And, finally, about everything Charlie had said about Tomas Czernak and her fears that he was targeting vulnerable women and getting them to take part in something awful.

"I mean, what if he's making S&M movies and things got out of hand with Krissy and Denise? Or maybe," she hesitated because she knew that what she was about to say seemed far-fetched, even to her, "maybe he's actually setting out to make snuff movies."

Kate took a long drink of beer and thought for a moment or two before answering.

"That's a bit of a leap, Jo. If Denise wasn't a prostitute, as you insist, then why would she get involved with this Tomas character? Or do you think she was into S&M as a leisure activity and got persuaded that way?"

"It could be that word had got around amongst the working girls and none would co-operate, that's why he went for someone who wasn't from that group." She was struggling and she knew it. "I don't really know why he would pick Denise, I don't know that he's making snuff movies, I'm just trying to explain it all. Make it fit." Jo admitted. "That's why we're here. The police believe Denise met her killer here and took him home with her. Unfortunately, no one remembers seeing her with anyone that night."

Kate looked around and shuddered.

"If Tomas was actively looking for someone into that sort of scene, why come here? This doesn't seem to be a major hunting ground for S&M enthusiasts. Not that I'd know one if I saw one, of course," she added hastily, "I mean, I've heard that Friday night's transvestite night at The Spotted Bull, but Karaoke and Bondage night at The Jolly Sailor?" She shook her head. "I don't see it somehow."

"The Spotted Bull?" Jo queried, "Who would have thought?" She sighed and looked around again. "I've never really understood the attraction of inflicting pain on someone let alone letting someone inflict pain on you."

"Me neither," Kate agreed.

Jo turned to the assembled men at the bar.

"Sad, desperate, lonely, yes, but nothing to suggest that any of them are pervs." A small, balding man, wearing a tracksuit for purely sartorial reasons, judging by his beer gut and double chin, caught her eye and winked. "Oh, God, I think I've pulled. Perhaps we should go."

And they both snatched up their bags and hurried out of the pub before he could make a move towards them.

They were almost running across the car park, laughing and looking round to check that they were not being followed.

"Wait! I've got a stitch." Kate stopped and clutched her side, still laughing as Jo went back to her.

"See? You are so out of condition you couldn't outrun a couch potato, let alone anyone else. We really should have gone to the gym."

"Absolutely. The men are much fitter there, and I mean that in both senses of the word, though I wouldn't want to outrun them anyway."

Once Kate had recovered, they set off down the hill towards the Old Town and home.

"Seriously though, I think you need to tell the police about your suspicions."

"I have," Jo insisted, but then corrected herself, "well, some of them and, as you said, some of my others don't actually add up. I mean, if I go and tell Miller that I think Denise might have been mixed up with Tomas, then he's going to say that he was right all along and she was a prostitute."

"True." They walked in silence for a while.

The downward slope of the hill steepened and the damp pavement made the going more treacherous, particularly given the high heels

Jo had put on as she wasn't on call, and she needed to concentrate to ensure she remained upright.

"You're sure Marcy is reliable?" Kate asked once the road had evened out a bit.

"No. In fact, I know the opposite. Marcy is hopelessly unreliable. But what she said, it had the ring of truth. Why would Krissy go home with a man who had beaten her up and run off without paying her before?"

"But you don't think Miller will believe her? Or you, if you pass the information onto him?"

"No. It won't change his view at all. He's so rigid, so set on things being the way he sees them that he won't listen to anything else. He desperately wants Jimmy Allen to be guilty because it excuses hitting him before. At least, in his eyes it does."

"I would suggest that most policemen and a pretty hefty chunk of the general public would agree."

"I know." Jo was frustrated. "But I also know that three healthy young women have died in a comparatively short space of time, and I think Miller is wrong to be so sure that Jimmy Allen is responsible."

"Then that is what you have to tell him. Convince him that Marcy is right."

"He's not an easy man to convince."

"But you will try?"

"All right. I will." Jo reluctantly agreed.

"And please tell me that you won't go off doing anymore investigating on your own. Goodness knows what might have happened in the Jolly Sailor if I hadn't been there with you."

"I know, I could have ended up sleeping with a man in a nylon tracksuit."

Kate stopped and looked Jo firmly in the eye. "I am being serious, Jo. I mean, what if he was there? In the pub tonight? Looking for another victim?"

Jo smiled.

"No way. I wouldn't have risked going if I'd thought that was possible. This man's much too clever to go back to a hunting ground after he's used it once successfully. I just wanted to get the feel of the place."

"And did you?"

"Yes. I realised what was going on almost immediately. The Vodka Bar and karaoke night at The Jolly Sailor are both regular singles haunts. That's what Krissy and Denise had in common. They were out on the pull. Looking for a man. The police need to concentrate on other singles venues because that's where he is, trawling for his next victim as we speak." Jo hurried on and Kate ran to catch up with her, grabbing her arm and forcing her to stop.

"Promise me you won't, Jo." Kate was frightened; she knew what her friend was like. "Promise me you won't go and try and flush him out yourself. Go to Miller, tell him what you just told me. He has to see it, has to realise that you are right."

"I will go and see Miller, I promise," Jo reassured Kate, but she didn't add that she was sure that he would not be convinced by her logic, and Kate was too relieved that Jo had agreed to go the police to notice that Jo hadn't actually promised not to visit singles bars herself.

They split up at the fork in the road, Kate heading further down the hill to her tiny house in All Saints' Street and Jo heading up to the top of the East Cliff and her flat. She was walking briskly, because the night was cold and she was feeling it, despite the several glasses of wine she had drunk during the evening. Whilst the days were still warm, if damp, the nights were beginning to get quite cold and wintry.

'Time to get out the warmer clothes,' she thought as she turned into the final stretch along the lane. Out of the corner of her eye she thought she caught sight of movement in the road below her and she turned quickly. There was nothing there. She listened for a moment but could only hear the distant noise of cars on the main road below. She turned back to the lane and hurried on, anxious to get home, to safety.

What was the matter with her? Imagining foxes were people. Thinking she was being followed. Perhaps she should lay off the alcohol she told herself, almost breaking into a jog as she kept checking behind her for any further signs of movement but not catching any. She was getting positively paranoid. Maybe a day out in the fresh air throwing up her guts into the sea would be good for her, help her to get her mind sorted out.

Only once she was back in her flat, with the door safely bolted and curtains drawn, did she admit to herself that what she really needed was someone at home, waiting for her to get back safely, or maybe walking back with her in the first place.

19

Jo was back at the police station, sitting outside Miller's office, twiddling her thumbs as she waited impatiently for him to see her and thinking that this was a complete waste of time. She was about to get up and leave, promise or no promise, when the door finally opened and Miller invited her in.

"You're making quite a habit of dropping in, Dr Hughes."

"She must like us, Guv."

Jeffries was lounging as far back as possible without falling off in an upright chair to the side of Miller's desk, leering at her. It was not an attractive sight.

Jo felt she managed to convey her actual feelings for the pair of them with a glare which left them pretty sure that 'like' didn't enter into it.

"Believe me, I don't want to be here," she added just to be certain that they got the message, "but I feel I have some more information that may help you with your investigation."

"Our friend Marcy been bending your ear again, has she?"

Miller silenced Jeffries with a look of his own.

"Let the lady finish." He turned to Jo and smiled encouragingly. "Please, have a seat and tell us. What's she got to say this time?"

Jo was tempted to walk out. She wasn't sure which was worse: Jeffries' contempt or Miller's patronising tone. She took a deep breath and brought her temper back under control.

"Krissy knew Jimmy."

They both sat forward: this was just what they wanted to hear, Jo realised, inwardly kicking herself. She wasn't there to reinforce their case against Jimmy but to destroy it.

"She had had dealings with him before. Professional dealings. He'd hit her and run off without paying. There is absolutely no way she would have taken him home with her that night. You've got to face up to it, you've got the wrong man."

Jeffries shook his head in disappointment and turned away, peering out of the window. Miller just stared at her as if he could not believe what she was saying.

"That doesn't fit the facts," he said simply.

"It doesn't fit your facts, which are wrong. Denise was not a prostitute, she was a lonely girl."

Jeffries snorted.

"Looking for love, was she?"

"As it happens, yes, that's exactly what I think she was doing."

Jeffries didn't look convinced but Miller at least seemed to be keeping an open mind, she thought, until he spoke, anyway.

"And exactly what evidence do you have for that?"

"If any," Jeffries added unnecessarily, and Jo could feel her face get hot. She just hoped she wasn't developing attractive red blotches. She was particularly prone to getting them on her neck, she knew, and she pulled at her collar in the hope that it would cover any that might be appearing there. She was acutely aware that Miller was watching her closely and that he was aware of her discomfort. What she couldn't work out was whether or not he was pleased to see her like this. Her instincts told her that he was not; indeed, he seemed more irritated by Jeffries and his withering comments than by her embarrassment, but her subconscious worked to destroy any confidence that thought might give her by insisting that he had been undermining her and patronising her from the moment she walked in the door.

She shot Jeffries another dirty look and spoke to Miller.

"Wherever Krissy picked up her man -"

"We know it was the Vodka Bar, we caught her heading towards there on CCTV and the barman confirmed it."

"Ok," Jo was grateful that Miller had given her that news as it confirmed her theory.

"Not exactly the sort of place Jimmy Allen would use, is it?" She couldn't help having a dig at their favourite suspect's credentials.

"He might do." Jeffries wasn't about to let her get away with that.

"Unfortunately," Miller cut in to stop the sniping, "we haven't got any coverage of her leaving."

"So," Jo continued to expound her theory, "the Vodka Bar and karaoke night at The Jolly Sailor, they are both well-known places for singles to meet, right?"

"As opposed to what?" Miller hesitated, "Working girls?"

"That's right." Jo was relieved and she hurried on before Jeffries could comment, "I know they can also be used by working girls, anywhere can, but they are primarily, well, pick-up places for single people."

"What's the difference?" Jeffries interjected unhelpfully.

"If you don't know the answer to that, you must end up paying for it more often than not." Jo couldn't stop herself from replying and was pleased to see Jeffries flush and, out of the corner of her eye, she thought she saw a glimmer of a smile from Miller, though it was gone before she could be sure, so she hurriedly continued.

"Look, I've got a theory. The killer isn't picking up prostitutes at all, it was just a coincidence that Krissy was one. He's hanging round singles bars. I went to the Jolly Sailor last night and, apart from the singers, it's full of men picking up women."

"Did you pull then?" Jeffries was being deliberately offensive.

"No problem, you should try it, Sergeant. Maybe even you would."

"Enough!" Miller finally exploded, unable to contain himself any longer. "What the bloody hell do you think you were doing?"

Jo was taken aback.

What do you mean?"

"You could have compromised a police investigation. Barging in with your mate. I presume you were," he glanced at the notebook in front of him, "the two single ladies, sat at a table at the back, pint of beer -"

"Not very ladylike." Miller silenced Jeffries with a look, again.

"- and a white wine spritzer, who left after only a couple of songs."

Jo was embarrassed.

"I had no idea you had someone in there."

"My point exactly. Fortunately it wasn't anyone you knew or you could have blown their cover. I mean, what were you thinking? What if the killer had been there?"

"He won't go to the same place twice. He's too smart."

"Really? You know that for a fact, do you? What are you, an expert on the criminal mind all of a sudden?"

"Amateur sleuth more likely. The Miss Marple of Hastings, only not as successful." Jeffries couldn't resist putting the boot in.

Jo was livid, embarrassed and confused all at once. She stood unsteadily.

"Right, well I'll leave you two professionals to it, shall I?"

"Please do, Dr Hughes and keep well away from this investigation from now on."

"Don't worry, I will."

And Jo left with as much dignity as she could muster.

She walked straight to her car and got in, but didn't start it straight away. She was literally shaking with anger and humiliation. She leant back and tried to take long, deep breaths. In through the nose, out through the mouth. And again. Slowly, steadily, she got her breathing under control. How could she have been so stupid? She hit the steering wheel with a clenched fist and had to start all over again. In and out. Slow and steady. She leant her head against the side window and concentrated for a moment on the feel of it. The touch of cold glass on her burning cheek felt good. Miss Marple, indeed. Compromising a police investigation? They wouldn't know how to conduct a proper investigation even if someone gave them instructions in triplicate. Their undercover officer must have been that really tarty girl at the bar, she thought. Not exactly discreet. If the killer had been there she would have frightened him off. She took another deep breath and blew away the tension. She had stopped shaking. She was under control. She would show them. She would show them how wrong they were about her. She put the keys in the ignition and started the engine. She'd show them that they should listen to what she had to say.

What had started as a bad day got even worse that afternoon. Timothy Lockwood's report from the paediatric specialist was not good news. His liver was failing fast and they were going through the process of tissue typing in preparation for putting him on the transplant list. Even with the progress that had been made, splitting donor livers so that they could be used for more than one patient, they were still rare. No matter how small a piece of a liver might be enough for a young boy like Timothy it would still have to be a close match and if they didn't find one soon, very soon, it would be too late.

Jo went on to have a fractious evening surgery. It was just that sort of day. Every patient seemed intent on irritating her. It was inevitable that she would eventually lose her cool and she did, with an obese patient with type two diabetes. She told her, rather too bluntly, to choose between losing weight or dying, because she was literally eating herself to death. The patient wasn't happy with her advice; if her diabetes was out of control it was Jo's fault. She wasn't looking after her patient properly. If her blood sugar was up she should increase the medication, not tell her to eat less. It stood to reason- well, her patient's sort of reason at least. For some people medicine will always be about what the doctor needs to do and never about what they can do to help themselves, Jo knew. She should never have let the woman get to her and on a normal day she would not have done.

Jo was relieved to get home though she didn't feel better knowing that her patients probably felt thankful to see the back of her too. Not to mention the receptionist and Linda, who had had to deal with the moans and groans and the formal complaint from her diabetic patient.

All she wanted, now she was back home, was to relax, have a glass of wine, listen to some restful music and prepare for her day out with Jonathan tomorrow. As she headed towards the kitchen she took the packet of sea sickness pills out of her handbag in readiness and then noticed that the answering machine was blinking. She had messages. Her heart sank. She knew the messages wouldn't be good news, not on a day like today.

The first was just a hang up again, but the second was Jonathan, crying off their day out. "Pressures of work" he said on the message, and didn't manage to make it convincing even over the telephone line. She knew he would have been squirming if they were face to face. However, once he stopped giving his excuses, he begged her to call him to make another date; dinner, he suggested, Monday night. He should have finished the paper he had to write by then. As he finished with another "please call me" she was half convinced he wasn't dumping her politely. But not completely convinced. Pressures of work was so lame. Apart from the excuse he seemed genuine, but how was she to know?

The next message was another silent one. She pressed delete irritably, not even waiting the silence out to be sure no one finally spoke. She was going to have to do something about the silent calls, she knew, but she wasn't sure what.

The final message was from her mother, inevitably, fishing for news of the great romance.

"Some romance," Jo replied to the empty room. "He prefers writing papers on obscure gynaecological conditions to taking me out."

She went back to the kitchen, opened the fridge door and grabbed the open bottle of wine, knowing that she was being unfair. Jonathan was a consultant gynaecologist, and a young one at that. He was ambitious. He would want to make his mark. Maybe move onto a bigger hospital, a teaching hospital. That meant doing research, writing papers and getting them published. That meant working weekends, even when they were supposed to be time off. Even when you were supposed to be taking your girlfriend out. Girlfriend? Jo questioned her thoughts; she wasn't sure she qualified for that status yet but she sincerely hoped she wasn't just casual sex. That so wasn't her style. Maybe she should call him? Clarify the situation. She headed towards the phone and then stopped.

Her pride got in the way and dictated that she should wait for him to phone again, not rush to reply. She didn't want to seem desperate. He'd blown her out and, what's more, he'd left the message on her home phone at five thirty according to the machine. He must have known she would still be at work then. Evening surgeries were always packed. So it stood to reason that he had not wanted to speak to her in person. And why would that be? Because he was lying through his teeth and didn't want her asking awkward questions, that's why.

She poured herself a glass of wine and took a sip, continuing the internal debate as she stared out of the window, watching the sun slowly sinking lower in the sky, dropping gently below the level of the West Hill.

Perhaps he just hadn't wanted to hear her whine about being stood up, even though he must surely realise by now that she wasn't a whiner. Or maybe he had heard about what happened at Cowes. Sailing people gossiped as much as everyone else, and she had been spectacularly sick. Maybe he had found another woman who liked sailing. Trying to look on the bright side, at least she wouldn't need the seasickness pills just yet. Jo could live with another woman in his life so long as he only went sailing with her.

She took another sip of wine. This wasn't getting her anywhere. The sun had almost disappeared behind the castle ruins. Call him? Or make him wait? Pride? Or pragmatism? It was time for a decision. She put the glass down, decision made. She wouldn't call him, she would make him sweat.

She put the bottle back in the fridge. She would call Kate and go to the gym. Make sure she was out if he called again. But as she picked up the receiver and went to dial Kate's number she had second, or third, thoughts. If he rang again and she was out he might think she was angry and not leave a message. He might decide she just wasn't worth it and give up, then what would she say to her mother?

She quickly started dialling again, Jonathan's number this time before she could talk herself out of it again. She was disappointed that his mobile went straight through to voicemail but told herself that he must switch it off when he was working. She left him a message.

"Hi Jonathan? About tomorrow? Don't worry about the sailing, I quite understand. Dinner Monday sounds good. Give me a call and let me know where and when. Bye."

She put the receiver down and tried to ignore the slightly sick feeling in the pit of her stomach. She had just done what she always swore she would never do, she had grovelled. Well, almost grovelled. She had let him get away with breaking a date at the start of the relationship and that, she knew, would probably set the pattern. She would always play second fiddle to his work, just like her mother before her. She closed her eyes. She was letting history repeat itself, she knew, but at least she had her own career, her independence. She just hoped that it was enough to stop her ending up as bitter about coming second as her mother had done.

20

Saturday brought that rare event, a bright and sunny autumn day, the sort of day that reminded Jo why she enjoyed living in Hastings. The seagulls were wheeling overhead, noisy and threatening, but she didn't care. What were the chances of being hit by a dollop of droppings? On a day like today? Low, she reckoned. At least she hoped they were low. She walked briskly along the promenade, dodging joggers and cyclists, letting the stiff breeze blow the cobwebs away, taking deep breaths of ozone-filled air and feeling her spirits lift. Okay, so her love life and working life were both pretty crap at the moment but there was more to her than that, wasn't there? She didn't allow her pace to falter with that question but kept striding on, past the pier and on towards St Leonards. There was, had to be, definitely more to her. She was young- well, youngish- good-looking, fit and healthy. She might not be rich, but she was certainly not poor. She had some good friends and a loving, if irritating, family. Make that intensely irritating. She still had more than most and should be grateful.

She picked up a little more speed and headed for Bexhill. Her plan was to walk there and visit the modern art exhibition at the De La Warr Pavilion, then get the train back to Hastings in the afternoon. A good long walk would do her good and help her to sort out her head. Jo had always found that she thought better when she walked. Something about the background rhythm of keeping a steady pace seemed to help order her thoughts, and walking along the sea front going west, even though she still had to detour inland for a short section, had the advantage of no steep climbs or flights of steps, unlike all the walks going along the cliffs to the east.

Jonathan had not yet returned her call and, knowing that there was little she could do about that, she decided to put him out of her mind and concentrate instead on what she could do to convince Miller that she was right about the killer stalking single women. It was only a matter of time before he struck again. Jo did some sums in her head. Denise must have been killed between four and five weeks after Krissy, and it was just over a week since Denise's body had been found and she had been dead two weeks by then, three and a half weeks since he last killed, as far as they knew. The killer would probably start looking for his next victim by the end of the week or early the week after - that was always provided he didn't speed up or slow down due to other factors in his life, like work or family. Jo knew it was never as simple as they made out in serial killer fiction.

As she walked she pondered the other factors that might affect how quickly the killer got the urge to kill again, or even if he would. Was it possible that he would stop at two? No, she thought, this one's going to go on until he is forced to stop. She didn't know why she was so sure, but she was. And it didn't seem likely, somehow, that he would have a family. Jo couldn't imagine living with a killer and being completely unaware of it, although she knew that it could and had happened. There was no doubt that this killer had committed both the murders at his victims' homes, which might mean that he couldn't take them back to his place because there was someone else there. Maybe there could be a wife, or a girlfriend? What a horrible thought.

'No,' Jo said to herself with some relief, 'He doesn't take them to his place because he might be seen and also because he would have to move the body. That would be a terrific risk, so he goes to their place and leaves them there to delay them being found, not because of any-one else at his home.'

She got a strange look from an elderly lady walking in the opposite direction and realised that she might have spoken at least some of that thought out loud.

"I hope she just thinks I'm a harmless loony or a crime writer plan-ning her next novel, and not some kind of homicidal maniac," she continued, but this time she made sure that she kept her thoughts completely to herself.

As she came into Bexhill and saw the magnificent white Art Deco building that was the De La Warr Pavilion ahead of her she had come to a decision. If the killer kept to his time scale he would be beginning to scope out his next murder already. Choosing his location for the pick-up, if not his victim. And it would be a different location from the last two, she was sure of that. She had decided to visit some of the potential locations herself, although she had absolutely no idea what she was actually looking for, or what she could do if she saw anything suspicious. She could hardly warn the women who spent their evenings in singles bars not to take any strange men home with them, could she? It seemed hopeless and pointless but somehow better than doing nothing at all. Even if Miller had warned her off. In fact, especially as Miller had warned her off.

Jo wasn't sure exactly what she should wear. She had never, in her recollection, been out with the express intention of picking up a man in a bar. A school disco when she was in the fifth form once, yes, but not a bar. It wasn't her style and she didn't think she had the right sort of clothes. And anyway, she didn't really want to pick anyone up, she just wanted to look as though she did. There was a subtle difference. She wanted to talk to a few people, find out about 'The Singles' Scene': where it was at, how it worked. She hesitated. Perhaps she should get it deliberately wrong to make sure she wasn't actually approached, but she might be spotted as a fraud and then how would she find anything out? In the end she opted for jeans, a skimpy, sequined top she had bought to wear with her black silk evening trousers but decided was too glitzy, and high heeled sandals. She thought that she had probably got it about right and would just have to practice her best "Get lost" look for any man who got too pushy.

Then came the question of what time should she go? She didn't want to start too early, as it would almost certainly turn out to be a very boring night and she would probably end up drinking too much. Not to mention that she might stand out like a sore thumb when she came into an almost empty bar alone. Equally, she didn't want to wait until the bars were packed and she wouldn't be able to get a feel for either the place or its clientele. She wished she knew about the etiquette involved. She had already decided that she would be visiting the town centre as the killer had not used a bar there, so far, and she knew there were several likely places she could choose from.

She started in the Sports Bar, two streets back from the sea front, at just after eight o'clock. Considering it was so early in the early evening, it was surprisingly full. It didn't take long for Jo to realise that it was full because most of the men had been in there all afternoon watching some rugby match or other. And drinking. Heavily. Whilst they were a very happy, good-humoured bunch, presumably because their team had won, Jo quickly came to the decision that the killer would not pick a bar where the men outnumbered the women to such a degree. Besides which, after ten minutes she had had her bottom pinched twice, a scrap of paper with a man's mobile number scribbled on it thrust down her cleavage and beer splashed over her feet. It was time to try another bar. Fast.

Her next stop was another chain bar just down the street. It seemed a little less busy and there was a more equal mix of the sexes too. Jo went to the bar and got herself a spritzer and then found a quiet corner. At least, it would have been a quiet corner if such a thing existed in the place. The music was blaring at such a high level, bouncing off the bare walls and wooden floor so that it echoed and reverberated, that it would have been impossible to hold a conversation with anyone, even if she had wanted. Jo didn't even finish her drink. The killer would not be able to chat up his victims, unless he used sign language, so she didn't think that it would be here that he chose his next victim. Besides which, Jo's head was beginning to hurt.

At last she found a modern funky bar, brightly lit and woman friendly, where the music was playing low enough to allow or even encourage conversation. There were plenty of single women in groups and one or two sitting alone or chatting to men at the bar. Several single men were at tables or perched on bar stools and they all looked up and as Jo came in. She tried to look nonchalant and even smiled at one or two as she went to the bar and ordered her drink.

"Let me get that for you."

She turned to see a man beside her, having appeared out of nowhere, apparently. He was probably in his thirties, not bad looking and wearing some expensive designer gear a little too ostentatiously for Jo's taste and he was waving a twenty pound note at the barman in a manner that Jo suspected would mean he might not get served too quickly, if at all.

"No, thank you. I prefer to pay my own way." She took the sting out of her words with a smile as she handed the barman the right money. "I hate to feel beholden to anyone."

"No problem. I like independent ladies. Bit of spirit."

Jo tried not to grimace.

"You on your own?" he asked.

She turned round and checked behind her.

"Looks like it. How about you?"

"Yes. Absolutely. Name's Simon. And you are?"

Jo resisted the urge to call herself something exotic knowing that if she started giving out false names she would only tie herself in knots trying to remember what she'd used.

"Jo. Pleased to meet you, Simon." She compromised by following his lead and only giving her first name as she held out her hand.

"Good manners as well as good looks. I'm impressed," he said as he shook her hand and Jo wondered just how long she could take his appalling chat-up act. "Not seen you here before, have I? No, can't have, because there's no way I'd forget someone like you."

He answered his own question leaving Jo needing only to simper insincerely.

"It's the first time I've been in here." She looked around at the dimly lit décor. "It's nice."

"So, if not here, where do you usually hang out, then?" he asked. "Pissarros? Yates's? The Vodka Bar?"

Jo mentally noted his suggestions as places she might visit, apart from the Vodka Bar, as that had been where Krissy had met her killer.

"The Vodka Bar. How about you? This your regular haunt?"

"Yeah. Classy but friendly. Just like me." He looked as if he meant it to be a joke, but Jo wasn't entirely sure.

Jo smiled again and wondered how quickly she could leave.

"What about the others? Yates's did you say? And Pissarros? What are they like?"

"Don't use them as much. Pissarros is mainly couples and regulars, jazz bar, not my kind of music, Yates's tends to be so noisy you can't, you know, hold intimate conversations." He leant forward and his hand slipped onto her knee and rested there. Jo picked it up and put it back on his own knee.

"No offence, but I'm not that easy."

He held both hands up in the air in mock surrender and smiled to show that he hadn't taken offence but Jo noticed his gaze had quickly shifted over her shoulder. She looked round and saw that another single woman had come into the bar. She was a little older than Jo, possibly a lot older, but careful make up and well-chosen clothes made it hard to tell her age more exactly.

"Excuse me." Much to Jo's relief, her new acquaintance picked up his drink and sidled up the bar towards this latest entrant into the game of pick-up. Either Simon already knew her or he reckoned that she would be less hard work than Jo. Either way she was grateful for the reprieve.

"Let me get that." She heard Simon suggest and smiled to herself. He must have a set routine, tried and tested, almost scripted and, judging by the swift acceptance he got this time, it obviously worked.

With Simon safely out of the way, and having finally got her drink, Jo spotted two women sitting together at the end of the bar, enjoying some banter with the barman. Maybe they would be more help than the testosterone-charged men that had proved so useless so far, she thought. So she picked up her glass and went and sat with them.

"Do you mind?"

Both women, one blonde, one brunette, neither natural, were slim and in their early to mid thirties, Jo guessed. They were dressed to impress the opposite sex, in high heels and short skirts, with plenty of cleavage on display but managing to stay just the right side of tarty or mutton dressed as lamb.

"Well, I suppose it's okay. It's not like there's anyone interesting here at the mo." The brunette didn't exactly give Jo an enthusiastic welcome, but she pulled up another barstool anyway.

"Except Simon." The blonde said and giggled.

"I said interesting." Her friend corrected her and turned back to Jo. "You got rid of him pretty quick."

"Not my type."

"He's not anybody's." The brunette looked over to where Simon was clearly getting on like a house on fire with his latest choice. "Well, not twice, anyway."

Jo was immediately interested.

"Why? Is he, you know, into anything odd?"

The two ladies laughed.

"God, no. Unless you call finishing before anyone else has got started odd."

"Actually, that's pretty normal round here." The blonde woman said wistfully. "Not that I'd know, of course." She added quickly.

There was a moment's silence whilst Jo's two new friends thought about the sad state of their sex lives and Jo fleetingly recalled her more than satisfactory night with Jonathan. Would she have a second chance? Or was he giving her the runaround because it was over? Maybe he hadn't been as impressed with their lovemaking as she was? Had her performance been deemed unsatisfactory? She'd never had any complaints before, but maybe no one could bring themselves to say anything. It was a very personal thing to do, tell someone they were rotten in the bedroom department, even worse than telling them they had halitosis or B.O. At least your best friend could quietly confront you about bad personal hygiene but they could only mention your sexual performance if you had slept together. So maybe that was her problem. She was crap in bed. Perhaps she needed to visit a sex therapist and have lessons. Would it be unprofessional if she asked her professional sex worker clients for tips? Would that work? Or was she destined to spend her life hanging round singles' bars having one night stands because no one would bother with a second one? Like Simon. Maybe she should check with past boyfriends and lovers? Would they be honest?

Jo's wildly spinning thoughts were thankfully interrupted by the brunette.

"I'm Louise, by the way, and this is Amanda."

"Jo," she reciprocated. "Do you come here often?"

"Not as often as we'd like, as you probably gathered." Louise grinned and both Jo and Amanda laughed, even though Amanda had probably heard that line a thousand times.

They chatted about men and their failings, where you could get a good waxing and the barman's cute bum. Jo was taking her time getting to the point of her visit; she wanted to establish a rapport before diving in to the subject of the killer. She bought both ladies a vodka and coke and managed to get herself a sly sparkling water, with ice and a slice - that most helpful of drinks for a woman wanting to give the appearance of joining in whilst also wanting to stay sober.

Half an hour later, she knew most of what there was to know about the singles' scene in Hastings. The Vodka Bar was busy at weekends but, as it was also an internet café, tended to have more than its fair share of geeks and nerds during the week. Apparently geeks and nerds were not very good at long term relationships and they certainly weren't good bedroom material. Pisarros was more of a niche market for the jazz aficionados and more intellectual sort of guy, or at least those that thought they were more intellectual. Yates's was strictly for the younger crowd, and those refusing to admit their real age. The Jolly Sailor was definitely for the lower end of the market, the blue collar worker, otherwise known as a bit of rough. The Adelaide night club was the place to go when the bars shut and you were still unattached.

"You know you must be a real loser if you leave the Adelaide alone." Louise confided. "Helloooo," she added, looking past Jo to the door and automatically smoothing her already well-ironed hair. Both Jo and Amanda swivelled to get a look.

"Don't be so bloody obvious, you two," Louise hissed as the latest prey approached the bar and looked around the room, checking out the available talent, his eyes resting on the trio of ladies at the end. He was a bit of a hunk, Jo had to admit, but she wasn't here to meet men and she felt she had probably learnt as much as she could without raising suspicions about her motive, besides which Louise and Amanda had suddenly looked at her and marked her out not so much as a sister, but more as competition, so she excused herself and made for the door.

As she left she saw Louise move down the bar, ostensibly to get the barman's attention but, more importantly, to put her within striking distance of the new man.

Jo smiled at the rather obvious move and headed off for the Vodka Bar. It may not be a future venue for the killer to pick up a woman but she might find out more about the sort of man that went there.

By ten o'clock Jo was ready to call it a night. The Vodka Bar was packed and spilling out into the pedestrianised street. She had spoken to a couple of groups of single women, both here and at another bar she had passed on the way which had looked a possibility, but had learnt little new. By judiciously ordering sparkling water more often than not she was still relatively sober and tired of the noise and pointless small talk. But had she learnt anything useful? As she went over every encounter and conversation, she rather thought not. There seemed to be an awful lot of sexually active single people in Hastings and they had peculiarly rigid routines and ways of getting together, which only meant that they probably met the same people over and over again. How was that ever going to work? The men, certainly, seemed only interested in getting laid but some of the women she had talked to, most of them in fact, were looking for a long-term relationship, although they knew very well that the men they met and went home with, weren't, even if they ended up going home with the same woman more than once. Despite this clear difference in goals, the women, somewhat optimistically to Jo's mind, kept trying.

Jo wondered if she had the energy to stay up and try the Adelaide, last port of call for the desperate, but decided not. The Adelaide would have to wait. She wanted her home and her bed, even if she was the only person in it. Jo knew that after only one night of this treadmill she'd rather be single than go through it again. Maybe she would change her mind in a few more years, when the biological clock was ticking louder than ever.

As she walked up the steep hill towards her flat, she allowed her mind to dwell on her embryonic relationship with Jonathan. Maybe she should fight harder for this one, to stop herself from ending up like some of the women she had met in the bars during the evening. Maybe she should call, ask him over for a meal, brush up her cooking skills, or would he think that was too pushy, too early? Too desperate, even? But she knew, more than ever now, that she didn't want to be alone, she did want a partner, a family too, and she didn't want to leave it too late. Her mother was right, on that count, at least. She checked her watch, it was early enough still, she could call him tonight, leave a message if his phone was off. Or maybe he had called and left a message at home. She quickened her pace but then slowed again. She mustn't be silly, build her hopes up. She was behaving like a lovesick teenager, and just because she was frightened, frightened of being a lonely old woman, just like her mother was always saying she would be if she didn't catch herself a decent husband. She'd always thought that it was better to be a lonely old woman than to be an unhappily married one but, after tonight, she wasn't so sure.

As she turned the last corner and started down the lane to her home she saw that a car was parked at the end. Her end of the lane. A Jaguar, she thought, although it was too dark to be sure of the colour. She walked faster. It was definitely a dark colour and it could be hunter green. She hurried towards it - perhaps he had finished his work early, perhaps he had come over to see her and was waiting, but as she got closer she could see that it wasn't him, that it wasn't even his car. She was so disappointed, and angry at herself, that she slammed the door to her flat when she got in and then made herself take off her coat, go to the kitchen and pour a glass of skimmed milk before looking at the telephone. Nothing. No welcome blinking light. No message from Jonathan. She felt a huge surge of disappointment. So she took herself off to bed and gave herself a stern talking to: she didn't need to panic, she had years ahead to find the right man. Desperation was as off-putting as being standoffish, if not more so. It was better to be alone than settle for someone who wasn't right. She was an independent career woman, she didn't need a man. If only she believed it.

She sighed as she finished her milk and put out the light. A cat was definitely looking like a good idea.

21

It was a pretty standard Sunday morning at the police station according to the whiteboard that covered most of the wall behind the custody desk. Five drunk and disorderlies had been brought in the night before, along with a couple of affrays, almost certainly the result of alcohol overindulgence themselves, and three soliciting, plus there was one shoplifting that was a probably a hangover from Saturday afternoon. Jo had been called in to check a couple of them out; one of the D and Ds because he was still reluctant to wake up, and one of the affrays because he was complaining of pain in his groin. Jo checked the board, looking for any reference to Jimmy Allen, but his name wasn't in any of the spaces, so that meant that he was not being held in the cells, nor was he in the hospital having treatment. He must either have been released or remanded elsewhere.

Jo dealt with the D and D first, as he was the one who could conceivably be a serious problem but, thankfully, he was already beginning to come to in his cell, albeit reluctantly, which wasn't surprising given the hangover awaiting him. He seemed surprisingly unworried by the fact that he had woken up to find himself in a police cell, but this was explained once he admitted to Jo that it wasn't the first time he had done so. The fact that he was able to remember previous nights in the cells, if not what had happened to get him there this time, left Jo reassured that this was not a head injury masquerading as inebriation. It was a perennial worry for police and medical staff alike that they would mistake someone who had had a knock on the head for a common-or-garden drunk. It was notoriously hard to be sure which was which until it was too late so Jo was meticulous in her examination of him, checking and rechecking his vital signs until she was absolutely certain this was nothing more sinister than drunkenness, after which she spent even more time making careful notes of all her findings. Just in case.

As she waited for the groin pain to be brought into the treatment room from the cells, Jo nipped to the custody desk where Jayne was busy trying to keep up with the paperwork.

"What happened to Jimmy Allen, then?" she asked innocently.

"Remanded to Whiteleas." Jayne told her.

"They had enough to charge him?"

"Not on the murders, no, but there was enough other stuff, from Cardiff and that, to hold him, for a while anyway."

Jayne didn't look exactly happy with this state of affairs, making out she was busy checking a form and not looking Jo in the eye as she spoke, leaving Jo to suspect that Miller had concocted some holding charges.

"Miller still convinced he's guilty then, is he?"

"Seems like it."

"How about you?" Jo didn't want to let it go.

"Look, the bloke's no angel, that much is certain."

"That doesn't make him a murderer."

Jayne looked down the corridor. "Your pain in the bollocks is waiting for you, doctor."

Jo diplomatically decided to leave it at that for now and returned to the treatment room. She was angry at Miller: he was still determined that Jimmy Allen was the killer after all she had told him, and as a result she was less than sympathetic to the young man with a bruised testicle.

"Next time you get into a brawl, wear a cricket box," she told him tersely after ascertaining that there was no permanent damage, and sent him on his way.

Jayne was on a break when she had finished, and Jo was pretty sure that the sergeant had timed it deliberately to avoid continuing their conversation, which told Jo all she needed to know. Jayne Hales didn't think Jimmy Allen was guilty.

22

Monday dawned grey and overcast but Jo was almost humming with contentment as she parked her car in the cramped doctors' private car park at the rear of the surgery. Her Sunday morning might have been spent dealing with the usual bunch of drunks and whores but she had come back from the police station to find that Jonathan had called her and left a message. It was just a brief message but full of nice words; kind, flattering, loving words, and fixing a definite date for Wednesday, with the promise that he would be able to stay over. Even though, deep down, she had never really believed that she was bad in bed, at least that was what she told herself now, it was an undeniable relief to know for sure that she wasn't so awful he wasn't going to return. Plus, she had a plan to stop the silent phone calls. She took the stairs up to the office two at a time, clutching her telephone from the flat, eager to start the day and looking forward to Wednesday.

"Silly question, I know," Linda said as she came into the office, nodding at the telephone answering machine in Jo's hand, "but we have our own phones here, so why do you feel the need to bring your own?"

"Had a lecture from Kate about not letting people know you are a single woman living alone," Jo lied blithely. "I thought I'd get Neil to use his most manly voice and record a new message for me."

Dr Sinha nodded her approval as she collected her notes for morning surgery.

"She is a very sensible girl."

Linda looked less convinced.

"You could use the generic recording that comes with the machine, you know," she pointed out.

"That horrible electronic woman? No thanks. Besides people wouldn't really know they'd got through to the right person, whereas if Neil actually says: "You have got through to Jo Hughes' phone," they will."

"Very confusing though, if they know you are a woman." Linda still seemed suspicious that there was something Jo was not telling her. "Is there some specific reason for using a man's voice? Like you've been getting dirty phone calls?"

"No. Not a one. It's just a precautionary measure."

Jo smiled and quickly picked up her notes. Convinced or not, Linda seemed prepared to drop the matter, for now.

As she hurried down the stairs she was determined that, no matter what kind of day it turned out to be, she wouldn't let it get her down.

The first test of that resolve was waiting for her in the office: a letter from Timothy Lockwood's consultant. Things were not looking good. His liver function was pursuing a relentless downward path and his name had not just been added to the transplant list but marked as urgent too, in the sure knowledge that he was going to need one in the not-so-distant future, unless they discovered what was causing the problem and treated it successfully. The consultant wanted Jo to visit to make sure that the family were prepared for what the future was likely to hold for them. She asked Linda to add Timothy to her visit list for that afternoon and to call his mother to make sure that was all right. Suddenly her day didn't seem quite so bright and shiny and lovely.

Timothy Lockwood's mother might have claimed poverty, but her house was hardly a hovel. It was a brand new executive-style house, complete with double garage, on a recently-developed site on the out-skirts of town. Jo couldn't be sure from the outside, but she would bet that it had at least four bedrooms and probably as many, if not more, bathrooms to boot. There were two cars parked on the drive, his and hers Mercedes.

Jo locked her car and approached the front door. The garden was impeccably tidy, probably because all the bushes and plants had only recently been planted. They had that slightly isolated look of plants waiting to grow into the space they were in, so there had obviously been no time for them to grow straggly or die or for weeds to grow rampantly between them like they did in the small communal garden at Jo's house.

She rang the bell and waited, listening to the sound of angry raised voices coming from somewhere deep inside the house. It was too faint to hear what was being said exactly but, once the door was timidly opened by Timothy, looking tired and frail, with eyes too big for his gaunt little face, she could hear it all too clearly.

"You haven't been here five minutes and you're already leaving."

"Do you blame me? I haven't been here five minutes and you've already had a go at me about money and women and -"

Jo cleared her throat and both Mrs Lockwood and the man she assumed must be Mr Lockwood turned and looked at her.

"Who the bloody hell are you?" he asked belligerently.

"She's Timothy's doctor," Mrs Lockwood explained belatedly, before turning and walking back towards what Jo thought was probably the kitchen. Jo put down her doctor's bag and held out her hand.

"Hello. You must be Timothy's dad." She gave him her best reassuring smile, and he hesitated only momentarily before taking her hand.

"I'm sorry, I don't know your name."

"Hughes. Dr Hughes. I'm a local GP. I've come to talk to you both about Timothy."

Timothy came and stood next to his father, looking awkward and more than a little lost, but Jo was pleased to see his father reach out and pat him reassuringly on the shoulder. Timothy could have been mistaken for being tanned and healthy if it wasn't for the yellowness of his eyes and the fatigue and lethargy that had replaced any childish enthusiasm and personality.

"What can we do for you?"

"His consultant asked me to pop in, have a chat about what's going on, make sure you both understood it all."

"We're not stupid, Dr Hughes. I've already spoken to his consultant and to other experts in the field, just to be sure. I think I can say that I'm fully informed." He turned to his son. "I'll see you later in the week, all right, Tiger? Be a good boy now." And with that he went out, leaving Timothy staring listlessly at the closed door. The sound of a car crunching across the gravel quickly followed his departure. Jo gave Timothy a reassuring smile but it didn't seem to have much effect.

"Has he gone?" Mrs Lockwood was standing in the doorway, large glass of wine in her hand. Timothy looked at her, transparently disappointed by both his parents' behaviour, and slouched off into another room, to watch television judging by the sound of it. "Why did you say you were here?"

She turned and went back into the kitchen.

"Good question." Jo muttered under her breath as she followed.

The kitchen was absolutely spotless. All bright and shiny stainless steel and black granite work tops. It didn't look as though it had ever been used.

"Can I get you anything?" Mrs Lockwood waved towards the fridge and Jo realised that the glass in her hand probably wasn't the first of the day.

"No. Not for me, thanks. I'm working."

Jo took a seat on a high stool at the breakfast bar, as Mrs Lockwood leant against the sink.

"It must be nice for Timothy to have his dad here."

"If you say so."

"A bit of support for you, too."

"Is that what you call it? Support? Huh. Swanning in here, laden down with expensive presents. Patting his son on the head and paying for doctor after doctor. He'll carry on, you know, getting more and more opinions until one of them tells him what he wants to hear. That's what he always does. He thinks money can buy you everything. Well, he's about to learn that it can't. Unless he can buy Timothy a new liver, that is, and I wouldn't put that past him."

She swallowed another gulp of wine. Realised that the contents of her glass were running low, went over to the enormous American style fridge and took out an almost empty bottle.

"It really isn't possible to buy livers here. Apart from anything else, it has to be compatible." Jo told her.

"That won't stop him. He'll probably decide the doctors here aren't good enough and whisk Timothy off to Hong Kong. Prove to the world that he loves his son more than anyone else can and certainly more than me. And I couldn't fight him. Oh no, that would just show how selfish I was, wouldn't it? Putting myself and my needs first. Putting them before Timothy's welfare. Health. When, in reality, he doesn't care, you know, he doesn't give a toss about his son. All he cares about is getting one over on me. That, and impressing his clients."

Jo realised too late that Timothy was standing in the doorway, listening to every word. She hurried over to him and put her arm around his shoulders, whilst his mother looked on dispassionately, making no move to comfort her son.

"Come on, Timothy, Mummy and I are just having a quiet chat, you stay watching the telly for a while, will you?" Jo led him into the television room where he had been watching the cartoon channel on the enormous flat screen television hung on the wall directly opposite a cream leather sofa.

Timothy flopped on the seat.

"Why does it always have to be like this?" he asked Jo. "Why can't they just get on, like my friends' mums and dad?" He sat on the sofa, looking small and lost.

She stroked his head.

"It's hard for you to understand, I know it is, but sometimes grown-ups can behave in a very childish way." She was glad that he managed a little smile at that. "It's just that they're both worried about you, you know." He didn't look convinced, so she hurried on. "It's not easy when your child is sick."

"No, I know that. When my eczema was bad, and I was all red and scaly, Dad really hated it. He wouldn't let me go out at all. He said it was because people might stare and I'd find it embarrassing, but I think he just didn't want anyone to see me like that."

"Must have been tough."

Timothy's attention had drifted back to the television so Jo gave him another pat on the head and went back to the kitchen.

Mrs Lockwood didn't look as if she had moved, except that her glass was almost full again, as was the bottle by its side.

"He's going to die, isn't he?" Jo was thankful that she was at least speaking more quietly now.

"I can't deny that he's very sick, but if they can find out why his liver is failing or, if it comes to it, if they can get him a new one, then his chances are good." Jo went over to her and took the glass out of her hand as Mrs Lockwood started to cry. "He needs you to be strong."

"But what if I can't be?" A tear rolled down her cheek.

There was nothing that Jo could say that would help, she knew, so she just stood there silently, letting the poor woman weep.

After her heavy and depressing afternoon visit it was not surprising that Jo was left with a residual feeling of sadness. What would she be like if it was her child in that situation? Or who had been killed by a sexual predator? Or, probably worse than either of those, committed suicide? How could any mother, or father, recover from the devastating loss of a child? But many did, in time, on the outside at least. She knew that inside they were permanently changed, that they never forgot, but most got to the point where you wouldn't know about past tragedies to talk to them, unless the subject came up. They functioned as normal human beings, went out, had a laugh like everyone else, but deep down inside, there must always be a bit of them that had been lost. An empty space, with them until the day that they themselves died.

The only way to get out of this slough of despond, Jo knew from experience, was to exercise. Some might turn to the bottle, food, or simply choose to wallow in maudlin thoughts but she craved the instant lift of a hard physical workout and went to the gym for the first time in several weeks. It was evenings like this that she realised that, however uneconomical being a member of a gym was, when one considered the all too infrequent visits that she made to it, it was still invaluable.

After an hour of the cross-trainer, treadmill, weights and some excruciating abdominal crunches on the mat, Jo felt, hot, sweaty and exhausted and she ached all over, but more importantly, she was happy and relaxed. And smug.

"God, I hate it when you've been to the gym." Kate later complained. "You positively glow with self-satisfaction."

"Maybe you should try it sometime."

"It doesn't seem to have quite the same effect on me. I just feel knackered. And what's with the fizzy water and salad?" Kate indicated the offending articles in front of Jo.

"It happens to be a fact that after exercise you don't feel so hungry, until later anyway, and you feel thirsty, so alcohol isn't good enough."

"Unless it's by the pint." Kate tucked into her pizza with gusto. "So what you're saying is: exercise and you not only use more calories and get fit, but you feel less depressed and actually crave a healthier lifestyle. Maybe you should get yourself a television slot, preach to the masses, or, better still, write a self-help book. But personally, speaking as one who has not yet been converted, it all sounds pretty depressing to me."

"Yeah, yeah, you might mock, but it's true." Jo continued to enjoy her grilled chicken and salad, but then nicked a slice of Kate's pizza. "No calories if it comes from someone else's plate," she explained.

"Hypocrite." Kate continued to eat. "At least your new hobby is healthier than your old ones. Hunting down serial killers and psychopathic pimps can seriously damage your health."

Jo sighed.

"I wasn't getting anywhere with those ones, anyway."

They were in an Italian restaurant on the sea front, sitting inside and watching the world go by through the large plate-glass windows as they ate.

An elderly man was walking slowly along the pavement, pausing every few steps to catch his breath and let the pain in his legs ease. Two girls, probably foreign language students, underdressed for the weather, were walking by, arm in arm, laughing and giggling, English lessons forgotten as they spoke rapidly in Spanish. A lad, in T-shirt, denim jacket and low-slung jeans, turned to watch them walk by from under the brim of his baseball cap. A couple in their thirties, cheap clothes, tired expressions, one carrying a small child, the other pushing a buggy, stopped and looked in the window, longingly, before moving on.

"So, this health kick, nothing to do with your sex life, is it? Getting fit for Doctor Love?"

"No." Jo said with exasperation. "Like I said, I was feeling a bit down, and needed to do something to get everything back in perspective."

"Has he dumped you?"

"No, he has not. We're meeting for dinner on Wednesday night. Firm date."

"Somewhere expensive I trust after letting you down on Saturday, although I imagine that was something of a relief."

"Mmm," Jo agreed, "But it's just a postponement, isn't it? There's going to have to be a time when he does find out I get seasick."

"Unless he dumps you first."

"You are such a pessimist, Kate Ward."

"I'm a realist. How's your mother taking it?"

Jo paused.

"She keeps bringing up weddings and dropping them, like miniature time bombs, into every conversation. Suzie from the pub had a quiet do in the village hall, such a disappointment for her family but not as bad as her sister Debbie who eloped to Las Vegas. Mrs Giles' daughter, however, had a traditional ceremony: dress like a meringue, white Rolls Royce, five bridesmaids and a sit-down dinner for a hundred and fifty, she looked a picture and it was the highlight of her mother's entire life. Subtle, my mother is not."

Kate laughed.

"You are doomed, girl, doomed. You might as well accept it. You're going to have to marry him, whether he asks you or not. Your mother has probably already put her name down for a smattering of dates in local venues. Just in case."

Jo sighed. She wished Kate was wrong, but she had a sneaky suspicion that she wasn't.

"I think a pudding is called for."

"I knew it. The health kick was never going to last long. Not with your mother in the background."

But Jo ignored her and studied the menu instead.

23

No one would have guessed that there was anything disturbing Jo's ice-cool exterior throughout Wednesday but inside she was alternating between excited anticipation and dread that something would happen again to scupper her date with Jonathan.

Her day had started early: she was called out in the small hours to take a blood sample from a man who insisted on disputing the level of alcohol in his breath sample. To Jo's mind he was hardly in a position to challenge the charge of drink driving, as he was barely able to stand, let alone drive. In fact, he ought to have considered himself lucky that the police stopped him before he did himself or anyone else damage but, needless to say, he didn't thank anyone, least of all Jo.

After returning to bed and managing to get another couple of hours of restless sleep, Jo faced a packed surgery, tackled her paper work, getting the pile down to an almost respectable level, and then managed four visits before almost falling into her flat, exhausted. It took a moment or two before she felt strong enough to look at her answer machine. Sure enough, it was blinking at her. She had a message, or rather two, the disembodied voice told her. She felt a sinking in the pit of her stomach. If Jonathan had cancelled again, that was it, she wouldn't give him another chance she decided. She really wouldn't. She held her breath as she played them back. One sales call, and Kate, advising her not to jump Jonathan until they had at least left the restaurant as she didn't want to come across as too needy. As if Jo would. She let out a long sigh of relief, Jonathan hadn't cancelled on her again- yet- and there were no more silent calls. The first day of her new butch answer phone message there had been one hang-up but nothing since, so it was clearly working.

She was very tired, but knew that there was no way she would manage a quick power sleep or even a cat nap, not because she was too excited, because she was not an excitable person, but she was just too worked up and tense after a disturbed night and a busy day. At least, that's what she told herself. She was definitely not excited. She decided to try and relax with a long, leisurely bath and then promptly fell asleep in it. So much for excitement! As a result she found herself running behind schedule and in danger of being late. Fortunately she had already picked out her clothes for the evening. Actually, she had picked them out several times, changing her mind as often as she had changed her underwear. Sophisticated but sexy was the look she wanted, hoping she'd she managed to achieve it with her final choice: an embroidered chiffon jacket over a black silk camisole and wide-leg evening trousers.

They had arranged to meet at The Stables, a restaurant closer to the surgery than her flat, and she was supposed to be there at eight. As Jo adjusted her hair one final time and glanced at her watch, she realised that there was no way she was going to make it on time if she walked, or even if she called a taxi. She would have to drive and leave her car in the surgery car park overnight. She grabbed her keys and hurried out.

Jonathan had almost certainly chosen The Stables because, ever thoughtful, it was the sort of place where Jo would not feel uncomfortable if she arrived first, but there was little chance of that tonight. As she walked in, Jonathan was already there, sitting on a crimson velvet-covered love seat in the bar area, perfectly dressed as always, in chinos, sports jacket and open necked shirt.

He looked up as Jo came into the anteroom and smiled, and at that moment Jo felt her heart lurch slightly. If her return smile was, as ever, small and controlled, his was a lovely smile, full and friendly, and he was definitely a very handsome man, she appreciated anew. He had such excellent manners too, so it was no wonder she felt this way, she justified her reaction to herself. He stood, helped with her coat, ordered her a drink and then not only asked her how her day had been, but seemed genuinely interested in her answer. Once they had ordered, they talked about life as a GP, her frustrations at the limitations of her job compared to his, and then they moved to a table and discussed her father's illustrious career. They ate delicately stuffed mushrooms and carpaccio of beef as entrees, roast venison and grilled swordfish for the main course and, although she noticed that Jonathan turned every enquiry she made about his own family into a question about hers, or a story about his career, she didn't push him. He would tell her why he didn't want to talk about them in his own good time. After all, it was not as if she didn't have things to hide about her own family. She wasn't going to mention her mother, for instance, let alone her obsession with weddings. She did learn, however, that he had been to medical school at St Thomas's and had done both his houseman and junior registrar jobs there. He moved first to Brighton for a senior registrar position and then to a consultant's post in Hastings. Over the grilled peaches and home-made vanilla ice cream that they both chose to finish the meal they discussed music: Jo's love of oratorio and the baroque, Jonathan's love of jazz and as they talked they touched each other, fingers stroking as they reached for their glasses, knees sliding against each other under the table, each not-so-accidental meeting of their bodies sending shivers of anticipation down Jo's spine.

He asked if she would like coffee and she was torn. She wanted to prolong the evening, the surreptitious touching was very erotic, but she was equally keen to go further, get closer, and they couldn't do that here.

"Perhaps we could have it at your flat?" he suggested, as if reading her mind, and she quickly agreed.

He paid the bill, waving away her suggestion that she pay, and again, she allowed herself to be over-ruled, thinking that now was not the right time to put the case for independence. Not when she felt this dependant. He helped with her coat and asked the waitress to call a taxi for them.

"I'm probably over the limit and anyway, I left my car at the hospital, I'm not going to risk leaving it outside your place again. Not after the scratch it got last time."

Jo smiled, but she was irritated; it had been an isolated incident, after all. Her car had never been scratched whilst parked outside her home and it wasn't as if hers was a wreck, it was just as smart as his. Well, almost, anyway. His comment, or her irritation with it, seemed to break the mood slightly and, as they waited outside in the cool night air for the cab to arrive and he put his arm around her she didn't lean into him, encouraging him to kiss her, as perhaps she would have done a few moments earlier.

"Is something wrong?" he asked and, as she thought about it, she knew there wasn't really, she was over-reacting, she told herself. Men and their toys. Cars seemed to mean more to the average man than wives, girlfriends and jobs put together and there was little point trying to change that. Instead, she made a conscious effort to recapture the mood by sliding her hand along the side of his neck to the nape.

He responded immediately, reassured that she was still willing, taking her other hand, stroking her fingers sensuously, pulling her close and nuzzling her neck. Jo could feel he was aroused and that aroused her. She turned her head towards him and their lips met. It wasn't her fault that at that moment there was a couple walking along the street and the man called out to his wife to hurry up. There was something about the way he treated her, speaking to her in a slightly bullying way, that reminded Jo of Mr and Mrs Jennings and she suddenly realised that she had been so busy worrying about her relationship with Jonathan and so distracted by her feelings for him that she had not asked after her patient's health. She had not contacted the hospital ward or spoken to Sister Ojo and once that thought was there she couldn't get the fact that she had forgotten to ask after the poor woman out of her head. She tried to respond as Jonathan's hand moved down her back and he pressed himself against her but her mind was now taken up with Mrs Jennings. She felt guilty for having forgotten her and, even though she knew her reaction was stupid, it suddenly seemed wrong to be here, enjoying this, whilst her patient was lying alone in hospital, quite possibly dying.

She pulled back again, and could feel him tense.

"What is it now?" he asked impatiently, which irritated her again, although she had to admit he had been pretty patient with her up until now.

"Um, I'm sorry, but it came into my head and I can't get rid of it. I need to ask, just so that I can put it to bed, so to speak, how is Mrs Jennings?"

She sincerely thought that once he had answered, probably by telling her that there was no change in Mrs Jennings' condition, she would be able to put it out of mind and get back on track, but that didn't happen, was never going to happen. Jonathan was running his lips up her neck, as he spoke and, at first, Jo couldn't quite understand what he said.

"What was that?" she asked, putting her hands on his chest and pushing him further away. "Stop it!"

"She died." He was clearly irritated now and, having given her this blunt answer, tried to pull her close again and continued to kiss and lick her neck, working his way around to her most erogenous zone, her earlobes, but she pushed him firmly away, the mood totally broken now.

"When?"

"This morning. Less than twenty four hours since I'd operated." He seemed to think that was a personal affront.

"How inconvenient."

"Indeed."

He seemed to have missed the sarcasm in her voice, or perhaps he simply chose to ignore it. He was aroused and he wasn't going to give up that easily, despite her clear reluctance now. He stroked the back of his hand against her stomach. She slapped his hand away.

"And you didn't think to tell me earlier?" She was clearly angry and he was clearly bemused.

"I was going to, in the morning, but I didn't want to upset you." He slipped his arm round her, tried to pull her closer. "Come on, Jo, don't be like this, just relax and enjoy yourself, it's not worth spoiling the night over this." He moved to kiss her but that did it for Jo. She was incensed.

"Not worth spoiling the night?" she hissed as she pulled away from him again. A couple came out from the restaurant and glanced curiously at them; other people's arguments are always fascinating when viewed from a distance. "A woman died. How can you be so crass?" she shouted and she almost went to slap him on the chest but he grabbed her arm and pulled her into a bear hug, forcing his mouth on hers so that she couldn't continue the argument. The couple hurried away, this was more embarrassing than a mere argument and they probably thought that this kiss was just a prelude to sex, even if Jo did seem to be struggling against it. She finally succeeded in turning her head away from his bruising lips, and dug the point of her elbow sharply into his ribs.

"Ow!" He still had hold of her wrist and Jo jerked that free, her bag going flying as she did so, the contents scattering across the pavement. "For goodness' sake, Jo. What's up with you?"

"Never, ever, do that to me again." Jo said with ice cold dignity as she picked up her belongings and thrust them back into her bag, not even bothering to close it properly in her haste to get away.

"Oh, come on, Jo, I had to stop you shouting like that, I mean in front of those people, it was embarrassing. Look, I'm sorry. I won't do it again but come on, get it in perspective." But Jo was already walking away from him. He chased after her, grabbing at her wrist.

"Don't walk away from me!" He was angry now, as angry as she was.

"What are you going to do to stop me? Tie me up? Get out the handcuffs? Is that your sort of thing, Jonathan? Your idea of fun?"

"Don't be ridiculous." He was struggling to calm down, speak to her rationally. "Look, we've had a lovely evening, I'm sorry if I came on a bit strong. Now I know you don't like it, I won't do it again. I promise. Come on, Jo, we can get back into the mood." The taxi pulled up behind them, "let's just go back to your flat and -"

"I don't think so. Not now. Just, go, please, and leave me alone." Her tone was glacial and he must have seen from the expression on her face that he was not going to succeed because he let go of her arm and turned to walk back to the cab, but not before a parting shot.

"Fine. Whatever you want." He was so angry that he seemed to be speaking through clenched teeth. "But I don't pay out for expensive meals and get nothing back, so don't think you'll get another chance when you've changed your mind tomorrow."

"I wouldn't go out with you again if you begged me."

The taxi driver was sitting there, uncertain what he should do having arrived in the middle of what was clearly a domestic argument, but Jonathan got into the car and Jo carried on walking away.

"The hospital. Staff car park, off Regent Road." Jo heard him instruct the driver as the taxi door slammed and the car then drove off. She didn't turn and look as it passed her, just kept on walking, but she was shaking and she wasn't sure if it was from anger or fear. She stopped once she was sure that he was out of sight and leant against a wall, legs trembling, tears streaming down her face. Once she felt more under control she walked on to the surgery car park and went over to her car. She was pretty sure she was still under the limit, as she had spent more time talking than drinking and anyway, the argument had sobered her. She looked in her bag for her keys. The light wasn't very good but she could quickly tell that they weren't there. She groaned inwardly, they must have been lost when her bag went flying. She couldn't get into her car and, even if she got a taxi, or walked, home, she couldn't get into the flat. She was half-tempted to call Kate and ask her to come to the rescue. Kate kept a spare key to Jo's flat and Jo had a spare car key at home but it was late and it wasn't that far from the restaurant so she decided to go back and look for the keys. It was always a hassle getting replacements and the chances of them still being there in the morning if she left them on the pavement, or wherever they had fallen, were slim. It would be best to at least try and find them and if she couldn't locate them quickly, well, then she would call Kate for help.

As she walked back to The Stables restaurant she was consumed by righteous indignation at Jonathan and irritation at herself for being so misled by a man. How could she have got him so wrong? She began to check out the physical damage to herself. Her lips were sore from the way he had crushed his against them to stop her talking and her wrist was bruised from wrenching it free of his grasp but that seemed to be all. She knew she had got off lightly, this time. If there was one thing that she could never forgive a man for it was the use of force, of his superior strength, on a woman. She had seen the aftermath of too many cases of domestic violence to fall for the age-old lies; that she had asked for it, that she had led him on, or that it was a one-off and would never happen again. A man that used force once would always use it when it suited him, when his twisted mind could justify it to himself, no matter how often, or how sincerely, he said sorry afterwards. And she knew the violence only got worse with time.

It was very late now, and there were few people around as she walked briskly along the quiet street to the restaurant, going over and over the incident in her head. There was no doubt the man was an arrogant bastard. He seemed to think she owed him. That she had to have sex with him just because he paid for the meal. Well, she had offered to pay. Maybe she should have been more forceful, maybe she ought to have realised what he was like earlier, but even if she had expected him to pay, he had no right to expect sex in return. That was little more than prostitution in her book.

As she neared the restaurant she sensed that she wasn't alone. There were footsteps behind her but when she turned to look she could see no one there. It was just her imagination, she told herself, but she walked faster, not entirely convinced.

The restaurant was shut by the time she reached it and the lights switched off. She could only see small patches of the pavement in the pools of dim amber light cast from the street lamps and those pools only deepened the shadow of the unlit areas. As she looked in the general direction that she thought her keys must have been thrown she heard the footsteps again, getting closer. She forgot her dignity for a moment and got onto her hands and knees, desperately scrabbling about on the pavement, feeling for the key ring in the dark. This had been a stupid idea, on her own, late at night, she told herself. She ought to have called Kate. Then it occurred to her that it might be Jonathan following her; perhaps he had come back, feeling guilty at having deserted her, to check that she was safe, or maybe he had come back for another shot at her and was hanging around in the shadows to grab her any minute. She stood up.

"Come on then, show yourself. You fucking bastard!" she shouted at the shadows. There was no reply, but she could almost feel the shock in that silence. Whoever was out there, he hadn't expected to be confronted like that just as she hadn't expected that sort of language to come out. It was a measure of how frightened she was. A light came on in a nearby house and the curtain was pulled back. A woman stared out at her and made Jo feel immediately safe and grateful. This witness obviously frightened the figure off as well because she heard his footsteps hurry away. In this new, added light from the window, she scanned the area and a glint from the gutter told her that the keys were there, half under a car. She bent down quickly and her hand closed on the set of keys. Hallelujah!

She stood up, clutching them, and waved at her saviour in the window, before hurrying back to the surgery and safety, holding the keys like a weapon, just in case. It was less than half a mile to the car park but it seemed to take her forever to get there. She stopped frequently to check for following footsteps but heard none and, once her destination was in view, she stopped in a shop doorway, watching to see if anyone was there, waiting for her, but it was quiet and still and she could not sense any other presence. It was then that she noticed that her car was sitting differently, awkwardly. One side seemed lower than the other. She approached the car park to get a closer look and it became immediately apparent that somebody, some bastard, had let down two of her tyres. All her fear was forgotten in the wave of anger that overtook her. How dare he? How dare Jonathan do this to her, just because she had turned him down? How dare he take out his sexual frustration on her car?

She almost laughed as she remembered that it was Jonathan's pride in his car that had started her irritation with him and here she was, acting in exactly the same way. She bent down and examined the tyres: they were undamaged but the valve caps were missing- someone must have removed them and pushed something into the valves to release the air. There was nothing she could do, she couldn't drive on tyres so totally flat and she had only one spare, so she couldn't change them both. She pulled her mobile out of her bag and finally called Kate.

Kate arrived only a few minutes later, coat hastily pulled on over her pyjamas, Jo noticed, as she sank thankfully into the front passenger seat.

"What the fuck's happened to your car?" Kate was too busy looking at the sad spectacle of the Audi TT to notice that Jo was looking far from her usual level of perfection.

"Someone let the tyres down."

"Kids, do you think?" Kate asked, unsure as she looked. "And where's your knight in shining armour, then? No, don't tell me, you sent him away in an effort to show your independence." She turned and looked at her friend and realised immediately that there was something seriously wrong. Jo's usually impeccable appearance was marred by streaked mascara, swollen lips, dirty hands and muddy, torn trousers.

"Jo, you look a state, what on earth's happened?"

"Thanks for telling me." Jo smiled despite herself and tried to check out her appearance in the vanity mirror

"No, I mean -"

Jo held up a hand to stop Kate's apology.

"It's okay. I know I do. It's been a bloody, bloody awful evening."

"Jonathan?"

Jo nodded.

"We argued and well," she held out her arm for Kate to see the bruises developing there.

"He did that?" Kate was horrified. "The bastard. You should report him, Jo, you know you should."

Jo leant back in the seat, physically shrinking away from that decision.

"I can't face it, Kate."

"How many times have you told me that you wished more women reported domestic violence?"

"And now I will have more sympathy with the victims. Look, I just want to go home, lock myself in my flat, and sleep for a week, or at least until the bruises fade."

Kate started the car and started to drive away.

"We'll talk about it again tomorrow. I'll come over and take photos of the damage, the bruises will have developed properly by then and if you change your mind, at least you'll have some evidence."

When they got back to Jo's house, Kate insisted on coming in and making sure her friend was safe and secure.

"I'll make cocoa, or hot milk." She hurried towards the kitchen.

"It's okay. I don't want cocoa. I don't have any. Go home, Kate, I'm fine. And thank you for coming to the rescue, picking me up, you are a true friend."

"It was nothing. Honestly." She looked at Jo closely, worried. "Are you sure you don't want me to stay?"

"He's not going to come here."

"No, but -"

"Honestly, Kate, I'm fine. I'll double lock the door as soon as you've gone. Promise."

Kate finally left, and Jo watched out of the sitting room window. Despite her belief that Jonathan wouldn't come to the flat, that his anger and frustration would all have dissipated once he'd damaged her car, she checked that Kate got to her own car and drove away safely before closing the curtains and sinking onto the sofa.

The shock and fear of the evening had left her feeling exhausted, but she was not sure that she would be able to sleep, or even if she wanted to, and one glance into the bedroom told her that she certainly didn't want to sleep in her bed tonight. Her bedroom, normally the place she felt the most safe and secure, was now a reminder of failure. Made up with fresh sheets, candles placed around the room, flowers on the dressing table, in anticipation of a night of love. No, she didn't want to sleep in there tonight. Instead, she pulled her duvet off the bed, grabbed a pillow and settled on the sofa. Not the most comfortable of sleeping quarters, but better than waking in her abortive love nest. She switched on the television, tuned it to a twenty four hour news channel, with the sound barely audible, so that she didn't feel completely alone, and finally fell asleep to a discussion about world economics.

He knew that she would come this way, and he'd been waiting for her, thinking about what he was going to do, getting excited. The anticipation almost as good as the act itself. She was just a substitute, of course, he wasn't ready for his real victim yet. He needed more time to prepare and to practice. Angry as he was with her, Dr Jocasta Hughes would have to wait, but this one, this one would keep him going. Help tide him over until he was ready.

She was young and pretty and pretty drunk. Too drunk to realise the danger she was in until it was way, way too late. Dressed for a night out, in a skimpy top and pelmet skirt. And having sex in the car the way she did, she was just another tart really, like them all, but still a good looking one. She'd be dead pretty, he giggled to himself. Serve her right for treating him like shit, humiliating him in public, turning him down like she did. Like all women did. Well, he'd have the last laugh now, wouldn't he? He'd show her.

She walked down the narrow alley without even noticing that he had broken the security light or that he was hidden by the doorway into the incinerator room. And she dropped her bag as soon as he grabbed her, so she had no weapon to hit him with. She struggled a bit once the ligature was round her neck, biting into it, but the smooth rubber tubing was impossible to get hold of, to get her fingers round, when it was digging into her flesh the way it was.

She did manage to land a blow though, well, a kick rather than a blow, and she was wearing stilettos which hurt as she scraped the heel down his shin and pushed it into the dorsal aspect of his foot. It hurt like hell, even through his boot. He pulled his foot away, sharply. It was a good job her shoe fell off after that first struggle or she might have done him some real damage. And losing the shoe made her lose her balance too;

201

she would have fallen if he hadn't been holding her up, by the tubing round her neck.

24

Jo woke up in the living room and it took her a few minutes to re-member why she was there. She switched off the television and swung her legs to the floor, assessing the damage. She ached in places that she didn't remember being hurt and thought that perhaps it was just the legacy of a night on the sofa. She certainly hoped it was, anyway. She could see the bruise on her arm coming up, a livid purplish welt, with circular fingerprints around. She would have to wear something with long sleeves to cover it up. She padded into the bathroom and peered in the mirror. Her lips were slightly swollen still but it was not particularly noticeable, she would be able to cover the worst with some lipstick. Her clothes from the night before were just left in a pile on the floor and she wearily sorted through them. The knees of her trousers were beyond saving, crawling over pavements was not listed under the garment care recommendations, surprisingly enough. She balled the trousers and put them in the bin. Everything else she bun-dled into the linen basket for hand washing when she had time, even though she was tempted to just stick them all in the washing machine and hope they survived.

It was still early but she didn't want to hang around the flat and, once she was dressed, she called the garage and organised for someone to meet her at the surgery before it opened. She had picked up her keys and was about to leave when Kate arrived.

"The pictures will have to wait." She said, "I have to get to the surgery and meet the very nice man who's going to sort out the tyres."

"I'll give you lift and we can do this whilst he changes them. I'm speaking as your legal advisor here, Jo, as well as a friend. Let me take the photos, even if you never want to use them, because at least they are there if you ever do, want to, I mean."

Jo had to admit that she didn't feel much like walking, and it was raining, so she agreed to be driven to the surgery.

As they arrived, so did Linda, always the first so that she could open up for the others.

"What happened to your car, Jo?"

"Just kids, I expect, serves me right for being lazy and driving down the hill instead of walking."

"Well, I think we should report it to the police, don't you agree?" She looked at Kate who looked as if she did.

Jo clearly didn't.

"I've got someone coming to change the tyres, Linda. If you call the police, and if they take any notice at all, which I somehow doubt, they'll want to see the damage and I'll end up being stranded. Not to mention that you will have a vandalised car sitting in the car park all day. I'm sure Hugh will love that. It's hardly going to give a good impression to prospective patients, is it? Honestly, reporting it will be more hassle than it's worth. I've got to get up to the hospital and then do my shopping and things. I need my car."

Linda looked at Kate, who was sucking her lip and looking disapproving. Linda threw up her hands in exasperation.

"Talk to her." she said to Kate, and went inside.

"I know. I know." Jo said. "I should report it. I should report Jonathan. But seriously, what's the damage? My pride's hurt more than my body and it's not as if he's going to come crawling back, begging to be forgiven. And believe me, I wouldn't forgive him even if he did. What can the police realistically do? We don't know he did this to the car so he can't be charged with criminal damage."

"And what about the damage to you?" Kate asked.

"If they charged him with actual bodily harm I'd end up going to court for a couple of bruises that will be long gone by the time I get there, photos or no photos. He's a pillar of the community, a surgeon. He saves lives, for God's sake. The most he'll get, even if he's found guilty, is a conditional discharge. A don't do it again slap on the wrist."

Kate kept quiet whilst Jo got all that off her chest.

"And in a year's time, when you read in the paper about him beating up some other woman, will you still feel the same?" Jo was spared from having to answer by the arrival of the man from the garage and Kate, realising she was not going to get anywhere, left, calling over her shoulder.

"I'll give you a call tonight, see how you're doing." And she was off to her own workplace, a small and incredibly untidy office in the town centre, where the stacks of files and briefs in the corridors and landings threatened to topple and crush anyone silly enough to hang around there. Health and Safety would have a field day if they ever visited Harriman, Sydenham and partners. Just as well Harriman and Sydenham had died many years ago, but perhaps Kate could still pass the blame for the mess onto them.

Once her car was fixed, Jo knew exactly where she was going. If Mrs Jennings had died yesterday, less than twenty four hours after surgery, then her body was in the morgue and she might well be being posted this morning. As she had died such a short while after surgery, it was mandatory for her to have a post mortem, just in case it was negligence or just plain poor surgery that killed her, rather than the disease. And that was what Jo needed to know as well.

As she turned into the road that ran past the hospital she came up against a queue of traffic. In the distance she could see police cars, some with their blue lights still flashing, in and around the hospital car park as far as she could tell. As she inched closer she could see that a policeman was standing at the entrance to the hospital, stopping every car and turning them away, which was the cause of the queue. Jo pulled into a side street and found a more-or-less legal parking space. She grabbed her bag and got out of the car; it was going to be quicker to walk.

At the hospital entrance she stopped and tried to ask the policeman what was going on but he was too busy telling each car in turn that they couldn't come in, they would have to park elsewhere. They could probably see that but it didn't prevent them all from pulling up to him and asking anyway and then try telling him they had to come in because they couldn't walk and had an urgent appointment.

"I'm sorry, sir, there's been an incident, you will have to park elsewhere or come back another time."

He was going to be sick of saying it by the end of the morning, if he wasn't already.

Jo made her way across the car park towards the mortuary building, surprised to see that the area of most intense police activity seemed to be around there. A small crowd had gathered and she could see Sergeant Barlow, Jayne Hales and a couple of other uniforms trying to push them back and put a tape up to keep them away, further from the incident, whatever it was.

"Hi, Jayne. What's up?"

Jayne looked surprised to see her.

"Body's over there, Doctor Hughes, I'm sorry, I didn't realise the Guv had called you in." Jayne lifted the tape and motioned Jo through. Jo didn't really have time to say that she hadn't been called before she was the other side of the tape and Jayne had turned back. Jo hesitated: should she admit she was uninvited? But Jayne had her hands full just getting people to move away.

"Keep back, will you? Or I'll do you for obstructing."

Jo wandered in the direction Jayne had pointed. She could see crime scene techies in their white suits and blue overshoes picking over the ground in a narrow alleyway between the mortuary building and the main hospital. They were looking for anything out of place, or otherwise, to put in their evidence bags. Every now and then there was a flash as the photographer took pictures of the scene, which seemed to be in a dim and damp recess off the alley. All Jo could see of the victim was a shapely bare leg, painted toenails on the exposed foot, and one stiletto sandal, lying on its side. Standing a little back, also suited and booted like the techies, was Miller. Jo was reluctant to go further without getting kitted up herself so she stopped and watched for a moment. There was something pathetic and sad about the lifeless limb and discarded shoe, speaking so eloquently of a life violently and suddenly cut short.

"Inspector?"

He turned and saw her.

"What are you doing here?"

"I was at the hospital for another reason and just wondered if I could be of any assistance?"

"No. Thank you. Professor Wadsworth's on his way. We won't be needing you."

"So it's another murder?" She was determined not to let his attitude get to her, and consoled herself with the fact that he had at least said thank you.

He ignored her question and she had to restrain herself from saying anything further.

"Guv?" Jeffries, looking like a refugee from a children's programme with his thin legs and beer belly cruelly exaggerated by the all in one suit, was holding a sequined evening bag in his gloved hand. "It was in a doorway just up from the body."

"Anything in it?" Miller seemed to have temporarily forgotten Jo.

Jeffries gingerly opened the bag and peeked inside.

"Make-up, hair brush, a little money and this-" He fished out a cash card, "name of Caroline Sharpe." Jeffries was putting the bag and its contents into an evidence bag when there was a disturbance at the crime scene perimeter.

"Let me through, you've got to let me see her." They all turned and saw Sergeant Barlow trying to stop a young woman in nurse's uniform from getting under the tape. Jayne hurried over to help.

"You can't come thro -"

"It's Caro. I'm sure it is. I was with her. She's dead, isn't she? Oh my God." Jo was already hurrying over to the distraught girl as Miller hesitated and followed, pulling off his bootees and disposable over suit as he walked.

"Carry on, Bob," he called over his shoulder.

Jo reached the girl and put her arms round her shoulders. The small crowd were watching closely, relishing how close they were to a real murder, how they would be able to tell all their mates they saw a friend of the victim, that they were close enough to witness her pain.

"Come on, let's go somewhere quiet."

"I want to see her." The girl insisted.

"Not now. Later maybe, but you don't want to see her now," she said and started leading the girl gently but firmly towards the interdenominational and interfaith Chapel of Rest, situated on the ground floor of the mortuary building. The crowd parted reluctantly to let them through, and regrouped behind them, as if they were walking through some viscous fluid rather than people. Jo suddenly got a glimpse of Mr Jennings in the crowd. She wanted to say something, to tell him how sorry she was about his wife's death, but he turned quickly away and walked to the car park exit. It would have to wait until later. Right now, the young girl she was with needed her more. Miller was closely following them and, as they reached the Chapel, managed to scoot in front and open the door for them. Good manners at a crime scene - Jo had never encountered that before.

Inside, the Chapel had been decorated blandly so that it could not possibly be accused of favouring or insulting any faith. No cross, no altar, no symbols of any kind. Just maroon velour and plastic flowers and abstract stained glass windows. For all its political correctness, it was still a peaceful, contemplative place, a place for the bereaved and frightened to collect themselves and their thoughts in difficult times.

Jo led the girl over to the front row of seats and sat down next to her, taking her hand and stroking it, as Miller pulled another chair round and fished a notebook and pen out of his pocket.

"Perhaps you could start by telling me your name?" He smiled encouragingly at her, taking a closer look as he did so. She was small and dark, about twenty, in a student nurse's uniform, hair tied back neatly. Neat actually summed her up, neat face, neat clothes, neat hair, neat hands, neatly manicured nails.

"Claire," she said hesitantly, "Claire Crehan."

"And you think you know who the, um, victim is?"

"Caro. Caroline Sharpe. When she didn't show up at handover I thought she was probably just still a bit hungover. I didn't - I never thought -" She dissolved into tears again.

"Hush now. It's okay." Jo put her arm around her shoulders and stroked her back. "It's all alright." Claire cried for a few moments before straightening up. Jo had a tissue ready for her and was surprised that Miller waited until after she blew, noisily, before he resumed his questions.

"When did you last see her?"

"Last night. Well, could've been early this morning, actually."

Miller was interested.

"You'd been out together?"

"Yes. We went to a couple of bars and ended up at the Adelaide. We didn't stay too late, 'cos Caro and I were on earlies."

"The Adelaide?"

"It's a club, well, more of a late night bar, really. Down near the front in the town centre, under the copyshop."

"What time did you get back here?"

"I'm not a hundred percent sure. We'd had a fair amount to drink.

Sorry."

"That's okay. Don't worry about it, but do you have a rough idea?"

"I know the taxi dropped me off at my place in Bohemia Road about quarter past twelve and we dropped Caro off here first." She turned to Jo. "She only had to walk across the car park to get to the nurses' accommodation. It wasn't far. I should've stayed and watched, made sure…"

"It's not your fault." Jo tried to be reassuring, but Claire was going to spend the rest of her life thinking that she should never have left her friend to walk those last few yards home alone, no matter how short the distance or how supposedly safe the location, or the fact that Caroline had probably done it a hundred times before without problem. No one should live their lives expecting a homicidal maniac round every corner but Claire would from now on, Jo suspected sadly.

Later, Jo was sitting in the mortuary office, sipping her Lady Grey tea and talking to Ian Dunbar.

"Much as we are used to death and treat it as an everyday occurrence, this is different. For a young girl to be so violently taken, literally on our doorstep, it's just dreadful. Dreadful."

With a shock, Jo realised that Dr Dunbar looked old and tired. Despite his work, he had always seemed so full of life that it was easy to forget the fact that he was actually a year or two older than her father.

"Did you know her?"

"I doubt it. We get nurses down here quite often as part of their orientation or to deliver samples or collect reports but I wouldn't know any of them by name. It's not as if we tend to mix with other hospital staff. They regard us as a morbid necessity and, in some ways, a repository of their failures."

Dave came in with some paperwork for Dr Dunbar to sign.

"Did you know the girl? The one they found this morning, Dave?" Dr Dunbar asked him.

"Dunno, Doc. Do they know who she was?"

"I believe her name was Caroline Sharpe. Caro to her friends," Jo told him and he thought for a moment before shaking his head.

"Name doesn't ring any bells." He turned to Dr Dunbar. "I'm presuming it will be the Prof's usual arrangements, so I'm getting room one and a full set of instruments ready for him." Dave went out and Ian Dunbar scowled.

"That means I'll have to slum it in the small room as usual. Can't understand why Dave thinks he's so great. The man's a pompous ass."

Jo smiled. Ian Dunbar's nose was quite clearly put out of joint. He noticed her smile.

"I know, I know. I shouldn't let it get to me, especially under these circumstances." He reached for the delicate china teapot. "More tea?"

"No thank you." Jo looked at her watch. "I really ought to get going."

Jo stood as Dr Dunbar poured himself another cup, using sugar tongs to put in a fresh slice of lemon and a cube of sugar, before stirring vigorously.

"Have you spoken to your father yet?"

She hesitated and replied carefully.

"Yes, he seems to think he hasn't missed any dinners."

Dr Dunbar stopped his stirring.

"Oh." He put the spoon down and picked up the cup. "Perhaps it's me, then. I must have forgotten."

Jo wasn't sure if he was covering for her father's confusion or his own. They were both getting older and it was easy to suspect some form of dementia as a cause for forgetfulness in either of them but equally, there could be a perfectly normal reason. Benign forgetfulness occurs at any and every age, she knew.

"Which reminds me, I almost forgot why I was here," she said. "Before I got distracted by the business upstairs I was coming here to ask about a patient of mine, Jean Jennings."

"Be doing her later, even though her husband's objected."

"Objected? Why?"

"Usual story. Seems he doesn't want his wife be messed about any more than she has been already."

"In his case, I can understand it." He had agreed to her being messed about against her will in her lifetime, perhaps now he was trying to make amends.

"But I've no choice, given how recently she'd had surgery."

"I know. It's just that she didn't want to be operated on in the first place, but we- him, me and the surgeon- persuaded her. Fat lot of good it did."

"Well, it seems pretty routine, I understand from the notes that when they opened her up the tumour was massive, with multiple secondaries. Someone who comes in as late as that, well, let's just say that there will be some who say that it would be better for the hospital mortality league tables if they didn't come in at all."

"Are you saying we shouldn't even try to save patients with little chance of surviving?"

"No, I'm saying we shouldn't have bloody league tables influencing doctors' decisions on whether to treat or pack the patient off back to their home, or at least out of the hospital, to die. Anyway, I don't think you'll have any surprises with your Mrs Jennings." He looked at Jo closely. "Do I detect a hint of disappointment?"

"No, not at all," she said defensively but then hesitated. Ian Dunbar waited, eyebrows raised expectantly, for her to admit the truth. "Well, let's just say I'm not overly impressed with her surgeon, but that's for personal reasons, not professional."

"Hmm, well, don't make the mistake of mixing them up. The best surgeons usually make the worst husbands. They think they're God and like to prove it not only by making decisions without even discussing it with their patients but also by exercising Droit de Seigneur over the nurses."

"Yup. That's Jonathan Kane," she said, and even managed a smile, but as she walked down the corridor to the exit she thought that she was possibly being unfair on him. If he was guilty of overriding his patients' wishes then so was she, and possibly more so. But as for his Droit de Seigneur: it was her he'd exercised that with, not a nurse, and she wasn't about to forgive him for it.

25

The press, understandably, really went to town on the story. Britain doesn't have many serial killers and, whilst the number of known victims didn't actually qualify this killer to be classified as serial just yet, the potential of one being at work in a picturesque seaside town was more than any self-respecting, or otherwise, journalist could reasonably be expected to resist. By the evening, outside broadcast vans had taken up residence in the streets around the hospital, making it almost impossible for ambulances to get in and out, and staff and patients were getting used to being stopped and asked for a comment, no matter how inane, and completely disregarding the fact that they knew nothing about the situation at all. Immaculately dressed female presenters and scruffy male journalists addressed the camera or spoke into microphones, trying to fill the demands of their twenty-four hour news channels. There were calls for more action by the police, calls for Scotland Yard to be called in, although it was many decades since that had been an option, and calls for women to "Take care out there". As always, there was an inversely proportional relationship between facts and speculation. The fewer the facts the more the speculation and the pressure on Miller to find the murderer, or at least someone to arrest and stop the mass panic, must have been immense. It hadn't escaped the press corps' notice, as it certainly couldn't have escaped Miller's, that Jimmy Allen was in custody at the time of this latest murder, meaning he really did have a cast-iron alibi this time.

Jo was sitting in her living room, curled up on the sofa, glass of wine on the coffee table beside her and only half-watching the news on her television as she sorted through Timothy Lockwood's previous notes. When they first arrived she had read the summary and briefly scanned the rest, but now she wanted to go through them thoroughly and make sure there was nothing she had missed in the hundreds of letters and test results. She looked up briefly.

"Is this killer some kind of psychopath?" one journalist was asking.

"Is the pope Catholic?" Jo replied to the television before switching channels. If they'd sunk to that level of puerility it was time for a change, but the other channels were no better. Most seemed to have concluded that the killer was a man, which was a fair bet, but one reporter had gone further and apparently consulted an ex-FBI profiler and she was putting out a warning for the women of Hastings to beware a man in his thirties or forties who probably lived alone, might have a dominant or dominating mother and who possibly had some sort of labouring or casual job or was unemployed. Jo burst out laughing. That description must cover a fair chunk of the men in Hastings and was almost completely worthless. She suspected that the enterprising journalist had put it together herself. As if any professional profiler would say anything with so little information available. It was ridiculous. She switched channels again, relieved to find a natural history programme about Africa. Nothing like a bit of death and gore in the Serengeti to take your mind off the death and gore in Hastings, she thought.

She went back to Timothy's notes. For someone so young, his file had a remarkable number of entries, all neatly summarised in a computer printout at the front: eczema, eczema and more eczema, with a little bit of hayfever mixed in for good measure. The boy was clearly severely atopic but there was little, if any, sign of the eczema now. What had happened to change it? She searched for more detail on the various treatments he had had and read through letters from his consultants, both NHS and lots of different private consultants, as if his parents or, as Mrs Lockwood had suggested, his father, had tried them out and then dismissed them and moved on to the next when they failed to deliver the cure he demanded. Timothy had certainly worked his way through every single medication and treatment that Jo knew. Some had worked for a while, some had not worked at all and, at the end of his notes, his eczema was as bad as it had been at the beginning, if not worse.

Jo went over to her desk and switched on her laptop. She signed in to a medical journal website and searched under eczema, then narrowed down her search to new treatments because she was wondering if he could have been given something new by a private doctor, something that she hadn't heard of but that worked. If so, she had several other patients who might benefit from it.

The phone rang as she trawled though the hundreds of article headings, looking for one that could possibly help. Jo waited for the answer phone to kick in to see who it was.

"Jo? Jo? Pick up the phone, it's your mother and I'm worried sick about what's happening in Hastings, I need to know that you're all right."

Much as she really didn't want to speak to her mother, she couldn't really justify letting her worry that she had been a victim of a serial killer. Jo picked up the phone.

"Hi, Ma. I'm fine, there's really no need to worry."

"I'm sure you are, darling, but you haven't replied to any of my phone calls." Jo realised that her mother had deliberately used the ruse of feigning concern for her daughter's safety to get her to answer, and she'd fallen for it.

"That's because there's nothing to say." She could feel a tight knot forming in her stomach, knowing exactly where this conversation was going and knowing she wasn't ready to discuss the disastrous date with Jonathan with her mother just yet. In fact, if she was honest, she was probably never going to be able to discuss it with her mother, but she hadn't had time to make up a suitable cover story for why he was no longer around.

"Look, I'm really busy just at the moment, Ma. My bleep just went off and I need to call the police station. Talk to you later. Bye!"

"But -"

But Jo had already put the phone down, immediately picking the receiver up again and leaving it off the hook for a minute or two. Making it seem like she was calling the station, because her mother was bound to try and call back.

She was pathetic, she told herself. No one else her age acted like this with their mother, she was sure but, she consoled herself, maybe no one else had a mother quite like hers. She went back to her laptop and sent off some enquiries to a few medical chat rooms, hoping that someone had heard of a new miracle cure for eczema, and then wandered back to the sofa and switched the programme back to the news channel. She would wait a few more moments before putting the phone back and then make sure she left the answer phone to screen calls. She wasn't about to get caught again.

On the television, the studio presenter was halfway through an interview with a forensic psychologist who was desperately trying to sound knowledgeable in the absence of facts, when the host stopped talking, touched her ear to better hear what was coming through her earpiece and turned to face the camera.

"We're getting breaking news from Hastings General Hospital. We'll go over to Tom Almay, our reporter on the spot. Tom?" She turned back to address a static picture of the hospital, which suddenly changed to a real-time image of their reporter, Tom, standing in front of the hospital entrance, looking pleased as punch that, at last, he had something to report. Jo stopped and watched, hoping this was more than just some minor revelation about the victims' sex lives, which seemed to have dominated earlier reports in lieu of anything more important. Perhaps they had found the killer; now that really would be a relief.

"Yes, Kerry, we've just been told that the police have a lead." On screen, Tom could hardly contain his excitement. "They've asked for the owner of a dark-coloured saloon car, probably green and probably an 'S' class Jaguar, that was parked here in the hospital car park last night, to come forward."

"Have they identified the owner of this car yet, Tom?"

"Not yet, Kerry. But they have told me that after examining CCTV footage, they know that the driver was here, in the car park, at eleven forty-five, when the nurse walked back to the staff accommodation, and that he may well be a witness to the murder."

Jo sat down quickly, her legs were shaking far too much for her to remain standing, but she was no longer listening to what Tom and Kerry were saying.

Jonathan had a hunter green 'S' class Jaguar. Jonathan had left her at the restaurant at around about eleven thirty and had told the taxi driver to take him to the hospital where, presumably, he had left his car parked in the staff parking area just by the mortuary. Just by the alley where the body was found.

26

The front reception area of any police station is a melting pot of people and emotions that can, at any time, threaten to erupt. Victims and witnesses waiting to be interviewed are left sitting next to the friends and relatives of those in custody, friends and relatives who may be desperate to get them out, certain that they are innocent or that their guilt has, at the very least, been exaggerated. To them, the victim is always a liar, their mate was provoked or misunderstood. The slightest word or look can trigger loud and often physical arguments and Jo had been there on more than one occasion when a verbal dispute about just who had started a drunken brawl had escalated into violence and she ended up not just a witness to the assault, but also having to sort out the, thankfully minor, injuries afterwards.

Usually she knew she would only have to wait a minute or two before the custody sergeant confirmed to the desk that she was expected down there, in the basement of the building, and she would be ushered through. With both the mortuary and the custody suite being hidden in the bowels of their respective buildings, it was no wonder she chose to live on the top floor of a house high on the cliff. The view through her home's tall windows was the antithesis of the claustrophobic, windowless rooms and the harsh artificial light she endured at her work places.

Tonight, though, she was unexpected, as she had come to give information rather than in response to a call, and everyone was busy so she had to wait her turn on a bad night to be hanging around the waiting area. The publicity around the Hastings killer had brought large numbers of the mentally unstable and just plain inadequate out of the woodwork and most of them were in the front office with Jo, all queuing, like her, to speak to the increasingly harassed-looking civilian desk clerk.

As she stood in line, she wondered again if she wouldn't have been better to have called Miller but she knew she wouldn't be able to find out what she most needed to know in a telephone conversation. She needed to see Miller's face, to look for non-verbal clues when she asked him: was the man in the Jaguar really just a witness? Or was he a suspect? Did her argument with Jonathan wind him up to the degree that he took it out on another person? Caro? Could she, in any way, be responsible for the young girl's death?

The line edged forward as an anxious-looking man was told to sit down and wait for someone to come and see him. Jo sighed. She could at least have called to alert Miller to the fact that she was coming in to see him so that she wouldn't be kept waiting but in some ways she needed this time of penance and preparation. Or perhaps she was just trying to put off the moment when she found out that if she had behaved differently, not fought with Jonathan, or had reported him to the police straight away and had him picked up at the hospital, Caro would still be alive.

So she waited, whilst a shabbily dressed woman told the young man at the desk that she wanted to talk to the detective in charge of the murder case, claiming that she had been the killer's first victim but had fought him off. She could give them a description, she said, in fact she could give them a name. As the lady, toothless and in her eighties, was a regular, repeatedly coming into the office to claim that she was a victim of every sort of crime and always naming her dead father as the culprit, she was well known to the desk clerk, who asked her to wait, in a resigned voice. Jo knew the old woman as well as she had examined her on several occasions after allegations of rape and molestation but had never found a mark or sign of trauma on her. No one knew what terrible crime her father had committed against her whilst he was alive, but it was clear she was never going to forgive him and that she remained determined that he would eventually be blamed for something, even if it was the one crime he hadn't committed.

Jo examined at the posters blutacked to the wall as she waited. There were the usual crimestoppers and neighbourhood watch ones, details of the nearest GUM clinics and drug and alcohol contact numbers, she was pleased to see, as well as several faded hand-written entreaties for information on lost cats, dogs, and even a stray hamster, the poster for which was written in multi-coloured pens and whose description, pale brown and answers to the name Fluffy, suggested that the distraught owner was likely still in primary school. Bored, Jo finally resorted to looking round at the other people waiting with her, making sure that she didn't catch anyone's eye. That was always a dangerous thing to do, as the paranoid would take offence, convinced that there was some sinister reason why she was staring at them, while the sad and lonely would take it as a signal that she was inviting them to start a conversation, telling her their dull life stories which, to Jo, was infinitely worse than being accused of being a police or government spy. Fortunately, no one was looking at her as they were all far too preoccupied with their own thoughts and were themselves trying not to meet anyone else's eyes. They were probably old hands at visiting police stations too and had been caught out before. A scruffy man in the corner was muttering to himself and a young lad, clutching his vehicle and driving documents to show at the desk, kept glancing at the man's feet nervously, doubtless so as to be ready in case the madman sprang up and attacked him, or maybe concerned that lunacy was catching.

When at last it was Jo's turn to speak to the clerk she was recognised as quickly as the old woman had been but at least the young man at the desk didn't give her the bored and resigned look with which he had greeted the rest of his clientele.

"You been called in, Doc?" he asked her.

"No, I'm here to see Detective Inspector Miller."

"He expecting you?"

"No, but I have some information for him. I should have rung first, I know, but…"

"It's been a busy night; you probably wouldn't have been put through." The clerk told her. "I'll give him a buzz now. Take a seat."

"Thank you."

The only place to sit was a metal bench, bolted to the floor and apparently designed to be as uncomfortable as possible. Jo checked the seat carefully for deposited chewing gum before she sat down. She'd been caught out with that before now, as well. She hoped that being known would mean that she would get shunted up the list of people waiting to be interviewed and that she would get to speak to Miller himself rather than one of the PCs in the incident room, a fate that was sure to await the old lady, if anyone bothered to speak to her at all, but as she waited, while a steady stream of people presented themselves to the desk, she began to wonder if Miller was keeping her waiting deliberately, either to teach her a lesson, or because he just thought she was a time waster. It was already late, she had morning surgery tomorrow, and there was always the chance that she would be called out in the night as well. Jo was fast coming to the earth-shattering conclusion that she was no longer as young as she used to be and that it was therefore getting harder to recover from broken nights. It had been a bit of a shock when she discovered that she could no longer rely on youthful vitality and enthusiasm to get her through the long nights on duty, as she had hoped that wouldn't happen until much later in her career and at a much more advanced age. Forty, at least. But here she was, in her early thirties and her body was already betraying her. Perhaps she should consider Dr Grantham's offer of a full time job and a partnership at the surgery? At least her on-call would be limited to one or two nights a month with the local GP co-op. Or maybe she should consider training in pathology, become a nine-to-five body cutter? That would please both her father and Ian Dunbar, not to mention his assistant Dave Ball, if nobody else.

She had just decided to give up and come back after surgery in the morning when the door opened and Sergeant Jeffries leant into the waiting room, giving a jerk of his head to indicate that she should follow him. She stood up and did so hurriedly, only just catching the door as it was about to slam shut, and pursued the sergeant briskly in the direction of the incident room.

"Busy night," she said to his back as he went through another set of double doors and left her to catch them as they closed. No one would ever accuse Bob Jeffries of being an old-fashioned chauvinist for holding open doors for ladies. They could say he was a chauvinist for a whole host of other reasons, but not for that.

"You could say that," he replied, making her think for a moment of confusion that he must have heard her thoughts before she remembered she had commented about it being a busy night before he had let the door swing in her face.

"Every nutter in the county's got urgent information for us," he continued. Despite the fact that Sergeant Jeffries was a small man, Jo was having to almost break into a trot to keep up with him, and so she didn't have spare breath to ask if he included her as one of the nutters, although she had a sneaking suspicion that he did. Fortunately, they arrived at the incident room without her having to make any further conversation.

Despite the late hour, most of the desks were still manned and people milled around, consulting one another about leads and reports. Jayne Hales was sitting at a desk with Miller standing behind her and looking over her shoulder at a TV screen. Jo had the chance to watch him for a moment or two without him knowing that she was there. He looked tired, and the closest to dishevelled that she had seen him. He was not wearing a jacket and his tie had been loosened at the collar with the top button of his shirt undone and the sleeves rolled up to just below his elbow.

"There," Jayne said, pointing. "You can see that the security light's on by the reflection in the chapel window, until this frame," she checked the time on the image, "twelve sixteen a.m. and then it suddenly goes out."

Miller looked at the screen intently, rubbing at his five o'clock shadow.

"So we know exactly when he broke the light. Have you spotted the nurse returning yet? Or any other movements?"

"Still going through the tapes, Guv"

He turned and, spotting Jo, self-consciously straightened his tie.

"Dr Hughes. What can we do for you?"

Jo hesitated. She had rehearsed exactly what she intended to say, over and over, in her head whilst she was waiting in the reception area, arguing with herself whether any of it was actually relevant, whether or not she should just go home and wait. Wait and see if there was a connection between Jonathan Kane and the dead nurse, if it was his car that was seen in the car park and if he was a witness or something more. In the end she had decided she had to speak out, tell them everything: about his car, about their disastrous date, his violent temper, but now that she was here she felt uncertain, her natural reticence coming to the fore. What he had done to her, hurting her arm, was hardly in the same league as killing someone, was it? Kate had said that she would regret not reporting Jonathan at the time, and here she was, doing just that. Why was Kate always right?

She realised he was waiting; they all were, Jeffries, Jayne Hales, and Miller, waiting for her to speak.

"The car. Dark coloured saloon. Have you found out who owned it yet?"

"We have a list of possibles. We're going through them now. That's the staff parking area so we'll find it, I'm sure."

"Good, well, that's it then." She knew it was ridiculous to try and leave at that point, even as she was doing it.

"That's it?" Jeffries was, as usual, the first to say what he thought. "You came all the way over here, hung around in reception with all the loons and tossers for half an hour or more, just to say that's it?"

"Well, if you think you know who owns it…I mean, it might not have anything to do with this." She was suddenly acutely aware of Miller moving forward so that he stood, almost toe to toe with her, so close that she could smell the last, lingering traces of his aftershave. She had to tilt her head to look up into his face, and his expression was not what she expected. He didn't seem angry, irritated or even exasperated with her like he usually did. For a moment, he looked as if he was worried, as if he cared. He touched her arm, just where Jonathan and grabbed it, and bruised it, and she instinctively pulled her arm back, wincing and stepping away from him, but he moved forward again, real concern in his eyes. Jeffries cleared his throat and they both suddenly looked at him and then stepped back, startled by the realisation that for a moment, just a millisecond, they had been mutually attracted, to the extent that they had forgotten where they were and just how many other people were in the room. It was Miller who recovered first.

"If you know anything that might help, that might save us some time, even if it is irrelevant, Dr Hughes, now is the moment to tell us."

She knew he was right.

"Jonathan Kane, the obstetric consultant. He, um, has a dark green jaguar."

Jayne Hales checked down the list.

"Here, Guv. 'S' class, hunter green, six months old. That could be it." Miller looked at Jo.

"There's more, though, isn't there? Something that made you connect him to this?"

"No, well, yes." Why couldn't she keep calm round this man? Be her usual detached, professional, self? "It's just that we went out, for a

222

drink, dinner, the night of the murder, last night and he left in a taxi, about eleven fifteen, eleven thirty, and I heard him tell the driver to take him to the hospital because he'd left his car there."

"Had you argued?"

"No, no, nothing like that," she lied. "It was just a, a business meeting if you like, we were discussing a patient."

"Over dinner?" He seemed unconvinced.

"Yes."

"Where?"

"The Stables"

"Pretty flash for a business dinner."

"That's Jonathan. Flash."

"Know him well, do you?"

She managed to look him straight in the eye and, seeing his interest and irritation with her, tilted her head slightly, defiantly

"You know how it is. Medicine's a small world, we all know each other."

"And you parted on good terms?"

She said nothing and was taken by surprise when he suddenly reached forward, grabbed her hand, and pulled her sleeve up with his other hand. They all stared at the bruises that were now fully developed, the purple prints of Jonathan's fingers clear where he had grabbed her wrist and twisted it trying to get her to go with him.

Jo pulled her arm back, away from him, embarrassed to have been exposed like that, not sure what she should or could say to explain. She glared at him but she could see that his eyes had darkened with anger, and when he spoke his voice was tight with the difficulty of keeping his emotions under control.

"That doesn't look like good terms to me."

When she finally arrived back at her flat, she was exhausted, too exhausted to go over what had happened or how she felt about any of it, but too wide awake not to. Jonathan was a bastard, and Miller, well Miller was more complicated. Confusing. When she had finally made a full statement, telling them everything that had happened the night before, no, it was two nights before now, he had been gentle with her, solicitous, coaxing out her memories, painful and humiliating as they were, getting the full story. He had seemed to care. About her, about what she'd been through. Then, as soon as she was done, story all told, he'd stood up, told Jeffries they were going to pick up Jonathan, and left her. Just like that. With hardly a backward glance. She groaned. He probably used that method on all the silly, girlie witnesses who came to see him. All the battered women. Made them feel like he cared, got every detail that he wanted out of them and then, wham, bang, thank you ma'am, high-tailed off to arrest his suspect.

Jo looked at the half-full wine glass on the table, and the flashing light on the answer machine and then headed into the bedroom. For once, they could wait, all of them, she needed to go to bed and get some sleep, even though she knew that that was probably the last thing that was going to happen.

27

She was finally woken by the telephone ringing and the vague feeling that it had been ringing for some time. She reached across the bed and grabbed the receiver, just in time to hear a click and then the dial tone. Seconds later the start of a Mozart piano concerto told her that whoever wanted her was trying her mobile number. So at least it couldn't be her mother.

Jo got out of bed and went searching for her mobile. It was in her bag where she had left it when she got in last night. By the time she extracted the phone out from the depths of her bag the ringing had stopped. Ten missed calls, half from Kate and half from the surgery. Her home phone started ringing again and as she leant over to pick it up she glanced at the clock on the mantelpiece. Nine o'clock!

"Yes, yes, Linda, I know I'm late and I'm really sorry. I must have slept through the alarm- I'm on my way, okay? Just pacify my patients, apologise to them, give them tea and biscuits or something. I'll be there as soon as I can."

She slammed the phone down and charged through to the bathroom. Nothing, but nothing, was going to stop her from having a shower, no matter how late that made her.

As she drove, just about within the speed limit, down the hill to the surgery, she talked to Kate on hands free.

"I know. When I left the police station last night they were on their way to question him."

"They said on the radio that they had actually arrested a consultant gynaecologist, Jo. That must mean that they suspect he was more than just a witness. Did you tell them about him hurting you?"

"Yes. I did, promise. They even saw the bruises, okay?" Jo didn't mention the fact that she hadn't initially volunteered the information. "And I admit it. You were right. I should have reported him at the time, it would have saved me the humiliation of having to tell Miller last night."

"Not to mention that it might have saved that nurse her life."

"Look, you've every right to be angry with me, Kate, but you can't lay that guilt trip on me. I don't honestly believe that Jonathan killed her. Maybe for a while last night I did but in the cold light of morning? No. I'm sorry, but it just doesn't ring true, and that's not just me trying to feel better about it and making excuses. Look, I'm at the surgery and I've got a waiting room full of irate patients, I'll speak to you later." She disconnected, parked the car and took a deep breath before getting out and striding in to the surgery, ready for whatever was waiting there for her. Knowing her luck, it was probably Mr Herring.

As she had expected, it was a long and difficult surgery. Patients who have been waiting more than an hour don't want to be fobbed off with a pat on the back and a prescription, they want to feel as though it's been worth the wait. They all wanted their full ten minutes, if not longer, and they wanted Jo to know that they were not happy about it as well. Her surgery started running at just over an hour behind, and got later and later as the morning wore on. She had apologised so often during the proceedings that it had become increasingly hard to make it sound sincere.

At last the final patient was gone and Linda arrived with a life-saving cup of coffee and some biscuits.

"I don't suppose you had time for breakfast."

"No." Jo checked her watch. "Or lunch by the look of it."

"And I know you've got all your paperwork still to do but," Linda looked uncomfortable, "Dr Grantham wants a word, if you can spare a minute?"

Linda withdrew and Jo sighed. On top of everything else she was going to get a reprimand and, what was more, she couldn't blame him for it. If she were in his shoes she would do exactly the same. She had behaved in a most unprofessional manner towards her patients and no matter what the excuse she deserved to be pulled up for it, at the very least.

"I don't need to know the reason for your late start, Jocasta. It is irrelevant." Hugh had almost reached the end of his speech about treating patients with respect, delivered from his imposing leather chair, beside his solid oak desk. His consulting room was larger than any of the others and more imposing, as befitted the senior partner, and his walls were decorated, not with Disney posters or pinboards covered with reminders and clinical bulletins like his colleagues' rooms, but with Russell Flint reproductions that he painted himself and that Linda maintained were bordering on the obscene and certainly not suitable for a family practice, though she never said this in Dr Grantham's hearing of course.

"The fact is," he continued, "that if something in your personal life means that you cannot fulfil your professional duties then you need to take some leave."

"It won't happen again, Hugh. I promise you."

He looked at her closely.

"Is there anything that I should know about?"

"No."

He waited in silence for a moment as if expecting her to change her answer.

"Honestly, Hugh. Everything is fine and I won't be late again."

"Well, that's okay then." He stood and so did Jo, hoping that that was an end to it. At the door he took her hand in both of his. "You would tell me if there was something wrong, wouldn't you, Jocasta? I mean, even if it was personal. I would like to think, well, you are like a daughter to me and maybe I have a little more experience than you in affairs of the heart so I could always offer you some advice, if you ever wanted advice from an old codger like me."

Jo smiled but she was embarrassed and could feel a flush running up her neck. Always a private person who drew a very distinct line between her professional and personal lives, when she was thinking straight, her senior partner was the last person she would confide in, particularly about her love life.

"It's okay, Hugh, honestly. I just overslept. All right?" He nodded and released her hand, but as she went out, he couldn't resist adding,

"And my door is always open if you change your mind…."

Miller was waiting for her when she went back down to her room and she involuntarily groaned out loud before she could stop herself.

"I take it you're not pleased to see me?" He seemed a little put out by it.

"It's nothing personal, inspector, it's just that I've had the surgery from hell this morning and then got a ticking off from the senior partner for being late. I am absolutely starving and I have precisely forty five minutes to eat and get my paper work done before I have a baby clinic. Three hours of screaming infants. I really don't have time to speak to you."

Miller stood up and she looked at him more closely. He had a slightly swollen and split lip and she wondered if he had upset Jonathan to the extent that he'd taken a swing at him. If so, she hoped Miller had hit him back. Then she suppressed the thought, shocked that she was musing about violence with approval. Even against Jonathan.

"There's a really nice café just down the road, so you can talk to me while you have your lunch. Kill two birds with one stone. And you never know, I might even pay. This way."

He led the way to the door and, too hungry to argue, she followed.

The café was not what she had expected from Miller at all, being a vegetarian, whole food establishment.

"Not that I'm a vegetarian," Miller assured her, "but they do lovely falafels, stir-fries and salads. Is it okay with you? Only it's not really the sort of place I can take Sergeant Jeffries."

Jo smiled.

"No, I wouldn't imagine you could. He's definitely the full English breakfast type of man."

"Not at all." Miller stood up for his sergeant. "I've seen him eat steak pie and chips on a number of occasions."

"I hate to think what sort of state his arteries are in," Jo laughed. Miller constantly surprised her. Just when she thought she had got him pegged he went and did something else that turned her opinion of him on its head.

Miller ordered a stir fry from the young, fresh-faced waitress and Jo asked for a hummus and salad-filled pitta bread.

Once the waitress had left, Miller looked at Jo, a serious expression on his face.

"I wanted you to know before you read it in the newspapers." He hesitated.

"I know that you have arrested Jonathan but I'm guessing that's just because he's being uncooperative."

From the look on Miller's face Jo knew that it wasn't just that.

What?" she asked him, "Don't tell me you're serious about Jonathan? That you really think he killed that girl?"

Miller flushed slightly, irritated that she wasn't taking this as seriously as he did.

"We certainly can't discount him. We suspect the killer is involved in medicine in some way, for several reasons."

"Like what?"

Miller was clearly reluctant to say but equally he wanted to convince her that Jonathan was a viable suspect.

"We believe the killer is wearing hospital theatre greens to keep the trace evidence to a minimum and also who would notice a set of blood body fluid stained scrubs going through the hospital laundry?"

Jo had to concede he had a point. If that was what the killer was doing then it was a brilliant idea.

"Also, the ligature this time was probably some sort of rubber or plastic tubing; it could be surgical in origin."

"So you are serious about Jonathan?"

Miller nodded.

"But what I wanted to warn you about is his alibi."

"Alibi?"

"He admits he went to the hospital to collect his car after he left you at the restaurant, although he denies laying a finger on you."

Jo snorted in disgust.

"Yes, well, I didn't say I believed him, did I? Anyway," Miller continued. "He also admits that he picked up the nurse, took her "for a spin in his car" before dropping her back at the hospital, although he didn't take her all the way into the car park, just dropped her at the entrance."

"What a gentleman." Jo sounded bitter, even to herself. "I take it that "for a spin" is a euphemism?"

Miller was looking uncomfortable.

"Yes. He did finally admit to having sex with her. Just a quickie as he put it."

"And to think I…" Jo stopped as the waitress arrived with their food. It looked lovely, which was a shame, because Jo suddenly seemed to have lost her appetite. She pushed the plate away and massaged the spot between her eyes that was the focal point of the tension that was building, making her feel as if her head was about to explode.

"You have to eat." Miller's voice was solicitous, gentle even.

"I'm really not hungry." She looked at him, saw the hesitant look on his face. "Don't tell me there's more?" She thought for a second. "You haven't got to whatever his alibi for the murder is yet, have you? Well, I can assure you he wasn't with me."

"No, I know. He says he was with his wife."

Jo felt all the anger and humiliation inherent in those words wash over her. She had been used, there was no other word for it; he was married all along and she was little better than some girl he took out for a "quickie". She felt hot and then cold and clammy; her breaths were too fast and shallow but she couldn't seem to slow them down, make them deeper, her head was spinning and she felt dizzy. Then she heard the sound of Millers' chair scrape as he stood up rapidly and pulled her chair round.

"Put your head between your knees. Now!"

Too dizzy to object, she did as she was told and the swimming feeling in her head slowly abated.

"Come on, deep breaths. Nice and slow now."

Jo would have liked to ignore him; it went against the grain, taking medical advice from a policeman, but there was no getting away from the fact that he was telling her to do exactly the right things. So she did as she was told and eventually managed to get her breathing under control.

"Is she all right?" The waitress seemed to be asking from a long way away.

"It's okay," Jo said. "I'm fine, absolutely fine, just a slight dizzy spell." And she lifted her head to see Miller, crouched on the floor in front of her, looking concerned.

"Take it slowly. That's it." He was watching her closely for any signs that she was still feeling faint. "I should have waited until you'd eaten." He turned to the waitress. "A cup of tea, with sugar." And she scurried off, glad to have something to do to help.

"I don't take sugar," Jo told him.

"You will today," he told her in a voice that said he was not going to take any argument from her. The sort of voice that she would normally have argued with for that very reason, but not today. Today, she really wasn't feeling strong enough.

The waitress reappeared with her tea and Jo sipped it, obediently.

"I didn't know," she told Miller.

"I didn't think you did. You're just not the sort of woman who would have an affair with a married man, are you?"

"Not knowingly, no. I'm sorry about that, coming over all dizzy on you. The number of times I tell my patients not to skip meals." She could tell he wasn't completely convinced that a lack of food was the sole cause of her faintness. How could she have been so stupid? She took another sip of tea; she was beginning to feel better for it already and beginning to allow herself to get angry again.

"Do you believe his alibi?"

"No."

"Is she, I mean, is his wife the sort of passive woman who would say whatever he tells her?"

"She's the sort of ball breaker who would happily lie, die or, better still, kill her husband rather than let him cause any kind of a scandal that affected her standard of living. My only consolation now is that she's giving him a far worse time than PACE would ever let me give him."

Jo smiled and had more tea.

"That's better," he said. "At least you've got a bit of colour back. Now, how about some food?"

She took a tentative bite of her pitta bread, as he went back to his chair and tackled his stir fry.

"What about the other murders? Do you honestly think he could be responsible for them?"

"He only has his wife for an alibi for Krissy's murder or for the night we think Denise met her killer and, as I said, I don't place much stock on her truthfulness."

"I just can't see it somehow. I know he's a, a -"

"Shit?" Miller interjected helpfully, as she was clearly struggling to find the right word.

"Over-sexed, two-faced adulterer," she corrected him and he smiled. "But that doesn't mean he is a serial killer or that he behaves in the

231

way that the killer did when he picked up his first two victims from the singles scene. That's really not Jonathan's style."

"Yet he fits the description of one of the men who was in the Vodka Bar the night Krissy was there."

"Really?" She was genuinely surprised. "Has he actually been identified? Or is it one of your leaps of deduction?"

Miller bristled.

"And that's always supposing I agree with your half-baked theory about the singles scene."

"Half-baked?" Jo counted off the murders on her finger as she spoke. "Krissy met her killer in a singles bar, Denise at a karaoke night, and Caro -"

"Met hers in a car park," he finished for her.

"Having just come back from the Adelaide, last resort of the desperate in singles scene terms, or so I've heard."

"And you'd know, of course." Jo flushed and Miller was suddenly apologetic. "I'm sorry. I shouldn't have said that, it was unforgivable." He looked round and realised that the waitress was listening open mouthed to every word before continuing quietly.

"Look -"

But Jo had glanced at her watch and she leapt up in a panic.

"I'm going to be late again, twice in one day. Hugh will be furious." She flung some money on to the table and rushed out.

"Wait!" But by the time he had paid the bill and hurried after her, she had gone.

28

It wasn't until late afternoon, after the last baby had been weighed, measured and jabbed, that Jo was able to get away and at long last go to the mortuary to ask about Jean Jennings' post mortem. She could have waited for the report but she told herself she ought to know sooner, for Mr Jennings' sake, if not for her own peace of mind.

Who was she kidding? She asked herself, as she searched for a parking place; she was really going to see if Ian Dunbar had any news from the post mortem on Caro Sharpe rather than Mrs Jennings.

As she slowly circled further and further away from the hospital, she wondered how long the car park was going to be taped off as a crime scene; at this rate she would have been better off getting a taxi. She finally found a legal space she could squeeze her car into about quarter of a mile away and began the trek back to the hospital. At least she wouldn't need to go to the gym to get her daily exercise, she consoled herself, it was just a shame that it looked like rain and she hadn't brought an umbrella. If she had to run back to the car later, she'd get drenched.

She found Dr Dunbar in his office, once again attempting to edit a report on his computer.

"Why don't you get your secretary to type it up for you?" she asked as she cleared a pile of reports from the only other chair and sat down.

"Because some bloody administrator with two P.A.s and a receptionist says I don't need a secretary anymore. I told him that I have much better things to do with my time than struggle with this infernal machine and he had the cheek to offer to send me on a course. Bloody whippersnapper. I've a good mind to get him in here and ask him to do the damn reports himself." He sat back and looked at her closely.

"Have you come to find out about your patient?"

"Yes, although if you've got any interesting news about the murdered nurse it would be an added bonus."

"Hmm." Dr Dunbar hesitated. "Just how well do you know our Mr Kane?"

Jo flushed.

"Well, let's just say better than I would like."

"Yes, all right, I'll accept that and pry no further, but you should know that he's involved in both cases. Do you still want to know what I know?"

"I, um, do know about his involvement and I've been questioned by the police, Ian, so you don't have to worry about all that. Jonathan Kane was having dinner with me earlier in the evening, and then came back here to pick up his car and, how can I put it, meet with Caro Sharpe."

Dr Dunbar looked relieved.

"I didn't want to break it to you that our Mr Kane is a bit of a ladies' man, and a bit of a bastard about it if the rumour mill is to be believed."

"I think I can vouch for both charges being true and no, I didn't know he was married."

"I'm sure you didn't, Jocasta. There's very little else I can tell you about the murder then. Old Wally Wadsworth is keeping his findings very close to his chest, but according to Dave, who is being irritatingly tight-lipped as well, it does look as though she's linked with the other two."

Dr Dunbar was all brisk efficiency now that he knew he wasn't treading in delicate waters.

"And on the patient front there really wasn't anything anyone could have done to save that poor women. She was absolutely riddled with cancer. Mr Kane did a total abdominal hysterectomy and a bilateral salpingo-oophorectomy and removed the worst of the growth but it had infiltrated most of the lymph glands in the groin, adhered to the peritoneum and grown through to involve the bladder and bowel. You could argue that chemotherapy would have shrunk the tumour prior to surgery, made it less of a trauma, but in reality this lady wasn't going to live long enough to see it through, no matter what. I'm sorry."

"No." Jo was relieved. "It's good to know that no one messed up, apart from the woman herself, of course, and possibly me for not managing to persuade her to come in earlier. I honestly didn't think that Jonathan -"

She looked up, suddenly aware that someone was standing in the doorway, listening to their conversation. It was Miller, leaning non-chalantly against the doorpost, politely waiting for her to finish. She blushed and was immediately irritated to have done so.

"Carry on, please, don't let me interrupt. I've only come to collect a couple of samples that need to go to forensics." He smiled, knowing that they all must know this wasn't true. The chain of evidence meant that all samples taken during the autopsy, as well as the victim's clothing and belongings, were bagged and tagged during the procedure and sent direct to the forensic laboratory.

"No, no. I've finished here." She stood up quickly and turned to Dr Dunbar so that her back was to Miller, in the vain hope that she could get her colour under control before having to speak to him again. She was even more irritated to see an amused expression on Dr Dunbar's face. He had always read her far too well. "If you could just send me the report, Dr Dunbar."

"Of course," he said and stood as well.

"Reports!" Miller almost snorted. "Your Professor Wadsworth is impossible. Hardly says an intelligible word during the P.M. and then sends me a report where he never knowingly uses one word when two, particularly two in a foreign language, would do."

"Ah, that's Wally Wadsworth, for you. He relies on people thinking he's intelligent simply because they can't understand what he's saying." Dr Dunbar was clearly pleased to hear criticism of his bete noir. "I'd be happy to take a look at those reports for you, Detective Inspector, see if I can translate them into the English language for you."

Miller smiled and whipped out a couple of folders from behind his back.

"These are the first two done by Professor Wadsworth." He handed the folders to Dr Dunbar. "I'll drop off the report on Ms Sharpe as soon as I get it."

He stood back to allow Dave to come in.

"The stock order, Dr Dunbar." He held out a form.

"Just put it on the side will you, Dave?" Dr Dunbar was already flicking through the folders. "What about the independent P.M. on the first victim? Have you got that?"

"At the office. It's a lot clearer but if you think it would be helpful to see it I can drop that off as well."

"I think it would be good to make sure that they both marry up. Nothing I'd like better than to catch Wally out, find something he'd missed." Dr Dunbar had a mischievous twinkle in his eye. As he leaned across Jo to put the stock request form on the side, Dave managed to brush some bits of paper onto the floor. He bent down to pick them up and Jo moved to the side in an attempt to get out of his way but the room really wasn't big enough for the four of them, particularly in view of the fact that Dave was by no means compact. Jo edged passed him towards the door.

"I'll say goodbye then."

"Bye, Jo." Dr Dunbar was already engrossed in the autopsy reports and barely looked up.

"I'll walk out with you." Miller stepped back into the corridor

"I thought you had some samples to collect?" she said as coolly as she could as she walked towards the lift.

"I think we both know the purpose of my visit was to get Dr Dunbar to decipher those ruddy reports for me."

"It was a bit obvious." She agreed, with a smile.

"I'm glad I bumped into you, though. Make sure you're okay."

"After I made such a spectacle out of myself, you mean?"

"Not at all. You hadn't eaten and you have had a difficult couple of days."

"Nothing I can't handle, Detective Inspector." She was damned if she was going to encourage his solicitousness; she was a strong independent woman, after all, she told herself, not some flaky neurotic. She punched the lift call button, the doors slid immediately open and they both got in.

"I'm sure. But -"

"No buts. I admit to an error of judgement in going out with Jonathan Kane but that's it. We only went out a couple of times and he proved to be unacceptable. End of story. Okay?"

"Unacceptable?" Miller wore an amused expression on his face.

"Yes, unacceptable." she snapped as the lift doors opened onto the ground floor corridor and she marched hurriedly away, pleased to see through the windows that at least the rain seemed to be holding off.

Jo had picked her time to visit home very carefully. Wednesday night was her mother's bridge night and nothing, absolutely nothing, stopped her from going out to play cards. Her father was guaranteed to be on his own.

He looked slightly confused as he opened the door.

"Jocasta? Come in, come in. Are we expecting you? Your mother's out, playing bridge."

"I know, Daddy. I was rather hoping to catch you on your own."

He ushered her into the kitchen.

"That sounds ominous." He put the kettle on whilst Jo got some mugs out of the cupboard.

"It's about Jonathan."

"Ah. You've found out."

"Found out what?"

"That he's married."

"You knew?" Jo was surprised.

"I looked him up in the medical directory first and then on the internet. I googled him, as they say." He was clearly quite proud of his grasp of the modern idiom. "He's written quite a few articles for the journals but there was also a piece about his marriage. She's a corporate lawyer, partner at one of the big city firms."

Why hadn't Jo thought to do that? It could have saved her so much time, trouble and pain.

"You never told me."

"I wasn't sure if you knew, or if perhaps his marriage was over…" He looked at her. "I didn't want to interfere."

She gave his arm a reassuring squeeze.

"That's okay. I found out eventually anyway and, to be honest, being married wasn't the biggest problem he had."

Her father raised his eyebrows and gave her a questioning look.

"Is that so? I think perhaps we'd better take these through to the sitting room, then."

He put the two mugs of coffee onto a tray and carried them to the sitting room, placing them on the occasional table in front of the open fire.

Jo settled herself in the comfortable armchair and took a deep breath.

"Have you been watching the news? About the killer?"

Her father looked confused.

"They've arrested someone, haven't they?"

"Well, he's helping them with their enquiries, anyway?"

"Who is?"

"Jonathan."

"They think Jonathan Kane has something to do with these murders? But he's a consultant, a gynaecologist, for goodness' sake, how can he be a killer?"

"The two aren't mutually exclusive, Daddy. And, for what it's worth, I think the police are wrong. I don't think he's the killer, not for one moment. Believe me, his being married would pale into insignificance if I thought that but even I have to say there's quite a bit of circumstantial evidence against him."

"Has his name been released?"

"No, but it's only a matter of time."

He sighed.

"Goodness only knows what your mother's going to make of this. As far as she's concerned you are as good as married to the man, so to find out that not only is he allegedly a killer but that he's already married as well - she is not going to take it well. How on earth are we going to break it to her?"

He shook his head, worrying about the problem.

"That's why I came over tonight, to tell you first."

The truth dawned on him.

"So that I can be the one to tell your mother? That's not really fair, is it, Jocasta?"

He was right, she wasn't being fair, but there were no two ways about it, she couldn't face telling her mother herself.

"No, but we both know that she'll take it better from you."

"Hmph." He seemed as unconvinced by that argument as she was, if she was entirely honest. Whoever broke it to her mother would have to suffer hours, if not days, of criticism. Her father for being of the male gender and therefore complicit in their tendency to have affairs and lead nice young women astray, and Jo for her infallible ability to pick men who were never going to marry her.

"Oh, all right. I should have told her the married bit when I found out so I suppose it's all my fault anyway. Finish your tea and hurry off before she gets back then. I'll do the honourable thing and take the flak for you."

She out down her mug and leant across to kiss him on the cheek.

"Thank you, Daddy. I owe you for this."

"You owe me for quite a number of things if I remember rightly, Jocasta, and I won't forget, you know. When I'm old and doddery and your mother's put me out on the street, I'll expect you to give me a home and look after me."

"Don't worry, I'll happily take you in." And she settled back to finish her tea, relieved that she wasn't going to have to speak to her mother just yet and also that her father seemed so well. No problem with his memory at all, in fact it was he who had had the common sense to google Jonathan and find out about him rather than her. It just went to prove that there was nothing wrong with his mind, after all. For now, anyway.

29

The drive back to Hastings was so familiar that she was able to let her mind wander as she drove, almost in auto-pilot mode, first along the narrow lanes from her parents' house and then the main road into the town. As she came down past the long strip of Alexandra Park and signalled a left turn to head up over the hill towards the old town she saw a familiar figure, dressed up to the nines in next to nothing: a tiny pelmet skirt, handkerchief top and white stilettos; Angel Stubbins was heading into the town centre. How she could possibly walk in heels that high, let alone hang around street corners all night in them, Jo didn't know, besides which it was starting to rain and the girl had no coat or umbrella with her. Not to mention that she must be absolutely freezing. Before she quite understood why or what she was doing, Jo cancelled her left turn signal and went straight across the roundabout, only mildly irritating the car behind she hoped, and pulled over to the kerb just in front of Angel.

"Can I give you a lift?" She leant across the passenger seat, talking as the window was still opening.

Jo was completely unprepared for Angel's reaction, which was far from grateful: the girl was petrified. It took her a moment or two before she realised the person driving the car was Jo.

"Oh my God, you scared me."

"I can see that. I'm sorry, I didn't mean to, I just thought you might like a lift, as it's raining." Jo was puzzled as to why the girl had over-reacted so badly but perhaps it was understandable, sensible even. After all, a serial killer was out there targeting women on their own and prostitutes particularly, if you took the police view, and the newspapers and television reports were all warning the women of Hastings to take care. Perhaps that was all that had spooked Angel, and it was certainly enough reason, but Jo wondered if there was something else worrying the girl. Angel was still hesitating, but a sudden squall helped her decision.

"Thanks." Angel said as she got in the car and taking a closer look at Jo, obviously trying to place her. "I know I know you, but can't remember where from."

"I'm the doctor from the police station."

"Oh, yeah. I remember. Talked about safe sex and that."

"That's right, Angel." Jo pulled away from the kerb and carried on towards the town centre.

Angel thought silently for a few minutes, remembering that there was something else about Jo, something that worried her, but unable to quite remember. Jo could almost hear the cogs turn as she tried to put two and two together. Jo finally lost patience and prompted her.

"I also asked you about Tomas, remember?"

"Yeah." The penny dropped and there was no denying it, Angel was scared, and Jo asking about Tomas had frightened her even more.

"Did you think any more about what I said? About Tomas being bad news? And that you shouldn't have anything to do with him or any of his plans?"

"Mmm." Angel was sweating slightly as Jo paused at the traffic lights. "Look, I'll get out here, it's not far." Angel had her hand on the door handle, but the lights very fortuitously changed and Jo quickly moved on before she could work out how the door opened.

"Sorry. Couldn't stop there. I'll pull over when it's safe." Jo quickly tried to think of something, anything to say to stop Angel from doing whatever it was that Tomas had asked her to do.

"Angel." What could she say? "You know that Tomas is not a nice man."

"But -"

"I know he's offering you a lot of money, but you have to ask yourself, is it worth getting injured, dying even for that money?"

"Dying?"

"Have you heard of snuff movies, Angel?"

"Snuff movies? Like when they kill people? What's Tomas got to with them?"

"That's what I, we, think Tomas is planning to do."

"Nah, you're wrong, it ain't nuffink that bad. He told me about it. He wouldn't hurt me, I'm going to make him rich, he said so."

Jo sighed, was the girl really this stupid? She pulled into the bus stop opposite the shopping centre.

"And how exactly is he going to get rich, Angel? He's going to sell the film to people who will pay a lot of money for it."

"'Xactly." Angel agreed, relieved that they were on the same hymn sheet. "And no one's going to pay a lot of money for a film about someone getting killed, are they? They'd have to be sick to do that."

"Yes. They will, Angel. They will pay a lot of money. Some people are really that sick."

Angel shook her head.

"It's all about fantasy, innit? Fulfilling people's dreams." She was clearly using someone else's words here, parroting what she herself had been told.

"And what if these dreams are more like nightmares, Angel? What then? Look, you don't have to do it, just tell me what it is he's making you do." Angel still didn't seem convinced. "Ellie died because of this, Angel."

"Ellie took an overdose. I know that. Tomas didn't kill her, she did it herself."

"Because she couldn't bear to do what he was asking her, because she was frightened. Look, talk to the other girls, Angel, ask them why they won't do it. Promise me?"

"Tomas said not to." Angel had her hand on the handle, had worked out how to open the door.

"Because he doesn't want you frightened off. Please Angel. Ask them. And here, let me give you my number. You can call me if -"

Jo reached for her bag, to get pen and paper, but Angel finally managed to get out of the car and hurried away.

"Wait!" But she had gone, and all Jo had was the certainty that Angel was going to make this film for Tomas and there was little she could do about it except keep her fingers crossed that Angel was right and she was wrong.

"So you think this girl's actually going to do it? Make the film?" Kate asked as she made Jo a cup of coffee. Troubled by her encounter with Angel, not to mention the rest of the day's events, Jo had dropped by for some solace and chocolate.

"I'm sure of it, and I don't know what I can do to stop her."

"I don't think that there is anything you can do. She hasn't broken the law, not yet anyway."

"But by the time the law is broken it will be too late."

They were going round and round in circles, and getting nowhere fast. Kate handed Jo the large mug of coffee and put a plate of chocolate biscuits on the generously-sized coffee table in front of her. Kate's home, like Jo's, reflected her personality perfectly, but where Jo's flat was minimalist and neat, and all about cool colours and clean lines, Kate's was full to bursting with rich, jewel colours: ruby, emerald, purple and deepest blues, over-stuffed chairs, plump cushions and sensuous textures, velvet, raw silk, and thick, deep carpets. It was a house that welcomed you warmly, tempted you to touch it and stroke it, and threatened to smother you in its embrace. Just like Kate.

"I really thought I was beginning to get through to her when she ran off."

"Have you told Miller about it?"

"Yes, but he doesn't honestly believe it's going to happen. I mean who would make snuff movies in Hastings, for Gods' sake?"

"He has a point."

They sipped coffee and nibbled biscuits as they thought about it for a moment or two.

"Couldn't you get this girl's address from the police station? I mean, you saw her there, didn't you? So you could say you have some test results back, have a legitimate reason for tracing her."

Jo looked at Kate.

"And have another go? That's brilliant, Kate. Trust you to come up with a plan of action."

"It might not work, of course."

"But at least I could put my hand on my heart and say I did everything I could."

Jo leant back and closed her eyes. A visit to Kate always worked, always helped her to solve her problems rather than let them get on top of her. They said a problem shared was a problem halved, but when it came to sharing them with Kate, more often than not they went away completely.

Back at her flat, there were fifteen messages on her answer phone. Two from her mother, demanding to know how she could so consistently let her family down, one from a reporter who must have heard something about her and Jonathan, however vague, and was fishing, and twelve hang ups. Jo dialled 1471, but the number was withheld every time. For a moment she wondered if it was the same person as before but they had seemed to stop calling once she had changed the message.

They were probably all from the reporter, checking to see if she was home yet, Jo thought, inwardly groaning. That was all she needed: her unsuccessful love life splashed all over the front pages. She would never be able to go out again.

As Jo was brushing her hair, getting ready for bed, the phone rang again. Nervous in case it was her mother, Jo left it for the machine to pick up.

She listened as the message kicked in: Neil from the surgery saying that the caller had reached the number for Dr Jo Hughes, and that they should leave a message after the tone. There was a bleep and then nothing.

Jo stopped brushing her hair. She could feel the hairs on the back of her neck stand up and a shiver run down her spine as the silence went on. She put down the brush and went through to the living room, standing next to the phone, listening. There was nothing but the faint sound of breathing.

In a sudden rush of anger, she picked up the phone and shouted into the receiver:

"Go away!" slammed it down, and pulled out the plug.

She didn't know what the person at the other end thought of her outburst, but it certainly made her feel better.

He smiled. He was getting to her, he could tell. He had known she was home. Standing where he was on the cliff top, he had seen the light come on in her living room when she got back. She shouldn't have answered but she couldn't resist it. Couldn't resist him. He dialled again, withholding his number like before, but got the engaged single now.

He was disappointed, like he'd been disappointed when she changed the message on the tape, got one of her boyfriends to speak for her so he couldn't hear her voice. She was such a whore, such a cock-tease. She probably had hundreds of men at her beck and call.

245

He tried again, and again it was engaged. She must have left the phone off the hook, but she couldn't do that forever. He would catch her out again, he just needed to keep trying, then he would hear her voice and maybe next time she wouldn't be angry. Maybe next time she would be frightened.

30

Next day, Jo deliberately didn't put the TV on and, when she drove to work, she didn't listen to the radio and even avoided looking at the newsagent's hoardings which she was sure were full of the arrest of a certain gynaecologist. She no longer wanted to know what was in the news because it was bound to be bad.

She had a quieter than usual surgery; the gaps were filled with the people who had rung and asked to see a doctor that morning- mainly the worried well wanting reassurance and children with viral infections- but some of her patients were no-shows who hadn't even bothered to cancel their appointments. She wondered if Linda had been proved right and the sight of her vandalised car had put people off or was it more likely that news about her being persistently late had got round? Either way, she was glad of the break and the fact that she had time not only for a coffee but also to make some phone calls. Firstly she rang the police station and asked to be put through to the custody suite.

"Hello, is that the custody sergeant? It's Dr Hughes."

"Hello, doctor, it's Sergeant Barlow here. How can I help you?"

Jo's heart sank. There was bound to be some rule or other that meant he couldn't give her Angel's address, either that or it would be too much trouble to try and find it for her, she was sure.

"I was in last week and saw a couple of working girls, sergeant. One of them gave her name as Angel Stubbins."

"I know Angel. She's a regular."

"Well, I sent off some samples and one of them has come back positive," Jo had her fingers crossed as she held the telephone, "however the address she gave me and that I put on the specimen label, seems to be wrong. I wonder if you can let me have the address you've got? Only I really ought to visit her today, get her started on treatment as quickly as possible."

She hoped and prayed he didn't ask why she hadn't used the address on her custody form at the time and was relieved when he didn't.

"Let's see." She could hear him clicking the mouse and typing things into the computer. He wasn't the most technologically minded of police officers but he was by no means the worst either. There was one PC she had come across who was a real technophobe and he had admitted to her that he was finding it increasingly difficult to do the job and it was causing him great stress. He loved his work and it was a shame because he was good at it, a real old-fashioned copper, but he was going to find himself on the scrap heap if he didn't get to grips with the computer system. Equally, she knew that, in this day and age of computer data and audits, it was no longer good enough to do a good job, you had to have a powerpoint presentation to prove it.

"Ah, here we are: Angel Stubbins, Flat three, eighty one Glenferrie Road. Do you know Glenferrie? It's up in Ore, I think, doctor. Hope that helps."

"That's great, thank you, Sergeant."

"No problem, can't have Angel spreading diseases willy-nilly round the men of Hastings, can we?"

Jo felt he could have put it better, or perhaps acknowledged that if Angel really had got a sexually transmitted disease then she would undoubtedly have caught it from one of those very men, but she said nothing other than a quick goodbye. Just as well, considering that as far as she knew Angel didn't have a disease at all, so not only had she broken confidentiality rules once again, she'd actually slandered the poor girl. The GMC would have a field day with her if they ever found out. She grabbed her bag and car keys and headed out the door. She had a couple of hours before her next surgery in which to get lunch and visit Angel. Hopefully, it was too early in the day for her to be out working.

Eighty one Glenferrie Road was a sixties eyesore set in the middle of a perfectly nice Victorian terrace. Whichever town planner had agreed to it should have been shot, Jo thought as she tried to work out which of the four bells related to flat three. Deciding it could be any one of the three unlabelled ones (the only labelled button being for a D. Kirkman in flat one), she rang them all and waited. There was no reply, so she pushed the button marked tradesmen, the door entry system buzzed and she was able to push the door open and step inside.

It always seemed strange to her that so many blocks of flats had an entry system that could be circumvented so easily by anyone. It was hardly any greater security than leaving the door wide open for all to see. Once in the hallway, Jo looked around. The floor was covered in free papers and junk mail: clearly the local delivery agents could not be bothered to distribute it to the individual flats. She hesitated, uncertain which was number three, the flat that she wanted. To her right was the door marked as number one, belonging to D. Kirkman, and number two was to her left. She had just decided that number three must be up the concrete stairs, when a querulous voice called down from the upper level.

"Is that you, Angie? Forgotten your key again, have you? How many times have I told you?"

Jo quickly took the stairs calling up to the unseen woman as she climbed.

"Is that Mrs Stubbins?"

As she turned to take the second flight, Jo could see the small, wizened old woman, bent over a wheeled zimmer frame. She had several layers of cardigan over her stained floral dress, her bare legs were discoloured by broken veins and poor circulation, and the battered slippers on her feet were comfortably misshapen to accommodate her bunions and bent joints but, above all that, the face staring down at Jo with an equal mix of suspicion and scorn was perfectly alert.

"My name's Dr Hughes. I was hoping to see Angel - is she in, Mrs Stubbins?"

"I'm Mrs Hill, Stubbins was her father's name, and his name was all Angela ever got from him. How my Jane picked him for a husband, I'll never know."

The old lady turned her walking frame with surprising speed and headed back towards an open flat door. Jo hurried after her, grabbing the door before it closed in her face.

"Is she in? Angel? Angela, your granddaughter, I mean?"

"If she was, I wouldn't have thought you were her, would I?"

The flat was hot and stuffy, and smelled of a mix of stale urine, blue grass talcum powder and cat, which was, sadly, the scent of the home of almost every elderly patient Jo visited.

She followed Mrs Hill into the lounge, with its pink velour covered sofa and profusion of floral patterns: the rugs, lamp shades, curtains and cushions accounting for at least six different varieties.

"Have a seat, doctor." Mrs Hill ordered before plonking herself down in an upright wingchair in a similar, but not quite matching, shade of pink.

Jo sat on the sofa, moving an over-stuffed cushion in order to sit far enough back to be comfortable. The cheap, glass-fronted, display cabinet opposite her was filled with china horses, every available space crammed, mainly with large cart horses but there were some rearing stallions and cute big-eyed ponies, probably presents from children and grand-children, as well as smaller models that had probably come out of crackers or been won in the seafront bingo arcades.

"Gosh, that's a big collection," Jo commented dutifully. Mrs Hill followed the direction of her gaze.

"Nothing but a dust trap, if you ask me. I keep telling Angie we should get rid of them, but she won't hear of it. She really loves them." She turned her beady eyes back on Jo. "Now, what are you doing here, doctor? I'm not expecting a house-call and you're not one of the usual ones from Heath Road Surgery."

"As I said, I'm here to see your granddaughter, Angela."

"Well, you are out of luck. She hasn't come home yet."

"Is she normally out this late?"

The old lady said nothing as she looked at Jo, wondering whether or not to trust this stranger.

"Sometimes." She hesitated. "How do you know Angie, doctor?"

"I'm the police doctor. I met her at the station when she was last arrested so I know what she does for a living."

"So you know that she sometimes gets 'unavoidably detained'. Normally rings though, lets me know why she hasn't come home."

"So this isn't normal? For her not to call at least?"

Mrs Hill gave Jo an appraising look.

"Tell me, why should I talk to you? Seeing as you come from the police?"

"Because I'm worried about her. Worried that she might be tempted to do something -" Jo hesitated, she didn't want to alarm the old lady, "unwise."

To her surprise, Mrs Hill snorted in derision.

"Well, she's not likely to do anything wise, that's for sure. That girl hasn't got the brains she was born with."

Jo smiled and waited as Angel's nan looked at her with those bright, intelligent eyes and made her decision.

"She went out last night. Said she'd be back usual time. Not seen her since."

"Does she do this often? Other than when she's been arrested?"

"No. It happened a few times when she was younger, before she was on the game, but not now, not recently."

Jo wondered if Sergeant Barlow could possibly have forgotten to mention that Angel was in the cells to her but she didn't think so. He knew she was going to see her, surely he wouldn't let her make an unnecessary visit?

"I don't think she's at the station. I rang earlier and they knew I was coming here. So where else do you think she could be?" Jo asked.

Mrs Hill shrugged, but she was beginning to look worried.

"She's a good girl, Angie, not the sharpest knife in the drawer, as you probably realised, but she looks after me. I don't need much help. I can manage to look after meself. It's getting in and out of bed that's my problem, and dressing. Takes me hours on my own and I can't get my elastic stockings on. So, every night before she goes to work she helps me to bed, and every morning when she gets back, she gets me up again."

Mrs Hill looked at her bare legs and then at Jo.

"I could help you with the stockings, Mrs Hill."

"And what if Angie doesn't come back, how am I going to get them off again?"

Jo didn't have an answer for that one.

Back in the front reception at the police station, waiting for Miller, Jo was fast learning to hate this place but she had checked with Sergeant Barlow and Angel certainly wasn't in the cells, here or at any other police station in the county, and she had called in favours at the hospital as well but no one fitting Angel's description had been brought in to casualty. She had even persuaded the charge nurse on duty to make a brief foray into the waiting room and she wasn't there, either.

So, once again, Jo was sitting with the dross of Hastings although, thankfully, the fact that it was early afternoon meant that there were few people there to share the bench with her, most of the usual suspects still being in the pubs and betting shops. As she waited she couldn't help thinking back to that awful moment in the café when she had thought she would faint. Hardly the cool professional image she worked so hard to present. Miller must think she was some sort of hysteric or even a neurotic. At least she had been more together in the mortuary, if a little snippy, but that could be explained by embarrassment, nothing more. She could feel a slight burning, a flush creeping up her neck as she thought of him and tried to convince herself that she was not developing anything remotely like "feelings", as her mother would no doubt put it, for DI Miller. She quickly tried to make herself think of something else. Going in to see him looking red-faced and apologetic would only make things worse. She must put it behind her and move on. Show him just how detached and unemotional she was.

If only life was that easy.

The door from the main police station opened and everyone looked up expectantly. Jo in particular was surprised to see Mr Jennings being shown out by a bored looking P.C. who, having opened the door, quickly drew back in and slammed it shut. There was no way he was going to give anyone else the chance to catch his eye and demand attention.

Jo jumped up.

"Mr Jennings, I didn't expect to see you here, I've been meaning to get in touch, I was so sorry to hear about -" The look in his eyes made her stop.

"Sorry? You don't know the meaning of the word. You pretend to care but you don't. I know. I know what you are really like," he said furiously, almost spitting at her in his hatred and it was a couple of seconds before Jo recovered enough from her shock at his words to say anything more herself.

"What on earth are you talking about?" she asked but he brushed passed her with a scowl and headed for the door, leaving her standing there staring after him. Aware that everyone else in the room was looking at her she sat down quickly. What had that been all about? Where had it come from? He had always been a little strange but perhaps the death of his wife had unhinged him completely? She would have to keep an eye on him, visit him, or maybe it would be better to ask one of her colleagues to visit him, as she clearly wasn't his favourite person right now. Perhaps he blamed her because she didn't act sooner, try harder to persuade his wife to go to hospital? But why come to the police? If he was concerned that she might have been negligent wouldn't he go to the surgery, speak to Hugh? Or perhaps he had? But then, wouldn't Hugh have told her? Her mind was going round in rapid circles again and she was relieved when, at last, Jayne Hales came to collect her and take her up to the incident room to see Miller.

"Jayne, I just saw one of my patients being shown out and, um, well, he's just lost his wife and he's -"

"A bit unstable?" Jayne finished for her.

"Possibly."

"What's his name?"

Jo hesitated; she had already violated medical confidentiality with his wife, she couldn't with him as well.

"No, look, forget about it. He was probably here for something innocuous."

"He's not why you're here?"

"No, honestly, it's nothing."

"Sure?"

"Positive." She tried to sound confident, but she certainly wasn't feeling it. She had a bad feeling about Mr Jennings.

"So why are you here, then?" Jayne asked Jo as they walked briskly along the corridor.

"Don't laugh, but a missing prostitute."

Jayne stopped and looked at her, a serious expression on her face.

"In the current circumstances, I'm hardly likely to laugh, am I?"

"I suppose not." They started walking again.

In the incident room, Sergeant Jeffries was less impressed.

"Angel Stubbins? It doesn't fit with what that trick cyclist said, does it, Guv? Mind you, you know my views on psychiatrists."

"Psychologist. He's a psychologist." Jayne corrected him and turned to Jo. "They lent us a profiler."

"Whatever. But what this bloke said was that the killer was getting more confident, leaving the body where he knew it would be found quickly, and that he was also getting more choosy. Picking steadily prettier victims. And I'll give him the nurse, she was a real looker, but Angel Stubbins? He's back at fucking Battersea Dogs' Home with Angel, isn't he?"

He looked round for everyone else's opinion. Jayne was staring fixedly at the floor, and Jo had closed her eyes but Jeffries seemed blissfully unaware that he could have offended anyone present.

"When did the grandmother last see her?"

"Last night, about seven." Jo replied, thankful that at least Miller was asking relevant questions. "But I saw her after that." She had their attention now. "Walking past Alexandra Park, about seven thirty. I was in the car and I stopped and picked her up since it was raining, then dropped her off at the shopping centre."

Miller and Jeffries exchanged looks.

"What?" Jo asked, well aware that something was going on that she was not privy to. Miller and Jeffries studiously avoided her eyes.

"Did she say anything about where she was going? If she had any clients booked in?" Miller was clearly changing the subject but Jayne cut in before Jo could answer.

"Angel's not the type to take bookings, Guv. She's strictly a street worker."

He nodded and turned back to Jo, who was feeling distinctly uncomfortable despite still wondering exactly what she had missed.

"Did she say anything else then?"

"We talked about Tomas Czernak."

Jo could see Miller's face tighten with annoyance.

"I thought I told you to leave him alone."

"That was what I was trying to persuade Angel to do. She was going to do the film for him. The one that Ellie killed herself rather than do, remember? I wanted to try and convince her not to do it."

Jo was angry but not as angry as Miller.

"The inquest found that Ellie Smith had died of an accidental overdose, if I remember correctly."

"Okay, so maybe it was accidental, who knows? But the fact is, she took a double dose, far more than she was used to and to me that means that either she was trying to kill herself or she was trying to get herself right out of it so that she wouldn't remember what she had done or was about to do."

"That is entirely speculation, Dr Hughes."

"Yes, but you see, don't you? I've said all along that these murders couldn't be down to Jonathan. I mean, you know how I feel about him and I'd gladly let you lock him up for a few years but, as Sergeant Jeffries so eloquently put it, Angel was a bit of a dog, like Denise, and there's no way Jonathan would have touched them with a bargepole. Besides which, you've got him in custody, so if anything has happened to Angie it's because of Tomas Czernak, not Jonathan Kane."

There was an uncomfortable silence before Miller cleared his throat and continued, more calmly.

"Mr Kane was released on police bail at six thirty last night."

"So it doesn't rule him out," Jeffries explained helpfully, just in case she hadn't fully understood what his boss was saying.

"Yes, but -" How many times was she going to have to explain it to them? "There is no way Jonathan would pick up a prostitute, not a street walker like Angel anyway, let alone an obese check-out girl from Morrisons."

"Fine, okay, we got that." Miller assured her, with only a trace of irritation in his voice.

"But you still don't seem to believe it"

"We can't discount anyone at this stage, Dr Hughes, you know that."

There was a moment's awkward silence and then Jayne cut it.

"Have you checked the hospitals?"

"Yes." Jo refused to be mollified.

"She's probably gone off to party with a bloke for the night and got lost. She'll be walking back into town and turn up at her gran's." Jeffries seemed unworried. "She'll stroll in with a sheepish grin and wonder why anyone was worried. She certainly won't thank you for coming to us."

Jo looked fit to explode.

"So you aren't even going to look for her?"

Jo looked Miller directly in the eye and he did at least have the good grace to look as if he regretted the situation.

"I'll be frank with you, Dr Hughes, we can get our patrols to look in all the usual places she hangs out, ask around a bit perhaps, but until we find something to give us a clue where to look, or some kind of evidence that something's happened to her, there's not much we can do."

"Well, thanks for nothing, inspector."

Jo turned and was about to leave but Miller stopped her.

"Wait!" She turned back and he continued, firmly: "And I don't want you going anywhere near Tomas Czernak, do you hear me?"

She didn't dignify that with an answer but walked out of the room instead, cheeks burning and a dangerous glint in her eye. Jayne had followed to show her out.

"He's right, you know, Jo. You mustn't go anywhere near Czernak, leave him to us."

"I'm not going to see him, it's okay, I'm not that stupid. But I did want Miller to at least agree to go and see him. What if Angel's being kept prisoner there? What if she's injured?"

"Look, I know the Guv and I certainly know Sergeant Jeffries, unfortunately." She smiled at Jo and Jo found it hard not to smile back, she could so understand where Jayne was coming from. "They will check out Czernak as best they can but they've got to act softly, softly, even if it isn't quite their usual style."

"The one time I want them to go in all guns blazing." Jo was trying hard to keep the frustration out of her voice but failing.

"I understand completely but with the press crawling all over the town they've got to be even more careful than usual. They don't have grounds for a warrant and if they go barging in, step over the line, they could mess up any future evidence or case they might get against him. Believe me, it's better to wait until there's something to go on."

"Until you've got another body, you mean."

Jayne said nothing, as there wasn't much she could say to that. They had reached the front entrance and Jo left, almost breaking into a run to reach her car. There were no two ways round it: she was late for another surgery on top of everything else. Hugh Grantham was not going to be pleased.

31

Between patients in her evening surgery Jo rang Mrs Hill to persuade the by now very worried old lady to report Angel missing formally and was surprised to hear that a policeman who fitted Miller's description had been round asking about her already. Every time she thought she had him pegged he went and did something surprising like this: taking her seriously to the point of checking up on missing girls. There was clearly more to him than she had thought.

Even though she hadn't been asked and had no authority in the matter, Jo then called Mrs Hill's GP and organised someone to call, explaining that she wanted them to arrange some kind of help at home while Angel was missing. Help with social care wasn't easy to get, she knew, as there was a desperate shortage of carers. She was always begging them to help with her own patients but at least she had alerted the surgery to the problem and felt as if she had done something, however small.

It wasn't until much later, once she had finished surgery and managed to avoid any confrontation with Hugh over her timekeeping by the simple yet effective expedient of giving his room and the office a wide berth, that she was able to give any thought to the problem of Jonathan and the silent phone calls. Now that she knew he had been allowed out of custody she was sure now that last night's batch must have come from him, not a journalist as she had suspected before. He was obviously trying to frighten her because he blamed her in some way for what had happened to him. Well, she wasn't to blame, he was, and there was no way she was going to allow him to intimidate her.

As she unlocked the door to her flat and placed her doctor's bag neatly in the small cupboard in the hallway, the first thought on her mind was how to get to the kitchen for a glass of wine without even looking at the phone but it was hopeless, her eyes were automatically drawn to it as she crossed the living room. She stopped dead in the centre of the room, the answer phone light wasn't flashing, in fact it wasn't even on. Then she remembered: she'd left it unplugged last night. Fantastic! What a stroke of luck, there wouldn't be any messages from her mother or reporters, or long silences from Jonathan Kane; she had nothing to dread hearing after all.

She was inordinately pleased with herself for not plugging the phone back in, even though it had been forgetfulness rather than a conscious decision to avoid unwanted phone calls. No matter the reason, it made for a much more relaxed evening as she settled down to a chicken Caesar salad that she had bought in Marks and Spencers on her way home, followed by a real treat: a slice of chocolate cheesecake, all washed down with a glass of chilled Pinot Grigio. She felt she deserved to be spoilt after the events of recent days. It was only after she eaten the last crumb, drunk the last drop of wine, and made a pot of coffee that she allowed herself to think about the day and its problems.

She really didn't know what to do about Angel. Much as Jo wanted to go after Czernak herself she knew deep down that she wouldn't. Couldn't. There was no getting away from the fact that, even though she had never met the man, he frightened her. More than that, he terrified her. She just wished that she had managed to convey some of that fear to Angel, enough to stop her going off and meeting him last night, because that was where Jo was sure Angel had gone and why she was missing now. Did she think Tomas was behind the other killings? she asked herself, and had to admit she wasn't sure. For the life of her she couldn't think of a coherent or logical motive but, from everyone's descriptions, he was the type who would kill and that there could be two people capable of murder in one small town like Hastings was equally difficult to imagine.

Try as she might, Jo couldn't think of anything more she could do to help the girl and so she decided to concentrate on her other life, as a GP, and see if she could find out any more about Timothy Lockwood's mystery illness. She plugged in her laptop and checked her mail. Apart from a large number of offers to enlarge the size of her organ, supply her with cheap medication, more slimming pills than Viagra these days she noted, the cheeky beggars, or congratulating her on winning lotteries she had never entered, there was little of interest so she deleted everything and logged onto the medical chatroom-cum-bulletin board she had been on before, asking questions about new cures for eczema.

She was surprised by the number of answers she had received to her initial inquiry; there were obviously a lot of doctors out there with nothing better to do than hang out in chat rooms. A whole conversation seemed to have taken place while she was out of the room, so to speak, so she skipped forward to the conclusion: Chinese herbal medicine used to be excellent but didn't work so well now. Most of the correspondents thought that it had never really worked or that patients probably became immune to it, in a similar manner to the way they became resistant to steroid creams and other mainstream treatments. There was a lot of discussion about alternative therapies in general with the participants split into two distinct camps: those who couldn't see the harm and those that could, and things were getting really quite heated.

Herbs, that old chestnut, she thought. There had been loads of activity in that area in the eighties and nineties, with even some respected hospitals running pilot schemes to assess various concoctions on eczema but, as far as she knew, the interest in it had died out. She typed in a query, asking if anyone knew why Chinese herbal medicine had stopped being so fashionable, was it just that it stopped working or was there something more? And then she waited to see if anyone was currently on line. Their use would certainly fit with the fact of Timothy getting better whilst he was in Hong Kong with his parents, maybe they had seen a herbal specialist over there? She was surprised at the speed of the response. Dr D told her that one of his patients had done wonderfully well ten or more years ago and had been distraught when the particular blend of herbs she used were withdrawn for safety reasons. The mix she had used had subsequently been banned in this country.

Jo asked him what were the safety reasons that led to the herbs being banned and the response came quickly: dangerous side effects, although his patient hadn't suffered any he hastened to add.

Jo thanked him and went back to med-online, searching on Chinese herbal medicines and side effects. There were numerous results and she slowly started working her way through them, but a pattern soon emerged. Mixes containing aristocholic acid obtained from the herb Mutong were associated with some cases of renal failure. Well, Timothy's kidneys seemed to be working just fine, so it wasn't that.

She read on and finally found an article that caught her attention: Chinese herbal medicine used for eczema was thought to have caused acute hepatic necrosis in six cases in one study, and two in another, although which of the commonly used herbs and alkaloids in the mix actually caused the problem was unknown. Dictamnus and Paeonia were concluded to be the main suspects, either on their own or in combination.

Jo knew that the liver was vital in detoxifying alkaloids and the report seemed to think that abnormal liver enzymes in some people might predispose them to acute reactions to certain alkaloids found in these herbs. This seemed not to be a problem in China or people of Chinese ethnicity so the article postulated that it could be a western liver enzyme variant that caused these acute toxic reactions. Whatever the cause, the result of these cases, and several other side effects from herbs used for sleep problems, had led to a severe clampdown on what was allowed, with some herbs and herb mixes being banned outright and others having their use severely restricted. The result meant that Chinese herbal medicine was much safer now but, in some cases, also much less potent and it followed on that they were also not so effective. So that was why they became less fashionable, in eczema at least.

Jo sat back and thought about this and what it meant in relation to her patient, Timothy Lockwood.

She didn't believe for one moment that the fact that his eczema cleared up whilst he was in Hong Kong and his parents would have easy access to herbal remedies that were banned in Europe was a coincidence. Jo looked at the carriage clock on her mantelpiece. It was eight o'clock and, it seemed to her, as good a time as any to visit the Lockwoods.

There were few lights on when Jo drove into the gravel driveway and parked behind one of the two cars already there.

'Good,' she thought, 'they must both be in.' And she rang the bell quickly, not giving herself a chance to change her mind.

The door was opened by Mrs Lockwood, looking rather bleary eyed and dishevelled, a large glass of wine in her hand as usual.

"Oh, it's you." It didn't seem to occur to her that it was strange a doctor visiting late at night without having been called and she held the door open wide for Jo to come in.

Philip Lockwood was in the living room, a half-empty whisky bottle open in front of him. They had clearly been drinking for quite some time.

Mrs Lockwood flopped into an armchair and indicated vaguely for Jo to follow suit.

"Would you like a drink?" His voice was slightly slurred but, thankfully, he still seemed to be in control.

"No thank you, I wanted to ask you some questions about Timothy, if that's okay?"

"Fire away, if you really think it will help."

Mrs Lockwood hiccupped and took another sip of her drink.

"They said he probably wasn't going to make it," she explained with a sniff. "Can't find him a new liver in time they said, as his own one's stopped working pretty much completely. They'll try but -"

"I'm sorry to hear that, Mrs Lockwood," Jo turned to her husband, "and Mr Lockwood, but what I wanted to ask about was Timothy's eczema."

"Didn't you hear what my wife just said, Dr Hughes?" Philip Lockwood was at that slightly belligerent stage of drunkenness that warned Jo that she would have to tread carefully, "Timothy is dying, as good as dead already, and you're worrying about his eczema? Believe me, it's not going to be a problem once he's been cremated."

Mrs Lockwood began to quietly cry.

"Pull yourself together for God's sake, Victoria." Her husband was less than sympathetic with her and then turned to Jo. "This isn't exactly helping, you know."

Jo bit back a retort that it was his attitude that was causing most of the problem, and tried to be more diplomatic.

"I understand, Mr Lockwood, but bear with me a moment, it honestly might help." She took a deep breath and started again. "Now, Timothy had really bad eczema and all the conventional treatments didn't seem to work, right?"

"It was awful." Mrs Lockwood fished a tissue out of her sleeve and wiped her nose. "He had these red scaly patches all over. He was teased terribly at school."

Philip Lockwood poured himself some more whisky, sighed and

looked at his watch pointedly. Jo ignored him.

"But it cleared up when you went to Hong Kong?"

"Yes, we went to a lot of doctors -"

"The best in the world. Cost a lot but they found it, the treatment that worked." Philip Lockwood cut in. "You should have seen him before, covered in all these oozing scabs, he was disgusting, I couldn't bear to be seen with him."

"You never were seen with him. Wouldn't have let him out of the house if you'd had your way."

"And who could blame me?"

"And what treatment was it? The one that worked?" Jo tried to stop the bickering.

"A herbal tea," Mrs Lockwood carried on, "tasted disgusting but it was like a miracle."

"And is he still using it?"

Even though Jo was addressing her remarks to Mrs Lockwood she could feel the husband tense at this question.

"Oh no, we stopped it once we left Hong Kong. The doctor there said he'd been on it long enough but we could have it again if Tim really needed it, once he'd had a break. But the eczema didn't come back. He'd been cured."

"He didn't give you a supply to bring back here with you?" Jo was puzzled

"No. But I was up in London and took the prescription into a shop in Chinatown, I thought I'd get some just in case, but they said they couldn't fill it, something about some of the ingredients not being allowed in this country."

"So you knew he couldn't take it over here?"

"Stupid red tape. Just because it comes from outside the E.C. or something like that. No real scientific reason not to allow it here, just bureaucracy."

Philip Lockwood gave her a look that challenged her to disagree, so she did.

"Actually, some Chinese herbal medicines were banned in this country a few years ago because of toxic side effects. Particularly liver toxicity in eczema remedies."

Victoria Lockwood looked closely at Jo, trying to focus her befuddled mind and work through the meaning of what she had just said.

"What rubbish." Philip Lockwood was less slow to see where she was heading. "It's just a few herbs."

"Deadly nightshade is just a herb, Mr Lockwood, belladonna, hemlock, strychnine: just a few herbs. That's why we insist on everything being tested. To make sure that it is safe."

"Yes but-" he was about to bluster but his wife cut in this time.

"Does it matter, anyway? Tim hasn't taken the tea since we left Hong Kong so, if it was the herbs that caused it, his illness, why did it take so long?"

Jo looked at Philip Lockwood and said nothing. The silence stretched on with Mrs Lockwood looking from one to the other until the penny dropped.

"He's still taking it? Philip?"

Philip said nothing.

"His night time drink. He always makes his own night time drink." Her voice was rising in volume and tone as she got into her stride. "You've been sending him the medicine and he's still taking it? Even when the doctor over there said not for more than six months? Philip, how could you?" She launched herself at her husband, fists flailing at his chest, her glass of wine, his whisky and the bottle all sent flying. She was shouting now, almost screaming at him.

"You've killed him, you've killed my son."

Jo pulled Mrs Lockwood back and held her as she sobbed, helping her back into her chair.

"There, there, now. It may be okay, if he stops taking it. His liver may recover." She glared at Philip. "I hope he's not got it with him in hospital or that, if he has, he can't make it for himself in there."

Philip Lockwood continued to say nothing.

"Where is it? What have you done with the tea?"

"I didn't know. I swear."

"Where is the tea?" Jo was not going to let him off the hook. "You can't seriously prefer your son to be dead than have eczema?"

Philip Lockwood seemed to sag as the full enormity of his actions began to get through.

"I made some up and put it in a drinks bottle for him, but he's so sick now, he's probably not drinking it anyway."

"Well, you'd better ring the hospital right now." Jo was tight lipped with anger. "And tell them exactly what you've done, Mr Lockwood, and you'd better hope and pray that the liver damage is not irreversible. If your son dies I'll make sure the coroner knows exactly why he did. He died because you couldn't bear to be seen with a scabby son."

Philip Lockwood looked as if he was about to argue but Jo was having none of it.

"Call the hospital, now!"

Obediently, he reached for the phone.

32

First thing the next morning, Jo called the liver unit at Kings College Hospital and spoke to the ward sister. Tim had lapsed into a coma, but she confirmed that Mr Lockwood had confessed to having been dosing his son with herbal tea and that the tea had been sent for analysis, although the mother had also given them the prescription, as written by the Chinese Doctor as well. It certainly contained some herbs that had been withdrawn from use. However, they weren't hopeful that the liver would recover because even though, according to Philip Lockwood, Tim hadn't had any of the tea for several days already, his condition was still deteriorating. It was the consultant's opinion that it was too late to save him.

Jo put down the receiver and closed her eyes. It was a real blow that the hospital didn't think Timothy was going to pull through. Overnight she had managed to convince herself that he would get better. If only she had realised the problem earlier. Maybe if -

"Looks like you are in urgent need of some chocolate." Linda interrupted her thoughts and Jo opened her eyes to see her holding out the biscuit tin.

"Somehow I don't think that's the answer."

"No but even if it doesn't help, it doesn't hurt, either."

Jo took a biscuit and Linda put down the tin and sat next to her.

"It's not your fault, Jo."

"Isn't it?" Jo was feeling really miserable. "I'm beginning to think Hugh is right. By trying to do two jobs, I'm not giving either one the time and commitment they need."

"How would you being a full time GP have helped the boy?"

"I would have spent more time trying to work out what was wrong with him and maybe I would have come to the right diagnosis earlier, in time to save him."

"And some GPs would have never bothered to look for the cause once they'd referred him on and others could have spent from now until next year checking out the internet or their text books and still never got there."

"I know, but I," she jabbed a finger at her own chest to emphasise her point, "I would have got there earlier if I hadn't been distracted by other things and that's what's important. I know I failed Timothy because of my other work and that's what I have to live with."

There wasn't really anything else Linda could say to make it better so she withdrew and let Jo sit there feeling guilty. The office phone was constantly ringing with people all trying to be fitted in to morning surgery or asking for visits, and the post had arrived and needed sorting. Life had to go on, no matter what: there would always be more patients needing help and she knew that Jo would snap out of it as soon as she was faced by another sick child, or adult, who needed her attention.

"Seaview Surgery, can I help you?" Linda asked into the phone, and listened to the person on the other end for a moment. "Are you one of her patients?" She looked across at Jo still staring at the wall, lost in her misery. "Okay, I'll put you through to her, Mrs Hill."

Jo snapped out of her reverie as the phone extension beside her began to ring and she picked it up. Tim, whilst not forgotten, was already on the backburner. Linda smiled. Jo would be fine.

"Dr Hughes. Oh, hello, Mrs Hill, any news of Angie?" she paused to listen to the woman on the other end, "Really? That is good news, you must be delighted. Have you let the police know? You have? Okay. Has she said what happened? No? Well, I'll pop in and see her later, see how she is, if that's all right. Thank you for letting me know." She put the phone down and looked at Linda with a grin.

"Angel Stubbins, the prostitute that went missing a couple of days ago, has turned up at home. She's a little confused but alive and well."

Jo knew her way up to the flat now and, as she got to the top of the stairs, the door was already open and she could hear the steady clump and thud of old Mrs Hill walking slowly back to the overheated living room using her Zimmer frame.

Angel was sitting in the arm chair looking half asleep and barely glanced up as Jo come into the room.

"Hello, Angel, how are you feeling?"

She just grunted in reply.

"You had us worried for a while there."

"Needn't have been," she muttered, apparently unimpressed.

"I'll make some tea." Mrs Hill clattered off towards the kitchen, leaving them alone.

Jo sat in the chair next to Angel and looked closely at the girl. Her eyes seemed even more vacant than was normal for Angel and she was definitely drowsy.

"Have you taken anything, Angel? Any drugs?"

"I don't do drugs. Never."

"But this time, to help you through, did you take anything?"

"Just some pills Tomas gave me. Nothing heavy."

"What were they like?"

"Small. White, I think. Dunno what they were, can't remember."

"You must be able to remember something."

Angel thought for a moment and then shook her head.

"It's all a blur, I took the pills and then…" She shrugged. "Can't remember anything, until I got out of the car, or taxi I think it was, outside here."

They sat in silence for a moment as Jo digested this news. She suspected that Angel had been given a strong benzodiazepine, maybe Flunitrazepam, also known as Rohypnol or Roofies, the date rape drug, to relax her and, as far as Tomas was concerned, they had the added benefit of inducing amnesia, at least partially.

"Do you feel sore, anywhere?"

"Skin feels like it's been scrubbed raw and," Angel looked embarrassed, "a bit bruised, down below, so I guess I had a good night."

"Nights." Jo corrected her. "You've been gone two days, Angel."

"So nan said. I didn't know it was for that long. Wouldn't've done it, if I'd known. 'Cos of nan being on her own, like."

"They must have given you several doses of pills during that time, to keep you sedated. Can you remember nothing at all?"

The effort of trying was written all over Angel's face as she did her best to recall something, anything, for Jo if not for herself.

"There's bits. All hazy. I remember this old bloke being there and Tomas, and someone else, I'm sure, but -" She looked apologetically at Jo, "Nothing much."

"The police need to know what -"

"No way! Tomas would kill me."

"He gave you drugs, Angel, the police need to be involved."

"I took them pills, okay, he didn't force me or nothing and he said they weren't even illegal."

Jo doubted that was true; they might be drugs that were available on prescription but trafficking in them or giving them to people for whom they had not been legally prescribed was still against the law.

"Look, Angel, we really ought to treat this as rape, you know, as you were clearly not in a condition to give consent, but if we don't know what happened…?"

"S'not rape, Doc," Angel reassured her, "I went there knowing it was going to be sex, and he paid me. Five hundred. Said that was just a start, that there could be more later too, so I don't want the police involved, right?"

Jo dreaded to think what might make a man like Tomas hand out five hundred pounds and promise more and why he felt he had to keep Angel drugged up so that she would probably never fully remember what she had done and what it was that made Ellie take the overdose. Had she known what was in store? Or was it just the anticipation of what it might be that made her take that risk? Jo sighed; in reality, she knew Angel was right, the police would do nothing. Could do nothing. She might not have gone in there with her eyes wide open but it did at least look like she had got off reasonably lightly, certainly a better result than Jo had expected, anyway.

"Sometimes, days or even weeks later, when the drugs wear off, you get flashbacks, remember bits of what happened. If you remember something and you want to talk, just call, okay?"

Angel nodded and Jo was pretty sure she'd heard but whether or not she'd remember was another question entirely.

"And I think we had better run a full screen. Check you out for all the usual STDs, and you will also need follow up, okay?" Jo was all business now. "If you can't remember what happened you certainly can't remember if you used protection, can you?"

She knew she shouldn't be here, standing outside Jonathan's home, it was the sort of thing that the worst bunny boilers did in films. It hadn't been hard finding out where he lived- if it had meant having to break into personnel and steal his records she wouldn't be here but she found the address on the electoral roll in the library. As simple as that. Jo had to see him, tell him what she thought of him. She could have accosted him at the hospital but the thought of a scene, in front of people she might have to work with again, would be far too embarrassing. She just wanted to say a few choice words and go, although she rather hoped that his wife would be there to hear it and, as there were two cars parked outside the elegant Victorian home, it looked like she might be in luck. Jo took a deep breath and pressed the doorbell. After a few moments, during which Jo began to change her mind and wondered if she could do a runner, the door opened and Jonathan stood there, expression changing from mild irritation to fury very quickly.

"What in God's name are you doing here?" he hissed.

"Who is it?" a voice asked from inside the house.

"Just someone from work," he called back inside, before pulling the door closed behind him and taking a step towards Jo.

"Go away, for Christ's sake."

Jo stood her ground.

"I wanted to tell you just what a sad, despicable excuse for a human being you are. A two-faced, violent, arrogant, bastard." Even Jo had to admit that bad language had its place and, mild as her language would seem to many, she could feel it help release her anger and let it go. "You led me on, letting me believe you were single -"

"Are you trying to say you didn't know I was married?"

"I don't go out with married men and you didn't exactly go out of your way to make the position clear, quite the opposite in fact."

"It's never polite to mention the wife to the mistress."

Jo flinched at hearing herself described as a mistress. It was an almost physical slap in the face. She would never allow herself to be one, not knowingly.

"Well, excuse me for not knowing the etiquette in extra-marital affairs, it is not a situation I've been in before."

"Don't tell me you actually thought our little fling was serious?" Jo flushed and he laughed at her. "You did, didn't you? You probably even had visions of white weddings and heard the patter of tiny feet. God, you're pathetic."

He hadn't noticed the door behind him open as he spoke and Jo was delighted to see the hard-faced woman behind him was not happy, not happy at all. Suddenly Jonathan realised that Jo was looking over his shoulder, or perhaps he had felt the sudden drop in temperature as the ice queen came out of the house, but he turned round and visibly paled.

"I'm sorry, dear, let me introduce you to Dr Hughes, from the hospital, she was just asking advice -"

"Get rid of the whore and come inside, Jonathan," was all she said before going back inside, but the look of disgust she gave her husband and the cringing fear on his face was a joy for Jo to behold.

"You'd better do as your beloved wife tells you," Jo said and walked back to her car smiling to herself. They deserved each other and she sincerely hoped that they would both be truly miserable together but now she felt she could move on. Jonathan was history.

Her feeling of elation at causing a certain amount of friction in Jonathan's marriage didn't last long. He might be in the dog house for a month or two, but she had no illusions; he would be out and about, having affairs again before too long. His wife probably knew that too. After a busy evening surgery, and having heard that there was no change in Timothy's condition, Jo decided the only way to lift her looming depression was exercise. She rang Kate, and after much cajoling and promises of a decent dinner afterwards, managed to persuade her friend that it really was a good idea to meet at the gym. Jo knew she herself hadn't been all that regularly, only once in the last couple of weeks but, judging by the fact that Kate didn't seem to remember how to sign in, or even where to find the changing rooms, Jo thought it must have been considerably longer since she last went.

The gym echoed with the noise of metal weights crashing against metal rests, the grunts of the more serious body builders and fitness fanatics and Kate moaning about how tired she felt as she ambled into the cardio section behind her. The air-conditioning was set low, causing goose bumps on Jo's arms as soon as she stepped out of the changing room in her T-shirt and joggers, but she knew it was only going to be for a short time; she expected to fully warm up in a matter of minutes so she tried to position herself as close as possible to one of the vents for maximum cooling effect.

After twenty minutes on the cross-trainer, Jo used some free weights and then moved onto the rowing machine. She noticed that Kate seemed to have disappeared; she certainly wasn't in the cardio section. Jo looked round and quickly spotted her, chatting to one of the fitness instructors. One of the young, male fitness instructors. He didn't look much over twenty one and was busy apparently showing her how to use one of the weight machines, but Kate wasn't looking at the machine and neither was he much. Jo smiled, that was so like Kate: Jo would leave the gym exhausted but virtuous and Kate would leave with a date.

After an hour, Jo decided she had tortured her body enough and she went back to the changing rooms to shower. Kate was already in the crowded locker room, drying off her voluptuous naked body with a lack of self-consciousness that Jo had never managed to achieve. She always used the curtained-off changing cubicles, or wrapped her body in a towel as she awkwardly pulled clothes on or off, even though her figure was nothing to be ashamed of. There was no way she could be like Kate, who seemed to have no qualms about walking around the room completely starkers and often teased Jo about being a prude.

"Go on, strip off. Let everyone look at you. If I had a body like yours I'd want everyone to see it and weep," Kate would tell her, but Jo just couldn't bring herself to do it.

Jo was still dressing after her shower when Kate was ready to go.

"I'll meet you in the bar next door," she called as she hurried out, clearly having arranged to meet somebody and leaving Jo to worry about playing gooseberry for the rest of the evening. She took her time dressing, to give Kate a bit of a start, and decided that if it was clear her friend was interested in the man- and when was she not?- she would politely make her excuses, plead work pressures or some such, and beat a hasty retreat. However, when she got to the bar, Kate was there, nursing a pint and a half-eaten packet of crisps, on her own.

"What's happened to him, then? Blown him out already?" she asked.

"Working. He joined me for his fifteen minute break but he doesn't finish until ten and then he's going to take me for an Indian. So," she looked at her watch, "you've got to keep me company for another hour and a half. What are you drinking?"

"What about food for me? I can't drink for an hour and a half and not eat, and I'm certainly not going to go with you for an Indian meal at that time of night. I wouldn't get a wink of sleep."

"One: you weren't invited anyway."

"Charming." Jo pretended to be hurt.

"And two: I certainly hope I don't get a wink of sleep." Kate grinned and Jo couldn't help laughing.

"You are such a -"

"Slut." Kate finished for her. "But you love me really." Kate grabbed a menu from the bar and passed it to Jo. "If you're starving they do at least do food here and I promise not to pick at your plate, well, maybe a bit but that rather depends on what you choose." Kate leant over and peered at the menu as Jo read it. The girl behind the bar came over, expectantly.

"I think I'll have the chicken fajitas with salad but hold the spicy potato wedges." Jo decided.

"Don't you dare!" Kate interjected and turned to the barmaid. "Make it a large portion of wedges, I'm starving, and how about a drink?" she asked Jo.

"Fizzy mineral water with a slice of lime." Jo told the girl. "I'm driving" she added as Kate looked aghast.

"You are way too healthy, you know."

"I'm a doctor, I have to lead by example."

"Quick! I need a doctor who smokes, drinks and is morbidly obese."

Jo laughed, although she could think of quite a few colleagues who would qualify.

"Did you really go to that slime-ball's house and give him what for?" Kate asked.

"Yes, although you probably wouldn't rate it as a what for, just a bit of a telling off. Still, it made me feel better, particularly the look on his wife's face when she saw me."

"I'll bet. I hope she makes his life hell."

"So do I. He certainly wouldn't want to risk losing all the status and money she brings to their marriage." Jo's drink had arrived so they clinked glasses and she spent a moment or two savouring the thought of Jonathan being made to beg forgiveness.

Once Jo's meal arrived, they talked of Angel's reappearance, safe, if not totally sound, and what might have happened to her, and of Timothy's chances but, whether it was Kate's cheerful common sense, or the endorphins released from exercising, Jo no longer felt quite so down about life.

"I'd hazard a guess that it's not been the best week of your life, what with that bastard Kane and everything." Kate spoke between mouthfuls of slightly soggy, and not very spicy, potato wedges.

"That is an understatement." Jo conceded.

"Have you heard anything more about the murders?"

"Not really. Obviously they know that Jimmy Allen can't have done them, seeing as he was in custody, but their new obsession seems to be Jonathan and I just can't see it."

"Be nice to see him banged up for life, though, wouldn't it?"

"Yes, but it won't stick I'm sure. I know they're going through all the CCTV footage: they had been concentrating on Krissy's usual haunts around town but they've collected everything from the Old Town as well, now that they know she was there, although a lot of it has gone, been recorded over."

"What about on the Priory estate? They must have cameras there."

"All moved to watch over where the renovation is taking place to catch people walking off with the building materials. So nothing covering Krissy's block or her way into the estate."

"There are loads of cameras around town, if they're going to cover the other girl, what's her name? Denise? Her route back from the karaoke, and the hospital as well, they've got tons of cameras there, they must have teams of people checking the footage."

"No, that's the problem, I think they've left most of it for poor Jayne Hales. She's been seconded into the team to help and has been given all the boring jobs. She'll be completely boss eyed at this rate. It will take her months to get through the relevant tapes, by which time the real killer will have disappeared."

"It's spooky, isn't it? To think that somewhere there's a CCTV camera watching you."

Jo pushed away her plate and let Kate finish the remaining wedges, which were now tepid as well as soggy.

"But they are what catches criminals, and will probably be what catches this man, rather than old-fashioned detecting. And if they concentrate on the hospital pictures they should catch him soon." Jo wasn't sure who she was trying to convince, Kate or herself.

"Question is, how many more girls will he have killed in the meantime?"

And that, Jo knew, really was the issue.

33

It was late Saturday morning, while Jo was busy sorting out her clothes cupboard, doing anything she could think of to take her mind off the sad state of her love life, that Angel called. She sounded distressed so Jo left the half-filled bag of clothes destined for the charity shop sitting in the middle of her bedroom floor and hurried over to see her.

Angel hadn't wanted Jo to come to her nan's flat so they met at the surgery. It felt strangely lifeless, eerie almost, with an empty waiting room and no telephones ringing but at least Jo would be able to talk to Angel uninterrupted for as long as she needed.

"I keep getting these, like, pictures, in my head. Flashes. All in bits." Angel was pale and frightened, her hair still damp from washing, her face scrubbed clean of make up. She looked much younger, fresher, even though there was no way she could ever be described as a looker. She was fidgeting with her bag, reaching for a cigarette and then putting it back constantly. Her eyes were flickering from one place to another. Never resting in one place. "They make me feel all… anxious… even though I can't really tell what they are, what's happening."

"This is all part of coming down after the drugs, Angel. You will get anxiety and later, maybe, a bit depressed but it will pass. If you want, I can give you a prescription, something to help you through, take the edge off it."

Angel nodded and then thought some more as Jo wrote out a prescription on the pad she used for her role as a police surgeon, making a mental note to let Angel's regular doctor know about this, just in case he prescribed something for her as well.

"Will it make it last longer?"

"Shouldn't do. Look, here's the prescription: use it if you need to but don't if you think you can manage on your own. Is that all right?"

Angel nodded, relieved to have the reassurance of something to help if it got too much for her.

"These visions, flashes, can you tell me anything about them?"

"Not much. I just know they make me feel real anxious when I get them. You know?" She hesitated and Jo kept quiet, sure that Angel could remember more than she was saying.

"It's just, like, a smell, then my heart starts racing, my belly sort of wobbles inside and I sweat, but I don't remember why," she finally continued, but she stared at her toes as she said it and Jo knew she was lying: not about how she felt, that rang true, but that she didn't know why. There was something that Angel was hiding, probably because she was ashamed of it, Jo thought.

"I'm not the police, Angel, and if you don't want me to go to them I won't, unless it involves children, or -"

"It weren't kids." Angel cut in quickly, which was good because Jo didn't actually want to start listing sexual deviances that she considered beyond the pale, there were so many. "It was horrible, filthy, disgusting and I won't be doing it again, no matter how much money he offers me." Her vehemence startled Jo, it was so out of character for her. Whatever had happened, it had clearly crossed even Angel's boundaries.

Jo went and opened the window, wide.

"Come and sit by the window and have a cigarette, Angel, if it will make you feel better." Jo had never, ever, let anyone smoke in her room before and it was very strictly against the rules, but she desperately wanted to get Angel talking, to find out exactly what the girl had been forced to do; she just hoped she didn't set off the smoke alarms in the process.

Angel lit up and blew the smoke out of the open window.

"I don't feel clean." Angel said quietly.

"Lots of rape victims feel that way."

"It wasn't rape, though, was it? I thought I knew what I was doing."

"Did you? I don't think so. You wouldn't have consented if you'd known what it was, would you?"

Angel sat quietly for a minute.

"I've heard about it, you know, and it takes all sorts, I suppose."

"Takes all sorts of what?" Jo still didn't understand what she was getting at.

"People." Angel explained patiently. "I mean, I've been around, on the game, for a couple of years now and I've heard of S&M and people who like sex with kids, animals, dead bodies. There's some as like to dress up as babies and shit theirselves, I even had a punter who liked me to pee on him, but this was the other."

"This what?" Jo was leaning forward, but then the penny dropped. "Faeces, you mean?"

Angel looked slightly confused.

"You know, poo," she said. "I can remember this really wrinkly old bloke, just wiping his shit all over me. It's the smell as keeps coming back. I was covered in it and so was he and then, when he finally got it up, he had sex with me."

Jo almost gagged, it was a repulsive thought. As Angel had said, it takes all sorts.

"Okay. Well, um," Jo was at a complete loss for words because of the horrible pictures she couldn't get out of her mind.

"Could I have caught anything bad from it, do you think? An infection?"

Angel's medical question helped Jo put the images out of her head and she kicked into doctor mode with relief.

"We ought to do a few more tests. The swabs I took should show if there are any, um, unusual infections in your vagina, but we ought to test your blood for Hep A."

"I thought you did that with the AIDS test?"

"No, that was Hep B, but Hep A is also carried in faeces." Jo got out a blood test form and was all business now.

"I'm still not going to the police, though, I wouldn't want to tell them lot what happened." Angel said as she took the test form.

"No, well, I don't blame you." Jo admitted, "Besides, I'm not actually sure it's illegal."

Angel left soon after, a little happier for having told someone what had happened. After wafting out what was left of the smoke, Jo closed the window and liberally sprayed her consulting room with the air freshener. By Monday, she hoped, her room wouldn't smell quite so much like an ashtray whilst she told her patients to stop smoking.

She set off home, intending to finish clearing out her cupboards before scrubbing her flat from top to bottom and probably herself as well. No wonder Angel looked like she had spent most of the day in the shower. Jo felt much like doing the same herself.

As Jo turned the Audi into her lane and approached the flat she could see her mother's car parked outside.

"Oh, Lord," she thought. "That's all I need." The cleaning would have to wait.

"But darling, it's just not good enough." Jo gritted her teeth and tried not to let her mother get to her.

"What isn't?" she asked, irritated as usual by the tone as much as the content, and the disappointment in her daughter it expressed so clearly.

"I feel as though you and your father have conspired to keep me in the dark."

"Don't be ridiculous, Ma, "Jo responded, although this was exactly what they had tried to do, "we just didn't want to worry you, that's all."

"You go out with a serial killer and you don't want to worry me?"

"I didn't know he was when I went out with him and anyway I don't believe he is guilty of that. Just of being -"

"Married and clearly sex mad, assuming the papers have got it right," her mother finished for her. "Honestly, Jocasta, you are so naïve. You always think the best of people. Take that wretched boy, what was his name? The one that said he was a pilot, but forgot to mention that it was with some obscure African airline because he couldn't get work anywhere else."

"Lee, and that was when I was in medical school." And he had been such fun. And so good-looking. And… Jo sighed, and went over to the fridge. There was no point trying to deflect this conversation, she knew, so she might at least be fortified for it.

"Glass of wine, Ma? I'm afraid I haven't got any G and T." It was going to be a long session. Jo knew that her mother was about to go through every single boyfriend Jo had ever had and list their faults because it was what she always did but somehow Jo didn't think she was ever going to top the latest failure. It was going to take something really quite spectacular to beat Jonathan. On a scale of one to ten of terrible mistakes for lovers, he had to score eight and a half or nine, at least, and a solid ten if he did turn out to be a serial killer, Jo decided.

It was mid-afternoon before Jo finally managed to get rid of her mother and went back to sorting out her room. She looked at the flimsy low-cut sequin covered top that she had worn on her trawl of the singles bars and was about to consign it to the charity bag when she stopped.

It was a Saturday night and she didn't have a date.

Nothing new there, she thought.

Kate was out with her new man, the fitness instructor. Jo was going to spend a night in, with just a baked potato and the television for company. She was a sad excuse for a human being who would die alone and single if she didn't do something desperate.

But just how desperate was she?

34

The Adelaide, last resort of the desperate, had an entrance that looked as though it was quite used to disgruntled customers kicking it on the way out. Jo assumed it was on the way out, because she couldn't imagine that anyone would be mad enough to try and kick their way in to the place.

Inside, the actual club was down a steep flight of stairs, and was dimly lit, presumably so that the customers didn't notice that it was in dire need of refurbishment or, failing that, at least a good clean. Jo approached the bar, perched on a distressingly sticky, vinyl-covered bar stool and surveyed the scene. It was still quite early, only eleven o'clock, and not many people had reached the level of frustration needed to end up here.

In planning how to play the evening, Jo had decided that getting there early would be a good idea and that had been pretty much the extent of her strategy. She had little idea of what she was going to do, just that she wanted to check the place out before many people had arrived and have a chat with the staff about last Saturday night when the latest victim, Caro the nurse and her friends, had come to the club. Eventually, having waited at the bar for what seemed like an eternity, a bored young man dressed in low slung jeans and a T-shirt declaring that he was a sex god in training came over to ask for her order.

Jo asked for a white wine and soda and attempted to engage the barman in conversation as he mixed her drink.

"Is it always this quiet in here?"

"'Til late, yeah."

"How late?"

"Late late, when everywhere else is closed, right?"

"Get a lot of nurses in, do you?"

He looked at her suspiciously.

"I charge fifty quid for interviews."

"Nice try but I'm not a journalist."

"Gotta try, haven't you? Worked on the other three." He nodded his head towards two middle-aged-but-still-trying to-look-trendy men and a hard-faced woman dressed for a night on the town, each sitting on their own and watching her intently. Jo thought she recognised the woman from the local television news. It seemed as though everyone had had the same idea as her.

She turned back to the bar as the barman leant forward.

"We get all sorts from the hospital in here, lab techs, nurses, porters. They all smoke like chimneys and boy, can they drink. And ready to jump anything with a pulse, too. Must be something about working with sick people, right?"

"And last week?" Jo persisted.

"Yeah, there was a group of four nurses in with the one that got killed. They were here about this time and they left about an hour or so later, said it was 'cos they had to be at work early but that's never stopped them before."

"So why do you think they left?"

He shrugged again.

"Dunno. Maybe there wasn't anyone interesting in, it was quiet that night, or maybe they were being pestered by a bloke they didn't like, a groper or something, but they didn't say nothing to me or the bouncer, I asked." He caught Jo's look of distaste. "Hey, it happens, all right?"

He wandered off to serve an overweight wannabe lothario who looked as though he had already had too much to drink and Jo took the opportunity to study the club. There seemed to be a lot of marks on the deep puce walls where notices had been put up and either taken down or moved elsewhere. The few notices that remained were so badly scuffed and, in some instances, graffiti covered, that it was hard to read what they said anyway. Ideally, she wanted to find herself a secluded corner where she would be able to sit out of sight and watch people come and go while, hopefully, remaining unmolested herself. One look inside the club had told her that she wouldn't be finding her soul mate and life partner in here but she would certainly find a wide variety of bacteria. All she was hoping for throughout the rest of the evening was to see if she could spot any likely regulars who might have been in last week and who might have seen what made the nurses leave early. She was already getting a picture of the sort of person who went to the club, although that impression might improve when

282

a few more people arrived; it certainly couldn't get any worse. She was pretty sure that her theory that whoever killed Caro had followed her back to the hospital from here held up: something had happened to spook the girl into leaving prematurely and it seemed too much of a coincidence that she should encounter a serious groper here and then run into a serial killer elsewhere, all in one night. But what did Jo know? Maybe there were millions of perverts out there, just waiting to pounce.

She spotted a table in a corner so dark she had to get quite close to be sure that no one was already sitting there and she surreptitiously gave the faux-leather banquette a quick wipe down with a tissue before sliding herself as far into the corner as possible. Taking a sip of her drink she settled back. She mustn't rush it, it was going to be a long night and she didn't want to have to make too many trips to the bar or the loo as both were the other side of the room and she would have to cross the currently empty dance floor in full, intensely scrutinising view of the other occupants of the club, to reach them.

The barman had been right when he said the place didn't get busy until everywhere else had closed. Jo glanced at her watch for the tenth time and was despondent to see that it was only just gone midnight. The club was still half empty; other than the journalists who clearly thought she was one of them, there were just a few sad singles peering dejectedly round, waiting for someone interesting to come in. Jo had tried talking to the couple of them who had ventured over and who looked as if they might be regulars but neither had been in last week. Both had been delighted to talk to her, and disappointed once she made it clear that she wasn't interested in them personally, but neither had been overly persistent or had tried to grope her. Clearly used to rejection by now, they had settled resignedly back on their stools and left her alone. Her fingers tapped against her glass and her head thumped in time to the music that was turned up way too high considering that there was no crush of bodies to soak it up. She was so tired she could barely keep her eyes open. How much longer could she stand it? At last the door burst open and a mixed group of thirty-somethings crashed into the room, excited to be in such a notorious club, laughing loudly and acting as if they owned the place. They were soon followed by a younger group of boys on a grab-a-granny night, a couple of women in their forties who might just do for them and a strangely mixed group intent on carrying on partying, or at least pouring as much alcohol down their throats as was humanly possible, no matter what.

The dance floor was soon full, and the noise level increased by an alarming number of decibels as the DJ pumped up the volume. If Jo's head had been hurting before, it now felt like it was going to explode. There was no way she was going to be able to talk to anyone over the music and she was about to write the evening off to experience and leave when one of the young lads came and plonked himself down beside her. Jo realised a bit late the down side of sitting in the corner on a banquette, namely that there was no way out if anyone sat next to you, not without climbing over them, anyway.

The lad looked as if he was barely out of school, with his spiky gelled hair and no-need-to-shave-yet look, and something about the way he kept glancing over at his mates at the bar told Jo that he had probably been dared to chat her up. She was not amused. She was not a granny.

"So what's your name then, love?" he bellowed.

"Emily." Jo replied. She had no intention of saying anything to this boy that might help him trace her later; a toyboy with a crush was the last thing she needed. "What's yours?"

"Paul." he replied and then looked round for inspiration as to what to say next. "Do you come here often?" was the best he could come up with, despite thinking hard.

"No, do you?" Jo was trying not to sound bored, just not very effectively.

"No. First time." he shouted and slid his arm along the back of the seat so that it was poised to drape over her shoulder. After a bit of long-distance encouragement from his friends he reached across and slipped his other hand onto her knee.

Jo picked it up and popped it back on his own leg.

"Excuse me." Her tone was distinctly icy. "I need the loo." There was an awkward shuffle as he had to get out of the way to let her out and she hurried across the packed dance floor, wanting to hold her hands up in the air in order not to touch anyone or anything too intimate, but restraining herself. Once she was safely in the ladies' room, she stood patiently in the queue and eavesdropped on the conversations of those in front of her.

She quickly realised that she should have been in the toilets the whole evening. Not only was it was quieter and certainly the best place to chat, or listen in on people who were chatting, despite being a little cramped it had the distinct advantage of being ladies only.

"She was always a bit of a slapper, that one. Surprised she pulled a doctor, though, even if she met him at work." an overweight and very under-dressed woman was saying to a skinny friend with a face like a plucked chicken.

"Yeah," her friend agreed. "You ever had a doctor?" she continued as Jo tried not to look as though she was listening to them. She was pretty sure they must be talking about the victim.

"Nah, his type don't come in here, I'd've thought, but I did have an X-ray bloke once. Nice bum, shame about the rest."

They laughed and moved forward as two women came out of the stalls, but continued their conversation from adjoining cubicles.

"I wouldn't want to shag a doctor, mind, it's like you don't know where their hands have been all day, do you?"

"You would've with him though, I heard he was a gynaecologist, you'd know exactly where they'd been, up some woman's fanny." There was some ribald laughter and Jo tried not to let her reaction to this coarse language show.

"You'd think it would be enough to put you off sex, wouldn't ya?"

"Nah, my Terry looks at them all day on the internet and he's still up for it."

"You lucky cow."

"Lucky? Have you seen my Terry?"

They came out still laughing.

"Did you know Caro?" Jo asked them, standing back to let the woman behind her go into the cubicle ahead of her. The fat one looked at her suspiciously for a moment.

"What's it to you?"

"I knew Caro from work." Jo half lied. "I just want to find out what happened to her. Did you see her last week?"

"Yeah, but she and her mates left early."

"Lucky for us." Her friend chipped in. "They always nick the good blokes, nurses do."

"Why did they leave, do you know?"

"Couple of them were really pissed." The skinny one was tweaking her rigid hair in the tiny mirror, whilst the fat one tried to see past to slap on more lipstick. Jo couldn't help but notice that neither had bothered to wash their hands.

"But they'd only just arrived."

"You must know what nurses are like if you work with them. Drinks are too expensive here, so they neck some supermarket vodka before coming out, only, like I say, a couple of them had overdone it. Even so, I think they might have stayed but that Caro had a go at some fat bloke who asked her to dance."

"Thought she was too good for him. Stuck up cow." The skinny one sniffed with disapproval, as if no one was too good for someone they met at the Adelaide.

"So she flounced out and her mates all followed."

"This bloke she had a go at, do you know him?"

They both shook their heads.

"Might've seen him here before but not to speak to."

"He knew her though, or claimed to, but she denied all knowledge, said she couldn't be expected to remember losers like him."

"And he left soon after they did, I remember," the skinny one added.

"Do you think it was him then? That killed her? Not the doctor?" The two women were clearly excited by the thought that they might have actually seen the killer.

"I don't know." Jo told them. "But it's possible, isn't it?"

When Jo came out of the ladies she had to restrain herself from punching the air in elation. At last! She had a lead. She would go to the hospital first thing tomorrow morning and find Claire Crehan. She needed to ask her if she knew who it was Caro had seen here at the club and, if Claire did, then she had to get her to tell Miller, if she hadn't already done so. It was quite possible that Miller knew all about the fat man and had discounted him as a suspect, or maybe he was just too obsessed by the thought that Jonathan was the killer to bother looking at anyone else. Jo suspected the latter. Either way, she needed to make sure he had found out who the man was and that he had checked him out thoroughly but equally, she didn't want to go to him herself and admit that she'd been out snooping again. She suspected he wouldn't be pleased. That's why she had to get Claire to do it.

As she made her way towards the door Jo's face dropped and the elation evaporated as she recognised Miller himself standing between her and the exit. She stopped dead in her tracks, trying to think what on earth she could do. He was the last person she wanted to see right now but she couldn't help giving him a second look all the same. He was casually dressed in black jeans, black T-shirt, and black jacket, bottle of Mexican lager, untouched, in his hand. There were no two ways about it, he looked good, and he was attracting a certain amount of interest amongst the ladies although he was acting as if he was completely unaware of their attention.

Why on earth did he have to be here? Now? He was almost certainly undercover, doing much the same as she had been, and if he saw her he was going to be very angry with her for getting in the way of his investigation again. Why, oh why, had she come? It had seemed like such a good idea at the time. And, in fact, it had been, she told herself, firmly. She had got some good information, hadn't she? All the same, she had to get out before he noticed her. She looked around for an escape route but there didn't seem to be one; the only way out involved passing right next to him to get to the main door. Jo turned to go back into the ladies' room, wondering how long she could feasibly stay in there. Maybe there was a way out from the back? A fire escape, perhaps? Surely there ought to be an emergency exit of some sort? As she hurried back towards the toilets, she felt someone grab her shoulder. She turned and found herself frowning straight into Miller's eyes. Miller's furious eyes.

"What the hell do you think you're doing?" he asked, shouting above the music.

"Going to the loo," she shouted back, as calmly as she could, given the noise.

"I think not. Outside. Now." And he pulled her firmly but gently towards the exit.

"I need my coat," she said, breaking free from his grasp and stopping at the cloakroom, seething. He had absolutely no right to treat her like this, as if she were one of his employees or a suspect. She was shaking with anger as she handed over her cloakroom ticket and waited for the girl to find her coat. When she located it at last, Jo grabbed it from her and was still pulling it on as she stormed out of the club.

Miller stood directly in front of her, forcing her to stop and look at him.

"So?" he asked belligerently.

"So what?" If he thought she was going to make it easy for him he was sadly mistaken.

"So what are you doing here?" Jo had finally managed to get her coat on and started to walk round Miller.

"I came out for a drink."

"Rubbish! You've been snooping again, like when you and your friend went to the karaoke evening." He was keeping pace with her, arguing as they walked briskly back towards the Old Town.

"There's no law against it."

"You're messing with things you know nothing about and interfering in my investigation."

"Really? Like your investigation is getting anywhere."

"And yours is?"

"Actually, yes." She couldn't keep the smugness from her voice and he knew she had something.

"What do you mean?" She had his interest now, no doubt about it.

"I just found out from one of women in there that Caro Sharpe had a confrontation with a man at the club on the night she died. A man who seemed to know her. And also that he left shortly after she and her friends did. Or did you already know that?"

Miller stopped walking and Jo turned and regarded him triumphantly. She had him there and she knew it: he hadn't known about the incident.

"No. I didn't know that, but I will look into it. You have my word on it."

"You'd better do that, Detective Inspector Miller, because I will be checking up on you, you have my word on that." She turned on her heel and stalked off, pleased with herself and with the fact that she had set him so completely and comprehensively back on his heels.

She wondered what he would do now. Would he follow her? Try and question her some more and get her descriptions of the women she spoke to? Or would he go back in and try and find them for himself? She didn't pause for one moment to find out, walking quickly away from him through the underpass and along the sea front without so much as a backwards glance. She couldn't hear his footsteps behind her so she assumed he had gone back into the club.

She slowed down a little as she walked passed the long-closed souvenir shops and cafes, letting her coat flap open despite the cool night air. After the heat and close atmosphere of the club it was nice to be out in the fresh, crisp ozone, warmed by the healthy glow of self-righteousness.

The Old Town was quiet; most people were safely tucked up in bed at this time of night but it wasn't until she hurried along George Street and the last of the drunken, late night revellers had disappeared that she began to feel a little uneasy. She felt a tingling at the back of her head, as if someone was watching her. She turned quickly but could see no one. Maybe it was Miller after all, making sure she went straight home and didn't visit any more night clubs. She hurried on. The feeling of being followed persisted. She hoped it was Miller. It was gone two in the morning, she was alone and she had been deliberately trying to look for a man who was a serial killer of lone women. Right now that didn't seem like it had been quite such a smart idea.

Jo turned right at the end of George Street, back to the sea front, thinking that she might be able to get a taxi from the rank there but it was empty. She looked up and down the main street and the promenade but there was no one in sight and no taxis around either. The deserted mini fairground was dark and the carousels and roller coasters looked vaguely sinister without their bright lights and loud music disturbing the peace.

Jo hurried along the front, towards the tall, dark shapes of the net sheds, silhouetted against the night sky. She wanted to get home as quickly as possible and there seemed little point sticking to the main roads when they were as quiet as the backstreets so she took the narrow stairway straight up the East Cliff. She would go the shortest possible route, through the twittens, to get to her home. To safety.

As she hurried up the steps she paused to catch her breath and then froze, hardly daring to breath. What was that? She was sure that she had heard something. She waited a moment, listening hard, but there was nothing now.

"Go away, I am quite capable of taking care of myself," she said clearly, half of her hoping that it was Miller seeing her safely home and that he would ignore her request to go away, the other half indignant that he would treat her as some sort of weak and vapid woman in need of seeing safely home. Who was she kidding? Right now she would be delighted to see him, even if she wouldn't necessarily show it.

She quickly ran up the next flight of steps and reached the road at the top. She looked along the street to the left and then back down the steps. There was no one visible but she could swear that she could hear footsteps some way behind her. She raced along the road and took the next short cut up towards her own lane and the safety of home, positive now that she could hear someone behind her. She was taking the steps two at a time, running along the roughly paved horizontal sections, hoping fervently that she knew the path well enough that she wouldn't trip on a forgotten step or miss a turning in the dark. She could hear that the footsteps were gaining on her, despite her almost headlong flight. Panicking, she ran on and, startled by a cat that jumped out of nowhere, caught her foot on a plant pot partially blocking the way, going sprawling and banging her knee and jarring her wrist as she fell. The cat had fled but the footsteps were louder, closer, accompanied by loud, wheezing breaths. The breaths of someone pretty unfit and unused to running uphill. Barely pausing, she sprang up and continued up the path at a run again. She was nearly there, nearly at the top where it opened out into her own lane, only a hundred yards from her front door and safety. She could still hear the heavy, laboured breathing behind her, but at a slightly greater distance; whoever was chasing her was finding it a struggle to keep up. She put in one last effort and broke out of the twitten and into the reassuring amber glow of a street light, gasping too loudly to hear if her follower was still close.

"You should go to the gym and get fit, Miller, then you'd be able to keep up." She shouted with the last of her breath and peered down the alley but could see no one in the shadows. She turned and was walking briskly towards her house, pulling her front door keys from her pocket at the same time.

"Are you all right?" Miller's voice shouted back at her from a distance.

She turned, relieved that her phantom, wheezing follower had been him after all but then dropped her keys in surprise. Miller was way down the far end of lane, running towards her. She looked at where the twitten opened out under the street light, where moments ago she had heard footsteps getting closer, almost on her, and the heavy breathing, so loud she half wondered if it was her own. It hadn't been him behind her, couldn't have been him, not if he had come up the road.

He reached her, barely out of breath, clearly fit. A worried expression on his face as he registered her muddy knees and how she held her injured arm against her body.

"Someone was following me. Through there," she said, looking at the narrow gap between the two houses. She was shaking, exhausted by her run up the steep hill and her heart was pounding, as much from the adrenaline released by her fear as from the exertion.

He went down the first couple of steps.

"Is there anyone there?" he called but there was no reply and Jo couldn't hear anything other than the slight echo as his voice bounced off the canyon-like walls of the alley.

"There's no one there now," he told her unnecessarily. "And it certainly wasn't me. I didn't think you'd be stupid enough to take the alleys, so I came up the main road."

Jo was far too frightened to take offence. Now that he said it, it did seem a bit stupid, more than a bit, in fact, and it wasn't even the first time she'd done something like that, either. Miller bent down and picked up her keys, took her firmly by her good elbow and walked her towards the front door of her house.

"There. Home safe." He had opened the door and was holding out her keys, looking at her with concern.

Probably wondering if she was going to come over all faint again, she thought.

Jo almost snatched the keys from him and stuck them straight in her pocket, trying to disguise the fact that her hands were shaking so badly that she was worried she might drop them again.

"Thank you," she said meekly, and went into the hallway before turning back. "Would you like a cup of coffee or something?" she asked, expecting him to refuse, to say he had to go back to the Adelaide, or home, or any other excuse he could come up with on the spur of the moment.

"Yes, that would be good. Thank you." She was too surprised to retract the invite and stepped back, allowing him to follow her into the communal hallway.

Jo wondered how on earth she got herself into these situations as she led the way up the two flights of stairs to her flat, and dug out her keys again to let him in. Why had he accepted? He clearly loathed her, she was nothing more than an irritant to him. So why subject himself to any more of her company than was strictly necessary?

It wasn't until they were both inside the flat that she remembered that she might have a slight problem with providing coffee. She switched on all the lights and closed the curtains, unable to resist a look in case there was anyone watching her or the flat but she couldn't see anyone. Only once the place was snug and secure did she go into the kitchen, anxious to keep busy, do anything to avoid dwelling on being followed home like that, stalked and spied on, beginning to see a pattern emerge. She filled the kettle, switched it on and then took a quick peek in the fridge. What a relief, there was a carton of milk. She gave it a shake and her heart sank. Yes, there was something in it but the contents didn't give a nice reassuring slosh as she shook it, there was a definite delay in the movement, a heaviness about it. She tried pouring a little into the sink and a bit of watery fluid came out before a lump clogged the spout. She wrinkled her nose in disgust at the rancid milk and turned to explain the situation to Miller, only to find him standing at the breakfast bar, watching her with an amused smile on his face. That was the down side of an open plan kitchen.

"I take it black," he said.

"Just as well," she admitted. She took two mugs from a cupboard and hesitated. "You don't take sugar, do you?"

"I can live without." She wished that she was more organised, more prepared for unplanned entertaining, or entertaining of any sort for that matter. The sad fact was that she hardly ever had anyone back at her flat except Kate and whenever she came round she always arrived with everything she thought she might want because she knew just how bad her friend was at shopping.

She put the cups on a tray and was about to carry it through to the living area when he came up behind her.

"Let me." He took the tray from her. "Your hands are shaking so much you are bound to spill it."

She swallowed the retort that came automatically to her lips because he was right, she was still feeling a bit shaky, so she followed him meekly through to the living room and settled herself on the sofa, slipping off her shoes and curling her legs up under her, as he carefully placed the tray on the coffee table.

"Have you got anything stronger? Brandy? Whisky?" he asked her.

She pointed to the cupboard where she kept her mother's gin, when she remembered to buy any. There was about an inch left in a quarter bottle of brandy left over from last Christmas and he brought it out.

"That's it, I'm afraid. I'm not really a spirit drinker."

"Well you are now." And he poured a healthy slug into her coffee before passing it back to her. She took it gingerly and cradled it in her hands.

"Are you warm enough?" He seemed concerned rather than irritated with her, confusing her once again. She wished that she could make this man out.

"I'm fine, well, better than I was, thanks," she reassured him. "It's just a bit of a shock to think that I was followed by someone. Other than you, that is."

He sat on the sofa, keeping a respectable distance between them, and sipped his coffee.

"I didn't see anyone follow you from the club, so we've no reason to think it's the killer."

"Oh great, it's just some other stray perv, that makes me feel much better."

He smiled.

"Now I know you're going to be all right." She gave him a quizzical look. "The smart alec comments are back," he explained.

She smiled back and closed her eyes, feeling the brandy begin to smooth down the rough edges of the night.

"Have you ever been to that sort of club before?" she asked him.

"No, not my kind of place at all," he told her.

"Me neither. There's an air of desperation around it, isn't there? All those sad lonely people, looking for someone, anyone more or less, to take home. Anything rather than spend another night alone. What they don't seem to realise though is that sometimes you're better off on your own."

"Not everyone's as bad as Jonathan Kane."

"Granted, it's just that right now it feels like I pick all the ones that are. They are all either bastards or married, or both." The brandy seemed to have gone straight to her head and she felt slightly woozy. She opened her eyes and he seemed closer than before, almost touching her and looking directly into her eyes. He had nice eyes, the brown irises flecked with amber, his pupils deep and large. In fact, he had a nice face, gentle and smooth, he must have shaved before coming out this evening and she could smell a lingering trace of his aftershave. His lip was no longer swollen and the split in it she had noticed at the hospital had healed to a scab. Almost without realising, as she stared at his face she was leaning slightly towards him, her shoulder touching his, tilting her head up, saying nothing, wanting him to kiss her. He seemed to be leaning closer to her, reciprocating but just before their lips met he caught himself and leant back, looking away. Breaking the moment. Jo sat bolt upright, mentally kicking herself. How could she set herself up for rejection again? She knew he barely tolerated her and, if he had seemed momentarily interested it was just because he was a man, and a man will always take advantage of a woman's weaker moments. Almost always. She could feel a flush of embarrassment rise on her neck.

"I'm sorry," she said.

"No. I'm flattered. It's just that," he hesitated for a moment, "I'm married."

"Oh." She inched away from him, clutching her coffee cup in front of her, cursing herself for being so stupid. "Long?" she finally spluttered. "Have you been married long?"

He stood up and went to the window, pulling the curtain aside and looking out; anything to increase the distance between them, she thought, sadly.

"Five years. We're trying for a baby."

"That's nice." She gave herself a mental shake. That was a pathetic reply, she thought. She had to pull herself together and think of something better to say.

"We've been trying for almost three years now," he continued.

"It can take a while, sometimes." That was good, she thought: when in doubt, go into your professional role, it was great for hiding behind, for concealing your feelings. If she was acting as his doctor she wouldn't feel like this, like she wanted him to hold her, kiss her, make her feel safe. "I can recommend a good fertility specialist if you need one."

He let the curtain go, apparently satisfied that there was no one out there but more likely feeling reassured that she wasn't about to get hysterical, and looked back at her, sitting rigidly upright on the sofa.

"It's not that that's the problem. Lizzie's bipolar. On lithium. She needs to stop taking it for three months before getting pregnant so that it's not in her system."

"She could try other medications. There are newer, less toxic ones."

"Lithium works best for her, sometimes in combination with other things, but they all have the same problem anyway, they are only ever slightly less toxic and she still ought to get off the drugs to get pregnant."

"She shouldn't take them during the pregnancy either."

He nodded.

"I know, but she hasn't even managed to go the three months without losing it mentally yet. I can't believe she would hold it together for another nine after that."

"A year off medication is a long time."

He nodded agreement.

"On average it only seems to take a couple of weeks before she starts getting manic. Just shopping crazily at first, I can cope with that, I'm used to taking all the stuff back, getting refunds, but then the anxiety kicks in, paranoia at times. She can get pretty violent." He touched his lip.

"It must be very hard." Kicking herself for having been so harsh, thinking that it had been a suspect who had hit him, when all along it had been his wife. He was a battered husband and she was a battered girlfriend - ironic really.

"I can cope with all that," he dismissed it all with a slight wave of his hand. "It's the depression I can't handle. When that kicks in, draping over her like a blanket, that's when I break. I can't see her like that, I can't. I love her so much."

He turned away from Jo and looked out of the window, pretending to check that there was no one out there again but she could tell he wasn't really looking at anything, just staring into the distance.

"So every time I'm the first one to crack, make her go back on her meds again, threaten to have her sectioned if she doesn't. Even though I've promised her I won't stop her, that I'll let her see it through this time. I can't do it. I never can,"

Jo stood and came across the room to him. Put her arms around him and held him, resting her head against his chest, wishing he hadn't told her all that, wishing that this was more than a comforting hug between friends. Eventually he put his arms around her, gave her a little squeeze and then pushed her gently, regretfully, away.

"I'd best be getting back before she gets it into her head that I'm having an affair. That really sets her off," he said with a tiny smile that didn't really reach his eyes. Jo walked him to the door of her flat. He stopped as he was going out.

"Promise me you won't do that again. Put yourself in danger like that?"

Jo nodded. She had almost forgotten about being chased home.

"I promise."

"And lock the door after me."

He leant down, brushed her cheek with his lips, and was gone.

35

After a night spent tossing and turning, wishing Miller had been with her, Jo felt tired and washed out in the morning and it wasn't entirely due to the late night brandy. As she read the Sunday papers, avoiding all the articles about the Hastings murders, her mind kept going back over the previous evening and in particular how it had ended: frustratingly. Why did she want such an irritating man? Why were all the men she wanted married? Was her mother right? Had she left it too late already? Was there any point in asking herself these questions? In the end she gave up on the papers. A brisk walk along the promenade, well wrapped up against the wind and rain, finally dispelled the circular questioning and self-recrimination and she was able to spend the evening catching up on paying her bills and answering emails and letters.

Next morning, after a better night's sleep, Jo was confident that she would be able to give at least half her attention to her patients. Even Mr Herring.

The first patient on her morning list was Mrs Lockwood, which was puzzling. Had something happened? Jo wondered if she had time to call the hospital, prepare herself for bad news, then decided against. Whatever the reason for the visit, knowing in advance wouldn't make it any easier.

There was a knock at the door.

"Come in." Jo called out and Mrs Lockwood opened the door, as beautifully turned out as ever. Every bleached hair in place, every manicured nail expertly polished.

"How can I help you, Mrs Lockwood? How's Timothy?"

"Much better the hospital says, although he still seems very weak to me. Apparently his liver is beginning to work again and they think he will make a full recovery."

Mrs Lockwood didn't seem as thrilled about this news as Jo thought she should be.

"He's a very lucky boy. And you're lucky, too."

"I realise that. It was a close call and I appreciate all that you have done for my son." For a moment her lower lip seemed to quiver, much to Jo's surprise, making her think that perhaps she had misjudged the woman when she dismissed her as completely self-centred. But it was only a momentary quiver and then she was all business again, pulling a sheaf of papers from her bag.

"I've been talking to my lawyer and he thinks we need to go back to court to alter the terms of the custody agreement. I mean, apart from anything else, this whole incident shows just how unfit Philip is to be a father."

Jo took the papers that Mrs Lockwood was holding out to her and started looking at them, unsure of what the woman was expecting her to do.

"Whilst Timothy's father undoubtedly behaved stupidly, I'm not sure how that alters the situation." She flipped to the back page, which seemed to be a breakdown of expenses, including the cost of a live-in nurse, housekeeper and nanny, private home tuition, a staggeringly high premium for private health care and the cost of regular stays in health spas in exotic locations around the world.

"It means I can get more money out of Philip, if he ever wants to see his son again that is." Mrs Lockwood seemed to think that it was the most natural thing in the world.

"And what if he doesn't?" Jo was horrified: this smacked of almost holding her son to ransom. "What if he decides it's not worth the money?" Jo looked back at the figures; it was an awful lot of money, a real test of a father's love, always supposing he ever really loved his son in the first place.

"He'll still have to pay more. After all, this is all his fault and it's going to be hard to care for Timothy at home- his insurance alone is going to go rocketing up."

"But you said the hospital think he will make a full recovery."

Mrs Lockwood was having none of that.

"That's easy for them to say. What about me? I nearly lost my son, thanks to Philip. The emotional toll, the strain of it all, has been con-siderable." Even Mrs Lockwood must have realised that this sounded a little selfish; either that or she caught sight of Jo's expression. "I've lost my confidence as a mother," she hurried on, in a more caring tone of voice. "Timothy might relapse at any moment, I'm quite sure of it. Who can say what these drugs have done to him? I can't let him go to school, it could be too much of a strain on him and the worry would certainly be too much for me." She pointed to the paperwork. "What my lawyer wants is a statement from you about how I need help to care for Tim as a result of Philip's actions, as per the list here," she pointed to the balance sheet, "and if you could put in á bit about the mental strain on me that would be good as well."

"I am happy to write about the strain on you and Timothy but I can't justify your need for all these expenses, Mrs Lockwood. I have patients with far worse problems coping with much less help and support." Jo pushed the papers back to Mrs Lockwood, who looked surprised.

"Yes, but they don't have rich husbands who damn near killed their child, do they?"

She did have a point, Jo had to concede, but she still didn't feel she could justify claiming such an obscene amount of money, even if Philip Lockwood had behaved like a total plonker.

"Look, I will write a letter, of course I will, but what you and your lawyer claim, that's down to you. I really don't want to know."

It was a compromise that seemed acceptable to Mrs Lockwood, and she left with a look of grim satisfaction on her face.

Jo had nearly finished morning surgery and was busy trying to explain to a reluctant patient the importance of continuing his blood pressure medication on a regular basis, rather than a week here and a week there, when she heard shouting, a metallic crunch and the sound of breaking glass.

"Here you go, Mr Golding," she snatched the prescription off the printer and thrust it at him as there another crashing noise came from outside. "And take them this time, ok? Every day. Now you'll have to excuse me." And she hurried out of the room to find out what was going on.

The waiting room was empty, which was unheard of, although the reason was quickly revealed. All the patients were huddled in the entrance hall, straining for a view into the car park, from where Jo could here Linda's voice shouting "Put that down!" before there was another crunch.

"Excuse me, let me through, please." Jo was trying to get out into the car park as Helen, one of the receptionists, was trying to get in.

"I have to call the police," Helen explained as they passed each other, without stopping long enough for Jo to ask what was going on.

As she pushed her way out, past patients with necks craning in their efforts to get a better view, Jo cold hear Linda pleading with someone to "Just put it down."

Who and what "it" was became all too clear once Jo broke through the throng and out into the open: Mr Jennings, with a sledgehammer, in the car park. It took a moment or two before she realised that the object he was bringing the sledgehammer to bear on was her car. Her beloved, midnight blue, Audi TT, now with no windscreen to speak of, a large dent in the bonnet and another in the passenger door.

"No! Stop!" Jo almost screamed as the sledgehammer swung again, this time taking out one of the headlight clusters, but Mr Jennings, a look of grim determination on his face, was already preparing himself for the next swing.

Jo and Linda exchanged looks: what on earth is this all about? Linda's expression seemed to be asking her and Jo shrugged: she had no idea. Behind Linda, Jo could see some of her colleagues emerging, resigned looks spreading over their faces as they realised that Jo was once again the cause of disruption in their orderly lives.

"Mr Jennings?" Jo turned back to her patient and decided to try a more placatory tone as she approached him, one hand held up as if to protect herself, although what she thought her hand would do to stop a sledgehammer in full swing, she didn't know. "Mr Jennings, can we talk about this?"

Her answer was another crash as the few remaining lights were smashed to smithereens.

"I know you're upset about your wife but ask yourself, is this going to help? Is this going to bring her back?" There was a slight hesitation before the hammer swung again, into the driver's door, giving her hope that he wasn't totally beyond reason- yet.

"Mr Jennings, nothing is going to bring her back. Not now. But maybe talking about it would help." Jo could hear a siren, still off in the distance, and it gave her renewed determination to sort this before the police arrived and made it worse.

"Please, Mr Jennings let's talk about this. About what happened to Jean. About how angry you're feeling."

He stopped mid-swing at that and turned to Jo, advancing towards her and the crowd of Linda, Dr Grantham and assorted patients in a not entirely friendly manner. There was a mass intake of breath and they all seemed to shrink back, moving away from Jo, disassociating themselves from her as he advanced, sledgehammer clutched in both hands and held in front of him.

"Angry? Bloody right I'm angry. My wife died because of you and your negligence."

Jo could hear the communal "ooh" behind her, followed by some tutting, led by Dr Grantham no doubt.

"Negligence?" she asked Mr Jennings, unable to keep the tone of disbelief from her voice but thankful that he had at least stopped hitting the car. "In what way have I been negligent?

"By not referring her to the hospital earlier."

He stopped about six feet from her, shifting the sledgehammer between hands, weighing it up, as if considering changing his target from the car to her. The sirens were closer now, much closer, she had little time left to diffuse the situation. Jo edged forward.

"That was your wife's decision, Mr Jennings, remember? I tried to persuade her but she didn't want to go. Didn't want to be messed about with. That's what she said, do you remember? When I called you into my room to get you to make her go, and you did."

A police car screeched to a halt in the street and two police officers leaped out, taking in the situation at a glance. Jo was relieved to see that they were a pair of older, more experienced policemen; the last thing she needed was a couple of hotheads deciding to take out her patient without giving her a chance to talk him down. And Mr Jennings did seem to be giving some thought to what Jo was saying, so she held a hand up to stop the officers from interfering and took another small step forward.

"In some ways I regret getting you in to persuade her to go into hospital, Mr Jennings. It was sheer cowardice on my part. She knew the situation, she knew she was going to die and she wanted to do it at home, alone with you, but I wouldn't listen. I became almost obsessed with trying to save her, even if it was impossible and not what she wanted anyway. I used you to force the situation and that was unfair of me, I should never have tried to pass the buck like that."

She took another step forward. He was looking at her, listening to every word, staring directly into her eyes, and Jo stared right back, unblinking, holding his full attention, holding the full attention of the silent crowd behind her as well. She could feel it. No one seemed to be breathing any more. The two policemen were looking worried: should they intervene, should they let her carry on? Linda gave them a reassuring look, she seemed fairly confident that Jo had things under control. Jo was close to Mr Jennings now, so close she could reach out and almost touch the sledgehammer if she wanted.

"To be honest, I don't think there was anything any of us could have done to save her by the time she came to me with the bleeding. It was an aggressive tumour and she could have had months of unpleasant treatment and pain, only to die anyway. She seemed to know that and it was her choice not to seek help- to refuse it, in fact, until it was unrealistic to even try and do anything. It was her choice, Mr Jennings, not to have her regular smear tests and check ups in the first place because she didn't want them. Not your choice or mine. Hers. And that's why it was wrong of me to interfere. I apologise for that and I apologise for making you do the dirty work when it was never going to succeed anyway."

She moved a little closer and reached out, inviting him to give her the sledgehammer and, to her surprise, he did just that. He seemed suddenly tired, deflated almost. As he passed it over, the sledgehammer was way heavier than she expected and she almost dropped it but then caught it in time. The two policemen leaped forward and grabbed Mr Jennings' arms, pinning them to his side just in case he decided to do anything else but Jo knew he wouldn't. All the fight had gone from him.

"It's okay, officers." Jo told them. "I think I need to have a chat with my patient, sort this out. If you could just give me a moment?" She handed the sledgehammer to one of them and took Mr Jennings by the arm. She hoped they stayed there, she didn't want them to be too far away, just in case.

"Why don't we go inside, have a nice cup of tea and a chat, hmm?"

She led him towards the surgery entrance, and was taken aback to see Miller watching her intently, concern etched across his face, with Jeffries beside him, surprisingly without his usual smirk, and she instantly blushed self-consciously as they silently stood aside to let her pass.

Linda had point blank refused to allow Jo to take Mr Jennings into her consulting room alone, even though he seemed passive enough and no longer had his sledgehammer, so Jo had settled for the smaller waiting area outside the treatment room most commonly used by the child health clinics. The floor was dotted with children's toys and the walls with happy cartoon posters not entirely appropriate for bereavement counselling. Jo knew very well that all four policemen were waiting, just out of sight in the main waiting room, in case Mr Jennings got out of hand again and she was in part comforted to know they were there but also irritated that no one seemed to think she was capable of handling him, or anything, on her own any more. She sat Mr Jennings on a chair and spoke soothingly to him.

"Linda's bringing us both a nice cup of tea, then we can have a little chat and you can talk to me about what's upsetting you." She patted his hand and smiled reassuringly as she spoke, realising that she had slipped all too easily into the patronising tone that she had heard nurses use on numerous occasions with distressed patients. But Mr Jennings didn't seem to mind; perhaps he found it soothing. Perhaps there was a reason why nurses spoke that way.

"I thought you were in it together," he blurted out, grabbing her hand and squeezing it hard.

"Who were in it together?" she asked, genuinely flummoxed by what he was saying. "In what?"

"That doctor, Mr Kane or whatever he liked to call himself. I thought you were in it together. You'd messed up and he was covering for you." Mr Jennings was speaking loudly, distressed by what he had been thinking.

"Why on earth would you think that?"

"Because I saw you together, holding hands and, you know, flirting. I thought you were using your body to buy him off. Stop him from telling me the truth."

Jo was shocked that he would think this but she was even more put out by the little snort of laughter that came from down the corridor and emanated, presumably, from Sergeant Jeffries, who was clearly listening in to every word. Jo went steaming into the waiting room.

"If you have to listen in to my private conversations, at least have the good manners not to laugh," she hissed at him and he had the grace to look suitably abashed. Miller was staring fixedly at the floor, desperately trying not to catch her eye, knowing that he wouldn't be able to control the threatening laugh if he did. As she turned to go back to Mr Jennings she could see, to her horror, that the waiting room was full of patients, all lapping up every word. This was clearly better entertainment than the telly. Jo grabbed the tray of tea and biscuits from Linda, who'd been about to bring them through, and stomped back down the corridor, trying to hold her head as high as possible under the circumstances.

"Now, Mr Jennings, let's both have a cup of tea." She handed him a cup. "Biscuit?" He took one and dunked it in his tea. He seemed remarkably calm now that he had got all his fears off his chest, and worked off most of his anger on her car. He put the soggy biscuit in his mouth and sucked on it as he listened intently to Jo, who had lowered her voice in an attempt to keep as much of this conversation from Jeffries, Miller and the hordes of patients as possible.

"Whilst I have to admit that I did go out with Mr Kane, it was only a couple of times before I found out that he was, well, not the man for me. I can assure you, there was no collusion between us over your wife's case, we were simply colleagues and acted in a professional manner at all times. However, because I was concerned to be absolutely sure about both my diagnosis and Mr Kane's treatment, I asked to see the post mortem report. It was quite clear, Mr Jennings, that your wife had a very aggressive tumour and there was nothing I or Mr. Kane could have done to save her. If you would find it helpful I can ask the pathologist to speak to you and explain it all."

Mr Jennings dunked the next bit of biscuit in his tea and popped it in his mouth before replying, giving Jo a ringside view of the soggy, beige paste, sloshing round his mouth and coating his tongue.

"I believe you now. I know you were right about Jean not wanting to be messed about. I remember it and I can see now that I got it wrong."

He took another slurp of tea, without biscuit, much to Jo's relief. "My head was all over the place. All I could think about was you and that Mr Kane, too busy having fun to look after my Jean, letting her die, covering it up but, deep down, I know she was dying anyway. Knew it all along, if I'm being honest with myself. But I didn't want it to be that way." He stopped for a moment, staring at the wall behind Jo's head before continuing. "In some ways, I think she wanted to go." He stopped again and thought about that painful but honest truth. "I'm sorry about your car," he finished, almost as an afterthought.

Miller sat in the patient's chair in Jo's consulting room and placed a couple of files on her desk.

"Tell me, do your patients often trash your car?" he asked, unable to keep the amusement from his voice.

Mr Jennings had been taken away by the two uniformed officers to be formally interviewed. Jo had been reluctant to press charges but they'd had to point out that her insurance company might well refuse to pay for her car, which was quite clearly a write-off, if she didn't. Mr Jennings hadn't seemed to care, so Jo let them take him away and charge him with criminal damage but she couldn't help feeling bad about it.

"Do you often attend minor incidents of criminal damage?"

"Touché." He held his hands up. "Although I hardly think that was minor, and you took a real chance, approaching him like that. He could have killed you with one swing of that hammer."

"He would never have done that, though, would he?" Jo wished she sounded more confident of it than she did. The truth was, it was beginning to come home to her just how much she had put herself at risk. What might, indeed could, have happened if he'd swung the sledgehammer at her didn't bear thinking about.

"Hmph." Miller clearly wasn't so sure that Mr Jennings hadn't been capable of taking a swing at her, either. "We were on our way to the mortuary when we heard the call, so we thought we'd drop in and see if we could help, particularly in light of what happened Saturday night."

Jo wasn't sure if he meant because of her being followed home or if he was referring to later in the night, when they had suddenly connected, almost kissed.

"Well, you can see now that it was just a patient going a bit mad, that's all." Jo was brisk and business like. "Nothing for you to worry about, nothing to do with the murderer. Oh, and Mr Jennings has admitted he let my tyres down and I'm sure, if you ask him, you'll find out he was the person following me, watching the flat and leaving the silent phone messages."

"Watching the flat? Silent calls?"

"I've been getting a few recently. Didn't I mention it?" Jo tried to sound as if those sorts of things were minor incidents, little irritants that happened all the time, instead of the major anxiety-inducing occurrences that they had been.

"No." Miller seemed put out that she hadn't told him about them. "But there seem to have been a few things that you've forgotten to mention, recently. Like the fact that your missing Angel has turned up, perfectly all right."

"I did check that her Grandmother had let the police know - it's not my fault if no one thought to tell you." Jo was offended that he seemed to think she was keeping things from him.

"Anyway, you must be relieved that she hadn't gone off with Tomas, after all."

"She had, though," Jo corrected him, "and he put her through a horrendous ordeal but she won't talk to you about it."

Miller leant forward, deeply interested all of a sudden.

"What do you mean?"

"I really can't tell you. I know she's not technically my patient but what she told me, she told me in confidence."

"But you are sure that it has nothing to do with the murders?"

"Absolutely." Jo nodded. "I'm not actually sure what you would charge him with, even if I did tell you."

"I'm sure Bob Jeffries could find something." Miller smiled. "He's good at that."

"I can imagine." Jo gave it some thought, "Under Health and Safety, perhaps: exposing your employees to noxious substance.s" Miller gave her a quizzical look. "No, let's just change the subject, ok? I really don't even want to think about it, but let's just say Angel won't be volunteering again. Getting rid of Tomas will have to wait until another day."

He smiled his acceptance. She knew he must be disappointed not to have something to charge Tomas with, something that would take him off the streets for a long time, but she also thought she knew him well enough to know that he wouldn't leave it there for long. She was pretty sure he was intending to bring it up again at a later date, maybe even to visit Angel and ask her about it himself and, so long as he made it clear that Jo hadn't sent him or broken her promise not to involve the police, she didn't mind.

"Well, seeing as you have everything under control, Dr Hughes, I'd best get back to work."

And he left her with no more excuses or reasons not to go upstairs to face her colleagues, so she followed him out and went up to the main office with a sigh. She was going to have to apologise profusely- again- she knew, and promise them that this was a one-off, never to recur, incident. She was going to have explain everything, in detail, to Hugh, so that he could feel quite sure that there was nothing likely to come back on the practice. Well, she had Jean Jennings' signed disclaimer, absolving Jo and the practice from any come-back from her decision not to have her regular smear tests and Jo's attempts to persuade her to have subsequent tests, even an ultrasound, in addition to her refusal to allow Jo to refer her to the hospital, were all well documented. Jo was pretty sure she was covered from a medico-legal point of view. She was just going to have to get used to grovelling and endure re-criminations from her colleagues for weeks, and she knew it.

It wasn't until later, much later, that she returned to her consulting room and realised that Miller had left the two files on her desk.

The files contained the second post mortem report on Krissy Trent and the first on Caro Sharpe, which Miller had been intending to drop off to Ian Dunbar for translation into simple English, and Jo couldn't resist the chance to be nosy.

She sat down, opened the first file and started to read.

36

Linda looked up from the computer screen behind the reception desk as Jo came hurrying out of her consulting room clutching the two files.

"That scrummy policeman is on his way over, said he left a couple of files on your desk."

"Tell him to meet me at the mortuary. There's been a mistake. I've got to speak to Ian about these." Jo hurried out to the car park, looked at the remains of her car still sitting waiting for her to organise its removal, turned and went back into reception.

"I don't suppose I could borrow your car, could I, Linda?"

Jo struggled with the unfamiliar car as she drove as fast as she dared to the mortuary. She had tried calling Ian Dunbar but there had been no answer. This was not unusual or worrying. He could be conducting a post mortem with Dave assisting or he could be cutting samples whilst Dave had been called away to collect a body from a ward. She just hoped that Ian wouldn't be too busy to take a look at the files and confirm the discrepancy that she thought she had found between the two post mortems. She remembered him saying- or was it Dave?- about the swabs being negative when they were talking about the first autopsy, she was sure.

She was relieved to see that the hospital car park was no longer a crime scene and managed to find a parking space not too far from the mortuary. Snatching up the two files and her handbag, she locked Linda's tiny Fiat and almost ran to the mortuary entrance.

The lift seemed to take an age and, as she hurried out of the lift into the mortuary proper, she slowed as she was struck once again by the stillness and silence of the place. She couldn't hear so much as the clatter of metal instruments on trays or the murmur of voices. It seemed almost indecent to hurry in a place as calm and quiet as this.

She walked at a more measured pace along the corridor, peeking through the porthole window into the first post mortem room, which was empty, and then the second, which was also empty, save for a shrouded body on a trolley.

'Someone must be around,' Jo thought, knowing that Ian would never allow a body to be removed from the fridge unless he was about to start cutting. She stuck her head around the office door but there was no one there either.

The silence was beginning to feel oppressive and unsettling rather than calm.

'Don't be so silly,' she told herself, refusing to let it get to her.

"Ian?" she called out. "Dave? Is there anyone here?" Her voice seemed to echo along the corridor but there was no reply, no sound or sign of movement from anywhere. She walked back along the corridor, opening doors into changing rooms and store cupboards, but still saw no one.

Where could they be? Jo went into the second post mortem room and walked past the body on the trolley, brushing lightly against it as she did so, to look into the adjoining store room. No one in there either. She was beginning to feel seriously spooked and she turned to leave.

That was when she saw it. The foot, or rather the boot. The sheet covering the body on the trolley had shifted slightly when she'd brushed against it, revealing the right foot, still in a boot. The fact that the body was still clothed was not unusual; bodies were often wheeled in fully dressed to have their clothing removed in the post mortem room in order to preserve evidence, particularly in criminal cases. But bodies for autopsy rarely wore white rubber boots, unless they belonged to someone who worked in the mortuary.

Jo edged slowly forward, reluctant to take a closer look but unable to stop herself from doing so.

She reached the trolley and put out her hand to pull the sheet back from the head, then hesitated.

'Don't be so ridiculous,' she told herself, and swiftly whipped back the sheet, before gasping in horror and stepping back.

Ian Dunbar was lying on the trolley, dressed in his green scrubs, eyes bulging, purple tongue protruding from his mouth, with the yellow rubber tubing of a Foley's catheter cutting tightly into his neck. He was dead, very dead.

"I knew you'd come."

Jo jumped and let out a small involuntary cry. She hadn't heard Dave Ball come into the room.

"You startled me," she said, hurriedly, almost guiltily, replacing the sheet, hoping that he hadn't seen her look under it.

"I knew you'd work it out and come to me." He was standing squarely blocking the doorway, filling it like he filled his surgical scrubs to bursting point.

"What do you mean?" She looked around, knowing already that there was no other way out, but wildly hoping that there might be one she had forgotten. But no, unfortunately not. There were only the two doors, one was the way out, currently blocked by Dave, and the other was the door into the store room.

"He caught me." Dave nodded towards Ian Dunbar's shrouded body. "With Caro. In flagrante, as they say. Very careless of me, but that's why he had to die."

"You didn't have to do that, you know, to kill him. I mean, okay, yes, you wouldn't be able to work in a mortuary again once it was known that you liked to, you know, have sex with them, the, uh, the dead, ah, bodies." She found it hard to even talk about it, something so awful, so alien to everything she held dear, that she couldn't even imagine what attraction there was to it. It takes all sorts, as Angel would say.

Faeces and kids and dead people, she thought, what is there left?

"Necrophilia. I love that word. Necrophilia." He savoured the sound of it and took a pace towards her. "It wasn't until I worked down here and saw the bodies, so cool and still, that I realised what I was, realised my true nature, as they say. They were so tempting."

"I understand." She couldn't, but she needed to keep him talking while she thought of a way out of here.

"The first one, she was only thirty, died from breast cancer, very sad, a little on the scrawny side but that's to be expected in the circumstances."

Jo couldn't stop a shudder.

"Trouble was, once I'd discovered what I wanted, what I liked, nothing else would do. I tried so many times because the standard of the bodies round here, well, most of them are horrid old bags, to be frank, not many are in good shape, scrawny and sick looking or the morbidly obese who've stroked out. And all so old. Not exactly a turn on, know what I mean?" He moved a step or two closer and it took all Jo's strength of will not to recoil in horror, to step quickly away, anything to keep her distance from him.

"Not really." She was surprised at how steady her voice sounded, under the circumstances. She put her handbag down on the shrouded body.

"So I kept trying with the living but, well, I just couldn't seem to get it up any more and then that Krissy bird, the tart, she had the nerve to laugh at me and I lost it. Strangled her with her own tights. And there she was. Dead. The ultimate turn on. Didn't have sex with her there, though, I know all about trace evidence, believe me, I even took her fake nails with me to make sure there was nothing left at the scene. I knew there was no hurry, you see, she was going to be with me, here, for weeks. I had loads of time."

"But you made a mistake, didn't you, Dave?"

Jo began to very slowly sidle round the trolley as she listened to him talk, trying to put it between them.

"Yes. I didn't know they did a second P.M. for the defence. Stupid mistake, really, but we don't get a lot of criminal cases here. And once that happened, I knew it was just a matter of time before someone put two and two together."

"What about Denise, the till girl? She wasn't exactly your finest hour, was she?"

Jo was at the head of the trolley now, her hands lightly resting on the side rail.

"Jocasta, Jocasta, you are so right." Dave moved forward again, smiling and shaking his head in admiration at her cleverness. "She was such a loner no one found her body until she was well past her use-by date. And she wasn't exactly a looker when she was fresh. You can be assured I let her rest in peace. Putrefaction isn't a turn on, I've found. Good thing I had that junkie of yours to tide me over."

Jo inched a little further round, moving her hands down to the trolley head, hidden from Dave's view by Dr Dunbar's body. She had known from the moment she saw the second post mortem report on Krissy Trent, where it stated that the vagina contained dead sperm, enough dead sperm for a swab to be sent for DNA testing, that someone must have had sex with her corpse. The first autopsy had found no sperm at all, the swabs were negative. There was only the trace of lubricant from a condom, or condoms more likely, given Krissy's occupation. The question Jo couldn't answer was who had done it, and it hadn't even occurred to her that it was happening on a regular basis, or to other corpses as well as Krissy. Well, she knew now and the thought of him, Dave, someone she knew and had worked with, shared a joke with at times, desecrating the dead, was horrific. Not to mention the fact that he was killing them in the first place in order to have access to the bodies for sex.

"That's when I got the idea that I didn't need to stick to the fat ugly dollops that I usually ended up with. No, you see, that's the beauty of this job. I could have anyone. Any girl in the whole, wide world I wanted. I could have Caro, even though she thought she was too good for me. She learned, she did, not to reject me. And of course, my ultimate choice, the one person in the world I really wanted, Jocasta. You."

Dave was moving forward again as he spoke and Jo had been ready to push the trolley into him, but this final revelation gave her pause for thought, just a moment's hesitation, and he started round the trolley towards her. He was at the wrong angle now, she wouldn't be able to push the trolley into him, she had missed her chance.

"All those nights I watched, I even saw that prick Kane stay with you."

"You scratched his car."

"I was tempted to do more than that, but I didn't want you to know I was watching you. I called you on the telephone, I liked to hear your voice on the machine, so I was disappointed when you changed the message, put one of your boyfriends on it, but I still called when I knew you were in because I liked the thought that you were there, listening to me breathe."

Jo began to work her way round the trolley again, slowly, a step at a time.

"Once you started going to those places, the bars and clubs, I knew you'd worked it out so I made my plans. Got ready. Ready to take you away with me."

"What on earth makes you think I'd go away with you?"

"You have no choice, Jocasta, believe me, no choice at all."

Dave moved forward again and Jo moved to the side and tensed, ready to push the trolley into him. The room was suddenly filled with the sound of arpeggios played on the piano. For one second it seemed, eerily, to be coming from Dr Dunbar's body, but then both Jo and Dave realised at the same moment that it was coming from her bag, that it was her mobile phone ring tone. Jo lunged for her bag but Dave got there first and threw it across the room. The contents of her bag scattered across the room and the ring tone stopped as the mobile phone hit the wall and clattered onto the floor.

Dave lunged for Jo but, in the time that he had taken throwing the bag across the room, she had moved round and taken a firm hold of the trolley rails and shoved it as hard as she could into him, not waiting to see the effect, to see if she had stopped him or not, before turning and running in the only direction left open to her, into the store room.

She slammed the door shut behind her and tried to drag a metal shelving unit across the door to block it. She had no idea how long it would be before someone would come looking for Dr Dunbar or herself but she prayed fervently that Linda had passed on her message to Miller to meet her at the mortuary and that he was on his way.

The door handle turned and rattled as Dave tried to push it open. Jo leaned hard against the door and pulled again, harder this time, at the shelving unit, complete with the stocks of sterile packs, couch rolls, and specimen pots that were on it. She had it half across the door when Dave threw himself at it from the other side, sending Jo and the unit flying across the room, the contents of the shelves skittering across the floor. Jo landed awkwardly, her head hitting another metal shelf and her wrist cracking, as she hit the heel of her hand against the floor. A wave of nausea and pain washed over her. Her eyes were closed but she could feel the wet and warm feel of blood trickling down the side of her face. She shook her head slightly to clear it and decided very quickly that that had been a mistake. The floor tipped away from her and she could feel herself sliding into unconsciousness. She took a deep breath and tried to open her eyes again.

"You can't get away. There's no way out." Dave was filling the doorway, looking at her with a small smile playing on his lips and a slight sheen of sweat across his brow. There was no doubt he was going to enjoy this. Jo recoiled, clutching her broken right arm to her chest, crouching, huddled against the far wall, and looked around desperately but he was right. There was nowhere to go and no way out past him. She reached out with her left hand, her fingers searching for something that she could use as a weapon, anything at all. As Dave moved forward again, her hand closed around a small plastic container, a cytology pot.

A couple of feet from her, Dave bent down and picked up a sterile catheter pack that had fallen from the shelves and opened it, pulling out the rubber catheter tubing and snapping it in his hands. There was little doubt in Jo's mind about his intent. She was to become the latest victim, strangled with a urinary catheter wielded by a necrophiliac mortuary attendant. What a way to go.

"You won't get away with this," she said desperately, as she tried to work off the lid of the specimen pot one handed, but it was closed tight and she couldn't shift it. She had to stall him. Give herself time to open the pot. "Miller knows I was coming down here, that I had found a discrepancy in the reports. He will be on his way here by now." She certainly hoped he was.

"He'll be too late. We'll be long gone by the time he gets here. I've got everything ready." Dave was getting closer, and Jo tried to shuffle to the right but her way was blocked by the drug cupboard. That was no use to her because it was not only locked but had to be fixed to the wall by law, so she would never be able to open it or move it. She tried the lid of the cytology pot again and this time it moved, just a fraction, but it was a start. It gave her hope. She had to keep him talking, just a little longer, while her fingers worked on it some more.

"Where are you taking me?" she asked.

"Somewhere no one will ever find us," he said blissfully, as he reached down to her, bending over her with the rubber tubing in his hands, leaning closer, so close that she could smell his rancid breath and the stale sweat that was beginning to stain his scrubs.

At last the lid came free and Jo jerked her left hand forward, throwing the contents of the specimen pot, the formalin used to fix the cells sampled, into Dave's eyes.

There was a moment of shocked hesitation and then he screamed

315

and lurched back, dropping the rubber tubing and scratching at his eyes, trying to claw away the liquid that was instantly killing and fixing the cells of his corneae, blinding him.

Jo took her chance to jump up and hurtle across the room and out of the door, straight into the arms of DCI Miller. She clutched hold of him, sobbing into his chest, relieved to feel his arms come round and hold her tight, only vaguely aware of Jeffries and a hospital security guard moving rapidly past them into the store room, to where Dave was still blundering about, screaming.

"In there." She heard Miller tell two uniformed policemen who arrived as back up, but still she didn't lift her head, keeping it deeply buried in his chest, and he didn't stop holding her, tightly, and uttering soothing phrases.

"It's over, you're okay now. It's all right."

At last, she felt strong enough to lift her head, and look round as Jeffries brought Dave, in handcuffs, out of the store room. His eyes were squeezed shut and he was whimpering.

"I can't see, that bitch blinded me, I can't see anything."

"You'd better take him to casualty. I chucked formalin in his eyes and it will have to be washed out if there's any hope of saving his sight," Jo told them.

"Right," Jeffries said as he pushed Dave forward, then turned and spoke to Jo. "And should we take him the short way or the long way?"

"The short way, sergeant, if you please," she said firmly but, as she looked at Dr Dunbar, lying on the trolley, dead through no fault of his own, Jo wasn't absolutely sure that she meant it.

37

Jo was shown out into the casualty waiting area by one of the staff nurses, who was looking a bit concerned that this patient didn't seem to be listening to her advice. Doctors: they always made the worst patients. Jo was surprised and relieved to see Miller waiting for her and the nurse was happy to hand her over to him.

"There's no way you're fit to drive," he explained in defence of his presence and Jo had to agree: it was nothing to do with the fact that her arm was in plaster or that she had six sutures holding her scalp laceration together, it was just that she felt pretty weak and wobbly.

"It's all that local anaesthetic," she agreed, "leaves you a bit shaky."

"Not to mention the rest." Miller clearly wasn't taken in by her excuses. He took her arm and began to lead her out to the car park. Jo stopped and looked around.

"Linda was waiting for me, to take me home and take her car back."

"I sent her away." Miller told her. "I hope you don't mind. I promised her I'd take charge of you."

Jo didn't mind at all, there was no doubt that it felt reassuringly good to have his strong arm to lean on.

As they walked across the car park, Jo could see Jeffries over by the mortuary, standing next to a large lorry, a low loader, onto which a white van was being lifted.

"What's that? Is it Dave's or something?" she asked.

"Um, yes." Miller seemed suddenly and uncharacteristically embarrassed. "My car's just over here." He tried to hurry her away but she, obstinate as ever, and alerted by his anxiety to move her on, out of the way, stopped to give the van a closer look as it swayed awkwardly in the air, ready to be lowered onto the trailer.

"It's a refrigerated van," she finally realised in horror. "He was going to kill me and keep my body in a refrigerated van so that he could, could carry on, with me for -." Like the van, Jo was beginning to sway slightly. Her hand came up to her throat with the sheer horror of what Dave had planned for her. Miller grabbed her good arm to steady her but quickly realised that that was not going to be enough, so he swept her up and carried her back to one of the benches just outside the main entrance doors.

"Put your head between your knees," he ordered.

"Don't start that again," she said, staying as upright as possible. "Anyway, I'd probably be sick." So she just closed her eyes for a moment, leaning slightly against Miller. She heard someone close by clear their throat and she opened her eyes to see Jeffries. She moved slightly away from Miller and tried not to blush, a hopeless task.

"Sorry about that, Guv," Jeffries said.

"My fault," Miller contended, "my timing was impeccable as always." He tossed his keys to his sergeant. "Fetch the car over here, will you, Bob? I don't think she'll make it that far." And Jeffries scurried away to bring the car closer.

Jo straightened her shoulders and composed herself.

"I'm okay, honestly, you don't have to drive me back, I could get a taxi."

"No." He was firm. "I'm taking you home and I'm not taking no for an answer." For once, Jo didn't argue.

As he drove her back up the East Hill, he told her that Mr Jennings had readily confessed to damaging her car on the two occasions, but not to following her or to the phone calls. This had set him thinking that perhaps she might be being targeted by the killer, that she might know him. So once he got the message that she had gone haring up to the mortuary because of problems with the post mortem reports, he'd put two and two together and realised that it could be someone from the mortuary.

"The stupid thing is, I never suspected Dave was the killer, I just realised that he was having, you know -."

"Sex with the corpses?" he smiled, still amused at her inability to talk about sex.

"That's right."

"We were ahead of you there, then, we had already worked out that it had to be someone from the hospital because the professor had been pretty sure the murder weapon in Caro's case had been surgical tubing of some sort, and I did listen to your opinion that it wasn't that prat Kane. So it was no great leap to realise that it might be someone from the mortuary."

"He was going to use a catheter, can you believe it?" She felt her lip tremble slightly at the thought, the realisation of just how close she had come to being the next victim, and they continued the rest of the journey in silence, each alone with their thoughts and fears. It seemed no time at all before they arrived outside Jo's home. Miller switched the engine off and came round to the passenger side to open the door and help her out.

"My keys!" Jo suddenly realised that she didn't have her handbag with her.

"Your bag is still part of the crime scene, I'm afraid, but I did rescue these for you." Miller held out her keys and Jo took them, her hand touching his momentarily. It felt good, that fleeting touch, the rough skin of his hand against her softer fingers. She opened the door and went reluctantly into the hallway and then turned. Miller was still standing in the street, looking in.

"You must have lots to do," she said, making his excuses for him.

"Are you going to be okay?" he asked, gently.

She nodded.

"You should call a friend or family member, ask them to come round and be with you."

"I'm fine," she said firmly. She was sure of one thing: if she wasn't going to be with him then she wanted to be alone, she didn't even want Kate and she certainly didn't want her mother round, not now, if ever. She would need to visit them, tell her father about his friend Ian Dunbar, but that would have to wait until she felt stronger. This evening perhaps, before he heard it on the news.

"I'll come and take a statement later, if you're feeling up to it."

She said nothing for a moment.

"Maybe it would be better if you sent Sergeant Jeffries to take it, or Jayne Hales."

He gave her a long, hard look but then nodded and turned quickly, going back to his car. She watched silently as he drove away, a little too fast, wheels skidding slightly on the loose gravel, before closing the door, and she made her way up the stairs to her own front door, tears slowly running down her cheeks. A married man, an honourable man, who loved his wife. She certainly could pick them, as Kate would say.

About the Author

Candy Denman trained as a nurse, and worked in the NHS almost all her life, until recently managing to disengage herself in order to become a full-time crime writer.

She has also written a number of scripts for such highly-acclaimed TV series as The Bill and Heartbeat.

Also by Crime Scene Books

The Inspector Truchaud 'wine and crime' mystery series by
R.M. Cartmel:

The Richebourg Affair (2014)
The Charlemagne Connection (2015)
The Romanée Vintage (2017)

'A well-crafted treasure of unforgettable characters.'
Jeffrey Siger

'R.M. Cartmel was born to write.'
Sharon Powell

*'After an explosive start, R.M. Cartmel's latest vintage offering slips down
very easily, with an intriguing finish.'*
Jasper Morris MW

A thriller by Michael Cayzer:

50 Miles from Anywhere (2015)

*'Michael Cayzer doesn't shy away from a truth
that is sometimes unpalatable, but he still
manages to show that, even in the most awful
of circumstances, there remains a relatively
good side to people.'*
C. Jeffries

Also by Crime Scene Books

The Amy Lane psychological thriller mystery series by Rosie Claverton:

Captcha Thief (2016)
Terror 404 (2017)

'Rosie Claverton has produced a highly original heroine with truly authentic strengths and flaws. Definitively recommended.'
Zoë Sharp, creator of the best-selling Charlie Fox series

'Rosie Claverton has played the alchemist, and created literary gold.'
Crime Fiction Lover

A historical thriller by S.W. Williams:

Small Deaths (2017)

True crime by Julian Hayes:

The Poison Cell (2017)